Praise for
THE GODS OF GOLF

"Golf is often a mysterious and magical game played more in the mind than anywhere else, and THE GODS OF GOLF will take you on such a journey. If you liked *The Wizard of Oz* as a kid, then you'll love THE GODS OF GOLF as a big kid."

—Roger Twibell, golf commentator, ABC Sports

"In THE GODS OF GOLF, David L. Smith and John P. Holms take a fresh look at an ancient game. Just when you think they're holding up a mirror, you find they've opened up a window. And you aren't just looking through it; you're walking through it, to a whole new wonderland, a place where bunkers are filled with quicksand, the fairway shifts beneath your feet, and your very existence is ruled by gods and bedeviled by demons."

—Bo Links, author of *Follow the Wind*

"THE GODS OF GOLF proves what theologians have doubted and golfers have always known: there is a golf god, a bunch of them, in fact, and they are a crafty, nasty lot. A fun read."

—Bob Schieffer, CBS News

"A rollicking romp of a novel that will charm anyone who has ever picked up a golf club . . . or, for that matter, anyone who has wondered exactly how otherwise-normal people can be entranced by such a cruel, senseless game. All of us duffers owe a vote of thanks for this wonderful novel."

—Warren Murphy, coauthor, *The Forever King* and *World Without End*

THE GODS of GOLF

DAVID L. SMITH
and
JOHN P. HOLMS

POCKET BOOKS
New York   London   Toronto   Sydney   Tokyo   Singapore

This book is a work of fiction. Names, characters, places, and incidents are products of the authors' imagination or are used fictitiously. Any resemblance to actual events or locales or persons living or dead is entirely coincidental.

POCKET BOOKS, a division of Simon & Schuster Inc.
1230 Avenue of the Americas, New York, NY 10020

Copyright © 1996 by David L. Smith and John P. Holms

Illustrations by David L. Smith

ISBN 0-671-54774-7

First Pocket Books trade paperback printing June 1997

10 9 8 7 6 5 4 3 2 1

POCKET and colophon are registered trademarks of
Simon & Schuster Inc.

Cover design by Matt Galemmo
Cover art by John Nickle

Printed in the U.S.A.

For my parents, Dorsey & Dorothy,
who taught me the importance
of love, faith, and family

DLS

For my mother, Elizabeth Louise,
who has always believed and
always stood her ground.
I will never forget.

JPH

ACKNOWLEDGMENTS

A great many people helped make this book possible. First of all I'd like to thank many of my playing partners of the years who have blamed their woeful performances on the interference of the golf gods. If they had played better this book might never have been written. In particular, I'd like to thank my regular playing partner, Neil Cohen, who patiently listened to me jabber about this book every Saturday morning for the last two years. I am especially grateful to my wife, Alison, whose love and support made the work possible. Finally, a very special thanks goes to the real Harry Brady, who not only taught me a lot about golf, but about friendship as well.

DLS

So many people deserve my heartfelt thanks for their support and friendship throughout this remarkable journey; they know who they are. But thanks especially to Steve, Tom, Will and Sil, Barb and Wilber, and to Pat, who listened. And, finally, to David, who reminded me how much I do love this game.

JPH

We'd also like to thank our friend and agent, Tony Seidl, who got us on the tee and helped us keep an eye on the ball. His encouragement and belief never flagged. And to Pete Wolverton at Pocket Books, an editor who is always willing to raise the literary stakes and whose vision and enthusiasm made *The Gods of Golf* a bigger and better book than it might have otherwise been.

DLS & JPH

CONTENTS

Contents

THE GODS of GOLF

THE GREAT GOD MACKENZIE
The father of the pantheon of Mount Augustus, he invented the game of golf eons ago as a diversion. Now he threatens to withdraw the game from mortal men, unless Harry Brady can find a pure heart who just loves the game.

MACTAVISH, THE GOD OF RULES
Scheming and compulsive, MacTavish is an auditor at heart. He devised the first rules of golf in order to give the Great God MacKenzie an edge over his ambitious sons.

MULLIGAN, THE GOD OF EXCUSES
Trained as a defense attorney, Mulligan knows an exception for every rule, and a million reasons why you can take your shot over again.

HORACE, THE GOD OF HAZARDS
A gentle outcast cursed never to set foot on the fairways or greens of Mount Augustus. Instead, Horace must live out all eternity in the rough, sand traps and water hazards.

EUNUCH, THE GOD OF LOST BALLS
A strange cherub with an enchanting voice who was left behind during a meeting with the Roman pantheon. An idiot savant who lives only to collect golf balls and sing, Eunuch is Horace's only friend.

WEYLAND, THE GOD OF EQUIPMENT
A woodland faun, Weyland rules over the dreaded Foundry, an underground factory where traditional golf balls and clubs are fashioned by dwarfs and mortal golfers who have failed "the test."

DIRK, THE GOD OF TACTICS
A highland warrior skilled in the arts of battle who believes that a golf course is a ruthless beast that must be brought to its knees.

The Fateful Nassau

In which Young Tom Cruickshank is introduced to Pine Valley
and the mysterious Harry Brady

My first invitation to Pine Valley was nearly my last. I
was drafted as a last-minute substitute for the firm's most
important client—an aging sybarite who had taken to his
couch with a nasty case of gout. Exercising his perogatives
as a customer, the old boy had waited until 4:45 Friday
afternoon to give my boss the bad news. At 4:59 I was
summoned to the corner office for the first time.

Why me? Well, it certainly wasn't because I was the
boss's fair-haired boy. On the contrary, I was one of a hundred junior associates scrambling to break out of the pack
at Hartless & Craven, a giant consulting firm in lower Manhattan. The only reason Craven remembered me at all was
that I made a complete fool of myself at the previous year's
Christmas party. Fueled by too many cups of high-octane
eggnog, I had cornered the old buzzard and regaled him
with preposterous stories of my prowess at golf—which
every junior associate knew was the old man's passion. The
next morning, hungover and full of remorse, I got down

on my knees on the cold bathroom tile and prayed to all that was holy that Mr. Craven would overlook my indiscretion and let me keep my job.

Apparently someone had listened, for five months later I still had my job and was standing in the senior partner's office getting the chance of a lifetime. Through a blue haze of cigar smoke, Mr. Craven explained that after much deliberation he had chosen me from a long list of partners and associates to fill out his foursome over the long Memorial Day weekend at "The Valley"—words that made my ambitious little heart beat like a snare drum.

Then in a gesture of false bonhomie perfected during a long career in client sales, Mr. Craven wrapped his arm around my shoulders and explained the ground rules.

"Okay, sport, here's the deal," he began gravely. "Don't get too familiar with the other members. As a rule of thumb, don't talk to them unless they talk to you first."

"Understood, sir," I answered.

"Great. On to the dress code. No tennis shoes, sweatshirts, or jeans. No white belts and no polyester. Better bring a jacket for dinner," he said. "If you don't have the right stuff, Brooks Brothers is open late tonight."

"All set, sir," I replied and made a mental note to check my credit card limit. I'd be needing a whole new wardrobe.

"Last but not least: no fuzzy animal head covers, and no giant staff bags—the caddies won't carry them. Got that?" For emphasis, he squeezed my deltoid like it was a ripe lemon and then sat down behind his desk.

"Gotcha, Mr. Craven," I replied crisply.

"Good. Now one more thing, buddy. What's your handicap?"

"A fourteen," I replied brightly.

"The Valley's no ordinary course, pal," said Craven. He did some quick math on a notepad and then gave me a wink. "So we'll make you a twenty-five."

In retrospect, it was a watershed moment for both of us. By attempting to gain an advantage in the weekend's betting, Craven had only edged a little closer to the truth. My handicap was in fact a fraud, a monument to self-deception crafted over the years by the indiscriminate use of mulligans and selectively submitted scorecards. I had no more business playing Pine Valley than trying to cross the Atlantic in a skiff. But ambition had won the day over common sense, and I was in too deep to back out. Like some drought-stricken rancher on a pilgrimage to Vegas, I was betting the family spread on one spin of the wheel. It was a bet I couldn't afford to lose.

Early the next morning, we rode out to Pine Valley in Craven's chauffeured Bentley, and for the entire three-hour drive the old man regaled me with tales of eviscerating his golf opponents in high stakes Nassaus. To hear Craven tell it, he had never lost a match unless it was good for business, and he didn't intend to start that weekend. Near the end of our journey, as the limo slipped past a tiny amusement park and entered the unpretentious gates of Pine Valley, Craven placed his hand on my shoulder and summed up his philosophy of the royal and ancient game.

"Cruickshank, golf is like business," he said. "You thump the daylights out of your competition, and then you use their money to buy the drinks."

Our prospective clients would not be arriving until Saturday night, which gave us the chance to play a warm-up round that morning. While I unpacked, Craven flushed a couple of "pigeons" from the men's grill to face us in a $20 Nassau. When we shook hands on the first tee, I felt a surge of confidence; our opponents were older than my grandparents. But as it turned out, I had greatly underestimated both their skill and the difficulty of "The Valley."

On the front side alone I was 15 over par. Even though Pine Valley's caddies are famous for always finding your ball, I managed to lose two sleeves going out, including three balls at the fifth hole—a 230-yard par three, where the saying is that "only God can make a three." But my Waterloo was the par five seventh hole where I carded a 10. T. E. Lawrence took less time to free Arabia from the Turks than I needed to hack my way out of "Hell's Half

Acre"—that monstrous stretch of unraked sand and weeds bisecting the seventh fairway.

After a short drive into the left rough, I caught my second shot fat, so that it floated weakly into the barren wastes, a mere twenty yards away. We found my ball nestled in the soft sand under a hawthorn bush—a near-impossible lie. When I asked my caddie what club to use, he shrugged with disdain. He had given up on me. My boss was so disgusted that he steamed ahead to the next landing area spewing plumes of cigar smoke in his wake. Full of fear and self-loathing, I took a halfhearted lunge with my wedge, burying the clubhead in the sand and managing to advance the ball only a couple of feet forward into an old footprint.

Knees quivering, I addressed the shot again, but before I could swing, a hand snatched my ball, moving it to a smooth spot in the bunker.

"Let's give you a decent chance this time, son." It was Harry Brady, the younger of the two old codgers my boss was trying to fleece. Although he had to be pushing seventy, Harry looked lean and fit in his Bermuda shorts. To cover his receding hairline, he wore a faded Pine Valley cap that had lost its shape years earlier.

Although I couldn't figure out for the life of me why the guy would want to help me out, I decided not to look a gift horse in the mouth. Once again I took a vicious cut at the ball, unfortunately getting the same results.

"You're trying too hard, son," said Brady soothingly. After making sure that nobody was looking, he moved it to another flat spot with the toe of his shoe. "Now take the club back slow this time and watch your tempo."

This time I caught the ball cleanly and managed to escape the giant bunker. While my heart swelled with gratitude, Brady nodded with satisfaction.

"There you go, son," he said.

These were to be the last words of encouragement I received from him or anyone else the entire morning. For the rest of the round, Harry and his pal Crockett did their best to beat our brains out. No matter how bad he might have felt for me, there was no way he was going to tank on a $20 Nassau. But from time to time I caught him standing off to the side giving me the once-over, like he'd met me before, but couldn't remember where.

Unfortunately, Harry's Band-Aid fell off pretty quickly. By the time we were on the eighth green, I was gathering speed on my downward slide. After I failed to extricate myself from the Devil's Arsehole, a vicious pot-bunker protecting the 10th hole, my boss did not speak to me again until we were back in the bar at the clubhouse. I had the distinct feeling that at best my miserable play had assured me a lifetime tenure on the lowest rung of middle management, or at worst, a place on line at the unemployment office.

And there were still two long days to go.

The ancient bar was silent as we shared the obligatory round of drafts. Decorated with dark wood paneling and somber oil paintings of past club presidents, the 19th hole should have been the site of one of my richest memories— recounting my first round at America's toughest course while enveloped in the beery warmth of male companionship. Instead, the bar was as somber as a funeral home, and I was the guest of honor.

After a decent interval, old man Craven tossed back his mug in two gulps, and gave his "Hale Fellow Well Met" combination backslap and shoulder massage to the two old codgers who had just eaten our lunch on the back nine to take the Nassau.

"Great seeing ya again, buddy!" he yelled in Forrest Crockett's ear. Despite a hearing aid the size of a conch shell, the old gentleman was nearly stone deaf. He smiled with rheumy eyes and a total lack of comprehension, looking like a dachshund being asked to fill out a 1040.

"And Harry, you old bastard. I'll get you next time!" said my boss, massaging his trapezius until the old man winced.

Then Craven turned to me. His huge florid face, which had only a moment before been a monument to joviality, was now clouded over with seething disgust. His eyes looked like two red dots nestled in a waxy mudslide of jowls and thinning hair. I knew in that moment I was no longer on the fast track at Hartless & Craven.

"Pay the sommitches, I'm taking a shower," he growled and then strode angrily out of the bar. On the way up to his room, my employer ran into another senior member, called the old gent "pal" and slapped him on the back so hard that he nearly tumbled down the stairs.

"If it helps, everyone knows your boss is a horse's ass," said Crockett in a stage whisper. Everyone in the grill room could hear him, and it most certainly did not help.

I counted out six twenties and shakily handed them over to Crockett's partner, Harry Brady.

"Thank you, son," he said. "I always enjoy a spirited competition."

"You're very kind," I replied. "I'm afraid I was no competition at all."

"Don't take it so seriously," he said. "It's just a game."

"No it's not," I muttered. "Not to me, and certainly not to my boss."

Brady squinted at me like a marksman looking down the sights of his weapon. He took another sip of his beer and sighed, slapping the bar with both hands as if he had just made an important decision.

"Let me buy you some lunch, son," he said.

We found a table for two in a quiet corner of the dining room and sat for a moment staring out the window at the course I had dreamed of playing for so long. I wasn't hungry but Brady insisted that I try the snapper soup, a rite of passage for all first-time visitors at Pine Valley. While I trolled through the reddish brown liquid with my spoon—wondering why anyone would consider snapper soup a delicacy—the old man continued to look me up and down as if fitting me for a new suit.

When it became abundantly clear that I was in no mood

for conversation, Harry put on a pair of reading glasses, unzipped his sports bag, and took out an old leather-bound journal. Its spine had been broken many years before from the look of it, and the book was held together with rubber bands and strips of tape. Scraps of paper of all sizes and colors were stuck between the pages like bookmarks. Harry Brady was in desperate need of a new diary.

"Let me guess, son. Once or twice a week during the season?" he asked, uncapping an old fountain pen.

It would have been easy to go along with the old man, play the "if I just had the time to get out more" routine and leave it at that. But for some reason, I wanted to tell him the truth.

"Pretty much every weekend except when it snows," I said, as I pushed pieces of congealing chowder around with my spoon to reveal the famous Pine Valley emblem on the bottom of my bowl.

"Is that so?" Harry whistled through his teeth and nodded with satisfaction. He made a notation in the margin of his book. "Well, then. How many sets of clubs have you owned during the past five years?"

I did a quick mental inventory of the storage locker in my apartment building, picturing three bags hanging on the wall and an old clothes barrel in the corner full of discarded drivers and putters. I could have funded a modest day care program with what I had invested in the tools of golf. But before I could answer, Harry held up his hand.

"No, let me," he said, raising his eyes heavenward as if the answer was written on the ceiling.

"My guess is three," he continued. "But you're still shopping for that perfect set of irons. Am I right?"

He was exactly right. "Close enough," I answered.

Harry scribbled another notation and then peered over the rims of his glasses at me. "Ever break eighty?"

It was a sore subject, but I couldn't hold anything back.

"No, but I shot eighty two or three times. Once without mulligans."

Harry leaned back to let the ancient waiter refill our

water glasses. Then he righted his chair and looked me square in the eye.

"Look, I know you've had a tough day, but I've gotta ask you just one more question. And this is important." He took off his glasses and closed his diary before continuing.

"Tom, how do you feel about golf? Do you like it, or do you really love it?"

Taken aback by his obvious sincerity, I hit a little defensive lob to keep him off balance while I tried to figure out what his game was.

"Well, of course I love it, Mr. Brady," I replied smoothly. "Doesn't everybody?" Then to cover my tracks, I began to babble something about all the tournaments I watched on television and how I used to play with my dad when I was a kid.

The truth was I had absolutely no idea how I felt about it at that moment. I suppose I liked the game well enough, but over the years golf had come to represent something more practical than knocking a little white ball around forty acres of park land. Golf was about clawing my way up the corporate ladder, and about wanting desperately to belong. Since I hadn't gone to a fancy Eastern school, I didn't have great connections. So, I had chosen golf as my ticket to the partner track at Hartless & Craven, and believe me, that had nothing to do with love.

As I rambled on, Harry's pale blue eyes seemed to alternately narrow and darken like a pair of powerful lenses, and I had the uncomfortable feeling that he was looking into my very soul. When I finally ran out of gas, he nodded and leaned back from the table. Apparently, he had seen everything he needed to see.

"Son, we've got some work to do," he announced abruptly. "Meet me at the driving range tomorrow morning. 6:00 A.M. sharp."

Harry signaled the waiter, and endorsed the check with a flourish. As he was leaving the grill, he turned and called across the room.

"And finish that soup! It's a tradition."

After a fitful night, I awoke early and sneaked down the stairs carrying my shoes. As I closed the front door behind me, I could hear the staff rattling around in the kitchen of the guest house starting breakfast. I had at least two hours before my boss would start wondering where I was, and a good three hours before our scheduled tee time. I only hoped that Harry could work his magic quickly—whatever it was.

When I got to the range, a secluded five-acre tract tucked away in the piney woods, the sun was just breaking over the tops of the trees. There was not a cloud in the sky. It looked like it was going to be a perfect spring morning.

Harry was already on the line, hitting some soft pitches toward the 100-yard marker. As I approached, he turned and smiled slightly.

"There's some coffee in the thermos and some buttered rolls in the bag," he said.

"Thanks just the same," I said. I was far too nervous to eat and the last thing I needed was a jolt of caffeine. I just wanted to get on with it.

"Okay, then let's see you hit a few."

After a couple of practice swings I addressed the ball and began taking back my five-iron low and slow as innumerable instructors had taught me. At the height of my back swing, I consciously paused, thinking of Cary Middlecoff, Nancy Lopez, and Steve Pate, hoping to prevent my usual over-the-top move. Next I rolled my left knee targetward sending my weight lurching onto my left side. I caught the ball just a little thin, but it still went out a good 170 yards before dropping perfunctorily to the turf.

Harry grunted knowingly and I quickly moved another ball into position with the clubhead. This time I tried to focus more on my tempo, picturing Al Geiberger and Larry Mize in my mind's eye. Beneath my breath I tried to hum a little waltz as I took the club back. "One-two." Pausing briefly at the top, I came down slowly humming "three-four." I picked the ball cleanly off the sod and found myself in a full follow-through, but the ball had very little steam and only went about 160 yards before it faded down to the turf.

"Taken a lot of lessons, have you, son?" asked Brady with a knowing smile.

"Just got back from two weeks at Vardon's Golf University down in Florida," I answered. "It's my sixth time."

"Well, you sure bought a pretty swing," said Brady. He smiled again and cocked his head to the side in down-home fashion. "Yessiree, Bob, a pretty swing!"

"Then how come I played so badly yesterday?"

"Son," he continued, "the s⌐ ⌐et to playing good golf has absolutely nothing to do w   now many lessons you've taken, how expensive your ⌐ ⌐ipment is, your biorhythms, or how many videotapes you've got sitting next to your VCR."

"So what is it then, luck?"

"Absolutely not," said Harry. "It ain't luck neither."

"Then what is it?"

"Magic."

"Magic?"

"That's what I said."

"Come on, Mr. Brady, don't waste my time. If you can't help me with my swing, just say so . . ."

"Cool down, son. Before you get your knickers in a twist, let me show you what I'm talking about."

Harry reached into the side pocket of his old canvas carry bag and pulled out a small drawstring pouch. Inside was a small metal tin with the word "Licorice" printed on its cover in antique script. It contained a foul-smelling brown goo with the consistency of crystallized honey. Harry scooped out a dab with his finger and smeared it on the face of his driver.

"Now what's your biggest problem, son?" Harry teed up a ball and took a gentle practice swing. Then he unloaded a picture-perfect drive.

I was thunderstruck. "What is that stuff?"

Harry ignored my question. "Biggest problem?" he asked again.

"My driver, it's been so bad I've been using my three wood off the tee, and I'm still duck hooking like crazy. What is that stuff?" I asked again.

"Nothing really. Little bit of this and that," Harry replied. "Let me see your driver."

Holding the string of the pouch in his teeth, he examined every square inch of my expensive doorstop with great care. First he sighted down the shaft to check its alignment. Then he tapped the face with a brass divot tool and held the clubhead to his ear so he could listen to its vibrations.

When he finished, Brady grunted noncommittally and handed it back. "Let's do a little experiment, son. Take some of the paste and rub it on like I did."

He popped the lid on the licorice tin and offered it to me.

"Won't this make the face of the driver slippery?"

"Just try it."

I took a small amount of the goo and rubbed it into the face of my $300 state-of-the-art, duck-hooking driver.

"Guess it can't hurt." I smiled.

I took it back deliberately as I had been taught, expecting nothing but the usual disaster. Coming down, I made the transition a little too fast—a classic over-the-top move. The ball would be headed sharply left as usual. Then I heard an unfamiliar sound—the sharp report of a fully compressed ball. It shot off the clubface like a bullet, on a low trajectory. After a hundred and fifty yards it seemed to gather speed as if an afterburner had just kicked in. After another fifty yards the ball rose softly to its apex before turning over and drawing—yes, drawing—softly down to earth.

"My God," I muttered softly. "What's in that stuff?"

"Afraid I can't tell you that." Harry chuckled softly. "It's a closely guarded secret."

"Well, then sell me some! How much is it?" I took out my wallet and pulled out the deck of new twenties I had gotten from the cash machine before I left New York.

"I'll pay you anything you want," I pleaded. "Just get some of that goo."

Harry placed his hands on my shoulders paternally. "Put your money away, son. It's not for sale."

"Then where can I get some?"

"Well, as they say on television, 'it's not available in stores,' " he said with a chuckle. "But tell you what I'll do. I'll pick some up for you at my other club. How's that?"

"I don't have time for that, Mr. Brady. I need it now."

"Call me Harry, son."

Mustering up all the earnestness I could manage, I looked him square in the eyes.

"I'll be straight with you . . . Harry. Hartless & Craven is downsizing. The geeks from human resources are already nosing around my department. If I blow another round with Craven, my career is over. You've got to help me."

He raised his hand.

"Okay, I hear you. Now, I don't normally do this, son. But you seem like a decent fellow and I'd like to see you get ahead. So, I'm going to take a chance. That is, if you'll work with me."

I nodded eagerly.

"Will you work with me, Tom?"

"Whatever you say, Harry. You just tell me what to do and I'll do it."

"That's swell, Tom. Just swell. But I gotta tell you that this isn't going to be easy," said Harry. "It might even be a little bit dangerous."

"You want me to sign a release or something?" I joked.

"No, nothing like that." Harry smiled. "No, for right now, your word as a golfer is good enough for me."

"You've got it," I said.

"Then we've got a deal," he said solemnly. "Follow my directions to the letter, and I can pretty much guarantee you'll win that Nassau this morning."

We shook hands firmly to seal the deal and then looked up toward the soft amber sky. "It's getting lighter," he said. "Let's get over to the first tee."

"But I don't have time to play a round," I said, tapping on the crystal of my watch. "Craven and I are on with the clients at eight o'clock. That's only an hour and a half from now."

Harry grabbed me by the shoulders and wheeled me around so that I was looking straight into his eyes.

"You've got to trust me, son, if I'm going to help you," Harry said slowly. There was a hint of reproof in his voice. "Do you want this or not?"

"Yes," I answered.

As Harry nodded and gathered up his gear, I shouldered my bag and started up the path to the first tee. But the old man had other ideas.

"I know a shortcut," he offered, pointing to a small break in the trees at the far end of the range. As we walked a warm breeze rustled gently through the leaves, and though it held the promise of a glorious spring day I felt a sudden chill.

CHAPTER 1

Mount Augustus

In which Tom discovers what lies beyond Pine Valley

Like most shortcuts, Harry's path through the forest left me wishing I had gone the long way around. Fifty yards in, the fragrant pines gave way to a virtual forest primeval—an older growth of heavy gnarled oaks, elms, and chestnuts. Their thick leaves formed a canopy that almost completely shut out the early-morning sunlight. Now it was not only darker, but colder as well, and I found myself wishing that I hadn't left my new Pine Valley sweater on the dresser in the guest house. Lost in my thoughts, I tripped over a tangle of roots and went tumbling down an embankment, spilling my clubs into a dense bed of ferns.

As I gathered them up and brushed the dirt and leaves off my new pants, I cursed Craven and his $20 Nassaus. I lit into H&C and the entire consulting industry, and finally, I ripped Harry Brady for knowing shortcuts. As I was raving, Harry appeared over the edge of the embankment and waved me up.

"It's not much farther, son," he said. After I had clawed my way to the top he pointed to a soft glow about fifteen yards ahead. "Over there," he said, clapping me on the back, "that's the clearing."

He didn't wait for me to pull myself together, but took off toward the light at double speed. His enthusiasm was so infectious I immediately forgot my anger and trotted after him like a puppy chasing a ball.

When we emerged from the trees we were standing at the top of a small hill. The world rolled outward like a verdant carpet, infinitely varied in its shapes and textures, and yet infinitely green. There were hues of deep forest, rich aquas and bright kellys in the foreground gradually giving way to muted olives, mosses, and darker earth tones until my eyes finally reached the horizon and I could see no further.

As my senses adjusted to the richness before me I began to pick out details in the magnificent landscape. The contours of what must have been the first hole began to appear. A soft mantle of fog hugged the gently rolling fairway, and shafts of sunlight broke through the trees, piercing the misty air like long swords wielded by medieval knights. It was beautiful in the way every golf course is in the early morning, all soft colors and gentle vistas full of promise and power.

A tiny footpath wound down the hill and then cut through a meadow of wildflowers that ended at the bank of a brook. A rude wooden footbridge crossed the shimmering water at its widest point and led to the gentle mound of the first tee.

"Wait a minute," I muttered softly.

Harry smiled and said gently, "Welcome to Mount Augustus."

"What happened to Pine Valley?"

"Nothing at all," replied Harry. "It's right where it's always been . . . in its own world."

Harry gestured toward the fairway that stretched before us. "And it's right here, too," he continued. "Only different."

"How do you mean?" I asked, following the sweep of his hand as he caressed the landscape before us.

"It's how it was meant to be, son, the very heart and soul," replied Harry. "Soak it in for a moment and then let's play."

As he spoke, the fog that obscured the hollows of the valley lifted like a curtain blown by a gentle breeze, and there was no doubt we were standing in a world very far from home. Pine Valley's venerable clubhouse on the adjacent hill had disappeared, replaced by a dense thicket of brush and trees, and where the starter's house had been was a mogul covered with thick sod and spring flowers. The paved road that had formerly cut right through the dogleg on the right of the fairway had become a simple meandering footpath. The fairway itself was different, too. Instead of carefully cultivated Bermuda fairways it was a wild mixture of native grasses, common weeds, and wildflowers.

The balmy spring air we had left behind at the driving range was now richer, colder, and cleaner. I took a deep breath, filling my lungs, and was instantly invigorated. But it seemed to have a different effect on Harry. He coughed and pulled an ancient sweater from his bag.

"You okay?" I asked.

"I'll be fine," said Harry. "It always affects me that way at first."

Before he could elaborate, the tranquillity was shattered by a loud "CRACK!" Harry grabbed me by the shoulder and pulled me down. An instant later, a projectile shot over our heads and crashed through the trees behind us. A man's booming voice echoed through the clearing.

"NUN SHA' PASS!"

"What's happening?" I whispered.

"Look on the bridge," Harry whispered back. "But keep your head down."

I gingerly parted the nettles in front of my face, and through the mist saw the shadowy silhouette of a man straddling the footbridge. It was impossible to make out his features, but there was no mistaking the fact that he was a man of extraordinary size brandishing a weapon in his right hand.

"NUN SHA' PASS!" the man shouted again. "Any man who dares tae sneak onto these hallowed grounds will ha' tae go through me furst. An' nae man alive has snuck pas' Angus McLeod!"

The giant who called himself Angus dropped a small stone onto the bridge and then took a flat backswing, wrapping the club caddy-style around his body. He swung down rhythmically and the stone shot off with a sharp report down toward the fairway—a good 250 yards—before it began to rise and then drop suddenly in the midst of several black-faced sheep. They scattered hurriedly as the stone thumped onto the fairway.

"NUN SHA' PASS," the man shouted again, his voice echoing through the quiet glade.

"We've got a little problem here," whispered Harry.

"Who is this guy?" I asked.

"You heard him. He's Angus McLeod," answered Harry. "And he's not happy."

"Who the hell is Angus McLeod?"

"AH KNOW YE'RE THERE," he shouted again, and I ducked as another stone flew in our general direction, taking the limb off a tree behind and to our right.

"He's the God of Starters," whispered Harry.

"The *God* of Starters? Harry, what the hell are you talking about?"

"You know, G-O-D, god! Deity, divine being, immortal,

prime mover, universal consciousness, the almighty." Harry rattled off the list in machine-gun fashion and then hugged the ground as another rock crashed through the foliage above our heads.

"Like Zeus and those guys who throw thunderbolts?"

"Pretty much," Harry replied, "and he doesn't want us here."

Another missile shot over our heads.

"Better hunker down, son. Those rocks are real."

"Why is he so angry?"

"Unless I miss my guess, MacKenzie's on the course today," said Harry. "Angus doesn't usually get this worked up unless the Boss is around."

"MacKenzie?"

"The Great God of Golf himself," Harry replied. There was a note of reverence in his voice.

"So what do we do now?" I asked.

"No problem, son. You're the guest of a member," Harry replied, smiling.

"You mean *this* is the other club you were telling me about?" Visions of magic and salvation were dancing in my head.

"That's right," replied Harry with a mysterious smile. "Mount Augustus is the Golf Club of the Gods."

Now I understood what was happening—I was dreaming and would soon awaken in a tangle of sheets back at the guest house, hopefully before the dream dissolved into the nightmare I'd been having since business school. The one where I'm standing buck naked in front of my mostly female study group explaining why I hadn't finished the financials on our term project.

But the "dream" was hanging on with incredible tenacity, and I was still fully clothed. There were only two possible conclusions: the golf gods Harry was talking about were real, or this near total stranger I had entrusted my career to was stark raving mad.

Harry leaned over and pinched me hard on the forearm.

"It's not a dream," said Harry with a laugh. "You should

The Fable of Angus—The God of Starters

In the beginning it was decreed by the Great MacKenzie that Mount Augustus hold its secrets safe from all those not invited to share them. And so he sought a god to stand as gatekeeper at the sacred entrance. But none would sacrifice the pleasures of the mountain to do his bidding. So MacKenzie bided his time knowing one of them would soon incur his wrath and could be punished. That it would turn out to be Angus, his favorite son, and the one destined to rule the mountain after him was yet unrevealed.

The fortunes of young Angus changed forever on a sunny summer afternoon when he was touring the lower 18 with some of the minor gods. Searching for an errant shot he chanced upon a beautiful young Goddess named Glenda who was bringing mead, wine, and sweetmeats to the other gods. Mistaking her for a wood nymph, Angus was pierced through the heart and fell helplessly in love. Little did he know that his father had cast his eyes on Glenda long before. A battle royal ensued with Angus challenging MacKenzie not only for Glenda, but for the throne itself. MacTavish, the God of Rules, proposed settling the dispute with a match over the upper 18, a treacherous mountain layout.

Angus had strength and youth on his side, but MacKenzie had experience and a deft touch around the greens. The Great God won 4 and 3, but so powerful was his anger at his once favored son that he damned him to stand guard outside the Kingdom's gates forevermore and bar the uninvited from setting foot upon the sacred links.

Banished from MacKenzie's sight and left to his own devices he became greedy, extracting tribute from all who would play there. According to legend, however, on Mondays when clouds completely cover Mount Augustus, the Great MacKenzie often sleeps late. Then Angus's stepmother Glenda descends from Mount Augustus and allows him to enter and play the sacred links.

---

see the look on your face. You're staring at me like I just escaped from Bellevue. Well, can't say as I blame you, son. Mount Augustus is a lot to deal with. But it's real—as real as anything gets."

"I don't know about this. All I wanted was a couple of pointers."

Harry turned on his side to face me. "Look, maybe I made a mistake here," he said. "If you want to, we'll turn back right now. No hard feelings. But if you stick with me, Tom, I promise you'll experience something only a few men in history have done before you."

Before I could reply, Angus shouted from the bridge, "Show yerselves like men or Ah'll cum an' drag ye out meself."

Harry waved his hat above his head and rose to his feet while I pressed deeper into the nettles.

"Well, what's it going to be?" asked Harry. "Are you coming?"

While I wasn't anxious to get up close and personal with a giant rock-driving starter god, I decided to follow Harry down the hill. There wasn't anything back at Pine Valley except certain disaster, and I still held out hope that Harry could help me. I stood, raising my arms above my head like a prisoner of war.

"Tae tha' bridge ye sneak thieves an' na a step further," Angus ordered.

When we were about ten feet from the bridge Angus raised his club, motioning us to halt. Harry gestured for me to stand behind him.

Up close Angus was no less terrifying than when he was smashing rockets over our heads. He was at least 6' 5", and standing astride the small wooden bridge, he looked a good foot taller. His face was craggy and flushed, and accented by a large mustache. He wore an old tweed jacket, decorated with tournament badges and golfing medals, and a Highland kilt with the soft blue and yellow weave of the McLeod tartan.

"Thought ye could sneak pas' Angus, did ye?" he shouted, raising the bushy brow over his right eye.

"Not at all," I said nervously. "We just didn't see you . . ."

"Dinna see me? Dinna see me!" The giant Scotsman jumped off the bridge and in three mighty strides was in my face like a demented drill sergeant.

Angus leaned forward and bellowed in my ear, "Ah've haff a mind tae scatter yer trespassing brains all oer tha furst fairway! 'Tis a terrible thing whin a body canna step intae tha bushes tae satisfy a call o' nature withou' sum mortal hacker tryin' tae slither on tae tha coorse like a thief."

Blood vessels on the enraged Scotsman's forehead bulged and pulsed. The force of his voice filled the valley and his face was so red that I was sure he would explode with fury.

"Do ye ken wha' Ah do tae weasels who try tae sneak onto ma coorse? Ah pool their limbs off one by one—like tha' wings off a fly, an' then Ah beat 'em about tha head wi' 'em! Ah tae every ball oot o' their bags an' droop 'em in tha nearest waterhole. An' finally, Ah write their name doon in ma wee book so tha' they'll niver get onto ma coorse, nae matter how many members they cum wi'. . . ."

He reached over and with one hand lifted me high into the air.

Just then, Harry spoke and I, for one, thought it was about time. "Whoa there, Angus. It's me, Harry Brady."

"Harry Brady?"

"Angus, I'd like you to meet Tom," said Harry with a wry smile. "Tom's a friend of mine from Pine Valley."

Angus considered this for a long moment, still holding me off the ground at arm's length. Though still suspended in midair, I offered my hand in friendship. He stared at Harry curiously.

"By tha Great God MacKenzie, 'tis really ye, Harry?"

"Yes, it's me, Angus," replied Harry. He removed his Pine Valley hat to reveal his balding pate.

"Ah niver thought tae see ye again, auld friend," said

Angus, smiling broadly as he dropped me to the ground in a heap. Then his craggy face suddenly clouded over. "Whin ye stayed away so lang, Ah thought MacTavish had won fer sure, Harry. Does MacTavish know yer on that mountain?"

"Well, I didn't send him an engraved note that I was coming, if that's what you mean," said Harry, hitching up his pants. "But I expect the little weasel knows I'm here."

"What's this all about, Harry?" I asked.

"Nothing, son. Just a little wager between some of the members," Harry replied dismissively. "Usual stuff."

"By tha by Harry, Ah've still ga' tha' woolen scarve ye brought me las' time, an' o' coorse tha' fancy metal driver," Angus resumed brightly. "But Ah canna' use it whin anyone's heer, or tha word wuild get back tae Weyland. But let's na' stan' heer prattlin'. Cum tae tha hoose, and we'll hae sum tea!"

Angus spun around on his heels. Harry winked at me, grabbed his bag, and followed. I looked back at the treeline, but the opening in the trees leading back to Pine Valley had closed. For the moment, at least, going back was no longer an option. So I fell in line behind Harry and followed Angus, The God of Starters, to his home.

Angus's house was really a grotto cut into the hillside off the first tee. The front of the cave had been sealed off by a rude wooden facade with a heavy door and one tiny window. A rusty stovepipe had been shoved through the sod on top. There was a tiny plume of smoke mixing with the misty air above.

"Cum in, an' warm yer bones," said Angus, taking off his tam-o'-shanter.

He moved toward the center of the room where an old potbellied stove glowed invitingly in the dark. A cast-iron pot with a heavy lid sat on the stove. Angus took a towel that had clearly come from Pebble Beach and lifted the lid. Although he smiled with pleasure, the odor was reminiscent of moldy sweatsocks left stewing too long in a gym locker. I thought I was going to gag.

"What is that?" I gasped.

"Haggis, me lad, and it's dun ta a turn. Wuild ye be joinin' me in a bit o' breakfast?" offered Angus.

Harry shook his head.

"What is haggis?" I asked.

"Food fer tha gods is all," Angus interrupted. "Ye get the sheep's stamach fresh as can be, an' stuff it wi' oatmeal . . ."

"Thanks, but I ate at the guest house," I said as politely as I could.

While the two friends warmed their hands and chatted by the stove, I began to quietly snoop around. I'm not sure what I was looking for, but when I saw some metal tins sitting on a crude shelf next to the door, my heart leapt. Although some were rectangular and others round, they were all roughly the same size as Harry's licorice tin. If they contained what I thought they did, the mother lode was mine.

My head began to swim and the future stretched out before me like a vision in a crystal ball. Using the goo, I'd win the Nassau and become old man Craven's fair-haired boy. Then I'd marry his lovely daughter—if he had one—and take over the firm when he retired.

Then I thought, wait a second. I'm selling myself short. With Harry's driving goo in my pocket, I don't need old man Craven. When he offers me a partnership, I'll tell him to shove his job! Then I'll take the stuff to a first-rate lab and have it analyzed. I'll set up an offshore factory and manufacture it under the name of Cruickshank's Miracle Cure—Good for Slices, Hooks, and Distance Woes. Then I'll go public and be the hottest golf stock since Callaway brought out the Big Bertha! In six months I'll be a kazillioinaire.

Harry and Angus were too deep in conversation to notice, so I lifted the stack of tins from the shelf. A tingle of excitement and a delicious rush of guilt flowed through me. I was a child again back in Illinois, playing soldiers with my aunt Gertrude's Hummel figurines while the unsuspecting adults drank tea in the parlor.

As I brought them down to waist level, the tins unexpectedly made a rattling noise, and when I opened the first one all I found was hard yellow candy. Every last tin was filled with lemon drops. Apparently The God of Starters had a sweet tooth. I quietly replaced them and continued exploring. The driving paste had to be around somewhere.

I figured I would look as long as possible and if I couldn't find it, hope there was enough on the face of my driver for a good lab to analyze.

As I moved further back into the dimly lit grotto I realized it was only the antechamber to a much larger cave, and along the rough walls as far as the eye could see, were softly glowing metal objects that turned out, on closer inspection, to be golf clubs. Hundreds—no, thousands—of sticks of all descriptions were hanging from hooks set in the stone. There were old long nose playclubs from the 1700s, hand-forged irons with hickory shafts, mashies, niblicks, mashie-niblicks, spoons, irons with exotic markings on their faces, and more modern clubs, too: forged and cast irons with hickory, steel and graphite shafts; and woods of every substance known to man. It was a private flea market, a bonanza of golf history, worth millions in the collectibles market.

I picked a George Low Wizard 600 putter and held it up to the light. In mint condition, it was probably worth five grand at least. Smiling in wonder, I began to practice my stroke on the floor of the cave.

"Wha' do ye think yer doin'?" Angus thundered suddenly.

"I was just trying out the putter," I answered.

" 'Tis na' tha bleeding pro shop!" Angus growled. He snatched the Wizard from my hands and returned it carefully to its spot on the wall. "An' I'll thank ye tae keep yer thieving hands off me booty. Ye're a snotty wee fellow an' deservin' of a blow."

Harry came between us, winked at Angus, and walked me over to a quiet corner.

"All this stuff belongs to Angus," whispered Harry. "It's the tribute he's exacted from golfers over the ages."

"You mean these things are 'tips'?"

"He may be a god, Tom, but he's still a starter, and a starter can't change his stripes," Harry explained patiently. "He'll be asking for something from us, too. That's why I picked up one of those new teardrop putters after lunch yesterday. The problem is you never know what he's looking for."

Harry turned to Angus, who was glaring at me with his arms folded across his chest.

"The boy meant no offense, Angus," Harry announced with a hearty smile. "We're just here to play a little golf. I know it's awfully short notice, but do you think you could get us out this morning?"

Angus's face dropped and he moved to a window, shaking his head dubiously.

"Weel, we're awfully backed up this mornin'...." said Angus as he looked out the window. The course was completely empty except for the dozen or so sheep that had resumed grazing in the fairway.

"We're the only ones here, Harry," I whispered.

Harry gave me a withering glance, and raised a finger to his lips.

"I'd sure appreciate it if you could squeeze us in," said Harry.

"Ah've ga' a big outin' due heer any time noo," Angus replied. "Sum o' tha younger gods are bringin' a whole party frum Elysian Fields an' ..."

"Think you could get us out before them, seeing as how we're a twosome?"

Angus picked up an old leather-bound accounting ledger from the table under the window and opened it. He ran his finger down the middle of the page and shook his head again.

"Ah'd love tae, Harry, really wuid," said Angus. "But Fergus says there's a terrible amount o' frost on tha greens

... and ye ken tha a Greenskeeper must answer only tae himself."

"It's sixty degrees out there at least, how could there be frost?" I muttered.

Harry shot me a glance that said, don't push it.

But Angus hadn't heard me. He was interested in something else.

"Tha's a fine pair o' trousers ye got on, mortal," said Angus. "Whar evir did ye find them?"

"Brooks Brothers," I replied.

Angus looked puzzled.

"It's a men's store in midtown," I explained.

"Noo, wha' color wuild ye call tha', laddie?"

"I think it's a sort of lime green," I answered.

"Ye dinna say," said Angus, bending over to inspect them. "How did they evir sew on all those wee whales?"

"A machine, I guess," I answered, not quite sure where this was going.

"Ah'll be go tae hell." The giant Scotsman sighed appreciatively.

"That's what they're called." I laughed.

"Called?" queried Angus. "What are called?"

"These pants, Mr. McLeod. They're what an upper-class WASP calls 'go-to-hell pants.' "

"Ga-tae-hell pants, indeed!" said Angus, with a giggle.

He reached out to feel the cloth and I jumped back reflexively. Angus let out a low guttural sound like a German shepherd who's just had a choice bone snatched from his mouth.

"Give him the pants," Harry whispered in my ear.

"What?"

"He wants your pants," said Harry. "That's the only way we're going to get onto the course. Rule number one: you always take care of the starter, especially if he's the God of Starters."

"What do I wear?"

"Put on your rain gear," said Harry.

As I began to slip off my trousers, Angus smiled broadly and rubbed his hands together in gleeful anticipation.

"Tha's awfully nice o' ye, Tom," said Angus, holding his prize out in front of himself. "Ah can call ye Tom, can' Ah?"

I was standing bare legged in my skivvies in a drafty cave, but apparently I had made a friend. After folding my lime green go-to-hell pants over a rickety old chair, Angus consulted his ledger once again and discovered that, wonder-of-wonders, there was a cancellation he had overlooked.

"But ye'll hae tae play wi'oot a caddie," he said tersely. "And ye'll hae tae keep yer own tally."

"It's good exercise to shoulder our own bags, Angus, and Tom here's a genuine MBA," said Harry. "We'll be fine."

"Keepin' tha tally 'tis a great responsibility, youngster. The God o' Rules will watch ye like a hawk an' tha price o' failure is dear," said Angus as he reached behind a counter made of rough planks and withdrew a leather pouch. He opened the drawstring and spilled a large pile of tiny stones on the wooden surface.

"Ye'll notice tha' tha bag ha' two sides," he continued. "One is red an' tha other green. Tha countin' stones rest in tha red side. Ah'll gie ye more than enough tae take ye through tha round. Noo, wha' ye mus' do at tha finish o' each hole is tae pull a stone fer each stroke ye hae taken an' place it safe in tha green side. At tha end o' yer round, tha stones frum tha green side will be tallied by tha God o' Rules, and ye will know yer score. But ye mus' do it wi'out fail at tha end o' each hole. Tha price fer failure is high. Do ye ken?"

"Sure, I get it," I replied. "You move the stones from one side to the other after every hole."

"Add well and honestly, newcomer." He glared at me to prove he was serious.

I couldn't help noticing that he didn't give Harry a scoring sack of his own. Perhaps it was nothing, but then, years of office politics taught me most things that happened in life were loaded with meaning.

"Shall we do it?" said Harry brightly.

"Aye, 'tis time, indeed," Angus chuckled.

And so, with a great flourish Angus escorted us out the door, and we headed out to the first tee. As we walked I asked Harry why he didn't have to cart a bag of rocks around, too, and he explained that members had a different system. Before I could ask what it was, he turned to watch Angus, who had been following us at a respectful distance but had stopped well short of the tee and was looking carefully around, his ear to the wind.

"Listening for MacKenzie," Harry whispered.

When Angus was certain all was well he strode jauntily forward and joined us on the tee.

The first hole at Mount Augustus was a par 4, dogleg right of roughly 425 yards. Like Pine Valley, it featured a large expanse of unraked sand just off the tee box. On the right side of the fairway was a large stand of trees making it necessary to keep the ball to the left rather than challenging the dogleg.

As the "member," Harry showed the way, cutting his shot softly into the fairway about 240 yards out. As I reached for my bag, I discovered that my new friend Angus was way ahead of me, already holding my driver in his hands.

"Tha's a fine bit o' craftsmanship there, laddie," Angus commented as he handed me the driver. " 'Tis a spot o' sumthin' sticky, though. Should Ah wipe it off fer ye?"

"No, no. Thanks anyway," I replied quickly.

I took a couple of practice swings off the box to warm up and my synthetic rain pants made swishing noises on my backswing. It was like doing the Lambada wearing a shower curtain. The raspy sound totally disrupted my positive swing thoughts, and I felt myself in the grip of a grand and classic case of first-shot jitters. My stomach tightened up like a drum and my knees felt like the joints had dissolved into semifrozen Jell-O. If there was a substitution rule in golf I would have asked Harry or even Angus to take my first shot.

As I wobbled to the front of the tee box, Angus leapt in front and pulled a large red handkerchief out of his hip pocket making a great show of dusting off the tee—like an umpire sweeping off home plate. I reached into my pocket for a ball, but once again, my new friend was a step ahead. I hadn't seen him go into my bag, but he must have, because he produced a pristine white ball decorated with the Hartless & Craven boar's head logo and proceeded to tee it up exactly 1¼ inches. Then he threw an arm over my shoulders and pointed down the fairway.

"Ye'll be wantin' tae fade on this hole, laddie," said Angus with a broad smile. "An wi' tha' fine driver o' yers, ye should hae na trouble." He stepped away from the tee, bowing and scraping like a French courtier.

There was no option but to hit away. I took as deep a breath as my strictured lungs would allow and went for it. The relief that coursed through my body as I hit the ball was as sweet as getting an unexpected tax refund. Harry's goo was still working, and once again I caught my ball flush on the sweet spot. It started out low, apparently heading toward the left side of the fairway and the trees, but as it began to approach the cluster of pines it began to turn, cutting sharply back and finishing twenty yards ahead of Harry's shot. Behind me there was a sudden explosion of applause and cheering. From all the noise I expected to see a gallery the size of Arnie's Army, but when I turned all I saw was my new friend Angus clapping furiously.

"Great sho', laddie, great sho'!" yelled Angus. "Ah seen Hogan, Ah seen Snead, and wee Tom Morris, too, but niver hae Ah seen a drive as fine as tha'! Ye will na be needing my friend Mulligan this day on tha mountain."

Harry acknowledged the drive with a barely perceptible nod of his head and a cryptic, "Shot."

"Ye ga' a purty swing there, Tommy boy," Angus continued effusively. "A purty swing indeed."

"Thanks," I replied, a flush of pride rising to my cheeks.

Being a junior associate at Hartless & Craven, I was not used to praise, especially not on the golf course.

Angus took the driver from my hand and placed the carry bag over my shoulder. Harry was already twenty paces ahead. I broke into a trot to catch up to the old goat.

"Hae a fine round, lads," said Angus.

"Thanks for everything, Angus," Harry called out without turning around.

"A pleasure as always, Harry."

As I turned to wave good-bye, I saw Angus was waving back with my brand-new $300 driver in his hand. I had just learned how to use it and now it was gone—taking with it the last traces of Harry's goo in my possession.

"Hey, he's still got my driver!"

"I know," said Harry. "Keep walking before he gets your shoes."

CHAPTER 2

Rub of the Green

In which Tom learns the nature of things

As soon as Harry and I were alone on the course some of the strangeness of Mount Augustus began to wear away. We were caught up in that initial burst of exhilaration that comes from being on a challenging new layout in the freshest part of the day. For a time, it was just like any other round; all that existed for us was the course and the next shot.

On the first hole, my approach shot had landed just short, but after a chip and a two putt, I walked off the green feeling smugly satisfied with a gentleman's bogey. Ever elusive par had been in my grasp, I told myself, and I had only missed it due to underclubbing on the approach shot. Even then, I was sure I would have gotten up-and-down if I had been familiar with the speed of the greens at Mount Augustus. Harry, on the other hand, had flushed a seven-iron over the back of the green. He recovered with a wonderful chip out of a clump of weeds on the down-slope that slid and skittered across the green like a billiard master's massé shot. It stopped a mere eight inches from the cup, leaving Harry with a simple tap-in for par. I counted out my five stones and dropped them in the green side. On our way to the second tee Harry grabbed my arm.

"How ya doing, son?"

"Better," I said. "But this is still pretty hard to believe. I mean, 'the Gods of Golf?' Geez, Harry."

"We can still go back if you're not up for it," Harry offered.

"There's time before Craven starts looking for me."

"Like I said, nobody will think the worse of you if you quit now."

"No, let's go on," I said, "at least another hole or two."

"Okay, but keep something in mind. This is *the Mountain*, Tom, not the world. Things may look familiar, but it's different as night and day. You'll see some things and you'll be tested. You'll learn about the game and maybe about yourself. You might find the price is higher than you think. Still in?"

"Yeah, I think I can handle it."

"We'll see," he said, smiling, "but I think so too." He put his arm around my shoulders, and led me to the second tee.

It was a tricky par four about 370 yards long. Once again, we had to drive over a forbidding stretch of sandy waste to reach a landing area. Since Harry still had honors, he served up a high fade that started left and then worked its way back to the middle of the fairway about 220 yards out.

It wasn't until I reached into my carry bag for my driver

that I remembered Angus McLeod had purloined it. Harry smiled and pulled a club from my bag.

"Use your three-wood, son," said Harry. "You won't really need a driver till the back nine anyway."

Maybe it was because the club hadn't been anointed, and maybe it was just the law of averages coming in to play, but for whatever reason, my trusty three-wood nearly deserted me off the second tee. Trying to make up for using less club, I took a mighty lunge and snapped off a low screaming hook that never got more than ten feet off the ground. The ball cleared the waste area off the tee with little to spare, but headed directly for a series of bunkers skirting the right side of the fairway. When disaster appeared certain, it miraculously hooked over the bunkers and hit the fairway hard, like a B–25 on a crash landing. After two gigantic bounces, the ball careened off the fairway at warp speed, finally nestling down in the first cut of rough on the left.

"Came over that one," noted Harry with a grin. "But you got away with it."

All I could muster in reply was a "yep" that would've made Gary Cooper proud.

By the time I reached my ball, my heartbeat had returned to normal, but there were still some cracks in the foundation of my newly acquired confidence. Despite landing in the rough, I had a reasonable lie about 160 yards from the green that was protected by a gauntlet of hazards that Rommel would have been proud to have at Normandy. The fairway ended abruptly some 25 yards short of the fringe, turning into another sandy waste area that rose abruptly into treacherous tiered bunkers that climbed the side of the plateaued green. It looked like a full six-iron to me.

"Take two clubs more," shouted Harry from the fairway. "It's a long way up there."

He was probably right. After all, he was a member and knew the course. But like most lousy golfers, I hated taking advice from better players, which probably explained why

I hadn't improved in the last five years. I was going to have to change my ways if there was any hope of keeping my job, so with a little wave of gratitude I pulled the four-iron from my bag. Before beginning my backswing, I took a quick look back at the green, and stopped. The flag was moving.

It wasn't just flapping in the breeze, but waving wildly back and forth. Suddenly it moved twenty paces to the right, and then it nearly disappeared over the crown.

"What the hell?" I exclaimed.

The flag was moving abruptly back toward the front of the green. Suddenly I could see the source of its bizarre gyrations. A dark furry figure on four spindly legs was moving about the surface of the green, and seemed to be carrying the damn thing in its mouth.

"Hey, Harry," I yelled, "there's an animal up there."

"It's not an animal, Tom," he called back. "It's Fergus and his damned goat."

"And Fergus is . . . ?"

"The greenskeeper," he said, walking toward me.

"What's he doing with the goat?"

"Riding it."

"What should I do?"

"No choice, son," Harry said. "He's not going to move, so you'll have to take your shot."

As I looked back up at the target, the figure on the green suddenly rose up and faced me, holding his hands limply in front of his abdomen. Although Harry had assured me that Fergus was not an animal, he looked exactly like a grizzly sniffing the air for prey—assuming grizzlies rode nanny goats. Even in the morning light, his eyes shone unnaturally like a deer caught in the headlights. He was staring at me with utter contempt.

I knew that look all too well. I had seen it on the faces of countless greenskeepers over the past ten years as they rode their giant mowers down the fairway toward me or continued snaking the greens long after I had hollered "fore" a half-dozen times. It was a look that said, "Go ahead, turkey. You couldn't hit me with a truck." And it made me mad.

"Fore, the green," I yelled, giving the creature fair warning. But he just kept staring at me mockingly. Animal or human, Fergus was undoubtedly a greenskeeper.

"Hit it, son," said Harry.

Although I caught the four-iron flush, it probably wouldn't have reached the green had it not been a flier lie. Just enough grass got between the clubface and the ball so that it came out hot and streaked directly toward the pin, easily carrying over the bunkers guarding the mouth of the green. The next thing I heard was a sickening *thwack* as the ball slammed into Fergus's furry body, sending him tumbling off the goat's back.

While his goat circumnavigated the green bleating cries of distress, Fergus lay like roadkill where he fell.

"That's a one-in-a-million shot, son," Harry said. "A lot of folks here would say he had it coming."

"I've killed him," I said. My heart was racing.

"No, you didn't, but before he's finished with us, you'll probably wish he was dead." Harry spat and shook his head after he hit a fine approach that flew straight for the pin. "Fergus is a pain in the ass, and not only that, the son of a bitch's immortal."

"God of Greenskeepers, right?" I was learning the ropes.

"You got it," Harry replied. "By decree of The MacKenzie himself."

As we reached the end of the fairway, the God of Greenskeepers suddenly sprang to life, glaring at me and breathing loudly through his nose. Fully erect, Fergus was about 4' 11"—a little diminutive for a god. His front teeth were large and protruding, and his hands—which he still held limply at his waist—were small and delicate like a child's. Wrapped around his body like a crude serape was a furry animal skin that Fergus had cinched at the waist with green vines. On his head was a strange crown of sphagnum moss interlaced with ferns, and tiny air plants. Attached to the sides of his headdress were two enormous divots that covered his ears. His cheeks were dark with a week's worth of stubble and his eyes were yellow and aflame with anger. He looked like a junkyard dog just daring me to climb over his chain-link fence.

I pulled my putter from my bag and held it aloft menacingly, but this only encouraged him. He sent my ball tumbling off the green with a swift kick, and it landed just above my feet in the second tier of bunkers.

"Hey," I yelled. I drew my putter back fully intending to heave it at him. But Fergus disappeared over the crown of the green.

"Get ahold of yourself, son," said Harry. "You can't hurt him. You can only make him madder."

Swearing under my breath I reached over to pluck my ball out of the bunker, but Harry grabbed me by the shoulder before I could reach it.

"Better play it as it lays, son."

"But, it was on the green," I protested.

"Here's your sand wedge," said Harry firmly. As I reluctantly took the club, I saw that his eyes were fixed on the trees to the left of the green. As I turned to see what he was looking at there was a rustle in the bush, and a glint of something metallic in the woods. Next, I heard what sounded like a wagon wheel crunching through the leaves and undergrowth on the forest floor.

"Is somebody out there?" I asked.

"You let me worry about that, son." Harry nodded toward my ball. "Just play it as it lays."

With one last look toward the forest, I stepped into the bunker and tried to clear my mind. Then I opened the blade of my wedge and scrunched my feet down in the unraked sand. I could just see over the top of the bunker to the hole some ten yards toward the center of the green. Fergus was nowhere in sight.

I took a full backswing and let the club slide neatly under the ball, sending it soaring skyward. My spirits rising, I climbed up the face of the bunker to get a better look. As the ball continued its soft ascent toward the hole, I heard the sound of snorting in the woods.

"Fore, the bunker!"

I turned in the direction of the shout to see Fergus riding his goat, hell-bent for leather in my direction, holding the flag like a jouster's lance.

"Lookout, Tom!" Harry shouted.

But it was too late. Fergus caught me square in the breastbone, knocking me head over heels back into the first bunker.

As I came to my senses, I was nearly overwhelmed by the musty aroma of rotting leaves and a crushing weight on my ribs. I opened my eyes to see Fergus standing on my chest holding the business end of the flag on my carotid artery. His goat was grazing happily on a hawthorn bush next to my carry bag.

"Yield, mortal!" Fergus growled.

"Harry!"

"Just lie quietly, son," Harry replied. "Everything's under control."

"Yield, mortal, before I run you through!" Fergus demanded again.

"Please take that thing off my neck," I pleaded. "I didn't mean to hit you."

"Perhaps," Fergus replied. "But I've still got a bone to pick with you, mortal." His voice had a high-pitched, throaty quality as if his vocal chords had not been designed for speech.

"I didn't do anything."

Fergus suddenly rose to his full height, and reached deep in the recesses of his serape, pulling out a crumbling handful of earth and grass.

"Haven't done anything? Then how do you explain this?" he demanded.

"I'm not sure what it is," I replied.

"It's murder, pure and simple, that's what it is," Fergus said, growing angrier by the second. "Look at these gentle shoots of rye and tiny buds of wildflower, so carefully nurtured by gentle evening rains and the warmth of the spring sun that ever shines oe'r Mount Augustus. And now, due to your reckless disregard, they've been cut off in their prime, never to go to seed, never to produce after their own kind."

Large tears began pouring down his cheeks. Fergus sniffed once and then threw the clods of earth in my face.

"Don't know what it is?" he moaned. "It's your bleedin' divot from the first hole!"

Out of the corner of my left eye I saw Harry above me, sitting casually on the apron of the green. He was rummaging through the side pocket of his carry bag, looking, no doubt, for some charm or amulet that would save my neck from the hairy beast standing on my chest. When he pulled out a foil package, my spirits soared, but when he peeled away the wrapper there were only two sandwiches on white bread. He began to eat.

"This sure hits the spot," said Harry.

Suddenly, Fergus relaxed his grip on the flag and turned his head back toward the green, sniffing the air.

"Watercress?" he asked.

"Tuna and watercress on white," Harry replied. "Want one?"

"Tuna and watercress!"

Fergus jumped off my chest and scampered up the embankment. Harry held out a sandwich at arm's length, which Fergus snatched greedily. He settled down on his haunches some twenty paces away, to enjoy his sandwich.

With Fergus off my chest, I exhaled and looked up into the sky that had gone from the muted grays of early morning to a brilliant azure, and the sun was almost at the ten o'clock position. Then it hit me: I was late for my tee-time with Craven.

"My God! Harry, what time is it?"

"Take a look at your watch," he said.

I consulted the genuine Swiss chronometer my mother had given me the day I took my MBA from the University of Illinois. Although I jokingly called it my "training Rolex," it hadn't missed a minute in five years. But now it had chosen to stop.

"Geez, Harry, Fergus broke my watch."

"Don't jump to conclusions," said Harry. "Take another look and tell me the time."

"It says six thirty-five," I groaned. "That can't be right. We left the range at six-thirty."

"Be precise," said Harry. "Six thirty-five and how many seconds?"

"It says, six thirty-five and fourteen seconds."

Harry took another bite of his sandwich and chewed for a moment, thoughtfully. Then he swallowed. "Sorry, how many seconds was that?"

I looked back at my watch and immediately realized I must have made a mistake. The sweep hand was now resting on fifteen seconds. I held it to my ear and heard the sound of works moving very, very slowly.

"Your watch is fine, Tom," said Harry. "Time's just different. You can spend a week here and when you get back home almost no time will have passed. Sometimes it's only a few minutes, sometimes a couple of hours."

I collapsed back into the trap in relief. "That sounds great, Harry. Just great."

"Suppose it does," he said. "But nothing's free in life. Always a price to pay."

"What do you mean?"

Harry unwrapped the other half sandwich and offered it to me.

"I've still got another half if you're hungry," said Harry cheerfully, putting an end to the conversation.

I rose and dusted myself off.

"How can you eat that stuff?" I asked.

"I'm really more of a ham and cheese man, but it's okay," Harry answered. "Fergus loves tuna and watercress. I guess it reminds him of his former life."

"His former life?"

"He used to be a beaver."

"That explains a few things," I said. Fergus's gamy odor was still fresh in my nostrils.

"Old Fergus used to dam up the creeks and rivers hereabouts and flood the fairways," said Harry in amusement. "To punish him, MacKenzie put him to work maintaining the course."

"So, he turned Fergus into a greenskeeper?" I said. "But that hardly seems fair, Harry."

"Life sucks, Tom," he agreed matter-of-factly. "It's no more fair here on the Mountain than it is back in New York."

"But he was just doing what beavers do," I protested.

"That's true of all of us, son. We just do what we do, according to our abilities and makeup. But that doesn't stop bad things from happening to us. Your boss is scum, and he makes your life miserable. My first wife cleaned out our checking account and ran off with her tennis instructor. Everybody has their cross to bear."

Harry rose and brushed the crumbs off his lap. "You're away, son."

My bunker shot had left me with a level putt of about 20 feet. I grabbed my putter and tried to read the line. But I was still thinking about what Harry had said.

"That's why I play the game, Harry—to get away from all that."

Harry laughed and shook his head. "Ironic, isn't it? To get away from life, we choose a game that's just as unforgiving as life itself. In the end, we all get punished not for what we do wrong, but for what we are. Just like old Fergus over there."

I fell silent. The conversation was beginning to depress me. Ever since I was forced to sit in the first pew and endure my Calvinist grandfather's sermons during our family summer vacations, the wisdom of my elders had always had that effect. I stroked the putt and surprisingly it rolled within a couple of feet of the cup, but I felt no real pleasure. Harry took a quick look at his line and lagged up about eight inches away. He tapped in for his par and I

The Fable of Fergus—The God of Greenskeepers

Shortly after the creation of the fortunate fields of Mount Augustus, and of course, the creation of golf, the Great God MacKenzie was enjoying a morning round with Mac-Tavish, the God of Rules, and Angus McLeod, who had yet to fall out of favor with his father. MacKenzie had recently finished the 14th hole and was in a fine humor, still exulting in the beauty of his latest creation, but that soon changed when they stepped onto the 14th tee. Instead of finding the pastoral expanse of wild-flowers and grazing sheep that he expected, MacKenzie gazed upon a swelling pond held in place by a complicated series of log dams and earthworks.

He flew into a rage and set out across the flooded meadow in search of the culprit. Just in front of the green, he found a large bull beaver who was ferrying a freshly cut birch toward his chez d'oeuvre—a huge log dam featuring a tumbling cataract spilling directly into the pond. MacKenzie grabbed the hapless beaver by the throat and shouted, "Ye arrogant bastard! Trying to change perfection, are ye? Weel, brother beaver, 'tis a mortal sin, and ye shall pay tha price!"

MacKenzie was in the midst of throttling the innocent creature when MacTavish intervened with a diabolical alternative. A proper punishment for the beaver's audacity, he suggested, would be not only to make him half-mortal but force him to labor in the Edenic garden where he had once frolicked, while others played around him. MacKenzie agreed, and to further punish the changeling, called him Fergus.

---

sank my two-footer for a six, including Fergus's foot mashie into the bunker.

If I understood him correctly, Harry was suggesting that there is an "elect" in the game of golf, just as there is in spiritual life, and that some of us are fated never to be any good at it, no matter how early we take it up or how many lessons we endure. If this was true, then after five years stuck at a fourteen handicap—and a bogus one at that, I was destined never to get any better. Not a lesson I wanted to take to heart. I must have looked as sad as I felt as I counted my stones.

Harry slapped me on the back, and laughed.

"Don't look so downcast, son. It's only a game."

"But what are we supposed to do? It all seems . . ."

"You've got to get an edge, son. That's why we're here on the mountain." Harry stood up and handed me the other half of sandwich.

"Give this to Fergus as a peace offering," said Harry. "I think it's time you started making some friends here."

I walked over to Fergus holding the sandwich in front of me as if I was offering a biscuit to an angry Doberman. He eyed me warily, then snatched it with his teeth.

"I'd like to apologize," I said as he devoured the sandwich. "I usually replace my divots, but I guess I got caught up in the excitement of playing here for the first time."

Fergus stood up and tossed the remains of his tuna and watercress delicacy down the embankment to his goat.

"A shabby and foolish excuse," he said. "But I'll forgive you on one condition."

"And what's that?"

"You must take the oath."

"The oath. Okay. What oath?"

"The Greenskeeper's Oath, of course. Kneel and raise your right hand."

I did as I was told. Harry was sitting on the edge of the green writing furiously in his old leather diary. He was barely able to contain his laughter. Fergus adjusted the divots that covered his ears and began.

"Do you, a mortal who is unworthy and kneels before me seeking worthiness, promise to respect and adhere to the greenskeeper's code of honor in all means and manners, including the replacement of all offending divots, removal of cut worms, and foreign objects from all fairways and greens in order to maintain the pristine and grassy surfaces intended for putting and playing of the ancient game? Do you further promise to report, without delay, sightings of burrowing rodents, birds of prey, and careless golfers who defile the mountain and destroy the greensman's sacred efforts?"

"I do."

"Excellent. Now, there's just one more thing," he continued. "What's your birth name, mortal, and where do you reside?"

"Tom," I answered as I started to rise. "Tom Cruickshank. I live on East Seventy-seventh Street in Manhattan."

"Remain on your knees, Thomas."

I rolled my eyes in Harry's direction. He was working very hard to maintain his composure.

Fergus then took the flag from the second hole and tapped me gently first on the right shoulder and then on the left.

"Rise, Sir Thomas Cruickshank of East Seventy-seventh Street," said Fergus. "You have now been invested in the Sacred Order of Greenskeepers and Superintendents."

I rose.

He reached once more into his fur wrap and pulled out a small canvas bag and handed it to me reverently.

"Carry this with you throughout your round at Mount Augustus. There will come a time when you're lying on a piece of hardpan, a patch of sandy ground, or in an old divot hole. Sprinkle the contents on the offending place and its beauty will be instantly restored, and you will have paid your debt to me."

"So, what is this? Seeds and fertilizer?"

"Seeds and fertilizer? What do you take me for, a gardener? If that's all it was, I certainly wouldn't be needing the likes of you to spread it around!"

I started to open it but Fergus grabbed my hand and shook his head. "You must never open the bag until the time is right, for you may only use it once. Choose carefully."

I nodded and placed it in the zipper pocket that contained my counting stones. I was acquiring quite a collection.

"Thank you for the fine lunch, Harry," said Fergus politely.

"It was my pleasure, Lord Fergus," answered Harry. "Let's do it again soon."

Fergus flashed a toothy feral smile, mounted his goat, and rode off to continue his sacred work.

As we moved on to the third hole, I thought of Fergus's gift tucked safely away in my bag, and felt that just maybe I had acquired something that Harry was talking about—an edge.

CHAPTER 3

Lucifer's Hammer

In which Tom views things from a startling perspective

We were walking through a stand of tall, scraggly pine on the way to three, but if Harry hadn't known the way, I would have been totally lost. Nobody had bothered to mark the path. Unlike most courses back in the world where space was at a premium, Mount Augustus seemed to cover a lot of ground. Logic or necessity certainly didn't seem to have been major factors in its design. However, the hike from green to tee gave me time to think. And what I was thinking about was my fancy driver hanging on the wall in Angus's hut.

"I ought to go back to that stupid cave and just take the damn thing," I said aloud as we walked. "He'll never miss it. Never should have let him take it."

"Thou dins't have a choice," Harry said, bowing low.

"Knock it off," I said.

"Beg pardon, Sir Thomas." Harry bowed again. "But 'tis true. Angus will protect his treasure with his life."

He was right. My chances of retrieving it from the kilted

giant were slim to none. And without the goo to fall back on, my future depended entirely on Harry being a man of his word. It was not a comfortable feeling. However, since I had just been knighted by a beaver, I decided to see if my elevation to the upper crust carried any weight.

"Well then, lackey, returnst thou to the hut and bring the driver back."

"Don't push your luck, son." Evidently Harry wasn't impressed by titles.

"I never wanted to be a knight anyway," I muttered.

"You couldn't hit it worth a damn," said Harry. "Stick to your spoon for a while."

"Spoon?"

"Three-wood. Anyway, the third hole's still a par three. Nothing much to it . . . except for a couple of little things."

"And what would they be?"

"Well, you should do your best to hit the green." Harry checked the wind. "A niblick or a mid-iron ought to be about right in this breeze."

"Harry, for God's sake. Niblick?"

"Five-iron."

"I know what it is, but it's also ancient history."

"I like the old terms," said Harry a little defensively. "They kind of fit on the Mountain. Wouldn't hurt you to get in touch with the history of the game, Tom. There's a lot of it here. And there's nothing wrong with indulging in a little nostalgia now and again. Keeps things in perspective, remembering the past."

"Let's say my 'niblick' doesn't make the green," I said. "Then what?"

"There's the sand devils," said Harry with a smile.

"What are sand devils?" I asked.

"Well, not sure exactly. Don't know what they look like—never actually saw one, but I know they're nasty little creatures who hate golfers and resent interruptions."

"Of what?"

"Their work," said Harry matter-of-factly.

"What work?"

"They construct the moguls and dunes in the fairway bunkers and greenside traps as tribute to MacKenzie. And they take it personally when poorly hit tee shots damage their masterpieces. Listen to me, son, even the gods themselves take the long way around through the woods to avoid the third-hole bunkers. And even then, they only enter the little devils' desert in groups of three."

"So it really is treacherous," I said.

"It gives the word new meaning," said Harry. "May well be the longest 175 yards in golf."

A series of noises from the direction of the third tee made me think Harry was probably right. We paused to listen and I began to distinguish the relentless crack of powerfully hit balls, the sound of something smashing against a rock and shrieks of rage that hung on the wind, echoing through the air.

Harry indicated that we should approach quietly, and as we stepped out of the trees I saw a short, stocky man sitting on a stone bench, holding a driver in both hands and mumbling to himself. He looked like a hand-colored lithograph of a golfer from a time when the game was elegant and the men who played it dashing and stylish. He was wearing brown tweed knickers, off-white knee-high stockings, a dark brown sleeveless cardigan sweater, and a starched white shirt complete with a firmly knotted school tie. His blond hair spilled out from under a tweed car cap that matched his knickers. Around his neck was a long silk scarf with fringe that was as white as his shirt and his kilted cordovan golf shoes glistened in the sunlight.

Maybe it was because of what Harry had said earlier but as I looked at him I felt myself growing nostalgic about an era that I had never known except through paintings, sepia-tinted photographs, and overheard conversations between my father and his friends. It could have been Gene Sarazan sitting there on the bench—except that Sarazan probably wouldn't have been talking so animatedly to his driver.

The club he was addressing was one of the most beautiful objects I had ever seen. A massive construction of highly polished wood, it sparkled with life. I found myself wanting that stick more than anything else in the world.

"Be careful what you wish for, son. You just might get it," intoned Harry, who knew exactly what I was thinking.

I started to set down my bag but Harry motioned me to silence and we stepped back into the trees. The young man rose from the bench and reached into his pocket for a tee, but came up empty. He swore in frustration and searched his pants pockets one by one. Then he rummaged through the compartments of his leather bag, his irritation mounting. He slammed the bag into the bench and knelt down to examine the broken tees that covered the ground like brightly colored confetti.

After selecting the longest of what was available, he placed his ball directly in the center of the tee box as far to the back edge as he could. It seemed odd to me because I was of the opinion that it was better to be as close to the pin as possible right from the start. He stepped back from the ball, holding the face of his driver in both hands, and cleaned it carefully with a terry cloth towel he had produced from his bag. When he was finished, the head of the club shone like a thousand suns.

The power in his arms and upper body was evident when he took a practice swing. The clubhead whistled as it snapped around, creating what could only be described as a minor sonic boom. I felt a rush of turbulent air as the man took another swing and then another. The clubhead soon became a shimmering object whirling in a perfect circle around the stationary but vibrating center of the young man's torso. A few more RPMs and I was sure he would rise off the ground like a tweedy helicopter.

When he wound down I could see that the frightening practice swings had taken their toll. The young man's hat was now on backward and his necktie was slightly askew. His face was tinged red from exertion or perhaps from something else. I felt as if I was witnessing a very private moment and felt a little guilty. He began to speak softly to himself.

"Light touch, Bertie, light touch. Pull it back slow and easy. Little draw, little draw. Set it down light as a feather." Bertie executed a couple of focusing waggles and became stony silent, concentrating totally on the ball.

Suddenly I realized he should be using an iron. Why would anybody in their right mind use a driver on a par three?

"Harry, this is still a par three, isn't it?" I whispered.

"It is," he said.

"But he's using his driver," I whispered again.

"It's all he's got, but anyway, it wouldn't matter. Any club's a driver in his hands. Grip and rip; that's his style. Old Bertie can't help himself."

"Is he a god?" I asked.

"Ssssh," answered Harry.

I didn't see the club begin to move away from the ball, so slow and imperceptible was its motion, but it gained speed quickly on the downswing and I heard the solid smack of clubface against dimpled surface, and the ball rocketed off the tee, disappearing into the cloudless sky before I knew it was gone. I had never seen such power— or such a roar of pain as Bertie dropped the club and rubbed his eyes vigorously with his massive hands.

The boom of the aftershock cracked the air and I stretched my jaw to relieve the pressure. Bertie looked excitedly in the direction of the green as if he expected his shot to appear inches from the pin. But even I knew that if the ball had yet touched the ground it was clearly several hundred yards past the green.

"Damnation," he screamed and smashed the driver against a rock, shattering the shaft and sending the head of the club spinning a fair distance out toward the third green. A screeching sound rose out of the scrub oaks and I could see swirls of dust spinning in the air. The head of the club was caught in the vortex of one of the swirls. It danced above the sand and was carried to a pile of club-

heads out about 40 to 50 yards neatly stacked in a triangular sort of arrangement. The swirl of dust deposited the clubhead carefully on the top of the pile, shrieked, and disappeared.

"Sand devils?" I whispered. Harry nodded.

Bertie evidently heard me because, still vibrating from his destructive frenzy and his face a mask of rage, he turned in our direction and spotted us standing in the shadows. I gulped. The transformation was instantaneous. The anger faded, and he smiled broadly, tossing what was left of the club over his shoulder into the woods.

"This guy's got to be a god," I mumbled again out of the side of my mouth.

"Bertie's in charge of the long ball," whispered Harry. "Sometimes we call him Crusher."

"One of you fellows spare a tee?" he asked in a gentle and understated Southern accent. "I seem to be out."

He walked to his bag where he pulled out a driver that was exactly like the one he just destroyed and several shiny new balls. Balancing the club casually over his left forearm he squinted at us.

"Well, sumbitch, if it isn't Harry Brady," said Bertie with a broad smile. "Haven't seen you for ages, Harry. Where you been, you old scoundrel?"

Harry just nodded as he stepped out of the woods.

"Yeah, it's been too long," Harry replied. "Demands of business, you know."

Bertie's eyes narrowed and his smile fell away. "So, who's he, Harry? The great mortal hope? Or just one of your developer friends?"

"What's he talking about, Harry?" I asked out of the side of my mouth.

"I've made a couple of bucks in real estate—you know, resorts, golf course communities, the usual stuff," Harry whispered. "But not everybody around here's real happy about it."

"No, Bertie, he's got nothing to do with real estate," said Harry with a laugh. "He's just a guest from Pine Valley. Shake hands with Tom Cruickshank, you rascal."

"Tom, pleased to meet you." He smiled and offered his hand.

I walked up onto the tee with a smile on my face and took his hand. He gripped me so tightly I nearly lost my balance. Bertie's meaty squeeze was a vise and I could feel the tender bones in my hand turning to popcorn. A simple and age-old gesture of goodwill had become a contest of strength, and I was losing badly.

The look on his face had turned from a gentle smile to a nasty grin. His eyes were cold. My head was swimming, and as I began to lose consciousness I heard Harry's voice from somewhere in the void.

"So, how you hitting 'em, big guy?"

The darkness left his face and the pleasant smile returned. He released my hand and turned to Harry.

"Poppin' 'em big time, Harry, big time. Got thunder in my club sure as hell." He put his arm around my shoulder. "Take a little advice, friend. Use a strong grip on your driver. Can't expect to hit for power without good fundamentals."

I rubbed the life back into my throbbing fingers hoping everything was in its proper place.

"You can play right through," offered Bertie. "I'm waiting for a fellow to come along. Bet you're up, Harry, always are." He looked over at me. "Harry's always up."

"Harry's up." I nodded.

"I knew it. Harry's always up." Bertie nodded.

Harry stepped up to the tee carrying his five-iron.

"Harry, Harry, Harry! Use your head." Bertie sighed, "Take out your driver!" He shook his head in exasperation.

"Take it easy, big fella. A niblick ought to do the job on a hole short as this one," replied Harry.

"That Harry," Bertie looked over at me and sighed again, "plays his own game. Can't tell him a thing." He was so tense that the cords in his neck were swelling. Clearly, Bertie wasn't used to people who didn't see things his way.

Harry stroked his usual fine shot. Whatever dangers lurked out there for the unsuspecting duffer just didn't seem to exist for him. He was a golfing machine. The ball sang straight and true, arching up and up into the blue sky in a perfect balance of line and speed. It hit the green with a stinging bite about five feet above the pin and spun back down the slope, easing to a stop so close to the cup it looked like a gimmie.

"Hell of a shot," I said.

"Thanks, looks like ol' niblick did the job." Harry nodded and walked to his bag.

"Looks like Harry got away with the iron." Bertie smiled through gritted teeth. "Lucked out again. Selection's gonna kill him one of these times though, mark my words."

The Fable of Bertie—The God of the Long Ball

 Bertie, the eldest son of the Great God MacKenzie, was blessed with the strength and skill only the offspring of a god could possess. This was discovered during the now famous Second Round when, without practice or instruction, he beat his father soundly, acing a 450-yard drive into a gopher hole nestled in a clump of poison ivy for the first "hole-in-one." He won 8 and 7 and soon Bertie was beating his dad on a regular basis.

Nymphs swooned and gods gathered on the tees to watch him hit his powerful drives, shouting, "You da man, Bertie. You da man." He came to love the feeling of "crushing the pellet," and his obsession with distance cost him his short game.

One day the prideful Bertie took it upon himself to alter the par 3, 13th, which was his father's favorite. He called to the gallery that "no 3 was worth its salt" and from henceforth he would deem it a 700-yard par 5, and would play past to the 16th green.

The gallery fell silent, for The MacKenzie had never been challenged. Bertie hit the pellet an easy 450 yards before it came to rest in perfect position for his approach. He took his bag and began to leave the tee. It was then that The MacKenzie stepped from behind a tree.

"Where ya goin', lad?" he asked. "Ye're outta bounds an' mus' hit again."

"Ah'll no' hit agin for my shot 'tis perfect."

" 'Tis na perfect on this mountain, while Ah'm The MacKenzie. For the Mountain is mine and will be mine till Ah gie it up. If ye step off the tee, ye mus' fight."

But Bertie recognized his own boldness for what it was and could not fight his father. He stood on the tee ashamed. So The MacKenzie softened, deciding not to banish his eldest son from Mount Augustus.

"Ye kin stay, lad," he spoke. "But Ah mus' punish ye, for yer pride and foolishness have caused great tumult." The MacKenzie decreed that Bertie would spend three years on the tee for each of the 700 yards of his so-called "new" hole and the beancounter MacTavish called it 2100 years.

"Ah hope ye kin learn ta find tha green in that time," was all The MacKenzie said as he walked away. The gallery abandoned Bertie as well, for they realized there was more to the game than the long ball.

"Born under a lucky star, Bertie, can't fight it," said Harry.

Bertie was silent but watched intently as I searched through my bag for what I hoped would be the right iron. I selected my club and stepped up to the tee.

"What's your weapon, Tom?" Bertie asked.

"I think it's a long mid-iron or something," I answered.

"Ah, speak English," said Bertie.

"It's a four-iron." I looked at Harry, who had a tight smile on his face.

"Nope." Bertie shook his head. "That ain't it."

"What?" I asked.

"You've got a strong breeze comin' right at you. Gotta have more club," Bertie said.

"There's no breeze that I can feel," I said, licking my finger and testing for direction.

"You're just used to it." Bertie's voice was a little strained.

"I guess a man has to make his own mistakes, Crusher," interrupted Harry.

"Well, that is true, Harry." Bertie folded his massive arms and waited for me to hit. "Give it your best shot, Tom."

Just as I was about to begin my backswing, however, he interrupted again. "Tom, excuse me, sorry to call you off, but I just hate to see you take the shot when you're under-clubbed like that. Why don't you give this one a try?" He was offering the monster driver and his gracious smile spoke of everlasting brotherhood.

From the corner of my eye I could see that Harry was shaking his head no, but all I wanted to do was try out that incredible club. So what if I blew it out of the park, I thought eagerly, I'll just take the penalty stroke and move on like I'd done hundreds of times before. It wasn't rational, but it was honest.

"I guess there is some wind," I said. "Hate to be short on a hole like this." Bertie stepped up on the tee and handed me the club. Harry was saying something but I couldn't hear what it was. I touched the grip and felt raw, angry power. The thing seemed to dance in my hands. It was alive. This wasn't about the game anymore—no logic, no skill, no combination of craft, wisdom, and experience. This was about power and the opportunity to smack the crap out of the ball with a god's perfect club just so I could watch it disappear in the far distance. I didn't care where it went. All I wanted was to see it go.

I took a practice swing and thought I was going to break the sound barrier. Bertie was laughing loudly, Harry was on his feet.

"I need . . ." I gasped, I couldn't finish the sentence.

"Right here, my man," called Bertie. He was pulling a tee and a handful of balls out of Harry's bag.

"Take your best shot." He laughed.

"Tom," Harry yelled, "hold on a second."

"Go for it, big guy," screamed Bertie.

"Better think about this," yelled Harry.

I pegged up the ball, set my feet, and wiggled the clubhead in preparation for what promised to be the shot of my life. In that moment I was a god myself. Nothing around me mattered. All I could see was the ball on the tee at my feet and the shimmering clubhead dancing behind it. I was the club, the club was me. It was Zen. I had discovered my third eye. It was smack dab in the center of the clubface. The ball loomed the size of a grapefruit right before my new center of vision, then the grapefruit became transparent and I could see the pin and the cup as if they were frozen in the crosshairs of a rifle scope. Grid lines expanded out before me, marking the contours of sand and scrub and leading me in precise formation to the green. I owned Mount Augustus.

I started my first backswing as a god.

"Tom!" Harry was trying to get my attention.

"Shut up, Harry. This one's mine," shouted Bertie as he grabbed Harry by the shoulders and sat him down forcibly on the bench.

The struggle between Harry and Bertie was coming into focus as I reached the top of my backswing, which was disconcerting since they were behind me. I was riveted to the ball, focusing intently on its shiny white surface, yet I could see Bertie was smiling broadly and holding Harry firmly on the seat. They were upside-down. I could see the ball on the tee below me and I could see them sitting on the bench upside-down. Then my third eye winked and I realized I was looking at them through the clubface. The upside-down Bertie winked back, encouraging me to swing through, but Harry had a terrified look on his face and he was shaking his head, side to side. Then, as I started my downswing, I realized why Bertie screamed after every shot. I was about to smack myself in the eye with a golf ball.

The world swung crazily as the club came down at the ball. My new third eye was wide with fear. I wanted to stop but I was consumed by the image of the ball soaring off through the cloudless blue into the far distance. I felt a scream rising in my throat.

At the last second everything went black and instead of a crushing impact, I felt the clubhead soar through the bottom of the swing with only the slightest click, and suddenly I could see the sky and clouds rushing up to me. I felt the club leave my hands and fly out toward the fairway.

In the moment of truth, I had blinked.

I looked off the tee and saw that Bertie's club had outdistanced my ball by a good fifteen yards. My shot was lying about ten yards off the tee in a patch of weeds, but Bertie's wondrous driver had landed smack in the middle of the sandy wasteland in front of the green. Within seconds, sand devils had emerged shrieking from their holes and were transporting the club across the sand. I turned and saw that Harry was already on his feet and that he had grabbed both our bags. Bertie was sitting on the bench with his head in his hands, shoulders heaving as he sobbed.

"Step off the tee box," said Harry calmly. "Let's play on."

"I blinked," I said. "I can't believe I blinked."

"Let's play on, Tom," Harry insisted.

I was staring at Bertie.

"Is he okay?" Tears were gushing between Bertie's fingers and cascading down his forearms into puddles at his feet. He must have heard me because he looked up.

"I thought you wanted to hit the long ball, buddy," he said through his tears. "We coulda hit the long ball, buddy." He rose from the bench and started walking toward me. "You coulda busted one, buddy. You coulda joined the gallery." Bertie was walking up onto the tee. The smile was still on his face but his eyes were cold as crystals on a glacier.

"Tom, I suggest you step off the tee box," said Harry quietly. "Now," he added.

As Harry spoke, Bertie sprang forward, reaching for my ankles. But Harry's warning was enough to give me an advantage. Instinctively, I sidestepped and felt him grab for the leg of my rain pants as I tumbled off the front of the tee box into the sand. I thought he was going to continue after me, but when he reached the front edge it was as if he had run into a wall of glass. Bertie could go no further. I understood why Harry was so anxious to move on. The most powerful hitter in the universe was trapped on a par three holding a scrap of fabric from my rain pants. The wind stiffened and it unfurled like a banner.

He looked at me, the rage still coursing through his body, then the passion and anger dissolved away and he seemed to forget we were there. He looked at the piece of Gortex as if he had no idea where he had gotten it and stuffed it absently in his pocket as he walked back to his bag. He selected another driver, sat down, and began to whisper softly to the clubface. He was as he was when we found him.

"You da man, Bertie," Harry said a little sadly. Bertie looked up as if he had heard something and he smiled, but he had no idea we were there.

As I walked away with Harry I looked back over my shoulder and realized that Bertie would remain there until passion overtook him and drove him once again to the tee. Bertie's curse was to live with an unrequited love: he had a thirst for power and control that could never be quenched. As frightening as his passion was, I understood his need more than I was willing to admit, and part of me would have given anything to know what it felt like to hit a drive with Bertie's club. I also understood that I owed my life to the mysterious Harry Brady—a man I barely knew. Golf might be a game on Mount Augustus, but the stakes were a lot higher than I had thought.

"Thanks, Harry," I said.

"It's a funny thing about golf," was Harry's cryptic response.

"What?" I asked as we stopped at my ball, which was sitting up rather nicely on a clump of dirt. It was still a long shot to the green.

"You can't let anyone, especially someone you don't know, tell you how to play a shot. If you do, then you're not playing your game. And if you're not playing your game, you might as well not play at all."

"But isn't that what Bertie's doing?"

"In a way, I suppose he is," Harry replied. "But he's missing an important piece of the puzzle, Tom. You not only have to trust yourself, you've got to see the course like it is, not like you want it to be."

"So how should I play this?" I smiled.

"Don't hit too far behind it and be aggressive." Harry laughed. "Make sure you stay out of the sand."

"But what about Bertie?" I asked Harry. "Won't he ever get off that tee?"

"He wants to play the hole, but he just can't let himself, Tom. He's trapped because a long time ago he tried to make the course something it wasn't. It made MacKenzie mad and he put the hammer down. For the last few hundred years Bertie's been paying the price. He gets up and something happens. His need to punish the ball is stronger than his desire to play the game. So, instead of being a golfer, Bertie's nothing but a big hitter, and will be till he figures it out.

"You see, Tom, the difference between the Mountain and the world is that you'll get exactly what you want—even if you aren't sure what it is or what the consequences are. You saw it. Hell, you felt it. You were a backswing away from spending eternity with him on the third tee. Bertie's been looking for a friend for a long time, and you almost made the cut."

That was a chilling thought and I was a little hesitant as I addressed the ball. But the third eye was only in the back of my mind and not on my clubface. Still, I could catch a glimpse of the vision that had overtaken me on the tee and swung the iron with freedom and verve. The ball was squarely hit and flew straight toward the pin, landing on the green a reasonable distance from the cup. Even Harry agreed it was a good shot.

As we walked toward the green on the edge of the huge expanse of sand, little whirlwinds spun along beside us like terriers nipping at our heels. But there was no danger of us disturbing the sacred moguls, because we were home on three. Harry missed his bird by inches but dropped what could easily have been a gimmie. I took what the course gave me, a two putt for another bogie. As Harry replaced the pin I counted four more rocks from one side to the other of Angus's leather tally bag.

As we shouldered our bags, we could still see Bertie pacing back and forth on the tee box waiting for us to clear the green. I wanted to wave but didn't.

Harry cleared his throat and picked up where he left off. "As I was saying," he began.

I was silent.

"You are expected to ask me 'What?' " Harry said impatiently.

"What?" I asked.

"Smartest thing you ever did back there," said Harry.

"What did I do?"

"You blinked."

"Yeah, I still can't believe I did that," I said.

Harry shrugged and chuckled. We were on to the fourth as Bertie unloaded another monster drive. The CRACK rang like an explosion in our ears.

CHAPTER 4

The Shepherd and the Squire

In which Tom acquires an unusual caddy

Harry was in a jovial mood as we approached the fourth and I started to share it. The chilly dawn had indeed revealed a glorious morning. The smell of pine and sand was a banquet and the gentle breeze carried the scent of flowers tinged with a hint of salt from the marshes. Birdsong filled the air, and as we passed, small animals rustled in the undergrowth, testifying to the incredible richness of life on Mount Augustus. In that moment, I knew what Adam must have felt that first glorious morning in Eden when the world was fresh and new.

These were powerful emotions indeed, so there was no way in hell I was going to share them with another man. I didn't want Harry to think I was getting all soft and sentimental on him. So, I fell back on shoptalk to pass the time.

"Still can't believe you missed the birdie," I said, glancing back at the third green. "Eight inches, hell, I would've given it to you. How could a putt that short just die at the lip? Geez."

"I'll take it any day," Harry replied. "Par's your friend."

"Yeah, but . . ."

"Beautiful morning, isn't it?" He smiled, signaling an end to the conversation.

"Sure is," I replied. We fell into the comfortable silence that can make a trek around a golf course so special when it's not about clients and scores and making deals. I was alone with my thoughts but not the least bit lonely.

A memory, long buried, struggled to the surface and I found myself thinking of the first time my father had taken me to his club and allowed me to follow along as he and his regular Saturday foursome hacked their way around the course. My father placed such importance on this weekend ritual that he regularly made preemptive announcements to my mother—just in case she had something else in mind—that only war with the Russians could cause him to miss his 9:30 tee-time.

One beautiful summer morning as we finished up our pancakes, my father suggested, quite out of the blue, that I might like to tag along and "walk the course" with him and the guys. It was like receiving an invitation to join Robin Hood and his band of Merry Men in Sherwood Forest. Later, I came to know that moment as a rite of passage but then it was just a dream come true. I made the most of that Saturday, running alongside as the men walked and laughed comfortably with one another. I waited respectfully as they drove balls into the woods, watched intently as they muffed approach shots, and sighed quietly as they missed putt after putt. I pretended not to notice as they stole occasional sips from the silver flask my dad's friend Benny carried in his hip pocket.

The cool, work-a-day demeanor of my father and his friends melted away as the round progressed. Without their suits, ties, and office game faces, they were more human and more real than I had ever imagined. And, when my father finally tipped an offered flask, lit a cigar, winked at me, and whispered, "Don't tell your mother," I felt a rush of pride at being considered trustworthy enough to share in their weekend fellowship. I knew that by participating in this conspiracy, my father and I were becoming friends. When the round was finished, debts paid, and trunk packed, we drove home to supper with smiles on our faces as broad as a mighty river. Over the course of that summer I became the official fifth member of the foursome and by September I had been designated Master Tallyman and Officer of the Nassau, positions of great importance and honor.

The fact that my father was a terrible golfer never bothered me, or him. He was a born optimist, so convinced that the next shot would change his luck and his life that he was willing to take as many leaps of faith as necessary to see his dream come true. "It's a grand game," he would holler as he sliced yet another ball deep into the woods. His passion for golf inspired me to sort through the stack of discarded clubs in the corner of the garage and take up the short game in our backyard, preparing for the time I would be old enough to give up my job as scorekeeper and join the foursome. As I struggled to master the fundamentals of the game, I shattered more than a few neighbors' windows and yard lights, but my father always took my side and never complained about the cost.

One morning before we left for the club, my father presented me with his old persimmon driver, in a backyard ceremony that would have rivaled the knighting of a new member of the Round Table. He had imbedded a shiny Indian-head penny in the insert between the screws and named the club "Thunderbolt," to "make it your own," and it instantly became my most prized possession. I asked him why he would do such a thing and he smiled at me, saying, "One of these times it'll be your turn." It didn't matter that I knew he had fallen in love with a new driver waiting for him at the pro shop, I understood that he had passed on something of great importance to him and therefore of great importance to me.

"It's why we play, isn't it, my boy?"

"What?" I asked, startled out of the well of memory.

"I said, 'It's why we play,' " he repeated.

"Why?"

"Oh, you know, nature . . . and all." He grinned.

As we chugged up a short rise to a stand of pines, I replied quietly, "Yeah, I guess." But my nonchalance was masking an undeniable surge of happiness.

I had begun to remember something forgotten long ago, lost in my joyless pursuit of business golf—the simple pleasure of chasing a small white ball through cut green grass. I was remembering a passion for the game itself, something my father wanted to give me long ago along with his old persimmon driver.

"Through here, son," Harry said, as he slipped through a narrow opening in the trees. "The tee is just beyond."

We stood on the fourth gazing at the layout, which Harry explained to me was sharp dogleg right ending on a raised green protected by bunkers left and right. From the tee the fairway sloped down into a small valley, more like a basin, cut by a narrow stream that ran down to the right and fed into marshy swampland. Where the stream cut through, about 240 yards out, the dogleg turned sharply to the right and the fairway ran uphill to a tightly defended green. Thick rough and tall pines lined the fairway on both sides. It was a birdie hole for a good hitter; for a guy like me it was yet another version of the last mile.

Harry studied the landscape for a second and pulled out his driver.

"I think we've got time, let's hit," he said as he teed his ball. "Play to cross the stream, it's a long poke but the ball'll roll and it'll pay off on the approach. You've got the muscle, you just need the will. Watch an old man and take a lesson."

Harry took a languid practice swing and then set up behind the ball. His shot was what I had come to expect, a clean low pop with just the right amount of draw that hit the dogleg on the upslope of the hill beyond the valley, about 250 yards out, leaving a foolproof approach to the green. He had barely noted where his shot fell. Harry watched as I worked through a couple of practice swings.

"Hit away, son," he said, handing me his driver. "Golf is a game of rhythm, don't interrupt yourself to chop the grass. That's Fergus's job." He smiled at me as he walked off the tee.

His nonchalance was annoying. I looked back and he was glancing at the treeline to the left. I took a couple more practice swings to show him I was my own man and then swung away, lifting up at the end. I caught the top of the ball, sending another weed cutter shuttling down the fairway. At least I had slugged it pretty good and when it reached the bottom of the basin near the stream it must have hit a rock or something because it took a very Presbyterian bounce, shot up in the air, crossed the stream, and landed close to Harry's picture-perfect drive. Not bad, I thought to myself.

"Damn," Harry said.

"So, it wasn't great," I said defensively, "but it'll play." But Harry was fixed on the treeline and some white shapes that were beginning to emerge onto the fairway.

"What's that?" I asked.

"Dammit," Harry said. "Sheep."

They were sheep, all right—a lot of them, streaming out of the trees and moving onto the fairway like a woolly blanket of fog. Soon they had filled the little basin at the turn, covering both our tee shots. I knew one of them was grinding my ball into the soggy grass.

"What do we do now?" I asked.

Harry just turned and walked to the bench where he arranged himself comfortably in the shade. He seemed in no hurry to continue. In fact, he seemed to have settled in for the long haul because he reached into his bag and pulled out his now familiar leather diary, the fountain pen, and a little cigar.

"It'll be a while," he said, lighting up and beginning to write.

"So, those are sheep, eh?" I said.

"You have a way of revisiting the obvious that could irritate lesser men," answered Harry.

The sheep now covered the fairway. At first they seemed motionless, but then I began to see little heads occasionally bob up, look around, and duck back into the midst of the crowd. They were lunching on the rich grass in the fairway and seemed in no hurry to leave—a lumbering lawn mower stuck in neutral.

"So what happens now?" I asked. "Do we play through?"

"You don't play through sheep. Eventually they go away."

"Isn't there a shepherd or like a sheep dog or something?" I asked.

"Yes," said Harry.

"What's he doing, then?"

"Tending his sheep," he answered. "What else?"

"I'm going to find my ball," I said firmly.

"What's the hurry?" Harry seemed puzzled.

"Because I've got to be back for breakfast with the clients before the round. It's part of the deal." I looked at my watch, which said 6:45. I spun it on my wrist so I didn't have to confront the face. It was too unnerving.

"Suit yourself," said Harry. "I'll be right here in the shade."

He went back to his writing and I decided he was right, the sheep would eventually go away. Time out for nature. I looked at the trees; they were nice. I gazed at the clouds high in the sky trying to find camels, landscapes, and movie stars as I had done when I was a child. In short, I really tried to sit there patiently until the herd decided to amble away.

But it was no good, I wanted the sheep to leave. The clouds became a *National Enquirer* spread of my boss being taken away in an ambulance after throwing a blood clot on the first tee waiting for me to show up. I was growing fidgety and distressed. If Harry wanted to sit and scribble away in his ratty old journal, that was his business—me, I was saddling up. I grabbed my bag and set off to rescue my ball before I had to go back and face the music.

"Good luck," Harry called after me. I didn't bother to answer.

The herd loomed in front of me. I realized I had no idea how to move a single sheep anywhere much less a mob of them. As I walked within sniffing distance I also learned sheep possess a pungent array of odors distinctly unpleasant to confirmed city dwellers like myself. All that fresh lanolin on the hoof made me question whether I would be able to wear a sweater again. An older fellow with runny eyes and drool matting his lips with flecks of grass, looked up at me with a vacant stare. He returned to his work without acknowledging my presence. I cursed at him and shoved his hindquarters with my foot, but still he refused to move.

Harry was right. The sheep would move at their own pace and it had nothing to do with me and my silly round of golf. Back up at the tee Harry was sitting with his cigar and book, passing the time in peace and contentment. But I became even more resolved to part this mass of dull-witted flesh, find my ball and play through. All the sheep had to do was cooperate. But they were as focused on their objective as I was on mine, chomping and chewing with a sense of concentration and dedication that would have inspired my boss to make them junior partners.

Making a path was like separating grains of sand; as I moved one, another immediately took its place. The sheep weren't against me, they just weren't for me. As a matter of fact, they didn't seem to care one way or another. After wedging my way in another two or three yards I stopped to catch my breath and a man rose up from the center of the herd.

"Hold right there, sir! Don't make another move!"

I assumed he was the shepherd, but he wasn't like the hardy peasant I conjured out of my enormous databank of Hollywood movies. Far from resembling the sinewy young Victor Mature, he was squat, like Bob Hoskins. And instead of a rough tunic and cape tied with leather bindings, he wore a tattered corduroy jacket with leather elbow patches over a gray sweatshirt that proclaimed, Property of the London School of Economics, in faded burgundy letters. Next came a pair of khaki flood pants hiked high enough above the ankles to satisfy the most conforming preppy, and on his feet were black Converse hightops. Completing the ensemble was a blue New York Knicks cap festooned like a pin cushion with colored tees and stubby yellow pencils.

"Don't make another move, guv'nor," the shepherd said with the utmost gravity. "Don't bat an eyelash. Just do everything I say, and all will be well."

The last time anyone had warned me not to move a muscle was in Scout camp when my counselor discovered a Timber Rattler curled up at the foot of my sleeping bag. The mere memory of it made me freeze.

"Where is it?" I whispered.

"Don't worry your head, sir. Reg is here now, an' he'll take care of everything, he will. Now breathe easy and raise your arms slowly to shoulder level."

As I started to raise my arms, Reg shrieked in alarm. "Slowly, I said!"

Shaking from head to toe, I continued until my arms reached shoulder level. Then he reached out, grabbed the strap of my carry bag, took it off my shoulder, and slung it over his.

The shepherd shook his head and let out a sigh of relief. "It's all over now, sir," he said, "but that was a close one."

He offered his hand. "My name is Reg, guv'nor. I'm the caddie master hereabouts, sir."

Still shaking, I took his hand and introduced myself. "Tom ... Tom Cruickshank."

Reg tugged on the bill of his cap in a gesture of deference and said, "Charmed, I'm sure."

"So, what happened to the snake?"

"Snake? What snake?" Reg asked as he arranged my clubs.

"You just scared me half to death," I shouted. "What do you mean no snake?"

"I was just taking the bag from your shoulders, sir," said Reg, seeming quite puzzled. "A gentleman like you has no business carrying a heavy thing like this." He lifted the bag and let the clubs clatter about for emphasis.

"No, sir," he continued. "It's asking for trouble, it is. The pressure a bag like this places on a gentleman's shoulders is enough to throw his sacroiliac out. I've seen it happen a thousand times, I have. Instead of playing golf with your mates, you're trussed up like a turkey in a butcher's window, hanging in traction the whole summer long. Now, where is the so-called caddie who allowed you to carry your own bag in the first place? I'd like a word with him, I would."

"My back is fine. Anyway, Angus didn't give me one."

"YOU DON'T HAVE A CADDIE?" Reg shrieked in disbelief. "By the Great God MacKenzie, why not?" A hundred sheep looked at me in alarm.

"It's simple," I replied. "They didn't have any and I don't need one."

"Don't need a caddie?" said Reg. "Every gentleman needs a caddie, sir."

"Why?"

"Despite what many people think, golf is not a solitary game, sir. It's a team effort, meant to be played in pairs. A gentleman and his gentleman's gentleman, if you will."

"Well, Reg, we're kind of uncomfortable with servants in my country."

He recoiled as if shot through with a crossbow.

"Sir, a caddie is many things, but he is not a servant. A good caddie is a boon companion; a collaborator in undertakings great and small; a friend and counselor when times are hard and everyone else has deserted you. No, guv'nor, a caddie is not a servant, he's your PARTNER."

Placing his arm over my shoulder, Reg continued, gesturing broadly in the air with his free hand. "Think about it, sir, where would Don Quixote have been without his

----

Fable of Reg—God of Caddies

One day MacTavish, who never gave up on a lost ball, ventured into a poor shepherd's meadow in search of an errant drive. The shepherd whose name was Reg, hid himself behind a patch of gorse to watch MacTavish stomp angrily through the meadow.

When MacTavish finally found his ball, the shepherd was thrilled to see him smack it with his strange walking stick so it soared through the air like a shooting star and disappeared over the crest of the hill from whence he had come. Reg, who despised his life, abandoned his flock and followed the old man into the cleft between two rocks. He was almost discovered by a divine foursome when he stepped onto the third fairway at Mount Augustus, but he jumped behind a bush and watched as the gods played through. The desire to join them overwhelmed him and he remained hidden for many days, unable to tear himself away.

One day Bertie became angry and hurled his stick into the woods. It fell at Reg's feet and he hid the miracle deep in the woods. Soon, a ball landed in the fairway within arm's reach and he took it as well. He then returned to his meadows to find his flock had deserted him. And so he began to learn the nature of the sacred and ancient game in his little meadow, creating a *links of holes* to make a course. News spread throughout the land and the people came from everywhere to learn the secrets of this pastime the gods had so jealously guarded.

When MacKenzie learned the gods' game was in mortal hands he was enraged. "Seek ye this evil shepherd and bring him before me," he cried. And Reg was returned to the Mountain by dryads disguised as sheep. "Explain yerself, pissant," shouted MacKenzie.

Reg told his tale and MacKenzie turned his rage on MacTavish. "Of course tha mortal would be enticed, were ye not enticed yerself when ye watched me play?" MacTavish said nothing but inside he seethed with anger at having been humiliated in front of the assembly.

"Do ye really love the game, shepherd?" MacKenzie continued,

71

not knowing he had planted a seed of bitterness in the God of Rules that would grow to cost him dearly.

"With all me heart," said Reg.

"Ah canna blame ye yer passion for 'tis mine as well. Yet ye stole from me. This Ah will do. Ah'll make ye immortal and ye shall carry ma bag and tend ma sheep. Fer 'tis watchin' brung ye here. If ye agree all the gud, if not Ah will send ye back with no memory and no desire fer the game. Wha' say ye, shepherd?"

So Reg took MacKenzie's bargain and became the God of Caddies. And sometimes when the sheep are grazing quietly and MacKenzie is asleep, Reg sneaks out on the back nine and indulges his passion for the Divine and Ancient Game.

Sancho Panza? Would Sergeant Preston have closed all those cases up in Canada without old King? Would those American blokes Lewis and Clark have crossed your great country without Sacagawea? I hardly think so."

Just then, he looked over at the bulk of the sheep milling around on the edge of the fairway. His eyes suddenly narrowed and his face turned a deep crimson.

"A'right, a'right! Break it up!" Reg yelled. "Don't think I don't see what you're doing, 'cause I do."

The sheep bleated loudly and scattered in several directions, leaving a circle of grass about fifteen yards in diameter. Where they had been grazing there was a distinct pattern in the grass. It looked like a series of concentric circles, some kind of giant diagram, like the sheep were sending a message.

"Bloody sheep," muttered Reg. "Can't leave 'em alone for a minute. Always making spirals and mazes in the grass when they think I'm not looking. One of them fancies himself as some kind of agitator—likes to stir up trouble. He teaches his mates the bleedin' patterns at night. Makes MacKenzie crazy when he sees that stuff. Then of course he takes it out on yours truly."

He glared at the herd and yelled, "I'll find you out, mate, and when I do I'll turn you over to the knitters. See if I don't. Now, where were we?"

"You were comparing caddies to Indian princesses, I think."

"Ah yes, so I was."

He pushed his cap back on his head and climbed up on a rock jutting out of the rough on the left side of the fairway. "Well, my point is that with a good caddie you always know where you are, sir," he continued. "You see, a caddie is like a compass that's always pointing north, or a lighthouse beacon on a stormy night at sea. A caddie is part campaign manager, part spiritual director. . . ."

"Look, I think I see what you're driving at," I said. "But shooting eighteen holes isn't like circling the globe, or sailing a ship through stormy seas."

"Oh, I beg to differ, sir," he shot back. "To the golfer, every new course is uncharted water, full of hidden reefs, whirlpools, and other hidden dangers waiting to engulf him. Take my word for it, you can't make a better investment than a professional caddie. You'll not only avoid a host of troubles, but on the practical side, you won't lose nearly so many balls."

That struck home.

"Just for the sake of argument, what kind of investment are we talking about?" I asked.

"Oh please, sir, you're money's no good at Mount Augustus," said Reg with a chuckle. "My, but that is a lovely towel you have on your bag," he said, suddenly changing the subject. "Where did you get it, if you don't mind my asking?"

"One of my friends picked it up for me in Scotland last year."

Reg raised the thick green towel and rubbed his face in it.

"Oh, this is lovely work," said Reg with a broad smile. "Lovely work, indeed. I love a good piece of terry cloth, I do. Tell me, how many threads per inch?"

"I really couldn't say," I answered, knowing I was about to lose my towel.

"I'll tell you what," he said brightly as if all this had just occurred to him. "I don't usually do this sort of thing, but seeing how you're a visitor to the Mountain, I'll make an exception. I'll give you the services of a professional caddie in exchange for this silly old towel. What do you say?"

"A stroke of genius," I replied coolly. After Angus and Fergus I was painfully aware that tribute and offerings were the main currency on Mount Augustus. Reg rubbed his hands together with glee.

"Maybe you can start by finding my ball."

"Excellent idea, sir, if I do say so myself. . . ."

We were interrupted by the clatter of clubs being dragged upon the ground. A large Angora sheep was trotting down the fairway with my carry bag hanging off his woolly back. As he moved through the herd, the other sheep protested with noisy bleating, but moved aside as he passed.

"Hey, those are my clubs!" I shouted. "Where does he think he's going?"

"To check your yardage, what else?" replied Reg matter-of-factly.

"I beg your pardon?"

"I mean, well, Raymond is your caddie, guv'nor. He's just going to where your ball landed."

"I just hired you to be my caddie. Come on, Reg, a sheep?"

"Well, sir, it would hardly do for the God of Caddies to be seen carrying the bag of an ordinary mortal, now would it?" Reg replied soothingly. "I mean, if I were to loop for you, tongues would wag in Mount Augustus. The other gods would make my life miserable and the sheep would be bloody impossible. I'm sure you understand, sir, you being in business and all."

"But a sheep?"

"I assure you, Raymond is an excellent caddie, sir. The best there is outside of myself. He knows every sweet patch of grass and every level lie on Mount Augustus. And there's nobody better than a sheep at reading greens. Of course, you do have to watch out that they don't do a little snacking on your line, if you know what I mean."

"That's all well and good, Reg, but I came here to play golf, not to keep my caddie from grazing the putting surface. Anyway, from what I hear sheep are dumber than rocks."

Suddenly there was silence. I looked around and saw hundreds of woolly heads turned menacingly toward me, their jaws grinding slowly back and forth. Thousands of little eyes closed in slits of pure meanness. I was surrounded by a herd of woolly assassins. Reg looked about nervously.

"Okay," I apologized loudly, "maybe I was wrong."

The herd began to close around me.

"All right, knock it off," Reg shouted. "The gentleman made his amends."

The sheep stopped. He jumped down off the rock and took me by the arm like a professor who wants a private word with a student. The killers seemed to relax.

"Listen, my lad, I can see you're upset and I want you to be a happy customer," Reg whispered sweetly. "So, let's do a little experiment, and I'll prove just how good a caddie Raymond is."

"This I gotta see," I replied skeptically.

Reg let out an earsplitting whistle and Raymond trotted back to where we stood, with my clubs clanking along behind him.

"Okay, Raymond, Tom here is 150 yards from the green on the second hole, and the wind is quartering into him at about two knots. What club should he use?"

Raymond cocked one of his black ears and then stared at me intently with his dark runny eyes. Then he looked back at Reg and bleated three times. Reg turned to me and said in all seriousness, "He wants to know your handicap."

"Oh for Pete's sake," I said.

"Humor me," said Reg.

"Okay, it's a . . . sixteen," I replied.

Raymond looked skeptical but turned his head back over his shoulder and grabbed a club from my bag. It was a six-iron. I was not impressed and it showed on my face.

"Is there a problem?" Reg asked.

"I'm usually 160, 165 with a six," I said.

Ray bleated another question.

"To an elevated green?" Reg translated.

"Didn't account for that," I admitted. "Is he that good all the time?"

Raymond shrugged.

"Blimey, that's nothing," Reg said, beaming with pride. "You should see him handicap a horse race. Nothing short of amazing."

"I'm sure it is," I replied. "Now, do you think we could find my ball?"

"Your ball? Oh, dear me, I know I've got it here somewhere," said Reg. He shoved his hands into the side pockets of his battered old corduroy jacket and after a minute of feeling around, came up with a golf ball that was completely encrusted in dirt.

"How do you know that's mine?"

"I know it's yours, sir, picked it up meself."

"You picked up my ball?" I shouted.

Reg smiled and began to clean the ball with a dirty hand towel.

"Local rules, mate," Reg explained. "Whenever a player's ball lands in sheep dung, you're entitled to a free drop."

"Oh. . . ." At least the towel he was using wasn't the fancy green one from Scotland I had just given him.

Satisfied that it was clean enough, Reg tossed my ball to Raymond, who caught it easily in his mouth, tucking it in the side of his cheek. Then he grabbed the strap of my carry bag with his teeth and expertly slung it up onto his back. It was official: a sheep named Raymond was now my caddie.

The sheep formed a long white corridor, sort of a woolly honor guard that led directly to a trampled patch of grass. Raymond proceeded down the path, and dropped my ball on the ground.

Meanwhile, the sheep had broken ranks and were milling around. Reg wove his way to where I was standing. He put his arm around my shoulders and gave me a fatherly hug.

"My guess is you've got a narrow window to take your second shot; otherwise my lads will go back for a second course, and only MacKenzie knows how long that might take. Trust Ray here with club selection and your life. You're gonna need him. Any questions, guv'nor?"

"Just one. Since you've got my bag towel, how am I supposed to clean my clubs?"

Reg laughed. "Oh, no problem at all. Just use the wool on Raymond's back. He don't mind. The mud keeps the bugs away, if you know what I mean. He's a great ball washer, too, if you can keep him from swallowing. I know you have your doubts about our woolly friends' abilities, sir, but just watch this. Might alter your mistaken impression."

He leaned over and whispered into the ear of an imposing black-headed ram. The sheep nodded and began to bleat in drill sergeant fashion. The herd began to mill around, then started to organize themselves into squads. What had been a herd of meandering animals became a disciplined battalion performing a complex marching routine accompanied by call-and-response bleating reminiscent of a military parade ground. Reg stood next to me, beaming as his charges strutted their stuff.

When the sheep had finished and rearranged themselves into squadrons, Reg moved them out, speaking to the squadron leaders in affectionate tones and occasionally slapping one on the haunches as they disappeared into the woods.

Raymond was still standing sentry over my bag a few yards away. My six-iron was lying next to my ball. I estimated the distance to the green and thought maybe the eight was a better choice.

"I think I'll hit the eight, Ray." He was a sheep, for crying out loud.

It was clear that he disagreed but wasn't going to argue. I addressed my ball, which was set up nicely on a clump of grass, which somehow had been missed in the feeding frenzy. My shot streaked straight toward the pin, but I knew it was going to be short. Ray had been right. I marveled at how well he shouldered the bag as we headed for the green; maybe this wasn't such a bad idea.

I remembered Harry when I found him standing next to his ball, which was about three feet from the cup. I saw that mine had landed in the frog hair at the front leaving a chip of about twenty-five feet to the pin.

"I see you've met Reg," said Harry. He gave the sheep a long stare and shook his head. "At least he could have given you one of the smart ones."

"Raymond's nobody's fool," I said. "How'd you get here, Harry? I thought we were hitting from the same place."

"You've gotta pay attention, son. Are you talking or chipping?"

"Chipping," I said, until I noticed my caddie shaking his woolly head and gesturing at the putter lying at my feet.

"Actually, Harry, I think I'll putt it out from here. Pull the pin, I'm feeling good." And I proceeded to jam the putt dead into the center of the cup to card my first birdie on the Mountain. As incredible as I felt and as excited as I was I also knew I had gotten away with murder and owed it all to my caddie. Raymond had done his job well and I was glad to have him on the team.

"Ray, you're okay," I said as I dropped my putter next to him, and a shocked Harry Brady rimmed the cup to miss his bird. I won the hole, but I noticed that when Harry bent down to pull his ball out of the cup he leaned heavily on his putter to support himself and seemed to wince as he stood up.

"You feeling all right, Harry?" I asked.

"Good enough to clean your clock from here on out, son. Don't you worry about me."

But I couldn't help it. Playing the Mountain seemed to have a draining effect on him. I didn't know how many times he'd been to Augustus, but I had to wonder whether the effect on mortals was cumulative—like the long-term effects of weightlessness on astronauts. I was concerned about Harry, but I was also worried for myself. There were strange things here and possible dangers. I needed a good pilot to steer me through the reefs and shallows if I was ever going to make it back to Pine Valley. I only hoped Harry would make it to the end of the round.

CHAPTER 5

The Breakfast Ball

In which Tom considers what's fair as opposed to what's allowed

Franklin Roosevelt once said that the only thing we had to fear was fear itself. Well, in my opinion, the fifth hole at Mount Augustus would have changed his mind. At 230 yards from tee to green, the fifth hole was not only a brutally long par 3, but a gauntlet of every hazard known to golf.

At the foot of the tee box was a lake strategically placed to swallow every dribbled, topped, or thinned tee ball. From the opposite bank, the terrain rose uphill through a wasteland of rough as impenetrable as the bouffant of a Texas prom queen. One hundred eighty yards from the tee the bunkers began—a nasty collar of unraked sandpits that nearly circled the green. Dense forest formed a second line of defense beyond the traps, leaving nowhere for hapless hackers like myself to bail out. In short, the fifth was a hole that demanded you hit your three-wood with the precision of a pitching wedge. It was a real nightmare.

"Your honors, son," said Harry. "You carded the bird."

But I was frozen in place, transfixed by the specter of a hole I knew in my heart I could not safely reach, much less hope to par. My saliva had turned to carpenter's glue, and every ounce of moisture in my body was pouring out through my palms, taking with it all the resolve I achieved by my spectacular birdie on four. While I may have looked like a hale and hardy thirty-year-old, I was brittle and porous inside—a giant sinkhole of fear waiting for the touch that would send me crumbling.

"You go ahead, Harry," I mumbled shakily. "I need to catch my breath."

"Whatever you say, partner."

He stepped up and smacked a low line drive. Forty yards short of the green, the ball slammed into a patch of bare ground and then skipped up to within ten yards of the apron. Not a bad play, all things considered, but he winced as though shot through the hip by sciatica.

"Damn," Harry wheezed, "your shot."

Out of the corner of my eye I saw Raymond pacing back and forth impatiently, which struck me as very sophisticated behavior for a sheep. Harry tapped me on the shoulder.

"Your shot," he repeated with surprising urgency.

My three-wood rested in Raymond's drooling mouth, but I couldn't breathe, much less move. My diaphragm was locked up under my lungs like the mirror of a broken camera. All the symptoms led to one conclusion: I was in the midst of a classic panic attack.

"Let's go," he said, a little louder this time. Somehow the club was in my hands. I attempted a waggle but was distracted by Harry shifting his weight impatiently back and forth between his feet.

Anxiety overcame common sense and rather than catch a breath, I took a hurried swing, missing the ball completely. Like the rawest beginner, I had whiffed. And then it got worse. Rather than take my medicine like a man, I pretended the whiff was merely a practice swing. Brazenly, I stepped back and took a couple more to cover up my crime. It was all so embarrassingly obvious. Even Raymond knew what was going on; he had turned his back on the pitiful spectacle and was chomping noisily on the grass at the edge of the tee.

"Tee off, for crying out loud," Harry snapped. But before I could swing again, he shouldered his bag and hurried off the tee box. Shame and guilt flooded through me. He hadn't been fooled for a second, and now he was leaving.

"Harry," I called, "wait a second!"

"Can't," he yelled over his shoulder. "My bladder's about to burst."

Sweeter words were never spoken! Maybe he hadn't seen the whiff, after all. He just had to relieve himself! Even if he had seen it, I told myself, he had decided to overlook it. Raymond, on the other hand, was leering at me with disgust. Things would never be the same between me and my caddie.

I gave Harry a thin smile and a wave as he made his way down the slope and into the bushes.

One of golf's unwritten laws is that a full-blown whiff will almost always be followed by a shot equally if not more embarrassing. Once Harry had disappeared into the bushes, I took another anxious swipe. This time I did manage to hit the ball, but just barely. My legs were as rigid as two giant redwoods, so I was unable to shift my weight to my left side. As a result, my three-wood merely grazed the top of the ball, sending it dribbling off the tee and down the bank to a watery grave. After blowing my first shot, I had cold-topped the second into a water hazard. This was the bottom of the pit, the nadir of golfing humiliation. I could sink no lower.

The wheels had completely fallen off and I still hadn't left the tee. Worse yet, there was no way out. I couldn't return to the clubhouse feigning injury or illness as I had done a few times in the past when things went sour. I was stuck out on the most unforgiving course in the universe with my game in tatters and thirteen holes still to play.

I let out a howl that was a combination of rage and despair. Then I fell to my knees and began to beat the ground with my three-wood. It must have been an embarrassing spectacle, and Raymond watched impassively until he'd had enough. Then he bleated disdainfully and disappeared into the bushes as well. Deserted by Harry and abandoned by my caddie, I buried my face in my hands and tried to disappear.

"Are you injured, sir?"

I opened one eye and peered through my fingers. A fresh

wave of humiliation swept over me. I had not only acted like a two-year-old, I had been seen doing so.

Although unable to move, I did manage a reply.

"No, I'm just fine. Thank you."

"I couldn't help but notice your predicament," the voice continued.

Since it was clear that my latest tormentor was not about to leave, I got up and dusted myself off. Before me was a disheveled and wiry figure of a man who looked like someone on the downside of a two-week bender. He wore a wool suit with plus fours that he had clearly slept in. A couple of buttons were missing from his jacket and one of his socks had slipped a garter, leaving the hose nestled around his ankle like a bird's nest.

As our eyes met, the little man touched the brim of his cloth cap and smiled. Greatly magnified by a pair of thick spectacles, his eyes were two giant robin's eggs encased in blocks of acrylic.

"When's the last time you ate, my boy?" he asked politely. "You're looking awfully pale."

He had a point. The night before I had weaseled out of dinner with my boss and the clients, then missed breakfast at the guest house and turned down Harry's rolls and thermos of coffee at the range. The bowl of snapper soup in the grill had been my last meal.

"Lunch yesterday, I guess."

"Ah hah! There it is!" he shouted. "It's not your game that's betrayed you, it's your blood sugar!"

The little man clasped a bony hand on my shoulder and escorted me to the side of the tee box where an ancient rucksack lay in the grass.

"You can't expect to play a demanding game like golf without fuel in your furnace," he continued solicitously. "I've got some scones and a jar of tea that should fix you right up."

The milky tea was sweet and the scone was lathered with a quarter cup of country butter. They acted like an elixir on my famished system. As I ate, my benefactor teed up a new ball and retrieved my three-wood from the slope in front of the tee box.

"Just as I thought, my boy," the little man cried. "You had no chance of hitting a good shot. No chance at all."

"What do you mean?" I asked.

He held my three-wood out for inspection like a prosecutor displaying the murder weapon to a jury.

"Look at that, the whipping on your three-wood is coming off," he said with outrage in his voice.

He was right. Two or three inches of the black twine that secures the clubhead to the shaft had indeed come unraveled.

"So what?" I asked.

"Well, for starters, it probably caused your club to kick early. No reasonable man would make you tee off with a piece of damaged equipment like that. Why, in all other sports, you'd be awarded an equipment time out. They wouldn't make you kick a football that had no air in it, now would they? Nor would they make you sail a cup race during a hurricane."

"No, I guess not," I said.

"Well then, by the powers invested in me, I officially declare that you are entitled to a breakfast ball."

"A breakfast ball?"

"Yes, a do-over," he continued grandly. "You're entitled."

"And just what powers are you talking about?" I asked. "Who are you, anyway?"

The little man suddenly became very agitated. His hands rushed to his cheeks and he stood there shaking his head in evident frustration.

"Oh, by the Great God MacKenzie! In all the excitement, I've forgotten my manners! Please forgive me."

"No problem, really." I smiled, trying to put him at ease.

He pulled a dog-eared business card from his waistcoat pocket, handing it to me with great ceremony.

I read it aloud, "R. P. Mulligan, Esquire. Counselor and Advocate."

"At your service, sir," he said, touching the brim of his cap.

"Tom Cruickshank," I said, offering my hand.

"Glad to meet you, Tommy boy," said Mulligan.

"Wait a minute," I said as it dawned on me. "You're not *the* Mulligan, are you? I mean ..."

"That I am, my boy," he answered proudly.

"I didn't think you were real."

"Of course I'm real. Now, sit down and finish your tea while I take a look at that pesky winding."

By the time I had finished Mulligan had repaired my club. The whipping had been carefully rewound.

"Now, let's start this hole over," he said.

When someone as legendary as Mulligan himself expunges your sins, you don't quibble, especially if the alternative is taking your fourth shot while still on the tee. So, with a new lease on life, I took another crack at the fifth hole. While not spectacular, the results were much more respectable. I hit a high cut shot that headed for the right apron of the green. With any luck at all, I'd be chipping for birdie. But as the ball reached its apex it suddenly begin to slice, entering the woods to the right of the green with a clatter.

"Take another," said Mulligan. "You were robbed."

"Excuse me?" I said.

"Golf should be a test of your skill, not your luck," he explained. "And by my reckoning, there was an unexpected gust of wind measuring at least fifteen knots on that shot," he said, wetting his finger and holding it aloft.

"I didn't notice anything," I said.

"Aye, it's a cruel crosswind. Much too strong for golf. You should be allowed another shot."

"No, I've got to play it," I replied. Mulligan's line of reasoning was tempting, but having already set foot on the road to damnation, I saw no reason to break into a trot.

"It's your choice, sir," he answered politely, "but I wish you'd reconsider."

Thanking him for the tea and scones I took my leave,

The Fable of Mulligan—God of Excuses

Mulligan is the offspring of the Great God MacKenzie and a cultural anthropologist named Margaret Mulligan who was doing field work during the late 1920s among shepherds that tended their flocks near the secret entrance to Mount Augustus. On one of his forays into the mortal world MacKenzie crossed her path and Margaret moved to Augustus to continue her research. Soon she tired of MacKenzie's godlike ways and left to found a women's agricultural commune in the Outer Hebrides where Mulligan was born. Part god that he was, Mulligan had a disturbing attraction to goats, and Margaret shipped her progeny off to live with his father at the age of nine.

Mulligan was the youngest son of MacKenzie, and the weakest and least athletic of the younger gods, so he had to depend upon his wits to survive. Sensitive to the plight of the weak and downtrodden, Mulligan often defended other gods against the wrath of MacKenzie and became so skilled he successfully handled his mother's divorce from his father.

Once, he was challenged to a match during the Annual Sons of MacKenzie Outing by older brother Bertie. Mulligan held up the start for the better part of an hour, complaining about the mortal weaknesses he inherited from his mother. He explained how the budding grass crippled him with allergies, and that he was congenitally short off the tee due to a thin frame and small, delicate hands. Impatient to begin, but more tired of listening, Bertie agreed to give Mulligan four shots a side if he would only get on with it and play—thus inventing the handicap system.

Bertie hit an enormous driver off the first tee that caused Mulligan to sneeze violently and his eyes to swell shut. Then, as one might expect, he cold topped his drive off the tee box into a patch of gorse. Rather than curse and cause the heavens to rumble like any self-respecting immortal, Mulligan fell into a swoon, causing further delay. When revived, he complained he was hypoglycemic and had not had time for breakfast. Mead and nectar were quickly summoned. After Mulligan assured all that his blood sugar was back to normal, he was given another drive—thus inventing the Mulligan. Due to histrionics too embarrassing to relate, he was granted two more "do-overs" during the match, driving Bertie temporarily insane and setting the stage for Mulligan's ignominious 9 and 8 victory over his older sibling.

----

determined to play the rest of the hole without further compromise. Raymond and Harry were nowhere in sight. I reached the point I thought my ball had entered the woods and proceeded to hack around for several minutes, without success. Just as I was about to drop another and take a penalty stroke, that reedy little voice piped up from somewhere behind me.

"You were playing a Maxfli, weren't you, my boy?"

"I really can't remember," I said, determined not to look at him.

"Look beneath the red maple," he said. "And I believe you'll find a Maxfli number 2."

Fifteen feet away, on a spot I was positive I had searched over several times, was a pristine Maxfli lying right out in the open.

"Where are you anyway?" I shouted.

"Why, up here, my boy," he answered brightly.

Mulligan was perched directly above my head on the bough of a giant chestnut tree forty feet off the ground. All I could see were spindly legs and the soles of his hobnailed boots.

"You put that ball there, didn't you?"

"Whatever would make you think that?" he replied.

"How else would you know that it's a Maxfli number 2?"

Mulligan gestured to his thick glasses. "The eyes of an eagle, my lad."

"The eyes of a bat, you mean," I yelled up to him. "If I play that ball, it's a two-stroke penalty."

"Says who?" said a voice behind me.

I wheeled around, expecting to see Harry, but was face-to-face with Mr. Do-over.

"The rules is who," I challenged.

Mulligan responded with a sneer.

"Do you mean the pusillanimous penal code written by those assassins at the USGA and their co-conspirators, the so-called Royal and Ancient?"

"Who else?" I said, startled by Mulligan's sudden burst of venom.

"Industrialists and corporate lawyers." Mulligan spat and made a face "They're nothing but a bunch of cut-throats and thieves all dressed up in fancy blazers. They sit around drinking sherry in the grand palaces they call clubhouses, but there's not a one of them wouldn't steal the pennies off a dead man's eyes."

"Wait a minute, whether that's true or not, golf is still a game of honor."

Mulligan laughed out loud, and did a little jig.

"I've heard the scribes back in your world prattling on about how golf is a game of honor," said Mulligan. "They say that because players call rule infractions on themselves. But that doesn't prove anything, my boy, because the rules are an abomination. Think about it. If you address a ball and it moves before you can hit it, what happens?"

"That's a one-stroke penalty," I answered.

"Now, I ask you, for what earthly reason would anyone concoct a rule like that—except out of pure meanness? There's only one plausible answer."

"What?"

"Why, to prevent your opponent from cheating!"

"Ah, come on . . ."

"No, if you think about it, and follow the logic of the so-called rules, you'll see that I'm right," Mulligan said, growing more excited by the moment. "You're assuming that your opponent is going to jump up and down near the ball so that it will roll to a better location. Or that he's going to use the toe wedge to gain a playable lie. In short, you're assuming that, rather than being honorable, your opponent is a lying, cheating scoundrel. And that, my boy, is who the so-called rules of golf are written for. Scoundrels!"

"Well, they're the only rules I've got," I replied and resumed whacking around the underbrush with my pitching wedge in search of my ball.

"Rules are made to be broken," intoned Mulligan with fake solemnity. "Play your shot and get on with it."

"It's records that are made to be broken, not rules," I said. He was beginning to annoy me.

Suddenly underneath a creeper was a flash of white. I moved the vine gingerly aside and saw the unmistakable Hartless & Craven logo. I had found my ball, but had virtually no chance of reaching the green from where it lay.

"You get a drop from there," said Mulligan, who had appeared beside me.

"Only if it's unplayable," I countered. "And then I have to take a stroke. Clear out, I'm going to give it a try."

"Suit yourself," said Mulligan. I had the dubious distinction of making a god sulk.

With a huge explosion of dirt and debris, the ball exploded from the undergrowth. But it carried no more than ten yards toward the green before catching a stout hickory limb and dropping into a greenside trap. After the shot, I swore I heard jeering laughter from the woods behind me and the unmistakable sound of wagon wheels crunching through the leaves on the forest floor.

When I got to the trap I saw my ball resting arrogantly in the middle of a large footprint and, while a great excuse to be upset, it really didn't matter because the shot would have been difficult under the best of circumstances. The lip of the bunker was at chest level and to clear it the ball had to come up fast and hard.

Before the sand wedge was out of my bag, Mulligan was at my heels.

"Go ahead, you can take relief," said Mulligan. "This trap should have been raked by the last player who came through."

"Not according to the rules," I said.

"Hear me out, lad," he said. "For every rule, there's an exception." He tossed a few blades of grass into the wind to gauge its direction.

"And for every exception, there's a situation. The situation here is that a rude and thoughtless hacker failed at the basic rules of fair play and good sportsmanship by leaving his shoeprint in the sand. All we have to do is put them together and it becomes clear that this is punishment far beyond the expectations of even those rascals at the USGA."

Good point. Why should I be penalized because of some other player's lapse of etiquette? The shot was hard enough anyway. The little man had worn me down with a relentless attack of godly logic. I was about to make things right when I heard a shout from the trees.

"Don't touch that ball. I didn't bring you all this way so you could blow it taking Mulligans."

When I looked up, Harry Brady's face was three inches from my own and Raymond was holding my bag a few feet away.

"You moved my ball twice yesterday, Harry. Besides, the lie was unfair."

I expected Mulligan to defend me but he was nowhere in sight.

"Why do I feel more like a baby-sitter than a player today?" Harry asked Raymond.

"Anyway, I'm afraid it may be too late," I said.

"What do you mean?"

I took a deep breath and told Harry the whole story, leaving out the part about the whiff on the tee. I wasn't ready to deal with that yet.

When I had finished, Harry was livid. "You mean Mulligan talked you into taking two shots over?"

Raymond shook his woolly head sadly. I could only nod yes.

"He's nothing but a damned ambulance chaser," said Harry, his voice rising. "Where are you, you little bastard?" he shouted, slowly scanning the perimeter of the green.

"He was right beside me in the trap, and then he just disappeared."

"Must have seen me coming," said Harry. "Stay away from me, you shyster, and leave Tom alone," he shouted as he shook his head and climbed back onto the green toward his ball, which lay some twenty feet from the pin. Harry was fuming.

To break the tension, I smiled and tried to give him a gentle ribbing.

"Golly, partner, seems like you've got more enemies up here than friends."

Harry didn't crack a smile. "Well, when you've been a member as long as I have, you're gonna rub some folks the wrong way—and vice versa. In some ways, it's not that different from New York. Steer clear of the counselor from now on." He looked at me closely. "Did he give you anything?"

"Yes, I almost forgot." I reached into my pocket and produced the dog-eared business card.

"Might as well hold onto it. Could come in handy later."

It took me three more strokes to get out of the bunker and another two to get down. Harry, of course, saved his par. As we walked off the green I examined Mulligan's card.

"So what is this, Harry? Some kind of 'get out of jail free' deal?"

Harry was pretty serious when he answered. "You're close, son. Closer to it than you know."

And then I was faced with adding up a big number. It's funny how often scoring becomes a moral dilemma. The way I figured it, I could have either an 11 on the hole, counting the whiff, or an 8 for snowman—which was embarrassing enough. But as I started to drop stones into the green side of the pouch I thought, "Mulligan forgave me two strokes and he's the God of Excuses. That ought to mean something on Mount Augustus."

The more I considered it, I wasn't so sure that whiff off the tee hadn't been a practice stroke after all. I was probably just feeling guilty because Harry was badgering me about getting on with it. Yeah, a fellow ought to be allowed a practice stroke, and furthermore, he should be allowed a chance to hit his drive in peace.

"Hey, Tom, hurry it up," barked Harry. "What's so damned difficult about adding up? I thought you were an MBA."

"Be right there, Harry," I replied, and closed up the pouch after depositing eight stones. For the moment at least, I was giving myself the benefit of the doubt. I rationalized my decision by telling myself I could always add more stones later.

We'll see how it goes, I said to myself.

CHAPTER 6

The Art of War, or Let Sleeping Beasts Lie

In which the ancient strategies and tactics are revealed

Even the pros find carding a big number unsettling, but for a weekend hacker like myself, taking that kind of a beating on a par three was enough to put me flat on the canvas. It must have shown, too, because Harry was worried. He stuck to me like a prison guard on suicide watch all the way through the woods to the sixth tee.

"Put it behind you son," he cooed soothingly. "It's just one hole. Besides, you'll knock 'em dead on six. Sets up perfectly for that big fade of yours."

Raymond, on the other hand, sensed the truth and had apparently given up on me altogether. My trusty caddie was dogging Harry's heels pretending to be looping for the old codger—just in case any of his woodland buddies happened to see us.

As we mounted the tee box, Harry paused to catch his breath. Then like a potter smoothing away an imperfection from his clay, he closed one eye and lovingly traced the contours of the hole with his fingers. A treelined dogleg right of about 390 yards, it featured both an elevated fairway and green. Harry smiled; the sixth hole was obviously one of his favorites.

"The smart play is to keep the ball left," said Harry. "It's a longer shot to the green, but you'll stay out of that mess on the right."

The "mess" that Harry was referring to was a deep ravine full of scrub oak, berry bushes, pines, and unraked sand. Although it was daunting, I figured any kind of decent drive over the ravine would cut off the dogleg dramatically, giving me a wedge to the green and a birdie opportunity, which would go a long way toward taking the sting out of the last hole. On the other hand, if I didn't reach the fairway, I'd be dropping another large fistful of gravel into Angus's scoring sack. It was a classic risk versus reward situation.

Again, Harry read my mind. "Don't even think about it, son," he said. "If you bite off the whole thing, it's two hundred twenty yards to the short grass, and all carry."

"Guess you're right," I replied. "Why don't you show us the way, partner?"

Harry slapped his drive out to the left according to plan, but it was a weak little cut-fade that couldn't have traveled more than 200 yards—a far cry from the crisp tee balls I was used to seeing him hit. He was safe, but had left himself a long iron to the well-protected green.

"Over the top," he muttered. "I guess my legs are a little tired from all the walking yesterday. Left myself a long way home."

"Yeah, Harry, but you'll make your par," I said as I teed up my ball. "You always do."

Harry cocked his head to the side and smiled. "Yep, always do."

At that moment, I had every intention of following his instructions and hitting away from trouble to the left side of the landing area. But as I took my stance a strong breeze began to swirl through the trees above our heads creating a haunting melody of rustling, squeaking, and groaning as the boughs bent to the insistent pressures of the wind. It was a melancholy and primitive anthem but it surged through my body and set my spirit on fire. Suddenly, I felt like I could do anything.

"Do you hear that, Harry?"

"Hear what?" Harry replied absently.

"The music. It's incredible."

When Harry answered by shaking his head from side to side, I saw that his ears had sprouted tufts of white hair—which I could have sworn were not there when we started.

Then just as suddenly as it began, the wind died away, the intoxicating melody faded, and I heard a voice in my head insisting that I take the challenge head-on.

"Go for it, Tom," the voice whispered. "You can do it, lad. Take it out over the left side of the ravine and let it fade back to the center of the fairway."

In fact, the voice was an old friend. It had been with me in a hundred late-night poker games when I was down to my last few chips, whispering that I could fill an inside straight if I only believed. It coached me to race traffic lights as they turned yellow hundreds of yards down the highway; and the same voice convinced me I could hook a low three-iron out of deep grass, around a stand of tall pines some 190 yards to a well-bunkered green. And now, the voice was urging me to drive over a ravine deeper than the Grand Canyon.

For reasons I cannot explain, it was a voice I *always* listened to.

My confidence soared, I adjusted my stance to the right, took dead aim at the fairway on the other side of the ravine, and unleashed a drive high over the sandy wastes. For a moment it looked as if I'd clear the chasm with plenty to spare, but just before the ball reached the other side, my fade began to degenerate into a garden variety slice and disappeared without a sound into the heart of Harry's mess.

Raymond released a low, mournful bleat and avoided my eyes. Then he disgorged a new Maxfli glistening with saliva at my feet. I couldn't decide whether he wanted me to hit a provisional ball or declare my tee shot unplayable until Harry stepped in.

"Listen to your caddie, son," he said.

"And be lying three on the tee? Not on your life, Harry," I replied obstinately.

"The ball is gone."

"I'm finding that puppy," I called back as I started down the hill toward the ravine.

"Okay, you've got five minutes," Harry shouted after me, "but if you find it, don't try anything stupid, just get the ball back to the fairway. I'll wait for you there."

"Gotcha," I replied, giving Harry a reassuring smile. Raymond was still standing on the tee box with my clubs slung over his back.

"Well, are you coming?" I asked impatiently. After exchanging glances with Harry, Raymond reluctantly scarfed up the provisional ball and lumbered down the embankment after me.

From the bottom, the ravine looked much deeper and more forbidding than from the tee box. It was a dense wilderness of coarse sand, prickly bushes, and stunted trees. Using my pitching wedge as a combination walking stick and machete, I began to poke my way through the undergrowth. After a couple of fruitless minutes, Raymond tired of the search and bleated impatiently. But just then, my eyes fastened on a patch of ultramarine blue that could only be the boar's head logo of Hartless & Craven.

All things considered, it was a pretty good lie. The ball was sitting up on a ridge of sand a couple of feet away from a hawthorn bush. However, as I stood over it, the surge of swashbuckling confidence I had felt on the tee finally petered out. Instead of opportunities, all I could see were obstacles. To my right, a stand of tall pines rose up like Hadrian's Wall to block me from the green, and to my left there was an embankment of sand as menacing as a forty-foot wave between me and the safety of the fairway grass.

This time, I was determined to take Harry's advice and limit my losses instead of going for broke, so I set up left to pitch the ball back up to the fairway. But the voice started in on me again with a renewed urgency. Louder than before, it seemed to be coming from a place just outside my left ear, and I noticed for the first time that my old friend had acquired a Scottish burr.

"Tha's right, lad," it whispered. "Set up wi' yer feet ta tha left. All tha better ta cut tha ball 'round tha trees. Yer target's tha top o' tha' tall pine across tha fairway. Now, open tha' blade a wee bit, an' yer sure ta hit tha green wi' yer big fade."

Despite my good intentions, I listened. I opened my stance, picked out my target across the fairway, and then adjusted my grip for a cut shot. Then it occurred to me that I was still holding my pitching wedge and it would take at least a six-iron to reach the green, especially using cut spin.

Almost as soon as I thought about it, I was given my six-iron and my pitching wedge was taken from my hands.

"Now, let's slay tha beast, laddie," said the voice excitedly. "PULL THA TRIGGER!"

Wheeling around, I came face-to-face with a wild-eyed man with a beard and shoulder-length red hair. His face was painted with broad stripes of cobalt blue and he held an ancient niblick in his hand.

"God Almighty!" I exclaimed. "Who are you?"

"Niver mind tha'," he rasped. "Pull tha trigger, mon. Surprise the coorse while she still sleeps!"

"You scared me half to death. How am I supposed to make a shot this tough when I'm shaking like a leaf? Who the hell are you?"

"Ah'm Dirk," said the redheaded man emphatically, as if his name should explain everything. "Now, calm doon, lad. An' lower yer voice."

"Tom Cruickshank," I whispered in reply.

I extended a shaky hand to introduce myself, but Dirk pushed it away and clasped my forearm in the ancient warriors greeting. He had a firm grip and there was nothing that wasn't masculine about him. He wore a heavy kilt with a sash of matching tartan and around his midriff was a broad leather belt in which he carried a short sword and an evil-looking dagger.

"So, what do you do here, Dirk?" I asked in my best Manhattan cocktail party manner. "Are you a ranger or something?"

He laughed. "A ranger, indeed. No, lad, Ah'm known ta all who do battle wi' this coorse as Master Strategist, Lord High Tactician an' General o' tha Armies—reserve, o' coorse."

"So, Dirk, do you always sneak up on people like that?"

"Evir chance Ah get," he said smugly. "Surprise, 'tis a powerful weapon, Tommy."

"Maybe in warfare," I said, "but I don't see how that applies to golf."

'Ye cuildna' be more mistaken, laddie," Dirk replied. "Consider yer situation. Raight now, tha coorse is sleeping, secure in tha knowledge tha' yer in trouble; niver dreamin' tha' while it sleeps, ye'll crawl up ta its stronghold an' slit its throat—figuratively speakin', o' coorse. Ah'm tellin' ye lad, ye hae a rare opportunity ta strike a killin' blow, ta brin' this coorse ta its knees!"

I had to admit Dirk's fire and enthusiasm were rekindling my confidence but I didn't fully understand what I was expected to do.

"And just how am I supposed to strike a killing blow from this ravine?"

"Ah though' ye'd niver ask, laddie," replied Dirk with a broad grin. He stepped over to a patch of smooth sand and began to diagram the hole with the tip of his gleaming dagger.

"Yer heer in this godfersakin ravine," Dirk began. "Tha green is heer, beyond tha trees. Now, tha green has protected herself wi' deep trenches all 'round, but she can be had, laddie. There are three ways ye can go: tha surprise attack; layin' siege; an' heavy ordinance."

The Fable of Dirk—God of Tactics

Like the royal families of Europe, most pantheons of deities are related in some way. Unfortunately, there is another similarity: rival pantheons not only intermarry, they do battle with one another. Dirk, the God of Tactics, came to prominence during the fateful Ten Thousand Year War between the Golf Gods and the Gods of Kolven.

Maindort, the Meister Gott of Kolven, had given his sister, Gretel, to be married to a minor functionary in MacKenzie's court, Visor, the God of Logos, thereby bonding the two pantheons together in peaceful coexistence. But unfortunately, Gretel was a spy, sent by her brother to destroy Mount Augustus and the game of golf from within. Within months, she had the entire court playing Kolven, an inferior golflike game designed to be played on the streets of towns, frozen ponds, and other domesticated surfaces. Instead of finishing the game by putting into a hole, Kolven players aimed their last shots at the doors of prominent houses. The Gods of Augustus proclaimed Kolven easier to play.

Soon, not only were the clubhouse doors of Mount Augustus being pounded by Kolven balls day and night, but the sacred links were virtually deserted. Worse yet, Gretel had imported a brigade of instructors from Kolven to "teach" the infernal game. So, MacKenzie decided he had no choice but to declare war on the Pantheon of Kolven. He chose Dirk, a wild young god who lived in the mists near the pinnacle of Mount Augustus as his commander and was not disappointed.

After laying siege to Maindort's clubhouse for many centuries, Dirk had his legions fashion a giant wooden Kolven ball and rolled it up to the Nether God's huge front door. Then Dirk withdrew his troops back to Mount Augustus. When the gods of Kolven were satisfied that Dirk had indeed left, they all gathered in the doorway to admire their trophy. At that moment, the Great God MacKenzie, in his guise as a fifty-foot titan, stepped up to the Kolven ball and drove it right through their clubhouse, decimating his enemies and effectively destroying the allure of Kolven both on heaven and earth. For designing the Kolven Ball Strategy, Dirk was honored with a hundred-year feast and was dubbed the God of Tactics.

"A surprise attack sounds fun," I ventured.

"Aye, 'tis tha warrior's choice," replied Dirk. "Ye cut a bush or wee tree an' use it fer cover. 'Tween each shot, ye advance evir so quietly an' evir so slowly up tha fairway, so tha coorse canna see ye. After ye hit yer approach shot, then ye drop yer cover and charge tha hole, screamin' war like a bloody maniac."

"Let's do it," I said.

" 'Tis a pity, but we canna," replied Dirk sadly. "Ye mus' be on tha fairway furst. Otherwise, ye waste too many soldiers. An speakin' o' soldiers, how many did ye leave behind on tha fifth hole?"

"Soldiers? I'm afraid I don't understand."

"Dead soldiers, casualties, strokes. 'Tis all tha same. Ah'm speakin' metaphorically, man!" Dirk replied with exasperation. "How many strokes did ye tae on tha las' hole?"

"Eight," I answered, choosing to forget the three extra strokes.

"Mus' hae been a bloody battle, indeed," said Dirk gravely. "Wi' all those losses, ye canna' afford ta lay a siege. There's only one choice ta be made, lad. Ah recommend heavy ordinance."

"What exactly is that?"

"Ye fire a bomb o'er these trees an' kill tha beast whilst she slumbers," said Dirk.

Shielding my eyes from the afternoon sun, I looked up at the trees. They didn't seem as tall as they were a few minutes before, but they still loomed as a considerable obstacle.

"I don't know, Dirk," I began to protest, but he quickly cut me off.

"Niver falter, lad, 'tis tha raight play. Dinna ye see tha openin' 'tween tha twin pines on tha' raight? Fire yer missile there, laddie, and tha day will be yers!"

I can't really say why I hadn't seen it before, but once Dirk pointed it out, it seemed like a perfectly plausible shot—even more compelling than the big fade he had first tried to get me to play. All I had to do was strike a clean six-iron out of the sand, taking the ball up abruptly through an opening roughly the size of a basketball between two mature pine trees. With a good release through the shot, the ball would naturally turn over after clearing the opening and then hit the fairway just in front of the green. The draw spin on the ball would then cause it to run up to the green, leaving me a tap-in birdie.

"I see it now," I said with growing excitement.

With Dirk urging me on, I took my stance once again, but as I drew back my six-iron, Raymond began to protest loudly with a series of staccato bleats. Dirk growled with anger and yanked his short sword from his belt. He whacked Raymond smartly across the backside with the flat of his blade, sending the sheep scurrying up the embankment, bleating wildly and scattering my clubs across the floor of the ravine.

"What the hell was that all about?" I asked.

"Yer caddie was tryin' ta persuade ye ta retreat," Dirk answered with fire in his eyes. "Niver trust 'em, laddie. Sheep are cowards—evir las' one o' them—an' traitors too. Mark me words, yer weel rid o' him. But ye'd better step lively, lad, tha traitor has no doot gone fer reinforcements."

Once again I took my stance while the wild Highlander talked me through the shot. As he whispered in my left ear, the small hole between the two trees began to grow in my imagination. Then when he was satisfied that I was as taut and ready as a bowstring, Dirk gave the order to fire.

In fairness to him, it was probably the best iron I've ever hit in such dire circumstances. There was a sharp report when I hit the ball, and then it rose quickly, streaking for the opening in the trees. But as almost everyone except Dirk and me would have expected, the ball hit a branch a couple of feet below the opening. It made a sound like Don Mattingly driving a single through the infield, so there was no doubt that the ball was coming back. We ducked involuntarily as my Hartless & Craven Maxfli whirred past our heads and landed with an explosion of sand twenty feet behind us.

"Tae cover, laddie, tha coorse is awake! Yer damned sheep has awakened her!"

Dirk grabbed me by the collar and threw me to the sand like I was a rag doll. Then we crawled behind a cluster of hawthorn bushes to plan our next move. Surprisingly, at that moment I didn't feel the least bit foolish. Call it personal magnetism, voodoo, or salesmanship, but for whatever reason, I was completely caught up in his vision of the world.

"Tha' beast kens tha' yer heer," said Dirk, "no doot aboot it."

"So what do we do now?" I asked.

"Create a diversion," Dirk replied. There was a wild gleam in his eye that should have told me to beware, but I was too far gone for that.

Once again the God of Tactics began drawing diagrams in the sand, laying out a plan of attack that, because I was under his spell, seemed positively brilliant.

"Furst, we exchange garments," said Dirk. "Then Ah'll throw a rock onto tha fairway an' clamber after it, pretendin' ta be yerself. Whin tha coorse has focused all her attention on me, then ye'll fire away frum yer hidin' place in tha ravine, strikin' a killin' blow."

"You're a genius," I said.

"Noo, Ah'm a strategist, laddie," Dirk replied smugly.

Moments later, we had exchanged clothes. Although we were roughly the same size, there were some problems. For one, I had never worn a kilt before and found the sudden draft a little unsettling—to say nothing of the rough, scratchy wool against my bare thighs. I had always wondered what Scotsmen wore under their kilts and now I knew. It took a moment to explain the basics of zipper safety to the God of Tactics and the exchange was complete.

"How do Ah look?" asked Dirk as he donned my baseball cap.

"Like John the Baptist on vacation," I muttered under my breath. "Shouldn't you wipe off the blue paint?"

"Frum a hundred sixty yards, tha beast will niver see it," Dirk replied crisply. " 'Tis time, laddie. Tae yer station."

When I had located my ball, Dirk heaved a small stone over the top of the embankment. Almost immediately, we were greeted with a shout of indignation.

"Watch what you're doing, for crying out loud! You almost took my head off!"

Harry Brady was standing on the crest of the embankment with Raymond at his side.

"What in the hell is going on here?" he shouted.

When I saw Harry, Dirk's spell began to break, and a flood of shame washed over me. In that moment, I knew what the Israelites must have felt when Moses caught them dancing around the golden calf, but Dirk stood his ground.

"Ah'll thank ye not ta interfere, Harry Brady," replied Dirk angrily. " 'Tis a military operation, an noone o' yer business. Go back ta yer wee little courses wi' tha stone highways runnin' through 'em an' leave us alone."

Dirk wheeled around and faced me while Harry and Raymond slid down the embankment. "Strike now, laddie. Strike now! 'Tis a trick. Tha coorse is tryin' a flankin' maneuver!"

"Drop your club, Tommy. And move away from the ball," shouted Harry. "Play it smart and we can minimize the damage."

"Shoot, mon! Shoot!" cried Dirk, waving my cap around above his head.

I set up once again over the ball, but before I could begin my backswing, a long, dark shadow covered the ball. Harry Brady was standing between me and the target.

Wheezing and out of breath from his climb, he reached out his hand.

"Give me the club, son."

"Don't let 'em tae yer weapon, laddie!" Dirk whispered in my left ear. "Slay tha beast wi' yer big fade!"

I addressed the ball once more. Harry stepped closer and looked deep into my eyes.

"Tom, can you hear me in there? It's Harry. Harry Brady."

I could hear him, all right, but I couldn't make myself respond. All I wanted was to hit a big fade around the trees and "slay the beast."

"This is worse than I thought, Raymond," said Harry. "He's damned near hypnotized." Raymond bleated his agreement and Harry grabbed me by the ears, staring directly into my eyes.

"You're wearing me out, son," said Harry. "If we were back in New Jersey, I'd lock you up in a motel room and deprogram you, but we don't have the time. So, I'm gonna have to pull rank on your friend. In the meantime, give me that six-iron before you hurt somebody."

Somehow he had reached me, and reluctantly I turned over the the club and stepped away from the ball. I was groggy and confused but trying to listen.

"And as for you, Dirk," said Harry in a booming voice, "I order you to release Tom Cruickshank from your power this instant."

Dirk laughed and whacked a scrubby pine in two with his short sword. "An' why should Ah listen ta ye, Harry? Tha game 'tis nearly o'er, an' ye've lost, auld mon. Ah've na luv fer 'em, but MacTavish has won tha day. As soon as MacKenzie gies tha word, ye'll be ruined. Yer fairways will be dryin' up, an' yer young men's fancy will turn tae other things. Soon gowf will be nuthin' but a memory in yer world."

"It ain't over yet, Dirk, and you'll listen because this soldier is under my command," said Harry, and poked Dirk in the chest with the butt of my six-iron.

Dirk laughed. "Under yer command, is he? Look at 'em, man. By tha Greet God MacKenzie, he doesn't evin ken wheer he is! Do ye honestly think this mewing mortal will finish tha coorse? Ye canna believe he's tha one. Do tha poor wee bird a favor, Harry, an' set 'em free before it's too late."

"He'll make it," replied Harry fiercely. "Now, release him before I have you brought up on charges!"

"Charges? What charges?"

"How about kidnapping for starters," Harry spat back. "You damn well know the warrior's code. If you've 'pressed a soldier under someone else's command into your service,' that makes you a kidnapper, a pirate, or both."

"Nae man can call me a pirate an' live," shouted Dirk, raising his sword above his head. "Ah'm a military man!"

"Then why are you out of uniform?" Harry countered.

"Are ye now suggestin' Ah'm a spy?" screamed the wild Scot. "Ah ought ta run ye through, Harry Brady!"

Harry raised his hands. "Dirk, there are rules in warfare just like in golf. By rights, since you're out of uniform, I should report this to Mars and Thor . . ."

Dirk looked appalled. "Ye mean you'd report me ta tha United Pantheon? Ta tha Council of Warriors?"

"Since you're an honorable man, Dirk," Harry replied, "maybe that won't be necessary. Can I trust you to do the right thing?"

Dirk stuck his sword in the sand and collapsed in a huff.

"Ye hae me word, Harry Brady," said Dirk. "Yer a silver-tongued devil."

"You'll live to fight another day," said Harry consolingly.

"Aye, tha' Ah weel," replied Dirk. Then he looked up at Harry with a sad expression on his face. "But weel ye, Harry Brady? Weel ye?"

"Don't lose any sleep over me, Dirk," said Harry. "Now give the boy back his clothes. He doesn't have the legs to wear a kilt, and Dirk, keep your yap shut till we clear the hole. I need this boy's head clear." He turned to me and said firmly, "Tom, change your clothes."

While Harry and Raymond collected my clubs, Dirk and I ducked behind a clump of scrub oaks. The old warrior was careful not to speak to me while we changed clothes.

I don't really remember getting out of the ravine, but I must have finally listened to Harry and taken my medicine, because the next thing I remember was standing in the middle of the fairway with a seven-iron in my hand. Between my feet there was a nice fresh divot hole that pointed directly at the green.

"Nice shot, son," said Harry. "You ought to play unconscious all the time."

As Raymond trotted forward to retrieve the divot, Harry took me by the shoulder and looked into my eyes until he was satisfied that someone was home.

"Tom, listen to me, and listen good. We're only a third of the way home, so you've got to get it together. I'm doing everything I can, but I can't watch you every minute. We're not playing miniature golf here. The stakes are high and they're going to get a lot higher. Do you understand me, son?"

"Yeah, Harry," I answered groggily. "I understand. I've gotta take my medicine."

"And use your head, Tom," said Harry. "I know you've got it in you."

Although I hadn't seen Harry's approach shot, it must have been a good one, because he was on the green in regulation as usual, some ten feet above the cup. My unconscious seven-iron had left me with an eight-footer that looked to be a nice straight putt, slightly uphill.

Raymond stood off to the side of the green with my putter clinched in his drooling mouth while Harry lined up his putt. Even though it clearly held some tricky breaks, he stepped up and stroked it without ceremony. The ball started slowly, then picked up speed as it took the slope. As it reached the vicinity of the hole the ball took a hard left toward the cup. I was sure that it was going to drop for a bird, but once again, the ball stopped dead on the lip.

"You were robbed," I offered, but as usual Harry didn't seem disappointed.

"Green in regulation; two putts: that's a commercial par," said Harry.

Raymond dropped my putter at my feet. He sauntered to the cup, grabbed Harry's ball with his teeth, and returned it. They stood together like brothers at the edge of the green waiting for me to hole out.

As I lined up my putt, it looked like there was no break, just a nice straight run to the cup that would save bogey and put me back on the road to respectability. As I took the putter back for a practice stroke, I thought I detected movement in the fairway. I turned and saw only a berry bush on the right side of the fairway that seemed to be shaking. Squirrels, I thought.

Satisfied all was quiet, I took my stance again and drew back my putter. But just as I began my forward swing, a large stone hit the green with a resounding thud, causing me to pull the putt hard left, sending the ball skittering past the cup. It didn't stop until it got caught up in the frog hair on the edge of the green, some fifteen feet away.

"What in the hell was that?" I cried, and then I remembered the God of Tactics.

At that moment, Dirk jumped out from behind the berry bush and began charging the green, screaming bloody murder.

"Sneak attack," Harry replied. "Better back away!"

As Dirk closed in on the green brandishing his short sword, Raymond looked down the fairway in alarm and then back at me, dropping my bag on the apron of the green with a resounding metallic clatter. Then he lumbered down the fairway toward the seventh tee. Raymond had cut and run.

"Traitor," I yelled after him, but he didn't even look back.

Meanwhile, Dirk had come within ten yards of the green, shouting at the top of his lungs, "death ta tha beast!" It was classic military tactics, choosing a flanking maneuver rather than rushing the hole head-on. So, as he crested the rise, he cut left, rerouting his charge along the apron. Unfortunately, the shoulder along the left apron was very soft, and as he veered to the left, it gave way, sending him

tumbling headfirst into the greenside bunkers. Dirk's charge had been repulsed.

"Guess the beast was ready for him." Harry laughed.

While he tended to the fallen God of Tactics, who as it turned out had more of a bruised ego than anything else, I set about trying to finish the hole. I'd like to report that I sank the comebacker—a miraculous double-breaking downhill putt of twenty feet off the apron, but Dirk had apparently awakened the sleeping course—if she was ever asleep. In the end, my bid for double bogey was repulsed and I moved a total of seven stones into the red side of the scoring sack.

CHAPTER 7

Hell's Half Acre

Where Tom learns what a really bad lie is like

When Harry and I climbed onto the tee box overlooking the seventh hole, I was still shaking the cobwebs out of my head, but images of the events on the last hole were starting to flash through my mind. I remembered something about fairways drying up and people not wanting to play golf anymore, but none of it made sense. In an effort to get my bearings, I checked the time and discovered only five minutes had passed since we left the driving range at dawn. But all around me afternoon shadows were beginning to lengthen across the tee. Harry got my attention by slapping me soundly on the back and speaking loudly into my right ear.

"How you doing, pal?" he asked. "You know where you are?"

"I'm fine, Harry," I replied, shaking my head. "Just trying to piece together what happened back there."

"Ole Dirk's a powerful fellow with that voice of his," said Harry jokingly. "He'd make a fortune doing commercials."

"He was saying something about golf disappearing, and something about you getting back to Pine Valley before it's too late. What's that all about, Harry? Are we in trouble here?"

Harry patted me on the shoulder and laughed gently. "Take it easy, son. You've got nothing to worry about. Some folks are just envious of my success. Like I told you before, I've done real well developing golf course communities, and I've made some good investments, too. The problem is, some of the members here just can't choke it down. They'd like nothing better than to see the stock market crash and a big drought dry up my investments, but it's just talk, son. Nothing but talk."

"I guess I can understand that, Harry," I said, "but what was that stuff about me?"

He spat and squinted down the fairway for a second before answering. "Well, Tom, it's a little early to be talking about this, but I've been thinking about cutting back on my schedule. Been looking around for a sharp young fellow like yourself to train. Sort of an apprentice to learn the business."

"You're kidding," I said, trying unsuccessfully to suppress a smile.

"Don't say anything right now," said Harry with a grin. "But let's talk about it at the end of the round—if it still feels right."

"So, this is sort of a test, right?"

"You might say that," he answered. "But you ain't passed yet, kiddo. Not by a long shot. We've still got a whole lot of golf to play. Are you up for it?"

"You bet, Harry," I answered eagerly. "So what are we looking at on this hole?"

"It's a five par, son," Harry replied. "Roughly 580 yards. Like the seventh at Pine Valley—but a whole lot tougher."

"Great." I smiled through clenched teeth. Since the seventh had eaten my lunch during the previous day's round, I wasn't looking forward to something even harder, especially now that I had something to prove.

Typical of Mount Augustus and Pine Valley, the hole featured a waste area off the tee box and a landing area beyond it. Further ahead, I could see the beginnings of another waste bunker. Foreshortened by distance, the far bunker didn't look particularly large or threatening from the tee, but I knew it was the prototype of Pine Valley's Hell's Half Acre—the most miserable stretch of sand and brush that any man has crossed since the wagon trains traversed Death Valley.

"Why don't you take the tee, Tom," said Harry with a pained expression on his face. "My dogs're killing me. Gonna sit down for a minute."

Still a little shaky, I had hoped he would show the way, but certainly didn't want to give the impression of not being with the program after what he had just told me. So, I gave Harry a big thumbs-up while he plopped down under a large chestnut and began to peel off his socks.

"Besides, you seem to play better when you're out of it," he added, grinning broadly.

One of golf's great ironies is that trying to avoid disaster is just as likely to get you into trouble as when you're jumping out of your shoes to crush a 300-yard drive. After my last fiasco, I was determined to avoid coming over the top and slicing my drive.

So, to begin my downswing, I consciously held my arms in check while violently thrusting my legs and hips toward the target. The good news was no slice or pull-hook but my body was so far out in front of my swing that I blocked the ball straight and right toward the trees. This was not going to be something I wanted to watch, so I closed my eyes and an instant later heard the unmistakable sound of a golf ball slamming into a tree trunk.

"Son of a bitch," said Harry.

"I'm dead, right?"

"You can open your eyes." Harry chuckled. "You got a ninety-degree kick off those poor defenseless pines. You're in the middle of the fairway, son."

After he laced up his wing tips, Harry joined me in the fairway with another poke that started out left, but then faded safely into the short grass. It was a reasonable drive, but Harry's backswing had gotten awfully short over the last couple of holes.

As we made our way toward our balls, our clubs were clicking together rhythmically in counterpoint to the brassy trills and chirping of the birds. After Harry's little bombshell about my future back on the tee, everything suddenly seemed brighter and my spirits were soaring.

I looked over at the old man and was swept up in a sudden wave of emotion. He was taciturn by nature and occasionally grumpy but there was a real warm spot in my breast for Harry Brady. Although his ways were sometimes unorthodox, he really had been looking out for me ever since we got to the Mountain. What sublime irony! After searching high and low through New York's forbidding canyons the mentor, the guru, the rabbi I had been searching for since business school was walking next to me, and I had found him on the golf course.

"It doesn't get any better than this, does it, Harry?"

"Dammit, dammit, dammit!" he shouted. "What's wrong with you lately? You'd forget your head if it wasn't nailed on."

"Was it something I said?"

"What?" asked Harry fuming. "No, it's not you. Left my seven-iron back on the green." He ran his fingers over his irons once more to be sure of the count. Then sputtering and swearing, Harry gave his bag a swift kick.

"I'll have to go back and get it," said Harry. "I'll catch up to you." He paused. "But, Tom . . ."

"Yeah, I know, stay out of trouble and don't do anything stupid."

As Harry slowly limped back toward the tee, there was a sudden flash of movement on the fairway ahead. Quick as lightning, a creature darted out from the copse of pines on the right side of the fairway and began to prance around my ball. It appeared to have the upper body of a man, and the lower body of some sort of animal. Then, as suddenly as he had appeared, the exotic creature shot back into the trees.

Harry's ball was sitting off to the left, exactly where it should have been, but mine was gone. Probably settled down in a little swale, I told myself, but a quick search revealed nothing except a few leaves and a couple of sticks.

"Lose something, mister?"

Standing in the shade of the pines on the right was a boy of twelve or fourteen. Sandy haired and freckled, and a little over five feet tall, he possessed a puckish grin made even more mischievous by the gap between his front teeth, a casting director's dream for Huck Finn—from the waist up. From the waist down he had the body of a goat.

"My ball. It should be right here in the middle of the fairway." Pleased with how well I was adjusting to meeting a faun, I pretended not to notice his tail and cloven hooves.

The creature laughed and began tossing a golf ball up and down with his right hand as he stepped out of the shade.

"No, it *should* be in the woods where you hit it," he said.

"Hey, that's my ball. Give it back!"

He cocked his head, arching an eyebrow. "And who exactly are you?"

"Tom Cruickshank," I answered.

"Ah, Harry's little fledgling bird. I thought you'd be taller. More heroic," the faun said tauntingly. "No matter. What happened? Mommy push you out of the nest?"

"If you're talking about Harry," I replied, "he forgot a club back at the last green."

"Sad what happens to you mortals as you age."

"Okay," I said. Enough was enough. "I've told you who I am."

"I'm Divot," he answered, rolling my ball across the back of his fingers like a sideshow magician.

"And what are you supposed to be, the god of stolen golf balls?"

"Stolen golf balls?" he snapped. "Divot never steals, and never lies!"

"Then give it back!"

"Your ball?" he answered. "Which one do you mean?"

He tossed my ball so high into the air it seemed to hang

114

for an eternity, and then began spitting golf balls of all descriptions from his chubby little cheeks. As they arched slowly over his head, I could make out ancient featheries, gutta perchas, wound surlyns, two-piece distance balls, orange and yellow winter balls, and tour balatas. As they fell he juggled them, chanting:

> *Pick a ball, any ball at all*
> *but never, ever let it fall . . .*
> *For if it falls, and fall it may*
> *You must play it where it lays!*
>
> *Pick a ball, any ball will do*
> *Any color, any hue*
> *White, yellow, orange, or blue*
> *But if it falls, and fall it may*
> *You must play it where it lays!*

As balls cascaded through the air I began to distinguish one from another. At the apex of their arc, one turned just enough for me to recognize the blue boar's head that signified a Hartless & Craven giveaway. As my ball dropped down toward the boy's left hand, I grasped it and clutched it to my chest.

Divot stopped juggling, letting the rest fall around his feet. The moment they hit the ground they were transformed into all manner of crawling and creeping creatures. Beetles, scorpions, grubs, silver fish, spiders, garden snakes, lizards, and salamanders all scurried into the bush with a chorus of squeaky laughter.

There was a tickling sensation in my palm and I opened it to see not the blue boar's head, but the six furry legs of a small tarantula. I let out a whoop and shook the spider off my hand—to another chorus of squeaky giggles from the forest floor.

As the laughter subsided, Divot thrust both of his fists in front of my nose. "Is it in my right hand or my left hand?" Before I could choose, he jerked his hands behind his back. "No, that's too easy—it's a game of chance." Like a Catskills magician, he pulled what had to be my ball from behind my left ear, squealing, "Let's make this a test of skill. Let's play golf." Then he launched the ball like a shot-putter out into the middle of the fairway where it bounced once and burrowed like a mole, leaving only a sliver of white. A chorus of high-pitched giggles echoed off the trees.

"You wanna play golf, I'll show you how to play golf," I shrieked.

Swinging my five-iron at the little beast, I tried to cut him in half, but if I was fast, he was faster. When I went for his head, he ducked and scampered back into the forest. Despite the fact that I had separated my shoulder two times playing JV ball in high school, I decided the only way to get the little bastard was to tackle him. But Divot had more moves than Gale Sayers and twice I hit the ground with a bone-jarring thud. Enraged, I began stomping around in the underbrush hoping to dispatch as many of Divot's little friends as possible.

"Hey, bug hunter," cried Divot from the fairway, "get a load of this."

The little brat was doing the flamenco on my ball, driving it deeper into the grass. "Do you think this is a difficult lie, mortal?" he shouted.

"It's an impossible lie, you little creep."

"*Au contraire, mon ami,*" replied Divot, gesturing at my now buried drive. "This is a mere inconvenience. Let me show you what a *bad* lie is really like."

He began to spin madly in a circle. Dust rose in clouds at his feet, and then he grabbed the end of my club, and I could feel myself spinning with him. The world around me became a blur of colors. First there were broad swatches of blue and green with traces of reds and yellows and then we began spinning faster and faster until everything became a blur of light. All my senses were overcome by a tumult of sound—a scream of pure white noise that obliterated everything else. Then everything stopped.

As the roar in my ears subsided, I opened my eyes and found that I had been transported into the heart of a desert wasteland. Enormous dunes as tall as office buildings loomed up in the stifling heat. Vegetation consisted mostly of dry weeds, brambles, and the occasional prickly pear. Divot had delivered me into the Mother of All Bunkers. It made the Sahara look like a sandbox.

My ball was sitting in an enormous swale, a gleaming white beacon in the shifting ochre sands. I walked toward it and began to sink. By the time I reached it, I was up to my knees. Club selection wasn't an issue; the sand wedge was my only choice.

"Give up! Give up! You'll never get out of this lie," called a large red scorpion, as it scurried up to my ball.

"Move it, bug, I'm blasting out of here."

"Take the penalty. Anyone can see it's an unplayable lie," it pleaded as its deadly stinger whipped back and

---

The Fable of Divot—The God of Bad Lies

The Great God MacKenzie remained a philanderer, much to the disgust of the Goddess Rowena, Queen of the Links and MacKenzie's original mate. Weary of his infidelities, Rowena turned a nanny goat named Muriel into a fetching maiden, and positioned her at the turn in the lower 18 of Mount Augustus with a chariot full of MacKenzie's favorite refreshments. Having set the snare, Rowena repaired to a wooded glen to watch the fun. As expected, MacKenzie led Muriel to a grassy hillside and had his way with her. At the culmination of their passions, Rowena restored Muriel to her original form hoping to humiliate her husband.

Not only did it not work, but in the fall Muriel gave birth to a litter of fauns—half goat and half man. MacKenzie was so taken with one of them that he took him back to the clubhouse to raise with his other children. He called the faun Divot.

Being half goat, Divot was trouble from the first day. When he wasn't knocking tables and other children down with his baby goat horns, he was busy placing snake or turtle eggs in birds' nests and vice versa. Soon the entire clubhouse and the nearby forest was in an uproar. But MacKenzie would not hear of disciplining the faun.

Then one rainy afternoon (yes, it does rain on Mount Augustus), Mac-Kenzie was practicing his putting on a carpet of fine white cowhide. Nearby, Rowena practiced polkas on her harp for the Annual Member Guest Ball. Unbeknownst to MacKenzie, Divot had replaced half of his balls with ripe serpents' eggs, and had hidden behind the curtain to watch. Each time MacKenzie putted an egg, he placed a hairline crack in its shell. All at once, the young snakes broke out of their shells and slithered madly across the floor. Rowena screamed and jumped on her stool, presenting Divot with a target no goat, half-human or not, could resist. Rowena was sent flying headlong onto the banquet table, which had just been set for lunch.

MacKenzie had no choice but to banish him from the clubhouse forever. But since he knew Divot could not stay out of mischief, he gave him a means of channeling it by making him the God of Bad Lies, and allowing him to keep the little creeping and crawling friends as helpers.

---

forth. "You'll only make matters worse if you try. Haven't you learned anything yet?"

"Don't say I didn't warn you," I said as I swung at the ball. But the blade bit hard and dug deep, sending a shovelful of sand and the scorpion high in the air. The ball itself merely dropped deeper into the excavation. Not only was the lie worse than before, but the exertion had twisted my legs even deeper into the sand.

"That was fun," said the scorpion, "but that's also one stroke. Give it up, mortal."

"Never," I answered, and drew back the wedge for another go.

The results were essentially the same, except now I was lying three and buried up to my hips. Two more strokes and I was up to my armpits. The ball hadn't moved an inch.

The scorpion crawled up close to my chest and looked up at me.

"You're an idiot," he squeaked. "Give it up and come with me. I've got refreshments just over the dune. I've got ginger beer, dates, and humus. And chocolate-covered termites for dessert."

"One last try," I answered and gave it my best shot. Not only did I fail to advance the ball, but slipped into the sand over my chin.

"As I said before, you're an idiot," said the scorpion. He flipped his tail two or three times in my direction and then moved closer. "I'd put you out of your misery, but long ago I swore an oath never to sting a defenseless creature. And you're not only defenseless, you're pathetic."

He wiggled around disdainfully and began to crawl away, his tail bobbing in the air. I watched him until he disappeared from view over the crest of the dune. My entire world was reduced to the shifting sands and the blue boar's head on the back of the Hartless & Craven golf ball sitting in front of my face. I missed that little bug more than I was willing to admit; it's nice to have someone to talk to.

To cheer myself up, I reviewed all my sexual conquests from high school through the most recent Christmas party. Not a smart idea since it turned out to be a short and rather dismal list. I tried to calculate my net worth, adding up the value of my 401K, checking account, a couple of moribund IRAs, and 500 shares of a Silicon Valley chip manufacturer that had sunk like a stone since I bought them. Completely depressed, I was about to move on to figure the total number of pounds gained and lost since high school when a trumpet sounded from the crest of the dune and Harry appeared like Lawrence of Arabia, wearing a burnoose and riding a camel.

"Harry, Harry! I'm over here!"

"Up to your neck as usual, I see," he shouted good-naturedly.

Harry dismounted like an expert and squatted in the sand.

"Pull me out of here, Harry," I cried. "I'm sinking."

"No can do, son," he replied.

"Why not?" I asked.

"Quicksand. If I came any closer, we'd both be goners."

"Then throw me a rope and pull me out with your camel."

"Where am I supposed to get a rope?"

"The same place you got the damn camel! Come on, Harry!"

"Can you free your arms?" he asked.

With a great thrust I pushed my arms free, but the effort screwed my body deeper into the mire.

Spitting out a mouthful of sand, I shouted, "Now what?"

"Use your edge."

"Wedge?"

"Edge, Tom, edge. Fergus's drawstring pouch," Harry replied impatiently. "Get it out of your carry bag."

I managed to grab the strap and drag it close enough to unzip the side pocket. The little bag was sitting right on top of my rain jacket.

"Now what?"

"Sprinkle it around," said Harry, stating the obvious.

The contents of the pouch were not impressive, just a dull, gray powder mixed with small flecks of yellow and white like ordinary pencil shavings. But as each grain of powder hit the sand, grass would sprout, take root, and send out runners creating a web of support. As the web grew thicker, it began to raise me up and before I knew it, I was standing on terra firma once more with only the sand in my trouser cuffs to remind me of Divot's bunker and my ordeal.

"Now you've got a perfect lie," said Harry, handing me a five-iron. He pointed toward the right side of the landing area ahead. "Go ahead, son. Take your best shot."

I cut a high soft five-iron into the dance floor some twenty-five feet to the right of the pin. Harry gave me a thumbs-up and brushed the remaining sand off my back in a fatherly gesture that both surprised and pleased me.

When we reached the green, I looked back and saw that Divot's terrible desert was once again the gigantic waste bunker I had seen from the tee—forbidding and dangerous, yes—but more like Hell's Half Acre than the vast Sahara. I wondered if any of it had really happened until I spotted something unusual in the shimmering sand—where we had stood, a small magnolia tree in full flower was waving gently in the breeze. I took Fergus's drawstring bag from my hip pocket and shook it. Nothing came out but a little puff of dust.

"There goes my edge," I muttered. "Got any more of the paste?" I tried to pretend I was joking.

"Maybe," said Harry evenly. "But it wouldn't do you any good."

"Don't tell me the stuff doesn't work," I said. "I used it back at the range, remember?"

"Of course it works . . . back in the world," Harry replied. "Just not here at Mount Augustus."

"What about magic, Harry? You said there was magic."

"Golf magic, whether it's potions, sacrifices, or incantations, is meant to do just one thing."

"And what's that?"

"Bridge the gap between our world and Mount Augustus," he replied with a smile. "But we're already there, don't you see? So all the hoo-doo has no effect."

"Explain Fergus's pouch then," I shot back.

"Ah, that's different," said Harry. "When a god directly bestows a gift or a dispensation on you, it's usually to counteract the interference of another god . . . like Divot. Get it? They're one-time gifts. Sort of like Mulligan's 'get out of jail free' card."

"Yeah, but . . ."

"Look, son. Don't you think it's time to take the training wheels off? If you're going to get anything out of Mount Augustus, you've got to be honest with yourself."

He reached over and playfully took a pinch of the spare tire that was growing around my middle—the result of too little exercise and too many late-nights eating takeout at the office.

"Otherwise, it's like weighing yourself on a bathroom scale that's been rigged. You might fool yourself into feeling a little better, but it won't make it any easier to get into your clothes. Are you with me, son?"

Harry was telling me there wasn't a Santa Claus, and that I had better get used to practical gifts like pajamas and underwear on Christmas morning. I knew he was right but it didn't make me happy and he knew it.

"Tell you what I'll do, son. When we're done, if you still think golf hoo-doo is so all-fired important, I'll teach you everything I've learned on the Mountain. All forty years' worth."

"Sounds good to me."

"But right now, Tom, we've got to play it straight," said Harry. "Local rules and all that. Deal, son?"

"I guess so, Harry," I replied. "I mean, I'll give it my best shot."

"That's the ticket," he said with a broad smile.

After putting out, I figured my strokes as best I could under the circumstances and dumped another handful of gravel in the old scoring sack with a couple extra to make sure. It was getting heavy.

"Got all your sticks?" I asked Harry as we were leaving the green. I was only joking but he looked suddenly anxious and began to inspect his bag. That he took it so seriously made me feel bad. After counting his clubs, he placed his left hand on my shoulder and steadied himself while he dumped the sand out of his shoes. There was a distant look in his eyes. I wanted to bring him back.

"Can I ask you a question, Harry?"

After a pause, Harry looked up at me. "Fire away, son."

"What happened to your camel?" I asked.

Harry slowly bent down to tie his shoes and chuckled.

"Parked next to the *Queen Mary*," he answered. "That's one for the books. A camel? You must have been hallucinating."

I left it at that. Maybe Harry had no idea what I was talking about. But one thing for sure, we had some kind of deal going and I was going to have to trust my mentor. Any way you cut it, magic was very much alive on Mount Augustus, and despite promising to play it straight, I would have done almost anything at that moment to get an edge to call my own.

CHAPTER 8

The Lie "Preferred's" Preferable to Fate

In which Tom is shown some practical solutions
to difficult problems

Seven holes on Mount Augustus was enough to send the average golfer to bed for a rest cure. After being speared by a deranged greenskeeper, hypnotized by a Highland warrior, and buried up to my neck in sand, I was pretty wrung out. So it wasn't surprising that I came down with a severe case of cement legs and almost whiffed again on eight.

My three-wood bounced off the turf a good four inches behind the tee, cutting a huge divot and managing to barely graze the top of the ball that dribbled slowly to the edge of the tee box before it rolled down the bank. End to end, it was a tape-measure drive of some nine feet.

Worse yet, the ball came to rest against a jagged piece of rock jutting out of the sandy soil. Harry, who had uncharacteristically snap hooked his drive into the woods, knelt to examine my life.

"Do you think it's a loose impediment?" I asked hopefully.

"No way," said Harry.

"Why?"

"Does it look loose to you?" he asked.

"Just asking," I said.

Harry looked out over the fairway as he awaited my decision.

"So I hit it where it lies, or drop and take a stroke?"

"That's about the size of it."

"What do you think?" I asked.

"If you try to hit it from there you better have an ugly club because you're going to do some damage," replied Harry.

My six-iron was already nicked up from playing soldiers with Dirk so it was the obvious choice. I was determined to have a go at it. But as soon as I addressed the ball, it began to roll away from the rock and down the slope, stopping in a wide patch of fine sand.

"How in hell did that happen?" I exclaimed.

"Got me," marveled Harry.

"Now what?" I asked.

"Take your stroke and hit away," he said.

"Take my stroke?"

"The ball moved, take your stroke."

"I didn't move it, Harry."

"Doesn't matter. The ball stopped and started rolling again after you addressed it, that's a stroke, that's the rule. Let's move on." Harry walked over to retrieve his bag.

"There's no justice," I called after him, and turned my attention to my lie.

Sand was flying around my ball like someone was digging. Expecting sand devils I approached cautiously, six-iron at the ready, and then stood and watched as two little men with shovels were digging sand away from my ball to create a tee. One of them stopped his work and waved at me.

"Done in a whiz, Tommy lad," said a shrill little voice.

"Stop that," I shouted, "you can't improve my lie."

"You might as well let us fix it up," a second, deeper

voice said. "We already rolled the bloody thing down here."

"And it cost me a stroke," I screamed.

"Why?" one of them asked.

"HARRY," I yelled.

"God in heaven, soldier, you could blow a bloke's eardrum like that," the first little man said, shaking his head.

"Harry, get over here," I called again. But when I looked up, he had shouldered his bag and was moving down the edge of the fairway toward trees where he hooked his drive.

"Dammit, Harry," I yelled, "wait a minute."

As he vanished into the woods he just waved at me to hit away.

"Compose yourself, Tom," a tiny voice called out from behind me. "There's no need to shout, old chap. We're professionals, after all."

"Well, excuse me," I said.

"Accepted," they said in unison.

"Allow me to introduce myself, Tom. I'm Wendell, the God of Winter Rules," said first little man.

"And I'm Ruppert, the God of Preferred Lies," said the second one.

"We've come to bring you joy," they said in unison as they flipped their shovels over their shoulders and planted them in the sand, leaning on the handles.

"And how do you know my name?" I asked.

"Don't be silly, Tom," Ruppert trilled. "Everyone at Mount Augustus knows who you are. After all, it's not every day a mortal plays the course."

"So you're not sand devils?" I asked.

"Heavens no," said Wendell. "They're horrible little creatures."

"Ugh," said Ruppert.

I knelt down in the sand to get a closer look at my would-be benefactors. The tallest one at about eight inches, who had introduced himself as Wendell, was thin and long limbed with a narrow face and a huge smile. He was wearing a morning suit complete with tailed cutaway and gray pinstriped pants, and his shoes shone like mirrors. A top hat was pushed back on his head and fine white gloves were on his hands.

Ruppert, the short one with the sensitive ears, was stumpy and round, like a bowling ball with legs. His cheeks were ruddy and his nose, red, lumpy, and lined with blue veins, was a road map to many pubs. He wore plus fours and a tweed jacket that was bursting at the buttons attempting to contain his enormous girth. He was sweating from the effort with the shovel and mopping his flushed forehead. Ruppert was bald as a cue ball.

"You look like a man with a troubled mind," said Wendell.

"You look like a man who needs a friend or two," said Ruppert.

"You look like a man who could use a laugh," said Wendell.

"Did you know why the vampire stopped playing golf?" asked Ruppert.

"No," I said.

"He couldn't get a decent bite on the ball," said Wendell.

"I'll see you guys around," I said as I rose and lined up my shot.

"Hello, wait just a moment," Ruppert said, "that was funny."

"You guys better move."

"No sense of humor," said Ruppert.

"None at all," said Wendell, as they stepped aside and gave me room.

I hit my iron without much conviction and the result was exactly what I deserved; a measley 70 yarder that stopped abruptly when the ball hit a scrub pine deeper in sandy hell. I grabbed my bag and left the comedians tsking and shaking their heads.

"Stay," I called over my shoulder.

Of course, when I reached my ball, which was solidly wedged against the base of the pine, there were Wendell and Ruppert, with tape measures and levels, examining the site.

The Fable of Wendell and Ruppert
The Gods of Winter Rules and
Preferred Lies

Wendell and Ruppert sprang forth from a meeting where the gods discussed how best to pass the long winter months when Fergus closed the links. After much debate they agreed that there should be two entertainers who embodied all that was funny. So the gods put quill to paper and wrote down every joke they could remember and put them all in a pile.

A wooden box was brought to the table and all the scribbling was placed inside. It was taken to the rear of the castle and buried in a cornfield. Each day the gods would pass by to see if their entertainers were sprouting. One morning many months later Mac-Tavish was taking his morning stroll around the castle and discovered a very tall thin man and a very short fat one sitting on a fence. He greeted them and asked if they were mortal. They replied that they had this funny feeling they were gods and stood on the muddy box to do a little soft-shoe. When they finished they said to Mac-Tavish that their names were Wendell and Ruppert and that was that. MacTavish took them to The MacKenzie who decreed they could be Wendell and Ruppert if they could make him laugh, which they did by telling a story about a philandering husband and a goat.

"Ye are who ye say," said MacKenzie, "and will be from henceforth. Now get ye back in the box until ye are summoned."

Wendell and Ruppert were dismayed but shrank themselves away into the box, and MacKenzie and the rest of the gods promptly forgot they were there. They were abandoned for many seasons, becoming angry and bitter and vowing to take revenge on the gods when they were finally released.

Late one night MacTavish stole into the great room while Mac-Kenzie was asleep and released the entertainers. They were grateful and pledged their services in return for their freedom. MacTavish accepted, saying that they must serve him in secret and aid him in ridding the sacred Augustus of mortals who, in MacTavish's eyes, were worse than the plague. He invested them with overseeing and maintaining Winter Rules and Preferred Lies, which were not difficult areas of responsibility since they were inherently unclear to begin with and offered great opportunity for interpretation.

When MacKenzie discovered that they had been freed by MacTavish he wished them removed from the Mountain. But when it was pointed out that he had deified the entertainers and that they didn't have to leave, he placed them in the keeping of the God of Rules. Many believe that MacKenzie took this action on purpose to create a little chaos in an otherwise perfect world.

"This is how I see it . . ." said Ruppert.

"We set the charges here and here . . ." interrupted Wendell.

"My feeling exactly . . ." interrupted Ruppert.

"The charges?" I asked.

"We'll blow this spiteful thing to kingdom come and your ball won't move an inch," they said. "We've done it often, don't worry."

"You can't do this," I said.

"Mortal, hearken to me," Wendell said with fatherly concern. "This abomination with needles shouldn't be here. It wasn't here yesterday, or the day before. Fergus planted this wretched bush just to put you in the soup. Ruppert and I saw him do it with our own eyes. It isn't fair and that's that. The dirty doings of mean-spirited groundskeepers should not be allowed to ruin your day on the Mountain."

"This tree wasn't part of the original course, anyway," chimed in Ruppert.

"Quite right," chimed in Wendell. "The original course had no obstacles at all."

"That can't be true," I argued, "all golf courses have obstacles."

"Claptrap," said Wendell.

"Hooey," added Ruppert.

"Anyway, how would you know?" asked Wendell. "Were you there at the beginning?"

"No, but that's not the point . . ." I tried.

"The Crown rests," said Wendell.

" 'Nuff said." Ruppert slammed the conversational door. He took some tiny sticks of TNT from a wooden box marked DANGER: EXPLOSIVES, humming the chorus of "There'll Be a Hot Time in the Old Town Tonight." As I watched, he placed them around the base of the tree. Wendell uncoiled a length of fuse and joined Ruppert in his work. They were whistling in harmony, the happiest demolition team in history.

"You'll thank us for this later," Wendell called out from the other side of the tree.

"Can we talk about this?" I begged.

"Well, certainly," said Ruppert.

They walked around opposite sides of the tree. Wendell was trailing the fuse behind him.

"We're finished anyway," said Wendell.

"After you, Wendell," said Ruppert.

"No, no, after you, Ruppert," said Wendell.

"Do you have a match, Tom?" asked Ruppert.

"No ..."

"Just kidding, Tom. Wendell's always got a match." Ruppert laughed.

"Yes, Ruppert, my arse and your face." Wendell went into convulsions.

"Oh, you got me that time." Ruppert pretended offense.

Wendell reached into the box and pulled out a large kitchen match.

"Let's move back a hair," said Wendell.

"Out of range," added Ruppert excitedly. "This kipper's gonna blow."

I suddenly realized if Ruppert stood on Wendell's shoulders the composite height would be slightly over a foot. There was no reason to be cowed by two men that I could swat like flies. Wendell stopped what he was doing and looked me in the eye.

"Tom, may I ask you a question?"

"Okay." I was plotting my move.

"You don't think we're too small, do you?"

"Well ..."

He didn't wait for my answer. Wendell looked at Ruppert and nodded. Before my eyes they began to grow like asparagus in a muddy field until they towered over me.

"We can be even bigger if you like," said Ruppert in a booming voice.

"But we prefer being smaller," added Wendell, and they instantly shrank down to their previous dimensions.

"It's more fun, all in all," Wendell continued.

"Easier to get around, find clothes," said Ruppert.

"What would you like to talk about, Tom?" said Wendell. There was just a hint of menace in his voice.

"Nothing." I sank back into the sand, defeated. It was out of my control. "All I ever wanted was to play pretty much by the rules, make a couple of good shots, finish, and go home, wherever that is. That's all I really want now. Please don't blow the tree."

"Well, it's just too big to pull out by the roots like a dandelion," said Ruppert huffily.

"Right now I don't want you to do anything to it at all. Let it sit there until I can knock my ball out, take another stroke, and move on. After that you can do whatever the hell you want. You can set the whole damn place on fire for all I care."

"You sound discouraged," said Wendell.

"Pity," said Ruppert.

"You've a problem with perspective," said Wendell.

"Born of misunderstanding and myth," added Ruppert.

"The rules are killing the game," Wendell continued. "This shot is impossible and unfair and should be improved. You have a perfect right to do so under our interpretation of Winter Rules and Preferred Lies. Now, don't get us wrong, mate. We're not suggesting you move the ball, or replay the shot as did that reprehensible Mulligan. We're merely suggesting you remove the obstacle."

"How did you know what Mulligan suggested?"

"It's the sort of thing that rascal always suggests," said Wendell.

"How did you know I'd seen him?"

"Everyone sees Mulligan," Ruppert said.

"You've been following me, right?"

"Why, no," they said in unison, and I knew they were lying.

"What do you really want?" I asked.

"We only want what's best for you and for the game," added Ruppert. "It's gotten far too difficult and the fun is gone."

"First of all," I retorted with as much conviction as I could muster, "Winter Rules haven't been in effect for weeks, and even if they were, there's nothing in them about bombing things out of your way. And furthermore, Preferred Lies are defined by course officials, not by midgets with explosives."

"Sticks and stones," sang Ruppert.

"You are being obstinate and offensive," said Wendell.

"No, I'm being honest," I replied.

"He's a tough one," said Ruppert.

"Most assuredly," agreed Wendell.

"Can I get my ball now?" I asked politely.

"Not until you hear us out," they answered.

"All right, I give up."

"Super," chortled Wendell. "Shall we, Ruppert?"

"Most assuredly." Ruppert smiled.

They dragged the box of explosives in front of me, reached inside and removed two poles, some canvas curtain, and two pairs of tap shoes, which they put on with great care. As they finished they began to shrink until they could stand on the wooden box. Next they attached the canvas to the poles and inserted them into holes at the front corners of the box, thereby stretching the canvas across the front and creating an act curtain, which they closed.

Wendell poked his head out and welcomed me to the show. A tinny overture sounded from behind the curtain. The music was up tempo, the kind of ricky-ticky sound that I associated with '30s movies. Wendell and Ruppert opened their curtain by hand in time with the music. They turned to face each other, bowed, doffed their straw sailor hats, and strode purposefully to center stage, where they turned sharply to me and bowed again. I had no choice but to applaud; I'd never had cheaper orchestra seats in my life. There was an easel on the left side of the stage with a signboard that read:

The Lie Preferred

And then they began to sing:

W: You with the club there about to take a stroke
R: We won't let you continue this folly
W: You are the butt of the gods' cruelest joke
R: And they think it's damnably jolly

The Gods of Golf

W: The legions who beat the little white ball
R: With the gleam of par in their eyes
W: Are blinkered unknowing at rule's beck and call
W: There are lies, lad, then there are lies...

Ohhh...
Our position here is simple, Tom,
We won't equivocate
The lie preferred's preferable to fate

The Gods of Augustus gave mortals this game
But the fine print was left to a Scot
Now we hack and duff in perpetual shame
Slaves to the comma and dot

With all the Scot's nagging, niggling laws
A simple game's too hard to play
When snared and scarred by rulebook's claws
A round is a waste of a day

All of us are mortal when on the links we meet
E'en the few of us who've overcome the sport
Not every drive is perfect, not every shot is sweet
And trouble lurks to bring us all up short

So why should we be punished for nature's little jokes
Say a rock or twisted branch that's out of place?
We're masters of our fate, Tom, no need to waste a stroke
Put a smile on every duffer's grieving face!

Our position here is basic, Tom
We won't equivocate
The lie preferred's preferable to fate

The team took a brief bow and segued into a lively, high-energy finale. To the driving beat of a snare drum and some snappy soft-shoe, they created almost every rotten lie I could imagine and all the myriad ways to make them better. It was a crash course in immoral and unacceptable behavior. Although devious and under-handed, I must admit I found it was pretty interesting— in an educational sort of way, that is. Wendell and Rup-pert's little presentation was giving me a whole new insight into the game.

Ohhhh...
There's always a better location
There's always a way to refine
There's no reason to settle for trouble
When a really big round's on the line

If you're stuck behind a tree
And there's no one there to see
Improve your lie

If you shanked it in the wood
But your opponent's shot is good
Advance your lie

If you hooked it in the rough
No need to make it tough
Enhance your lie

If you've landed in a trap
Don't play it like a sap
Amend the lie

If you're stymied in the rocks
Pull the spare one from you socks
Refine your lie

This really isn't cheating, Tom,
No matter what they're saying
There's little time and life's too short
To play it as it's laying

The Gods of Golf

(Big finish, Ruppert)
(Ready and, set, Wendell)

We're not just talking movement, Tom
We're talking self-improvement, Tom
The Lie Preferred's Preferable to Fate.

I was beginning to get the point. Dynamiting an obstacle to get a better shot had potential. Don't like the depth of the bunker? Get the Construction Corps in there and fill it up. Don't like the sand? Sod it over. Water hazard? Cover the son of a bitch with pontoons. Too much roll in the green? Get a bulldozer and level that bastard flat as an Iowa farm, and, while you're at it, add a lip like a pizza pan to keep the ball from rolling off. Hell, drop the center of every green until the cup is like the drain in a laundry-room floor.

Rolling Thunder Golf: it was a concept. It had appeal. I wouldn't be cheating. I'd be performing a public service: I'd be making the course safe for duffers everywhere.

"Blow it," I said quietly to Wendell. He looked at me and saluted.

"Yes, sir," he answered crisply.

"You won't regret it, sir," he added.

Wendell did an abrupt about-face, gave Ruppert a military embrace, stepped back, and handed him the kitchen match. Ruppert wiped a tiny tear from his eye and leapt to the sand with the kind of grace one is always surprised to see in men of girth. I was proud to have him on my team. He marched past holding the match in front like a company flag. Wendell interrupted him just as he was about to light the fuse.

"I say, Ruppert, safety first." He motioned to his head.

"Right you are," answered Ruppert.

"Shall we wear the tins?" said Wendell.

"First rate," answered Ruppert.

"None to fit you, I'm afraid," Wendell apologized to me. They walked to the wooden box, flipped open the lid, rummaged around inside and came up with metal dough-boy helmets circa 1915. Wendell had Ruppert's and Ruppert had Wendell's so they made a fumbling exchange that sprang full blown from a Laurel and Hardy short. Not only were they funny, they were going to help me.

It was then I realized the whole thing was wrong.

I have always believed myself to be a basically honest man. Sure, Harry had given me a couple of mulligans back at Pine Valley and I'd taken them. Hell, there'd been a lot of liberties with the rules over the years. Maybe I'd taken my first step over the ethical line a long time ago. But one thing for sure, I wasn't going to become a willing accomplice in the world's first Multi Megaton Mulligan. It wasn't much of a position but it was all I had.

Wendell and Ruppert were rummaging in the box for protective vests and leaning over the edge arguing about whose responsibility it had been to pack them. Ruppert's spindly little legs were dangling off the ground and his egg-shaped body was tottering on the box's lip. I grabbed their little feet, toppled them inside headfirst, slammed the lid shut, and sat on it, looking for the latch. They were yelling and banging on the sides of the box like terriers.

"Settle down, you lummox," Wendell cried.

"But we're trapped," whined Ruppert.

"Only because we're small, idiot," countered Wendell.

"Right as rain," said Ruppert.

"On three," Wendell shouted.

The lid shot open beneath me and I exploded high into the air like a Hogan sand shot with a lot of backspin. I was curled into a little ball and was spinning backward as I flew across the sand toward the treeline, landing with a thump in the thick rough.

I lay there a moment wondering how much was broken, then opened my eyes to rest them on two of the most beautiful feet I'd ever seen.

I looked up into the kind of eyes that make grown men lose control. They were as blue as liquid sapphires and as cool and soothing as pools in a forest glen. And I was completely suspended in those deep blue pools—weightless and hopelessly enchanted.

"Are you all right?" she asked. It was a voice made in heaven.

"Uhhh . . ." I mumbled.

"Wendell and Ruppert are responsible for this, I assume."

Even if I hadn't been at Mount Augustus, I would have known she was a goddess. Her loveliness was so perfect in every detail it was almost painful to observe. Tall, with a river of golden hair flowing down her back, she wore a gown of diaphanous white that revealed nothing and everything at the same time. Beads of perspiration began to form on my forehead, a sure sign that my face had flushed a bright red. I ached for her. I wanted her. I longed for her with a passion that knows no equal in our world, except possibly by the unrequited love of the science club for a high school beauty queen. Once again I was a teenager on prom night.

"Excuse me," she said, "there is something I must know."

"Whaa." I was stuttering like a fool.

"Have you succumbed?" she asked.

"Oh, yes," I answered.

"No," she said with a hint of exasperation, "I mean to the trickery of Wendell and Ruppert?"

I could see her moist lips moving, but I couldn't really make out the words. At that moment, I wanted nothing more in the world than to ask her to go steady.

"Excuse me," she said, shaking me gently. "I must hear from your own lips whether you succumbed."

"Well, almost, but no," I answered finally, averting my eyes.

"It is an honest answer, Thomas. I think you are a good man," she said gently, and a rush of fire shot through my body, nearly scorching my soul.

"WENDELL . . . RUPPERT," she bellowed, "stand before

me this instant or suffer the fate of Innings and the Band of Nine."

Wendell and Ruppert appeared.

"Now, Glenda . . ." Wendell began.

Her name was Glenda. Now I knew my true love's name. It was Glenda.

"Explain yourselves," said the Goddess. I grew weak listening to her voice.

"We were doing nothing," said Wendell petulantly.

"This I doubt," said Glenda.

"It was his fault," accused Ruppert, pointing his fat little finger in my face.

"Sssssshh . . ." hissed Wendell.

"I thought as much," said Glenda.

"Goddess . . ." started Wendell. But Glenda raised a slim and perfect hand to silence him.

"One question," said Glenda.

"Ask," said Wendell.

Ruppert shifted his weight uncomfortably from one foot to the other. He looked like a tweed weather balloon waiting for a good wind.

"Did you overstep your charge and come forth from the woods to toy with and tempt this mortal on the orders of the God of Rules, or did you do this of your own volition? Before you speak, think well for I will judge your punishment on your answer. You both well know that you must only watch."

Wendell's eyes danced back and forth as he weighed his reply.

"This was done without MacTavish's knowledge," Wendell finally answered. Ruppert groaned and staggered like he'd been struck in the side of the head with a Brassy. Wendell silenced him with a firm hand on the fat man's shoulder.

"I know that you lie." Glenda spit the words at him. "Hear me now. Since you are gods of a sort I cannot banish you from the Mountain. But I can assign you tasks to occupy your time and keep you from temptation."

Wendell and Ruppert looked as though they had both been stabbed in the same heart.

"From the northeast corner of Augustus begin a journey to the west. With great care and thoroughness catalogue each nook and cranny, limb and leaf, rock and rill, stream and lake in which a player could potentially find themselves in difficulty. Seek these hazards even in those places where the sacred game is not played, for we can never know where The MacKenzie will choose to place a hole. Also note where bogies hide and mark nests of bag demons with the sacred lightning bolt so that we may drive them off the Mountain in the fall."

"Goddess." Wendell was ashen, and his already long face seemed to droop below his bony knees.

"This will be most difficult," said Ruppert, in perhaps the classic understatement of all time.

"As well it should be." Glenda smiled coldly. "Be gone and hope when you have finished you will have learned some self-control."

Wendell and Ruppert turned, and with hanging heads walked back into the sandy rough to collect their belongings. Wendell looked once over his shoulder and caught my eye with a look that was pure meanness and rage.

"Have you enjoyed your round thus far?" Glenda asked with a beguiling smile.

"Yeah," was all I could say.

"Would it be all right if I walk with you to the turn?"

"Oh, sure," I replied, nodding like an idiot. "Absolutely, you bet!"

"Excellent," said Glenda, again flashing the smile that made my trains run on time.

Of course, I still had to move my ball from behind the scrub pine, being extra careful not to disturb the dynamite, and had to take the stroke, but I was in a transcendent state. Nothing mattered except sharing the fairway with Glenda, the true Goddess of Golf. The club felt like an extension of my arms. After years of hacking, I had finally

----

The Fable of Glenda—Goddess of Golf

Glenda and the Great MacKenzie are intertwined and have been so since ancient days. Before Glenda, the Mountain was a wild place and the Eighteen was a rough and tumble of native grasses and rock-strewn meadows. The MacKenzie had not yet begun his work and was unsure how to do so.

He was a Northern soul, weary of the stark beauty of the wasteland, and desired nature in a more tended and bountiful state. So he pledged to the assembly that the Mountain would be transformed into a place of lushness complete with rich grasses and tall stands of pine and oak to mark his fairways and shade his beloved greens.

But The MacKenzie could never make up his mind, even to choose what vine should cover a stone wall or what flowering bush should mark a tee. He feared of never attaining the perfection he sought, and became melancholy. Alone, he strode the limits of his Mountain kingdom seeking inspiration.

Once he paused in a glade on the Western edge to rest himself and noticed a budding flower that had not been there before. The MacKenzie, who appreciated such things, decided to watch it bloom. When the blossom revealed itself, MacKenzie wept, for he had never seen such beauty and he despaired. "Ye should niver die, flower," he said through his tears, "fer sech beauty holds secrets tha the world mus' know." And he buried his head in his hands, shedding salty tears for the passing of beauty in the world.

When he raised his head he beheld the most beautiful woman he had ever seen standing where the flower had grown. Her arms were folded across her chest and she was peeved. "Well," she said, "it's about time you looked up. Pick me, for God's sake."

"If Ah pick ye, ye will die. Ah canna."

"Then how will you ever choose the roses for the garden or the manner in which the vines will curl around the ball washer?"

"Ye kin do tha'?" The MacKenzie asked. "Wha is yer name, flower?"

"My name is Glenda. Pick me, you fool."

"All who see yer beauty will fall in love. Think of tha distractions."

But MacKenzie picked her and together they made the Mountain into a fitting place for the Gods to play.

----

entered that blessed state known as "the zone," and it was all her doing.

After taking my drop, I cracked a five-iron with effortless grace and the ball sailed to the turn of the dogleg and then rolled to A-number-one position in the center of the fairway. My approach to the green was equally flawless, a crisp pitching wedge hit so pure that I merely brushed the grass instead of taking a divot. The ball landed about six feet above the flag and spun back to within inches of the cup. Glenda laughed with glee and clapped her hands like a schoolgirl. It was the most thrilling moment of my life.

After my tap-in, she replaced the pin and caught my arm as we walked off the green toward the ninth tee.

"May we sit for a moment?" she asked. "We'll wait for Harry."

"Holy cow, I forgot all about him. Maybe I should go and take a look."

"He'll be along."

There was a small wooden bench on the path. I leaned my bag against the back and we sat down. We were so close I could barely contain myself but I could also barely speak. Wendell and Ruppert seemed like something safe to talk about.

"They wanted me to cheat so they could nail me, right?"

"Yes, that is correct, Thomas," Glenda replied. "Since you would not compromise yourself, they tried to compromise you."

"This course is tough enough without that. I'd be happy just to play a couple of holes from the fairway," I said.

She laughed invitingly and I wondered if it was polite

to address a goddess directly by name. Finally, I gathered enough courage to ask.

"Is it okay to call you Glenda?"

"Call me what you will, but whatever you do, do not call me late for the feast," she said, laughing.

I stared at her.

"It's a joke, Tom." She smiled wryly. "You understand jokes, do you not?"

I smiled back and nodded in appreciation, but inside I was burning up with passion. The goddess had actually tried to tell me a joke! Her delivery was so sweet and so clumsy that she seemed almost human and of course, that made me love her all the more.

Back down the fairway, Harry emerged from the trees and began to walk slowly toward us.

"Tell me about Harry," I asked.

"I'm afraid there is nothing worth knowing about him that can be told," Glenda replied. "He is Harry."

"That's not much of an answer."

"I always speak truthfully, Thomas; you must endeavor to ask the right question," Glenda said. "But let us talk of more important things."

"Like what?"

"Why do you desire the safety of the fairway?"

The question surprised me.

"It's the smart way to play the game—the easiest route to the green," I answered. "Why wouldn't you want to stay in the fairway?"

"What can you learn of life, if safety is your only goal?"

"I want to learn how to win," I replied. "That's what Harry knows, even here. He hooked his drive into the woods on this hole, but ten to one he'll pull out a par. He succeeds."

"Yes, Harry succeeds. But ask yourself if he relishes his success. Does he find joy in the consistent execution of his game? Does there exist for him a challenge each time he addresses the ball? Yes, Harry knows how to win, Tom. But where is his joy?"

I started to reply, but she placed her fingers over my lips. "Enough," she said. "Remember this, Harry may have flaws, Tom, but he is your friend. There may come times when you doubt it, but he is your friend."

She stood and offered me her hand. I took it gratefully.

"Glenda?"

"Yes?"

"I know you're a goddess, and I'm just a man," I stammered, "but do you think you could, you know, be . . . involved with a guy like me? I'm just a junior associate at my firm right now, but I'm thinking about a career change that could . . ."

"Tom . . ." Glenda silenced me with a smile so sad it nearly broke my heart in two.

We waited in silence while Harry hit his approach, a nice little shot that left him a level ten-footer. Glenda walked down the fairway and embraced the old man, taking his arm to help him up the slope to the green. He'd had a tough time in the woods.

"You found it," I said.

"Took a while," he said as he lined up his putt and sank it easily.

"How'd you do?" I asked as I replaced the pin and retrieved his ball.

"Pulled out the par. You?" he asked politely.

"Pretty good all in all. Ya know, Harry, we should try playing a whole hole together one of these times," I joked. Glenda laughed so I knew it was funny.

"All you gotta do is keep up." Harry chuckled as he pulled his driver from his bag and walked up the path to the tee.

CHAPTER 9

Nectar of the Gods

In which Tom experiences a miracle and Harry tells his story

Looking back on it, I'm convinced that I birdied the ninth to top Harry's par, and in the process, made one of the few brilliant shots in my speckled career, simply because I didn't want to leave him alone with Glenda. Even though Harry was clearly exhausted and was seeming to grow old before my eyes, I was jealous of his relationship with Glenda, and at the same time, so smitten with her that the notion of a second's separation was intolerable. It wasn't rational; it wasn't even fair, but jealousy is a powerful tonic for an ailing game.

So, I played the ninth like a pro, ripping my drive straight down the middle of the fairway and outdistancing Harry by a good twenty yards. I was walking on air, bantering with Glenda who inspired a second shot that under other circumstances would have allowed me to hang up my spikes a satisfied man. My drive left me about 190 to the pin, or 188 as Harry pointed out to ruffle my feathers. It was a distance that required a high, soft three-iron—a shot I usually pull off two or three times a year, and then only on the driving range. Harry had cut a little five-wood into the front of the green and the ball rested about twelve feet from the flag. At that distance there was no going to school on his shot, so I went with my heart and pulled my five-iron from the bag. Usually this would have left me severely underclubbed. But my love for Glenda had made me so confident, I could have reached the green with a willow branch.

Glenda held my bag and Harry stood quietly behind and to my right, smoking a small cheroot and jotting notes in his journal. The wind freshened as I took my practice stroke and the flag was starching in the distance. I started my backswing and the outside world slipped away. I savored it all in minutest detail. For the first time on a golf course I had the feeling I was wearing my game like a comfortable sweater. I knew exactly what was going to happen, as if I had done it a thousand times before. If I really wanted to, it was in my power to hole out from the middle of the fairway for that rarest of feats, an eagle on a par four.

The clubhead came through on line, the sweet spot eagerly searching for the ball, catching it perfectly. Glenda gasped and even Harry watched its flight with interest. The ball arched into the late-afternoon sun and seemed to glow as it fell toward the pin. It was indeed a golden shot. Unable to contain myself, I started to run for the green with the ball still in flight, hoping to see it land. Glenda dropped my bag and followed. We got close enough to see it hit a mere six feet from the pin, bounce once, and roll lazily forward. It was going to fall for eagle, but at the last second it gained speed and ringed the cup, spinning out to stop five feet away. Just a gorgeous shot in spite of the fact it didn't fall. In some respects, it was even better this way, because there would be the chance to putt it out. My birdie would be entirely of my own making; the gods could watch, but I wouldn't need their help.

Glenda looked down at the green, now deep in shadow

with two little white spots inviting us to continue pla, was so achingly beautiful. And when she smiled at me and kissed me on the cheek in congratulations, I almost collapsed. Harry joined us with my bag over his spare shoulder. He was showing the strain, but smiling. Embarrassed, I quickly relieved Harry of the extra burden.

"Nice shot, Tom," he said.

"Thanks, Harry," I answered. "I'm buying the beer."

"Your money's no good here, son," he said, laughing. "But I appreciate the thought."

Though he protested, I shouldered his bag along with mine and the three of us walked the fairway in triumph like the leader group coming up the eighteenth at the Masters on final Sunday. We basked in the golden light of late afternoon and it was a glorious experience.

Glenda sat on the edge of the green. Harry left his putt short and took par on a two-footer. It was all up to me. I squatted behind the ball to see my line. It looked like a straight putt most of the way, which broke slightly to the left near the cup. I took a soft practice swing and was reminded of the hours I'd spent as a child putting at a plastic glass in our living room. Every putt was for a championship, and if one rolled home I imagined Arnie or Jack fitting me for my very own green Master's jacket.

While something inside me didn't want this moment to end, I finally stroked the putt to cover the left break and it rolled into the cup with a loud clatter that caused Glenda to applaud. I had gotten my birdie, taken another hole from Harry, and for a second, it felt like I had won the girl. I would play this hole in my mind for the rest of my life. Harry shook my hand and Glenda embraced me.

But my joy was to be short-lived—reality will always intrude. Angus's warning back at the starter's hut came to mind and I realized I hadn't counted for the disaster on eight. In our moments of triumph we are reminded of our weakness. As I took three stones for my recent bird I added another nine for my adventure with Wendell and Ruppert. Harry informed us that he had finished the front nine at even par, and politely asked if I wanted him to check my score. I thanked him but didn't want to waste my bird dwelling on bad news.

"Anyway," I said, hefting my scoring pouch, "it's in the bag." Harry chuckled and put his book carefully away into its zipper pocket.

"Well, folks," he said with a sigh, "I could eat a bear! Why don't we take a break for dinner?" Harry was more tired than hungry, but he wouldn't have admitted it.

"Good idea." I smiled. I stole a glance at my watch. Most of Pine Valley was still deep in sleep. Even though the light was fading fast on Mount Augustus, I still had all the time in the world.

"We will eat," said Glenda, "and drink. What do you prefer?"

"How about mutton?" I suggested, still irritated by Raymond's cowardly desertion back on six.

Glenda gave me a look of mock censure and walked ahead to prepare.

As I started to follow, Harry grabbed my arm. It was hard to tell whether he was stopping me or using me to catch his balance. I took his elbow and we walked to a bench. Harry eased himself down and sighed with relief.

The sky was turning into a spectacular high-altitude sunset. It was clear that if we were to play eighteen holes on Mount Augustus we would have to face the back nine in the morning. Besides, Harry desperately needed to rest, so it was fine with me. In fact, I was glad.

"Son, now that we've made the turn, you've got a decision to make," said Harry.

"Is this where you tell me again that I can go back to Pine Valley if I want to?"

"That's right, Tom. If you go back now, nobody'll hold it against you. But this time there's a difference. If you decide to play on, you've got to stay to the finish and accept the consequences, whatever they are. No choices from here on."

"Why now?"

"It's the turn, son. The logical place. Things get tougher from here on out. The front is a piece of cake compared to what's ahead."

"What would you do?"

"Doesn't matter, Tom. It's your round, not mine."

"Don't you want me to finish?"

"You know the answer to that, Tom. But it's not for me to decide."

Of course, he was right. Not so long ago I had been ready to give it up and return to the world. Maybe it was the effect of being around Glenda, but playing on the Mountain was changing me. The disguises I learned in school and the workplace were stripping themselves away to reveal glimpses of the kid who once played Master Tallyman and Officer of the Nassau to his father's foursome so many years before. I liked it. And in that perfect moment, sitting with Harry at the turn on Mount Augustus, nothing else mattered but remaining. Not my budding career as a consultant at Hartless & Craven; triumphing in the morning Nassau with old man Craven; nor even the possibility of becoming Harry's apprentice. I felt alive and full of promise and wanted nothing more than to see where the rest of the journey would take me.

"I want to play it out, Harry."

"You sure?"

"I'm positive," I said. "Wouldn't miss this for the world."

"What if I wasn't there to bail you out?"

"What are you saying?"

"Nothing, just asking the question."

"Harry, right now I feel like I could do anything! You saw my bird back there; I've never shot like that in my life and hell, it even cost you the hole!"

Harry smiled broadly and patted me on the back.

"It was a wonder, all right." He smiled, patting me on the shoulder. "Why don't we find something to eat?"

Harry led us slowly up the path to a bower of flowering trees near the ruins of an ancient castle where refreshments had already been laid out on white linen tablecloths. Glenda seated us on thick cushions and we were immediately offered bowls of water and towels to wash our hands and faces. Once that task was completed we were given a sweet but refreshing drink from large stone pitchers by young men and women who paid special deference to Glenda, greeted Harry with tiny smiles of recognition, but seemed shy and refused to raise their heads as they served us.

The view of the ruins from the bower was sublime. The fallen stones that marked the buttress walls were worn smooth by years of rain and wind. Oak and hickory grew to fantastic heights from every crack and cranny. Vines scrambled up the standing walls and a single turret still reached to the sky. Atop the turret was a flag stiffening in the breeze and revealing a crest of lightning. The vision was so lush and so fantastic that I felt I had stepped into a landscape conjured by Coleridge or one of the other Romantic poets who occupied a dusty corner of my mind.

The castle, I was told by Harry, served as the second clubhouse on Mount Augustus, but nobody actually lived there. Glenda went on to say that she had no idea how long it had been there or for whom it was built. The Mountain was host to many spirits before it became MacKenzie's home. It has always been thus, she said.

The food was plentiful and delicious; fruits and game, a multitude of cheeses and coarse bread that was still soft and warm from the baker's oven. We lingered over the meal and as darkness fell the fire became the center of our world. We continued to drink the dark red wine from MacKenzie's special vineyards. From somewhere deep inside the ruined castle soft music began to waft on the gentle evening air. The fire was warm, we were comfortable, and it was time for a story.

"If you don't mind me asking, Harry. How'd you get to Mount Augustus—the first time, I mean?"

"Fair question," said Harry. He poured himself a goblet

of wine and settled back against a tree. Glenda nestled comfortably on her pillows, and in the flickering glow of the fire Harry began to speak.

The Story Harry Told Me

"When I was about your age my life was pretty much in the crapper. Marriage on the rocks, in debt up to my ears, and about to get canned—which was pretty pathetic considering I was married to the boss's daughter. I had pretty much run out my string, but wasn't facing up to it.

"What I was doing, was playing the ponies, betting on the dogs, and investing in real estate deals with impossible odds. Like most gamblers, I was counting on the 'big break' to save my bacon and instead of cleaning up my act I was getting in deeper every day."

Harry paused. "You see the same thing on the course everyday," he continued. "Guys with twenty-plus handicaps trying to cut the corner on a dogleg in the hopes of breaking 90 for once in their lives. They keep upping the ante till there's no way in hell they'll break 110.

"One Saturday morning I came home after an all-night poker game and found my wife's side of the closet empty except for a couple of rusty hangers. Ironically, the reason I had stayed out all night was that old Dad had come close to axing me that afternoon. Said the only reason he didn't was because of his little girl. Now she had cleared out. The way I figured it, I had till Monday to pretend I still had a job.

"So what did I do? Call my wife and beg her to come back? Call my father-in-law and promise to turn over a new leaf? Hell no. I threw the sticks in my old Chevy convertible and took off for the club. I knew I wasn't going to turn my marriage around in an afternoon, or my career either. But I had a hunch I might break 80 that day, and if I did, somehow everything was going to turn out right." Harry shook his head and laughed.

"When I got to the course, I had to change my shoes in the car. The club was dunning me for unpaid dues and I hadn't tipped anyone in so long I couldn't show my face in the locker room. I met the guys on the first tee and told the starter that I had signed up in the pro shop. Old Mike knew it wasn't true, but he also knew my foursome was good for a ten every Saturday morning in exchange for a tee-time he would have given us anyway.

"That fine morning I had nothing left to lose. World-class hangover, a busted marriage, and I was down to the only clubs I hadn't busted over my knee or tossed in the lake: driver, five-iron, seven-iron, and an old five-wood with the whipping coming off. But when we teed off I knew my hunch was dead on the money because I was in a zone! After four I was only two over, and just beginning to find my putting stroke.

"As we made the turn my cartmate, Tony the Taxman, did the totals. 'George, you had a 45, Charley a 47, and I had a 50, but Harry, baby, you went out in 39!'

"George slapped me on the back. 'The gods are with you today, ol' buddy.'

"Then Charley, a real wise-ass, jeered, 'Yeah, big deal. Wanna double the bet?'

"Everybody jumped in; they all expected me to tank. Hell, I always had before. But not today. We stuffed down some dogs and beers and ran to the tenth, a downhill par three of 170 yards with a couple of mean traps guarding the green. I cracked a beautiful seven-iron toward the pin that turned over and drew softly down toward the hole. The ball stopped about ten feet short and I sank it for the bird.

"Six holes later, I had racked up four more pars against two bogies. The gods were finally smiling on me. But as we climbed to the elevated tee on seventeenth, a long par four with a dogleg left, the ominous basso profundo of distant thunder echoed through the sky. Tony shook his head and said, 'Oh boy, check out those clouds. Two to one we don't finish.'

"Off to the west there was a pale yellow flickering against an advancing blue-black wall of clouds. An icy breeze swirled around my feet as the front reached us and then large drops of rain began to fall. Charley, Tony, and George scampered back to the carts like frightened rats, leaving me standing alone on the tee.

" 'Aren't you coming?' asked Tony.

" 'There's only two holes to go,' " I answered.

" 'It's a thunderstorm, Harry,' pleaded George. 'Use your head.'

" 'I'm only six over par,' I yelled over the gathering wind. 'Come on guys, don't wimp out on me.'

" 'You're nuts,' screamed Charley.

"I heard the unmistakable thump and clatter of a golf bag falling to the turf. Tony the Taxman had dumped my clubs.

" 'So long, Pardsie,' he yelled as he sped off to safety.

" 'Screw 'em,' I said, hitting a line drive that bore through the gale like a missile, never more than six feet above the fairway. It settled in position 'A,' a nice flat lie on the right side of the fairway 175 yards from the pin.

"By the time I reached my ball the rain was a steady torrent. I pulled out my five-iron and dried the grip. Because of the soggy turf, I caught it a little fat and the ball landed ten yards short of the green in some thick rough. But after an acceptable chip and two putts I was off to eighteen with a bogey still only seven over for the round.

"Visibility was down to less than a hundred yards, but I knew the obstacles by heart. A slice would end up stymied by a grove of pines on the right side of the fairway, that is, if it didn't catch one of the two traps eighteen shared with seventeen. A hook usually ended up in thick rough on the left and a wasted stroke. A long straight drive could also be trouble if it caught the downslope in the center of the fairway. From there, everything dropped precipitously to the left and fed down a murky green waterhole roughly the size and shape of Rhode Island. The only smart play was a fairway wood to the center of the fairway, then a five- or six-iron to the center of the well-bunkered green.

"With the wind behind me, I pulled out my battered five-wood and stuffed the head cover in my bag. In my back pocket was a brand-new Titlest I had found in the rough back on twelve.

" 'Be the right club, be the right ball,' I chanted as I peered into the gloom. A bright yellow bolt of lightning struck somewhere near the clubhouse illuminating the green. The pin was cut in the back right behind a slight swale.

"As I took the club back my mind was absolutely blank. I was unconscious. I heard the sweet crack of full compression and then found myself in a complete follow-through, standing tall with my arms wrapped over my left shoulder. The ball exploded heavenward like a prayer. But instead of dropping softly into the fairway, it was caught in an updraft and continued to soar forward. The bottom dropped out of my stomach; the ball was headed for the downslope and Rhode Island.

"As I trudged down the muddy fairway, I swore at my rotten luck and prayed that my ball hadn't made the water.

"At the top of the rise overlooking the downslope, I could see nothing but puddles and soggy fairway. A deep rumble of thunder overhead seemed to underscore my gloom. I had hit my drive too well, and now the shiny new Titlest was resting at the bottom of the water hazard.

"I stopped praying, began to curse, and stumbled on something solid underfoot. There was a dark, muddy glob attached to my spikes. Enraged, I yanked it off and started to toss it in the water hole when I realized that there were dimples under the muddy ooze. It was the Titlest. Rather than rolling into the hazard, my ball had plugged in the fairway. I began to laugh hysterically. The gods were still with me!

"Following the rules, I lifted, cleaned, and placed my ball on a spot turf a foot away from my pitch mark. I stretched on a dry glove and pulled the seven-iron from my bag. Without hesitation I swung, catching the ball first and then cutting a huge divot out of the wet turf. The ball streaked toward the green with a hum, spinning sweetly—a career shot if ever there was one.

" 'Be as good as you look,' I prayed.

"The ball rose majestically over the green and then began to drop softly through the rain toward the limp yellow flag in the back.

" 'Go in the hole,' I shouted. 'Go in the hole!'

"I had visions of an eagle and a magnificent 77. But, as the ball started down, the wind suddenly gusted, slamming it directly into the stick, and it careened wildly, bouncing into the decorative garden behind the green where it hit something solid, maybe a sprinkler head or a rock, and exploded out of the garden like a mortar shell, landing on the cart path to the left of the green. As I watched helplessly, it bounced down the cart path toward the water hole gathering momentum as it came. On the last bounce the ball peaked at fifteen feet and then began its descent, arching toward the center of Rhode Island where it split the water with no splash at all.

"As the ball sunk to the murky depths it took the hopes I had for breaking 80 and a new life. I stared into the water like a gypsy looking into her crystal ball, seeking to divine the indecipherable, to understand the immutable, and when the widening circles in the water finally played out, I snapped. Obscenities spewed out of my mouth over the pealing thunder and I shook my fist at the sky. I whipped my seven-iron through the driving rain toward the water. It made a whoosh, whoosh, whoosh sound like a helicopter rotor before it splashed down and sunk into the muck. It was a lovely cathartic sound, too lovely to hear only once. So,

I tossed the rest of my clubs in after it—all except my five-wood. After squashing its head cover into the mud, I made for the willow tree at the base of the water hole. With a savage swing, I slammed the shaft into the base of the tree. It bent like a pretzel, but the old persimmon head snapped clean off and caromed off the trunk, catching me smack in the middle of the forehead. Stunned like a heifer at the slaughterhouse, I fell backward, arms outstretched, into the murky green waters of Rhode Island.

"The extra weight of spikes and waterlogged clothing made me sink like a millstone. It was almost a relief. Underneath the surface all was quiet, and as I descended into the dyed green waters it grew steadily darker. With a mighty explosion of bubbles my lungs emptied and I resigned myself to oblivion. Then something grabbed me roughly by the hair. At first, I thought I was being rescued, but then we were going deeper into the hazard away from the light. I slipped into unconsciousness.

"When I woke up everything was pitch black, and my head was pounding. Then I opened my eyes and everything exploded into tongues of orange and yellow. I was staring into a crackling fire.

"I won't kid you, Tom. I was scared out of my wits. Couldn't sit up because the defensive line of the Dallas Cowboys was doing the Cotton-Eyed Joe on my forehead. Then I remembered slamming the five-wood into the willow, getting cracked in the noggin, and sinking to the bottom of the water hole. Figured I was dead. Then I heard a voice.

" 'Yer on tha uther side,' it said in a strange but recognizable accent, and it belonged to the largest man I had ever seen off a basketball court. He was over seven feet tall and garbed in a bizarre mesh of nets and water plants. In his right hand was a three-pronged staff with ball retrievers on each fork, and in his left was a bullfrog the size of a house cat.

" 'Am I dead? Is this purgatory?'

"A peal of dark laughter rose from my left. 'Purgatory, tha's a good one,' said the voice. 'As if a six-hour round wasn't punishment enough.'

" 'Nay, ya silly twit, yer on tha uther side of tha pond,' said the giant.

"And then it hit me. 'You mean I'm in Scotland?'

"My question was greeted with another rumble of laughter, even louder than the first.

"The giant then produced a jeweled goblet and gestured for me to sit up. 'This'll put ya right.'

"I took a drink and nearly spit it out. 'God, that's vile. What is it?'

" 'Vile, is it?' exclaimed the giant. ''Tis only the nectar o' tha gods.'

" 'You mean this is mead?'

" 'No, ya silly twit, 'tis na mead,' said the giant. Indignant, he snatched the goblet back from me. ''Tis unpasteurized ale!'

'Ye gods, he's thick,' said a second voice. 'Wha evir did ya choose him, Mac?'

"After another chorus of laughter, the little man on the other side of the fire stood up and spoke. "Tha's enough, Horace,' he said. ''Tis time to go.'

"He emptied the dregs of his goblet into the flames. As the first drop reached the coals it exploded into a million sparks, dissolving the darkness of the cave and everything in it into a swirl of light.

"Suddenly I was enveloped in a dense white cloud of smoke from the dying fire. I was pulled roughly to my feet and escorted through the mist.

" 'Open yer eyes and see,' said the presence. Then with a sweep of his arm, the fog dissolved, revealing the most wondrous sight any golfer has ever seen.

"I was standing near the top of a mountain at the end of a long, winding trail. Stretched out below us was an unspoiled world of incredible beauty. There were no freeways, factories, or housing developments—just an endless vista of greens and blues. Lush meadows filled with wild-flowers. Ancient forests with giant oaks, elms, and chestnut trees. There were sparkling lakes, rivers, and ponds. And far off in the distance there was the shore with its wild grasses and white sand."

The fire danced and flickered on Harry's face and his eyes sparkled as he continued.

"There were golf courses everywhere, each more breathtaking than the last. Soft mists were rising off the fairways and sunbeams were breaking through the trees. Black-faced sheep gamboled on the meadows, and no-where could you see the hand of man, Tom. There were no cart paths or railway ties, and the traps looked as if they had been excavated by the power of wind and rain over eons of time.

"One of them said, 'Welcome ta Mount Augustus, mortal.'

" ' 'Tis tha birthplace of tha ancient game,' the other chimed in.

"For the first time I could see the speaker clearly. He was also a giant of a figure, as big as the man with the bullfrog. But he was a Scotsman top to toe, decked out in Highland garb, right down to the kilt."

"Angus McLeod?" I interjected.

Harry nodded.

"Who was the other one, the one on your left?" I asked.

"It was the Great God MacKenzie, himself," he said. "Although I didn't realize it at the time. When he introduced himself he just said his name was MacKenzie and that he and Angus were guardians of the great game of golf."

"Well what happened next?"

"MacKenzie and Angus led me down a narrow mountain trail to the valley below, and on the way, MacKenzie talked about the pitiful condition of the game."

"Why? Nothing's wrong with golf."

"That's just what I said, son," Harry replied. "But MacKenzie looked at me and said that times are dark in your world. While more people were playing, no one understands the game. He poked me in the chest with his forefinger and said, 'In tha beginnin', gowf was na jist a game, but a fire ragin' inside tha few mortals who played it. Now 'tis down tae a pitiful ember. Ye mortals think tha' gowf is a grand way tae sell bloody insurance or climb tha social ladder or to git a bit of fresh air on tha weekend. Ye've lost yer way.'

"He clasped me on both shoulders with his powerful hands and said, 'We've chosen ye tae carry back tha true meanin' of golf tae yer world so tha fire will nae go out completely.'

" 'Why me?' I asked.

"He simply replied, 'Who else, man?'

"Angus, of course, went off the deep end. He rapped me on the back of the head with his old shillelagh and said, 'Why you? Because we already hae all yer clubs! We wanted tae see yer face an' meet tha man what would toss his dear sticks intae tha murky depths like a half-wit.'

"MacKenzie raised his hands, but Angus shook his stick in my face threateningly and said, 'Why you? 'Cause we were tired of yer bellyachin', mon. Dunna ya think we hae nuthing better tae do than listen tae yer constant whining? Oh please, let this ball go in. Oh please, dunna let it slice. By the Great God MacKenzie, man, hae ye nae pride? Git a grip on yerself.'

"The Great God MacKenzie?" I stuttered.

" 'Calm doon, Angus, ye've let tha wee cat outta tha bag fer sure,' said

MacKenzie. 'Rimember, Harry's our guest. And, son, if ye refer tae me as a god Ah'll box yer ears.'

"I guess I don't have to tell you the rest. With MacKenzie and Angus as my guides, I played Mount Augustus for the first time."

"And you broke eighty?" I asked.

Harry chuckled. "No, I didn't break eighty that day or even the next couple of weeks. But it was only a matter of time. To make a long story short, my handicap was down to five by the end of the summer. And I made up with my wife long enough to have three children. Oh yes, and my father-in-law made me a full partner with the firm. And that's how it happened."

The hour was late and the fire was dying as Harry brought his epic to a close. His story had the unmistakable patina of a tale polished and refined by a great many tellings. From the semisweet smile on Glenda's face, I could tell that she had heard it all before and while she never tired of hearing it, there was more to it—as there always is. More that Harry didn't feel like telling or had conveniently forgotten over the years. Glenda excused herself in order to attend to other duties and Harry began to doze. I leaned back on my pillows but couldn't sleep. Except for Harry's quiet snoring the Mountain was still. So as not to wake him I stole silently from the bower to explore the world of Mount Augustus on my own.

I walked for hours and then just before dawn I stumbled onto a huge arched opening on the far side of the castle. Two giant torches stood in holders on each side of the main entrance. When they were fresh and burning brightly they must have sent light hundreds of feet into the night. Now they were smoldering and almost extinct. The moon, however, was bright enough that I could see quite clearly. Next to the opening on the left was a barrelful of smaller torches standing in a mixture of tar and oil. I lit one and ventured inside and found myself in a walled courtyard. Before me was the entrance to the castle proper, a large doorway at the top of a short flight of steps. I ascended and entered the great hall.

It was the size of a football field and because the roof had fallen in long ago the stone floor had become a grassy meadow. In the center was a pedestal on which was sitting a huge stone urn. Shafts of moonlight streaked over the high walls outlining the urn in silver and blue. As I approached I could see that the pedestal had recently been decorated with garlands of flowers and that the grass around it had been trampled by many feet.

Another garland of flowers had been laid out on the ground in a large circle around the pedestal. I guessed it marked a boundary to keep revelers from coming too close. I stepped over it to examine the urn more closely and heard the achingly pure sound of a single tiny bell. As I drew closer the bell rang again. Somehow I knew it was calling me closer, not warning me away. I circled the column, which appeared to be a single section of a much larger whole, examining the deep fluting that ran up and down its sides. It had the rough and pleasant feel of history and was cool to the touch. I reached up and placed my hand on the base of the huge stone urn, which immediately grew warm and began to glow. The light worked its way up the sides and when it reached the top it brightened until the urn radiated heat like an old potbellied stove in a country schoolhouse.

As it grew hotter the urn cast an intense white light that spilled outward until it reached the ring of flowers where it stopped abruptly. The bell rang again and the urn became translucent and then disappeared altogether to reveal its contents. Before me were hundreds of golf balls standing on the pedestal holding the shape of the urn. A kind of static electricity danced around and through them and they moved about like particles in an atom. The wind began to blow and the balls moved faster and faster. One of them began to glow more brightly than the rest as it worked its way to the top where it shimmered and bounced. The bell rang and the ball was shot high into the air; it was as

bright against the night sky as a shooting star. It fell gracefully and landed softly at my feet. The wind stopped. The
sudden stillness was a challenge. Without hesitation I
picked up the ball and its energy flowed into my hand,
then my arm, and then through my whole body. Until that
moment I had never really believed in magic. This was
something beyond even Harry's paste.

Who could have given me such a wonderful gift? I hoped
it was Glenda. I looked up and saw that the urn had taken
solid shape again and its contents were concealed. I tossed
the sparkling object into the air and caught it, placing it
carefully in the snap pocket of my rain pants.

The bower was as I had left it so many hours ago. Harry
was sleeping soundly, and Glenda was nowhere to be seen.
I nestled down in the thick blankets and as sleep began to
overtake me I found myself looking forward to the morning and playing out the back nine on Mount Augustus.

When I opened my eyes Harry and Glenda were sitting
comfortably on their pillows, smiling at me. Harry looked
refreshed, as if a good night's sleep was what the doctor
ordered and Glenda was a vision as usual.

"How about some breakfast?" Harry asked.

"I'm not exactly in the mood for mead and ambrosia."

"Don't be ridiculous, son," replied Harry. "The only
place golfers have fruit salads for breakfast is in California.
On the Mountain, we have sausages, eggs, and lots of
fresh coffee!"

True to his word Harry and I sat down to the most wonderful breakfast I have ever had. There were English bang-
ers and spicy Tennessee patties. Choices of Canadian or
American bacon. Eggs sunny-side up, scrambled or folded
into luscious omelets oozing cheddar cheese and mush-
rooms. Sides of hash browns, fried applies, and cinnamon
toast. And last but not least, there were vats of steaming
black java. Halfway through our second helping, I broke
the comfortable silence.

"Harry ..."

"Uh-huh . . ."

"Well, I . . ."

"Fire away, son."

"Well, Harry, I get the feeling there's a little more to this story. Why did they really choose you?" I asked. "I mean, out of all the hackers in the world, why you?"

"That's a lot of questions, Tom," Harry answered, "but I'll see what I can do. First off, it had something to do with me hitting rock bottom. On that particular Saturday, there was nothing left between me and the experience—whatever it was going to be."

"So you're saying that it happened because you were ready for it."

"Guess you could say that."

"Just like I was ready for you?"

"That, too."

"Okay, I see what you got from them, but what did they get from you?"

"Nothing I wasn't willing to give 'em," Harry said coolly as he walked over to his carry bag and began rooting through the side pocket for a fresh shirt. I had struck a nerve.

"Well, what if you're ready for something and instead of a teacher, a con man gets his hooks into you?" I asked.

Harry pulled two new balata balls from the pocket and then zipped it closed. "What's the difference?" he replied. "Either way you're probably getting what you asked for—a lesson, or an experience. Depends on your perspective."

"So, what do you get out of this deal, Harry?" I asked. "What do you get from me?"

Harry tipped his cap back on his forehead and looked off in the distance for a moment before answering.

"Well, Tom. This game has been pretty good to me over the years. Let's just say that helping a young fella like yourself is my chance to give something back."

"You're kidding," I replied.

Harry smiled and cocked his head to the side.

"Look, I know it sounds corny, but that's a big part of

it. That plus the fact that I never had any sons. Three wonderful girls, but no boys to pass things along to."

"So, I'm supposed to be the son you never had?"

Harry smiled again and seemed genuinely embarrassed. "Something like that," he said. "And you remind me a little of myself at your age. You know, hungry to get ahead, but not able to get out of your own way."

Although I smiled, Harry's answer was unsettling.

"So what are you, Harry?" I asked again. "Con man or teacher?"

"Like I said, depends on your perspective. Or maybe it's up to you, son. Which one do you need?"

"This is getting too deep for me, Harry." I smiled.

"Then let's play golf," he answered. I got the distinct feeling he was relieved.

And so as the sun traced the morning on Mount Augustus, Harry and I saddled up and headed for the back nine on the Golf Course of the Gods.

CHAPTER 10

The Devil's Arsehole

Young Tom is reunited with an old friend by an old god

The night's layover had done Harry a world of good. Not only was his color better, but he seemed to have his old strength back. While I fumbled for balls in the pocket of my carry bag, Harry was pacing around the tee box like a thoroughbred before a stakes race. So, even though I had the honors, I let Harry take the tee. Without so much as a waggle, Harry stepped up and "pured" a seven-iron 155 yards to the back of the tenth green, some fifty feet beyond the flag.

"Wow, got all of that one," I said.

"Yep, feeling frisky this morning," Harry replied.

"Any suggestions?" I asked.

"Don't attack the flag, it's sucker pin," said Harry. "Play for the middle of the green and keep away from that big pot bunker up front. Son of a gun makes the Devil's Arsehole look like a dip in the road."

Of course, as soon as he mentioned Pine Valley's infamous Devil's Arsehole, my entire focus was on its older brother—the cavernous pot bunker that lay directly in front of the pin on the Mountain's tenth hole.

Now, of all the hazards in golf, only pot bunkers can be considered truly evil. Land in one of those diabolical craters, and not only is saving par out of the question, but double bogey or worse is a virtual certainty. They're often so deep, you need a ladder to get down into them, and once inside, you have to thump your ball out at a ninety-degree angle to clear the lip—a shot not one golfer in ten thousand has ever practiced. Frankly, the only shot I can routinely pop straight up in the air is a driver off the first tee. Even then, I need a teed-up ball and a gallery of important clients in order to pull it off.

Don't get me wrong. Like all fair-minded people, I believe that good shots should be rewarded and bad shots punished. But the punishment should also fit the crime, and the eight-iron I blocked off the tenth tee was only a matter of inches from being a pretty fair shot. After carrying 130 yards in the air, the ball just caught the fringe on the right front of the green before trickling back into that godforsaken sand pit.

"Thanks for the advice, Harry," I said.

"Next time, try following it," he replied with a devilish grin.

While Harry paced off the distance from the cup to the back of the green, I slid down into the bunker to find my worst fears confirmed. Even though my ball hadn't plugged in the sand, it was still tucked well under the lip of the bunker. Worse yet, there was a large flat stone embedded in the sandy floor just behind my ball. I had encountered yet another "loose impediment," and couldn't move it or my ball without penalty. On the other hand, I wasn't inclined to ruin a perfectly good wedge just because Fergus the greenskeeper was falling down on the job. Mulligan was right about this one—it wasn't part of the game and it wasn't fair. Anyone in their right mind could see that.

Still, if Harry saw me he'd make my life miserable. So I grabbed the lip of the bunker and pulled myself up to the level of the green to reconnoiter. Harry was hunkered down near the back fringe plumb-bobbing his monster putt while he waited for me to pound my way out of hell. Opportunity had knocked. Balancing my wedge on my shoulder I pondered the situation.

Admittedly, it would have been easier to move the ball than to try to dislodge the stone. But that was more of a liberty with the rules than I was willing to take. No matter how unfair the lie, I had to draw the line somewhere, especially after the holier-than-thou act I had pulled on Wendell and Ruppert on the eighth hole. However, the stone was a different matter. As a clear and present danger to both my personal safety and my $65 sand wedge, it would have to go.

The end of the rock was protruding from the floor of the bunker, so I grabbed it with both hands and pulled hard. The first couple of inches were easy, but then the resistance seemed to grow incrementally and I strained with the effort until abruptly the stone began to ease back toward me as if on a hinge.

"What's happening down there, son?" I heard Harry call, and reacted by giving the huge rock a solid yank just as his curious face appeared over the lip of the bunker. Our eyes locked as the stone clicked into place with a loud metallic clank. That's when the bottom literally fell out from under me. In the next second I saw Harry's expression turn from shock to disappointment and then to a kind of benign indifference as I tumbled backward through a shower of sand and pebbles into a well of darkness.

"Harry," I yelled.

"Dammit, Tom," was all I could hear him say.

Obviously I had pulled the trip mechanism on some kind of animal trap and probably was going to pay for it with my life when I hit the sharpened stakes that surely lined the bottom of the pit. But what kinds of animals pull stones out of bunkers? Certainly not lions, bears, or elephants. Only people play golf, I thought. Wrong, gods play it, too. Maybe the whole solar system plays the game. Maybe the Milky Way was just a big hazard in deep space. Perhaps Mount Augustus wasn't a golf course at all, but a Venus flytrap designed to capture humans for alien experiments. I saw myself strapped to a gurney surrounded by alien vivisectionists with eyes like prunes and began to scream. This accomplished nothing except to hurt my throat and my ears so I stopped and considered how the media would treat my disappearance.

My position at Hartless & Craven was too junior for the *Wall Street Journal* to cover the story, but surely *Unsolved Mysteries* or the *National Enquirer* would be interested. I could see the headlines on the checkout counter already: JUNIOR EXECUTIVE ABDUCTED BY ALIEN GOLFERS. What would they do with my office? Surely, they wouldn't give it to that devious MBA in strategic planning? Five long years it had taken to finagle an office with a window and three more to get a second one. It was outrageous to think that a phony little climber like her should get two windows only a year out of Wharton.

There had to be better ways to spend my last moments than whining about my job, but nothing else came to mind. Was the sum total of my existence a shaky hold on a work space with two windows I couldn't even open? If by some miracle the fall didn't kill me I would work very hard to get a life.

A blast of hot air blew over me and my feet hit a slope. Instead of freefalling, I was now sliding down an incline, still at great speed, but sliding nonetheless. Seconds later I slammed buttocks first, not into poisoned punji sticks or a steaming cauldron manned by alien chefs, but something soft and very familiar.

Even though the impact nearly knocked the breath out of me, I was quite comfortable, floating on soft cushions. After recovering from the impact I realized I was sitting in a chair—a fully extended BarcaLounger to be precise.

What a lounge chair was doing at the bottom of a pit was a mystery, but where there was a lounge chair there also had to be a side table. This was an immutable law of the universe. I began groping around in the dim light, first with my left hand and then my right hoping to find some means of survival—a table lamp, a bowl of mixed nuts, or at least a remote control unit. I found it on my right. A small oval-shaped affair—probably a Queen Anne knockoff from the feel of it. The table was quite bare except for a small metal bell. Now the question was, should I ring it?

In the end, there was no alternative. So I picked up the bell and shook it heartily. The sound was surprisingly delicate, like the tinkling of a crystal chandelier moving in a sudden breeze. It reminded me of the bell that had led me to the magic ball back at the castle. I was about to ring a second time when the wall in front of me moved aside with a great groaning and clanking of metal. The darkness of the pit dissolved in a glow of orange light. Silhouetted in the opening was a short, thick-bodied creature who barked at me in a gruff voice.

"Cruickshank?"

"Yes, that's me." I collapsed the lounger forward into a regular sitting position to get a better look.

"You're late!" the creature stated emphatically.

"I didn't know I was expected."

"You were supposed to be here yesterday afternoon," he replied. "What happened? Get lost in a bunker? Too much mead at the turn?"

"Something like that," I stammered.

"Not the first time, won't be the last," he said. With that

he struck a match and lit a long clay-stemmed pipe. The flare revealed a creature with a broad face, thick features, and a coarse red beard. He was clothed in a tunic of coarse green cloth and leather leggings that buckled along the sides.

"You're a dwarf," I said, stating the obvious.

"Ah, another college graduate. You fellows are so quick," he replied with a slight nod of his head. "Noopes is the name."

He turned and began walking toward the orange light.

"Better get a move on, Cruickshank," said the dwarf over his shoulder. "Weyland doesn't like to be kept waiting."

"Who's Weyland?"

"Only the God of Equipment," Noopes replied with a hint of irritation. "Where've you been?"

"Why does he want to see me?" I asked.

"I didn't ask," Noopes replied and ducked back through the doorway. "Mind your head," he said. "Tight squeeze for most mortals."

By getting down on my hands and knees, I managed to follow the dwarf through the doorway that led into a passageway carved out of the rock. A couple of yards later, the passage widened to reveal a long, narrow cavern lit by torches. Noopes had to throw his arm across my chest to keep me from tumbling off the trail into the cave below.

"We'll have to take the crossover to Weyland's lab," said Noopes. He pointed at a narrow suspension bridge of rope and wooden slats stretched across the width of the cave. "Too bad you came to the back door."

As we inched our way across the swaying bridge, persistent tapping and whirring sounds echoed through the cavern. "What's that noise?" I asked.

"Just the shop," Noopes replied matter-of-factly. "We're right over the finishing area."

I leaned gingerly over the edge of the bridge to witness a flurry of frenzied activity in every corner of the main cavern. In one area, shadowy figures were stripping hickory saplings for shafts, while in another, clubheads were being carved out of blocks of persimmon. Then I was startled by a loud sneeze, which almost shook me off the bridges.

"Aah-choo!"

Directly below us two men were crouched over a rude wooden bench in the corner. There were so many feathers in the air above them I thought they were plucking chickens. But closer examination revealed they were stuffing the feathers into small leather containers with awls. But why? Then it hit me. Featheries! They were making featheries— the preferred golf ball of the nineteenth century. Brushing floating feathers away from my face, I leaned over the ropes to get a better look.

Just then one of the craftsmen sneezed again, sending a fresh burst into the air. As he raised his head our eyes met for the briefest of seconds. Although I couldn't place him right away, he was familiar. He must have recognized me, too, for he quickly turned away and pulled down the brim of his cap. Unless I was mistaken, there was a look of fear on his face. Noopes grabbed me forcefully by the elbow.

"Weyland's waiting!" he growled.

Noopes picked up the pace as we made our way across the bridge, but I continued to peek over the side at the wheels of industry turning below. The cavern had been carved into a series of work areas and each of these spaces was dedicated to some aspect of club or ball making. In one space workers were splicing clubheads to hickory shafts the way it was done a hundred years ago. Then the clubs were passed through a hole in the cave wall to the adjacent space where the splice was reinforced with whipping cord. In another area, two wood nymphs were molding guttie balls from real gutta percha—the rubbery sap dentists use today in root canal procedures.

"Mind yer head!" Noopes barked suddenly. We had come to the end of the bridge and were about to duck through a narrow portal in the rock.

A couple of yards later and the passageway opened into

another much larger cavern. While torches were fastened every few yards along the walls, there was another more powerful source of light in the center of the great cave. Crouched like a great dragon was an old-fashioned forge. Manned by a team of workers, the forge glowed angrily each time they pumped the bellows, casting their shadows eerily on the cavern walls. Piles of discarded clubheads were strewn about the floor. A small figure stood near the head of the forge wielding a blacksmith's hammer. As he plied his craft, showers of sparks arched above him and a deafening echo reverberated through the cave. We walked down rough stone steps onto the main floor. Noopes was taking me to the forgeman himself.

When we drew closer, I could see that the master was a faun and a rather ancient one at that. The fur on his flanks was streaked with silver and he was wearing spectacles. On his chin was a snow-white goatee, giving him a severe, but very distinguished look. He lay down his hammer and turned to me, wiping his hands on a clean towel supplied by a waiting apprentice.

"So, you've decided to play on," said Weyland.

Surprise must have registered on my face. Everybody seemed to know my business.

"Don't be shocked, mortal," replied Weyland. "We who toil below the ground hear things as well. Everyone at Mount Augustus knows of your decision to finish the course. And we applaud your courage, Mr. Cruickshank. The question is, do you have the tools to make it all the way to the house?"

He turned to Noopes. "Where are his clubs?"

"Brogan took them to your workshop," Noopes answered with a bow.

"Well then, let's have a look."

My clubs were on a small bench in the middle of the cavern. Weyland pulled each one out of the bag and gave it a brief examination before tossing it to a waiting attendant.

"You've heard the old saying, 'It's a poor workman who blames his tools'?"

The Fable of Weyland—God of Equipment

Every organization has its visionaries and its hands-on people, and the pantheon at Mount Augustus is no different. The Great God MacKenzie is the prototypical visionary who can't be bothered by details—a god who thinks things happen just because he has an idea. Being a god, sometimes it happens this way, but all too often, his big ideas have been poorly executed. Take rain, for example. Designed originally as a means of keeping Mount Augustus lush and green, MacKenzie has a hard time regulating the amount of rain that comes. Which is why Mount Augustus has the occasional hurricane or whirlwind when a gentle drizzle would do the job.

MacKenzie's attempts at creating the implements of golf fared no better. Clubheads fell off during the middle of rounds, shafts twisted wildly during swings, and balls exploded upon impact. When the frustration grew to enormous levels, the gods at Mount Augustus formed a search committee to find a craftsman. After a prolonged and expensive process (consultants don't come cheap even at Mount Augustus), the committee discovered Weyland, a dwarf working as a midlevel manufacturing deity in the Norse god Odin's pantheon.

Weyland was lured away and ensconced as God of All Equipment and Course Operations, and his work was far beyond expectations. New and better implements were designed, and the gods imagined that their games improved. They stopped using MacKenzie's equipment, preferring that of the new god on the block. Even MacKenzie's wife, the Goddess Rowena, was reported to be hanging around Weyland's forge day and night watching him pound away with his hammer. Finally, MacKenzie blew. In a jealous rage, he caused an earthquake to swallow the newcomer and his forge. For one thousand long seasons, Weyland was trapped in the underworld—until all of his wonderful implements had worn out. Frustrated by the lack of decent equipment, the gods pleaded with MacKenzie to release Weyland. Remembering the impressive quality of Weyland's clubs, MacKenzie admitted his error and released the dwarf, but placed on him the following curse: that he was to stay underground in his workshop during the daylight hours. Weyland would be allowed in the overworld only at night, and then he must appear in the shape of a woodland faun.

I nodded yes.

"Well, we like to add, 'It's a stupid bastard who buys cheap ones to begin with.' You can't buy a good golf game, Mr. Cruickshank, but you sure can buy a bad one. From what I can tell, these are passably good irons."

The last iron in the bag was my eight, the club with which I had blocked my tee shot into the pot bunker in the first place. Weyland pulled it from the bag and then suddenly recoiled, dropping the club to the floor.

"By the Great God MacKenzie," swore Weyland. "How long have you had that infernal instrument?"

"About two years, I guess," I replied. "It came with the set."

He circled the eight-iron warily as if he was approaching a sleeping viper.

"Have you ever shanked a shot with this club?"

"A couple of times probably."

"How many times did you hit it fat or thin?"

"Quite a few, I guess," I answered. "I'm not really that good a golfer."

My answer was greeted with a rumble of laughter.

Weyland shook his head and winked at me. "Well, it's no bloody wonder with that club in your bag."

"Is it out of alignment?"

"No, there's nothing wrong with your loft or lie!" said Weyland. "Nor your shaft frequency either. Your eight-iron is possessed!"

"My eight-iron is possessed? Listen . . ."

"Hear me out, mortal," said Weyland. "This is not uncommon. Many individual clubs have spirits. In your world you might call it a virus or in some circles a demon. Here we call them by their true names. Hoselwiggs."

"Do you mean they live in hosels?"

"Precisely. They're similar to your Mexican jumping bean. Except when a hoselwigg moves, it throws off your club. Not much, but just enough for you to shank or top your ball."

Weyland picked the eight-iron off the floor carefully and executed a slow-motion practice swing.

"There, can you hear it?"

"Hear what?"

He swung the club again. "If you listen carefully you can hear the hoselwigg scream. The centrifugal force hurts its ears and causes it to jump."

"Okay, how do you get rid of it?" I asked.

"Feed it, starve it, or burn it out," Weyland replied with a twinkle in his eye. He brought the clubhead close to his lips and spoke directly to the hosel.

"But personally I prefer to burn it out!" he said. Suddenly the clubhead began to dance in his fingers and Weyland let out a loud laugh. Wiping away tears from his eyes, he handed the club to an assistant.

"Are you really going to burn it out?"

"Don't fret, mortal. Brother hoselwigg will be fine. The lads will coax him out with a bit of cheese and then give him a new home in a trophy club where he can't hurt anyone.

"Now on to the woods!" said Weyland, rubbing his hands together. He sorted through my remaining clubs with a puzzled look on his face. "But where's your driver, man? You can't play Mount Augustus without a driver!"

I explained how Angus had purloined it at the first tee— a story that had him alternately chuckling and shaking his head in disapproval. When I had finished, he walked around his workbench to a stack of clubs identified with bright red tags.

"Angus brought this in for me to repair only hours ago," said Weyland. "Seems he got into a donnybrook with Dirk over tee-times. Said he liked the funny sound it made when he whacked the "wild Highlander" over the head."

"That's my driver!" I cried excitedly. "I just got it in New York last Tuesday. I can prove it. See, look at the head. It's milled out of a solid titanium block. And the shaft is made from a special new graphite fiber. . . ."

Weyland cut me off. "Titanium block, graphite shaft? Space-age materials, eh? Good god, man, where were you planning to send your ball with this monstrosity? To Mars?"

"No, not really, I only hit it 240 or so on my best drives," I answered.

"If you're not planning to send your ball into space, then why in the world would you want to be using these so-called space-age materials?"

He picked up an old balata from his workbench and held it between his thumb and forefinger gingerly as if it were as fragile as a freshly laid robin's egg. "What do you think this is, a satellite? A rocket payload? Or perhaps a warhead, for godsakes? No, it's a bloody golf ball, made of the sap of trees, designed to be hit by blocks of wood or iron mined from the earth. And where is it supposed to go?"

"In the hole?" I answered.

"And where is the hole?"

"In the ground?"

"More precisely, it's in the *earth*, Mr. Cruickshank. Golf is a natural game, meant to be played in natural surroundings with natural implements—not space-age materials! You see, wood, iron ore, and rubber have a natural affinity for one another. They're all natural elements, son. Like attracts like, my boy. Like attracts like."

Weyland reached into a rude wicker basket sitting on the hearth and pulled out another ball.

"Now, here's your modern so-called distance ball." There was an edge of contempt to his voice.

Using a small penknife, he carved off a sliver and held it up to the light. "And God only knows what this stuff is. It doesn't come from the earth, or the trees, or even the birds of the air. It comes from laboratories. From chemists, not golfers."

He spat in disgust. "And where does a ball like this want to go? Certainly, not in the hole, that I can tell you. It wants to go bounding into parking lots seeking its own kind—looking for plastic seat covers, and fake wood grain dashboards. It wants to go careening along asphalt cart paths and soaring over greens into rubbish heaps. Slicing off fairways into patios and swimming pools made of fiberglass and other so-called miracle materials. Don't you see, man? Like attracts like! It's one of the secrets of golf."

"Can you fix my driver?" It was rude to interrupt, but I was getting impatient.

"If that's all you want," he answered brusquely. His eyes were suddenly smoldering. "I'd be more than happy to fix your driver."

Weyland snatched the mangled club from my hands and walked over to the glowing forge. Without hesitation he tossed it in and cranked the bellows to raise the heat. In seconds it had been reduced to molten sluice.

"There, it's fixed." The old faun laughed.

"Now what am I supposed to play with?" The damn thing cost a fortune and I was angry.

"How about an old friend?" He answered. He rummaged through a dark corner of his workshop and then returned holding an old persimmon driver, which he presented like a babe for christening. In the light of the forge, the polished head of the driver glowed familiarly. Inlayed into the center of the red insert was an Indian Head penny, dated 1917.

"That's Thunderbolt!" I cried. "Where did you find it?"

"Right where you threw it in 1979," he answered. "In the water hole off the fifth tee at Greenwood Country Club. You can have it back under one condition."

"What's that?"

"That you never, ever throw another club into a water hole," he said.

"It's a deal," I said gratefully.

Weyland beamed and the glow of the forge made him seem the warmest and friendliest god in the world. With the exception of Glenda he appeared to be the only deity who didn't want something from me.

"But there's just one thing," he said, raising an eyebrow as he caressed Thunderbolt's glistening clubface.

"What?" I asked.

"There's the small matter of the labor it took to restore poor Thunderbolt. It was in frightful shape when Noopes hauled it out of that pond. Frightful shape."

"Okay," I said. Clearly there was no free lunch on Mount Augustus.

"You understand, this is not for me; it's for the lads in the foundry," said Weyland, rubbing his beard thoughtfully.

"I've got a few twenties left in my wallet," I began, but I knew it wouldn't come down to money. He had to have his eye on something else.

" 'Tis a fine timepiece," said Noopes, rubbing his barren wrist.

"And shiny, too," piped a tiny voice in the assembly.

"Look, you can have anything else," I replied. "But I can't give you my watch. I need it."

"For what?" asked Weyland.

For what, indeed? It was a good question. So I could know for sure that my boss was in apoplexy? I had already decided to finish the round, so there was no going back until it was over, no matter how late it got at Pine Valley. I was pretty sure Mom wouldn't mind trading it in for something Dad actually made. Maybe it was time to let it go. Just maybe it was holding me back. After reading her inscription one last time, I handed my watch to Weyland, who gave me Thunderbolt in return. It was more than a fair trade.

"Wait till Harry sees this." I smiled.

"Now that you are properly armed with a block of stout persimmon, Noopes will escort you back to the course," said Weyland, smiling. Then he placed a rough hand on my shoulder in a gesture of fatherly concern.

"But first, a word of warning," he continued gravely. "There are rumblings in the world above. We hear that Mount Augustus is being rent asunder by a conflict between the Great God MacKenzie and his rulemaker, Mac-Tavish. And I fear that Harry Brady is trapped between them."

"Are you talking about the bet?" I asked. "Harry said something about a bet with some of the other members."

"A wager it may be, my friend, but it is no small matter," Weyland replied, shaking his head wearily. "While many of the gods are loyal to the great god, more and more every day are siding with MacTavish."

"But what does this have to do with me?"

"MacTavish has no love for mortal man," answered Weyland. "And even now he stalks the world above like a bear looking for something to devour. Make sure, my boy, that you're not his next meal."

"Thanks, I'll be fine," I replied. "I've got Thunderbolt."

"Then play on, Mr. Cruickshank," he said, shaking my hand. "The Mountain is waiting."

The cavern rumbled with the sound of the workers' polite applause, and I was whisked away by Noopes and a company of a dozen or so workers. As we wound our way through yet another dark passageway, I felt a tug at my sleeve.

It was the featherie worker I thought I had recognized from the first cave.

"Play it straight, Tommy boy. Play it straight!" the man whispered.

"How do you know my name?" I asked.

"Don't you recognize me? It's Dick Jackson from New York."

"Toe Wedge?" I turned to get a better look at him. He was much thinner and older, but there was no question about it. It was Toe Wedge Jackson, the most notorious sandbagger and do-over artist that ever played the links at

Hardpan Harbour, my weekends-only club on Long Island. "I wondered where you went."

"Don't turn around, or Noopes will see us talking," he said.

"What are you doing here?" I whispered as we walked.

"Same as you, Tommy boy. I was just trying to improve my game, but they caught me improving my lie instead. And now I can't leave!"

"Can't leave? That's kidnapping!"

"And slavery," Toe Wedge added.

"You ain't in Kansas anymore, Dorothy," rasped a familiar voice to my right.

"Ken Hoeffer? I thought you retired to Florida!"

"That's what everyone thinks," he replied. "They even made me fill out postcards to my buddies in the men's grill."

"This is insane," I whispered. "Harry and I'll get you out of here."

Hoeffer shook his head and grunted.

"It's too late for us," said Toe Wedge. "Just watch yourself up there. They want you bad."

"Weyland's right about McTavish," added Hoeffer. "Unless I miss my guess, he's been with you since the first tee."

"And if it ain't him," offered Toe Wedge, "it's his pet weasels Wendell and Ruppert."

"I thought we were being followed," I replied.

"Followed and watched," agreed Hoeffer.

"Have you been keeping score?" asked Toe Wedge.

"Mostly," I answered. "I'm not playing that well, anyway."

"Keep tally, for God's sake," implored Hoeffer.

"Wha's going on out there?" a voice cried from the depths of the foundry.

"Go, now," whispered Toe Wedge.

"Just one more question. How did you guys get to Mount Augustus in the first place?"

Before Hoeffer or Jackson could answer, Noopes stopped

short and glared back at us. "Stop your lollygagging," he said.

The front entrance to Weyland's foundry was another deep shaft in the earth. The workers strapped me in a large oaken bucket and tied my clubs to the side. Then Noopes gave the order and they hoisted me up through the shaft on a creaking block and tackle. As I looked back, I could see Hoeffer and Toe Wedge working the rope, their faces illuminated by the light streaming from above. They were chanting something over and over like a mantra. Leaning forward I strained to read their lips. Just as the bucket broke into the sunlight, I realized with a chill what they were saying. It was:

Harry Brady
Harry Brady
Harry Brady
Brady
Brady

CHAPTER 11

The Gauntlet

In which Tom learns that hell hath no fury like a Harpy scorned

The front door to Weyland's foundry turned out to be an ancient stone cistern hidden by a stand of birch trees just beyond the tenth green. As I cleared the top of the well, I was shaking, and my mind was reverberating with the implications of Toe Wedge and Hoeffer's warning. If what they were saying was true, then Harry Brady was not the kindly mentor I had taken him for. He was a devious peddler of human flesh whose sole purpose in luring me to Mount Augustus was to enslave me in the underground foundry. And my round at Mount Augustus, far from being a mystical journey or character-building exercise, was just a game of foxes and hounds—featuring yours truly as the beleaguered fox.

But how could it be true? Hadn't Harry rescued me from the clutches of Dirk and Mulligan? Hadn't he pulled me out of the neck-deep sand of Hell's Half Acre? Perhaps he was just saving me until the time was right, like a shepherd guards his flock until it's time for slaughter. On the other hand, while Harry wasn't perfect, I was seldom that wrong about someone's character and Glenda had told me to trust him. Still I knew I had to be careful. There was no way I was going to spend the rest of my natural life stuffing golf balls or pumping bellows. If I had to be anybody's galley slave, Hartless & Craven still had first dibs.

Holding the shafts of my clubs so they wouldn't rattle, I walked the perimeter of the green, staying in the trees and watching carefully for signs of life. All was silent and still. I took a deep breath and boldly crossed to the pot bunker that was responsible for my introduction to the underworld.

Nothing had changed, except that the stone doorway was back in place. My ball was still sitting just in front of the rock. As I let myself down into the bunker I knew that it would be some time before I saw Harry again. Maybe that wasn't such a bad idea. At any rate he was nowhere to be seen and I was alone.

I examined my options. There was no choice but to hit away from the green and pitch back to finish the hole. I considered packing up and heading into the woods to find the entrance to Pine Valley. But that wasn't realistic; the forest that surrounded each hole was dense and impenetrable. I didn't have a prayer of finding my way back to Angus's footbridge without walking the fairways where I could be seen by anyone. Any way you cut it, I was going to be a sitting duck, so I decided to press on. I hadn't come this far to turn tail and run.

Something began to bubble up inside me and I realized that in all my years as a golfer I had never taken the risk of testing myself against a course without a group of buddies along to share the misery. The situation I found myself in now was classic. I was alone in an unfamiliar place with no idea what lay ahead. I had lost my guide but gained a link with my past. The fact that Thunderbolt was safe in my bag was magic in the purest sense. I had been set free either by circumstance or design and the result was an opportunity to make or break it on my own. It was an unfamiliar and powerful feeling. Suddenly, the pot bunker was just another obstacle and all I had to do was take my medicine and move on.

It took four strokes to get over the back lip and then a bladed pitching wedge sent my ball sailing over the back of the green into a sandy waste area. The road back was relatively open so I chose to chip the ball out of the sand rather than attempt a splash shot. The ball clicked crisply off my eight-iron and bounced on the green twice before releasing and rolling to a stop five feet from the pin. I drained it and felt pretty damn good. It's funny how a couple of decent shots can erase the memory of a disastrous hole. If there's any real magic in golf, that's it.

"All right, Harry, MacKenzie, and all the rest of you," I said aloud. "I'm Tom Cruickshank and I came to play."

The path climbed sharply through the trees and I found that the eleventh tee was located on one of the highest parts of the course. The wind was to my back and so brisk that the ball wavered on the tee. I closed my eyes and created good and powerful swing thoughts. Thunderbolt felt like magic in my hands. My drive would sail out into the future straight and true.

Suddenly an icy gust nearly knocked me off my feet and I was startled by a shriek and the flapping of huge wings. I opened my eyes and looked upward as a massive black cloud passed over the sun, leaving behind a gray and desolate sky. Whatever had caused the unmistakable sound of beating wings was nowhere to be seen. Then I took a closer look at my surroundings and was sure I had lost my mind or was in another place.

The rocky turf at my feet was covered with brownish yellow grass, clearly uncut and very sparse. The high country spread before me. This was the top of the Augustus range, far above the treeline, a rugged and barren place, punctuated with dramatic outcroppings of black rock that thrust out of the hills and created a valley rolling before me like a wasteland. I was standing high on the crest of a windswept hill. There were low mountains on the horizon and dark clouds above the peaks promising a cold and driving rain. Fog as thick and white as freshly picked cotton rolled down the sides of the mountains and filled the distant valleys. I could see it move, covering the hillsides like a living, breathing thing. It was a wild and lonely place.

My chin itched and when I scratched it I was shocked to discover a beard, full grown and bushy. I had never had a beard in my life. But it didn't stop there. My clothing was roughly woven wool, short pants buttoned at the knees, leggings of an off-white, shirt of rough cotton, and a jacket without lapels that was closed against the wind with a sturdy leather belt. My rugged boots were ankle-length and leather with rough laces.

It was then I realized that Thunderbolt was gone. I looked frantically around to see if it had fallen from my hands and then felt my back pocket for the magic ball. But the pants had no pockets and the ball, my last remaining edge, was gone as well. My bag had become a sleeve of leather with a strap and my clubs were transformed into gnarled sticks of varying shapes and lengths. Lying next to it was a smallish kit from which spilled a single-edged knife, flint, and dried grass, and some perfectly round stones, painted in a grayish white. A rough blanket rolled into a bundle and tied with a leather thong lay on the ground with the rest of my belongings.

Several feet away was a group of rocks that created a shelter from the wind. Wisps of smoke curled upward from the dying embers of a fire and I threw myself to the ground in case the bandits who must have stolen Thunderbolt, the rest of my clubs as well as my magic ball were lurking there. There was only silence and the wind. No one was nearby. I walked around the rocks, but instead of making me feel better it only raised more questions. If there weren't any bandits had the fire been mine? Had I spent the night in this godforsaken place and not even known it? I wanted Harry to jump up and say "Gotcha, buddy," but that wasn't going to happen.

There was no way around it. I was in another time on another part of the Mountain and had gotten exactly what I had asked for. You wanted to test yourself against the course, Tom old buddy, I thought to myself, well, have at it. Hit away and see what happens. The problem was, I didn't know where I was going.

I knew I was standing on a tee but there was nothing else except the commanding view of the valley below to indicate it as a starting place. No markers defined the area. No freshly painted white arrows revealed the direction of the pin or the number of the hole. No benches with peeling green paint were placed in perfect position to sit and view a drive. No ball washers offered themselves to clean the sand and bits of grass from dimpled surfaces. This was the essence of the game, a field, a stick, and a stone.

Then a thought struck me. What if I allowed the lay of the land to reveal the target as I played? What if the natural roll of the hills would guide my shots to some logical place, say a curling root at the base of a tree or an animal hole on a level spot of grass? What if my objective would be simply to see where my shots would take me? I took the longest of the ancient clubs and resolved to become a hunter. I would learn by my play what the land would tell me and where the end would be. In the process of discovery I would carve a links for future generations of golfers out of this virgin hillside. To be the creator of something new, something that others who followed me would use for journeys of their own was satisfying. To hell with Harry, I was about to invent a golf course.

High in the sky a flock of large birds sailed over the horizon and circled far above my head. They shrieked and cawed as they flew above me. Vultures, probably, although I had never actually seen a vulture before. They disappeared into the clouds.

I teed up a rock on a mound of dirt. The wind was beginning to rise at my back again. It was damn cold but the heavy woolen clothing was good protection. I studied the terrain and decided to aim for a spot on the right about

200 yards out where two hills created the possibility of a long roll into the valley. A little draw to catch the wind and maybe I'd be "home in two" as the caddies say, hoping that flattery would ensure a larger tip.

It isn't easy to hit a stone with a knobby branch, as I discovered after gathering my thoughts and swinging through. I wondered how Angus did it. 200 yards was optimistic by 125, but it was still a decent shot, considering the technology. The stone didn't draw as I had intended and I was still well short of the hills that would be the turn of my dogleg left. I gathered my belongings and set off over the rough ground.

The lie for my second shot was good. The ground was firm and the grass was short. The problem was that the stone had cracked on impact and was sitting in several jagged pieces and there was no choice but to replace it with another from my bag. Not being sure what the rules might be for switching a damaged stone, I set the replacement carefully on the ground amidst the shattered remains.

The second rock was a real improvement; it was rounder and didn't have any obvious flaws. I hit it squarely and it caught the wind quite beautifully, topping the side of the second hill and rolling over the crest out of sight.

From the top of the hill I had been unable to see the sheer drop into a sandy pit about ten feet below the edge. In and of itself, no big deal. In fact, it was a devious and natural fairway bunker waiting for a sloppy shot from a careless golfer. The problem was that the pit was full of tiny round rocks ground to the surface by some ancient ice age. I slid down the embankment and began to hunt. At least, I thought as I rummaged through the thousands of stones, there'll always be plenty of balls. It was clear why mine were painted in that peculiar grayish white. The prize was sitting up nicely near the back edge of the pit in a difficult but playable lie.

After an inventory of my bag, I selected a short stick with a smaller but more angular knob than my driver. Whoever put this set together had spent a lot of time in the woods eyeing trees and sorting through fallen branches. It was amazing how much these rough sticks resembled modern golf clubs. Did Weyland walk the forests of Mount Augustus at night seeking models for his forge? I walked to the edge of the pit and looked for my next shot. A dogleg left was still the right choice, because an out-cropping of rock split the valley and the area to the left was clear. About 100 yards out was a large and ancient tree, with huge limbs that seemed to beckon me. The tree was out of place in these spare and rough surroundings and it was the perfect target.

As the architect of the hole, I decided to walk the line toward the tree and set a spot for the cup. I approached the tree from the right, imagining how the slope of the hill would allow a ball to bounce and roll to my green. Closer inspection revealed the area beneath the tree was everything that could be desired. Because of the shade from the huge limbs of the tree, which I decided was an oak, the grass was short and, while not thick and lush like the greens of Pine Valley, was already a desirable putting surface. It was relatively flat, but with a slight slope to the left that would require a precise approach so the shot could roll down to a well-placed cup. The left edge of my green fell steeply away into another sandy pit that was also filled with tiny rocks and was a perfect spot for a bunker to catch an over-zealous chip. The hole was a natural. I walked onto the surface of the green searching for a place to dig a cup when I discovered to my surprise that one already existed. Some burrowing rodent intent on shelter had done my work for me.

It was a perfect circle about four inches in diameter and at least four feet deep because I was able to stick my root-wedge in as far as it would go without touching bottom. As I poked around I expected a howl of disturbed rage but heard nothing. This home was abandoned and the tenant's departure was my good fortune. It did mean that a holed putt was lost forever but there were plenty of replacements available and, I noted smugly to myself, the price was right.

I returned to the fairway bunker and prepared to hit for the green. There was a good chance to make it with a well-placed shot. My tools were primitive and simple but they would have to do.

I took the wedge stick and assessed the situation. My rock was sitting up on a pile of similar stones far enough away from the back wall of the pit that I would be able to swing through without worrying about hitting anything. I walked to the front edge and looked down at the green. Something was missing—there was no flag. A brisk jog back to the tree and a quick search of the area revealed a branch long enough to serve as a pin. As I placed it in the hole a shrieking sound filled the air; it startled me and I searched the sky for the hunting bird but could see nothing and soon was back in the bunker preparing to swing away.

As I lined up my shot the limbs of the large tree began to sway and bounce as if a heavy wind was buffeting them. But I was safely protected by the back wall of the bunker. Blow winds, I thought to myself with a smile and prepared to strike.

I hit the pebble smartly and it sailed out of the bunker on a dead line to the pin. At that moment the tree erupted and a gigantic winged creature with the head of a woman reminding me a lot of Claudette Colbert burst forth flapping her wings madly to the left side of my rock, causing it to slice badly and fall far off to the right of the green in some deep weeds. She swooped down and grasped it in her claws. The creature wheeled in flight and soared toward me with a malevolent look in her beautiful brown eyes. I ran back to the wall of the bunker and prepared to protect myself as best I could with my puny stick.

The bird-woman circled above me, shrieking what sounded like *ssslllllliccceee*. Then she dropped my stone into the sand, and landed in the bunker, folding her leathery wings to her sides. She began to pace back and forth, staring at me intently. I held my stick in front of me in what

I hoped was a threatening manner. The face was heaven but the body was straight from hell.

"Do I know you?" she asked after what seemed an eternity.

"I don't think so," I replied.

"Argonaut?" she squealed.

"Consultant," I stammered.

"For Jason, yes?" she asked angrily.

"Hartless & Craven in Manhattan." I swung my stick like a cop in a riot drill.

"Not Jason?" she hissed and tossed her head, flinging her curls in an amazingly attractive manner. It made me sorry for a moment that she was a monster bird.

"Jason who?" I asked. I was noticing that something didn't smell right, and as she moved closer I realized it was her. The odor of decay and rotten food filled the air when she spoke, and when she flapped her wings it was clear she had never been within fifty feet of a birdbath.

"My name is Tom."

"And mine is Lorena. You must know of me."

"Sorry, no, but pleased to meet you," I said with as much bravado as I could muster, still holding my stick as menacingly as I could.

"No matter," she hissed slyly. "Anything to eat?"

"No thank you, Lorena," I answered politely. "All I want is to play through."

"No," she cried, "do you have anything to eat for me and my sisters? We are Harpies and must be fed."

"You're a Harpy," I stammered, "and you have sisters?"

"Yes, of course, is something wrong with that? Hei-diiiiiii! Sssisters!"

She began to flap her wings and scream bird noises at the top of her lungs. I was frantically trying to remember what I knew about Harpies from my few and ancient trips down mythology lane. All I could recall was that they were bad news and blinded some king while they were stealing his food. But I also remembered that Jason of Golden Fleece fame figured out how to get rid of them, which must have been why she was curious if I had any connection to him. For the life of me I couldn't remember how he did it. Then the tree erupted and a whole band of Harpies circled high above us; the flapping of their wings was like thunder. They wheeled in the air, plunging out of the sky, claws extended, only to pull back at the last minute and soar away. I waved my stick blindly, striking and defending myself as best I could. But they were fast as lightning and my few connected blows fell on wings with feathers as strong as steel. My hands vibrated with each impact and I knew I didn't have a chance without a bazooka. They were simply toying with me until boredom set in.

The demons flew in screeching circles above my head and settled in the pit in a random flurry. I had to admit, terrified as I was and preparing to die, that they were all as beautiful as every uptown sorority-girl type I ever wanted to date except, in the end, they would break more than my heart.

There were now twenty or more of the creatures milling around in my bunker, hissing, belching, and emitting foul odors. They were pawing absently through the pebbles with their claws looking for something. To say I was trapped was an understatement.

"Sisters," shrieked Lorena Harpy, "what do you desire of this mortal? Shall it be food, blood, or practice?"

One of them raised her beautiful blond head; she reminded me of Sharon Stone. "They wish to feed, but first . . ."

"Go on, Heidi," said Lorena.

"They wish to learn. They wish to chase the stone and change its course with their wings as you did and as they will someday do on Augustus. It is a rare opportunity," Heidi answered. Murmurs, shrieks, and bellows rose from the throng in what sounded like concensus.

"Well said," mused Lorena. "So it shall be. Mortal, hear me now. My sisters wish to play the game of chase the stone with you. And they are right. For they must prepare for the time when they will travel down the mountain to chase the shots on Mount Augustus. My sister, Heidi, prefers a clumsy arc to the left, but she is a fool. I myself prefer to chase it to the right, the flight is much more beautiful. The others do as they are told, for they are not goddesses but merely fledglings who hope to master the sacred tasks."

"You and Heidi are goddesses?"

"You dare to think of us as mere Harpies?"

"Wait a second. Hooks and slices? You're in charge of slices and Heidi's in charge of hooks? What are you doing up here? People are hooking and slicing all over the world."

"There are many of us who have gained the skills and have been sent into the world to practice what we know. You have found the sacred place of learning. And we are lucky that a mortal wandered here, for usually we must do the work of hitting ourselves."

"Why haven't I seen you before? I hook and slice all the time."

"We are invisible, silly." She giggled, then got down to business. "Where were we?" She pecked and scratched the stones beneath her as she tried to remember. "Ah yes. Mortal, you shall hit stones from this pit for them to chase and as long as you can do so you shall live. But if you stop, the game ends there and you shall die most horribly and with great suffering. Will you play with us?"

"Do I have a choice?" I asked.

"You may die horribly and with great suffering now," she answered sternly.

"But for it to be a game both sides should have a chance to win," I said. "What could I do to save myself?"

"Why do you hit the stone?" she asked.

"To reach the green and knock it in the hole," I answered.

"If you can do so you will live," she said. "If not..." The Harpies cawed and screamed with pleasure and anticipation.

The Fable of Lorena, The Goddess of Slicers, and Heidi, The Goddess of Hookers

In the ancient days when the game of golf was new and played by gods, every shot was, for the most part, straight and true. The MacKenzie discovered, to his dismay, that devious rules and laws devised by the weasel MacTavish were not enough to ensure victories over his sons. He plotted with MacTavish to invent other means to make the game more difficult for everyone except himself.

MacTavish knew of an island far away where there lived two sisters, each half bird and half woman of extreme beauty, and that they feasted on rotten meat stolen from kings and that the power of their wings could create a wind that changed the flight of lesser birds.

"If they can do that," posited MacTavish, "think what they could do with a stone driven by an unsuspecting god. To the left. To the right. The possibilities are endless, the penalty potential profound. It boggles the mind. Imagine a place that would be 'out of bounds.' "

So The MacKenzie sent MacTavish to seek them out. And after some years, MacTavish returned and told the god that there was interest but also terms.

"Tha seek ta bargain with a god?" The MacKenzie shouted.

"I think you should hear the deal," MacTavish answered.

MacTavish then told MacKenzie that the creatures, called Harpies, possessed great skills but were unwilling to relocate without improving their lot. They desired to become goddesses and also required an oak tree from their native island in which to live, for they would surely miss their homeland. In exchange they would chase certain shots and cause anguish and despair for the gods who earned MacKenzie's displeasure, but they also reserved the right to freelance.

"Believe me, they can produce. One prefers to chase to the right, the other to the left. The best part is that they can become invisible. They are perfect," finished MacTavish proudly.

"How are they called?" The MacKenzie asked.

"Lorena and Heidi," answered MacTavish.

"Can we na git Immortals fer the mountain wi' proper names?" MacKenzie cried.

So it came to pass that Lorena, who chased to the right, became the Goddess of Slicers and her sister, Heidi, who chased to the left, became the Goddess of Hookers. And their arrival on the mountain changed the game forever, causing otherwise rational gods to throw Weyland's works of genius into rivers or smash them into trees, screaming to deaf heaven about the unfairness of it all.

And the MacKenzie was pleased, for he enjoyed a little chaos even when it affected himself.

"We shall begin," shouted Lorena. The Harpies rose abruptly into the air and flew to the tree where they disappeared into the leaves. I had no idea how they all fit. It was a little like fourteen clowns stuffing themselves into a Volkswagen at the circus, but they were gone. The hills looked just as they had before the birds appeared, but the smell of decay lingered in the air like the signature on a bad deal memo.

Lorena poked her gorgeous head out of the tree and was followed by several others. They looked at me eagerly, impatient to begin. If I had not known that monsters lurked behind those pretty faces suspended in the leaves it would have been an oddly beautiful sight.

"Why do you wait?" she called sweetly.

I couldn't think of a single reason, so I wound up and swung away, hitting the stone solidly and sending it soaring into the air. Amidst much cheering and encouragement a Harpy flew out of the tree, sent it hooking badly left with the flapping of her wings, chased it down, grabbed it in midair, and nimbly dropped it just off the edge of the green. Heidi flew out of the tree and gave her the Harpy equivalent of a high five.

"More," they shouted and I hit another that was

promptly shunted right in a soaring slice, then caught and once again deposited on the edge of the green. Thus began a game of catch that went endlessly forward. I lost myself in the rhythm of hitting until it became an automatic function. I roamed the pit finding stone after stone to sail into the waiting talons of the circling Harpies who sent them hooking and slicing before they dropped them on the edge of the green. Single stones became visible piles that grew slowly higher and higher until they were a short but solid wall encircling the front edge. Lorena and Heidi would roam about, offering encouragement and tips. They were nothing if not supportive.

My arms were burning with exhaustion and my back ached from the constant repetition, but I was grooving my swing. Never in my life had I hit with such consistency and, in spite of myself, I was becoming involved in the game. On several occasions I had almost gotten one past a mediocre flyer and a backup, usually Heidi or Lorena, had to explode out of the tree to save a shot that was sure to hit the green.

Suddenly, I realized that I was running out of stones. It was becoming increasingly difficult to see over the edge of the pit. I was digging my own grave. As the peril of my situation became evident I also noted for the first time that the accumulated stones around the green had grown to a wall of at least ten or twelve feet high in the center and tapering as it trailed toward the sides of the green. Although I knew with some certainty where the cup was located, I could no longer see the pin.

The Harpies noticed the lull and were screaming for the game to continue. I found a few usable pellets and sent them over the top, but knew that soon the game would be over. I had been foolish to think I could defeat or even outlast them in competition like this. Suddenly I was exhausted, my arms were leaden, my hands raw and bloody from the constant friction of the stick, and my legs were shaking uncontrollably. I knew what a mighty game fish hooked on a strong line must feel after giving its all in a battle it could not possibly win. I had done my best and from this point on it was no longer up to me.

The Harpies were beginning to realize that the barrage of stones had ceased and this phase of the game was all but over. I wondered how it would feel to be plucked into the air and carried away on giant wings to some Harpy communal picnic ground. I decided I was too tired to care. The birds were calling for more stones and I could hear the thunder of their wings as they rose from the tree and flew in agitated circles around the green.

"Have you done, mortal?" Lorena screamed as she appeared over the wall and flew toward me.

"To hell with you," I cried. She cackled and flew back to the tree to collect her sisters for the endgame. As I was preparing for the worst a flash of lightning filled the air and from behind me there came a rumbling sound. I turned to watch a section of the bunker wall fall away revealing a cleft in the rocks. At least stuffing myself into it would make it harder for the Harpies to finish me off. I ran to the opening and saw something glistening inside. It was the magic ball. How it got there was something to consider another time; all I knew was that I had one last chance.

"Wait," I cried, "I've got one more."

"It is foolishness. You buy but a moment and we tire of the game," called Lorena.

"A deal's a deal, Harpy." I walked to the edge of the pit and shouted, "I've got one more shot."

"As you will," said Lorena. She was perched on the topmost point of the wall shaking her head and smiling sadly. "For a moment I had admired your courage and had decided to ease your inevitable suffering, but you are prideful and arrogant. Play the game with us one last time, mortal, we are patient and can wait for our pleasure."

"You better move fast, sweetheart, 'cause I'm cumin' atcha," I called out.

One edge of the pit was still almost level with the ground and there was just enough room to get a shot off. I ran up and dropped the ball gently in the sand. It almost seemed to jump as it waited to be hit. Lorena was still sitting on the wall watching me. Then a crash like lightning splitting a mighty tree exploded behind me and a flash of blue light curled over the top of the pit flowing down the wall where my bag was leaning. For an instant the leather sleeve glowed like a Roman candle and then the light curled back over the wall and was gone. Sitting there with my wooden sticks was Thunderbolt. Somebody up there liked me.

I ran back down to my bag and pulled my trusty driver. My last shot was going to be a good one. The rest of the Harpies had begun to fly from the shelter of the tree and perch on the wall with their sister. They lined up like ravishingly beautiful crows on a telephone wire watching a farmer finish his harvest. Flapping their wings impatiently, the Harpies stared at me with cruel eyes.

I took a practice swing and several of them leapt off the wall in pursuit. I laughed loudly to let them know I had tricked them. The gullible ones fluttered about clumsily for a moment and flopped back on the wall accompanied by the jeers of their sisters. When no one was fooled by the next try I knew it was time.

Confidence was the key and, by God, I had it. I had never been more sure of a shot in my life. There's nothing like hitting a few hundred midlength approaches to groove a swing and improve the old game; I should've thought of it before. The stones had been taking off straight as strings; the harpies were making them change course. Practice makes perfect. I would have to remember that. The ball was ready, Thunderbolt was ready, and so was I. My chaffed hands and tired back were forgotten. The backswing had to have been picture perfect because I belted a ground-to-air missile that hit the wall dead center, shattering the stillness with the crash of its impact. A fraction of a second later the wall exploded in slow motion sending rocks and startled Harpies careening into the sky. Where there had been a wall was once again an open shot to the green for all who would follow me. I had blasted my way home and all I had to do was get it down.

Like Dirk charging a sleeping green, I grabbed Thunder-bolt and went over the top, running a gauntlet of screaming Harpies, who were zigzagging back and forth as they tried to pelt me with stones and grab at me with their claws. I leapt over the rubble and turned a perfect shoulder roll that brought me to my knees in the middle of the green. I scanned it quickly looking for my ball, which I saw to my delight was only about three feet from the pin. I had executed the shot of a lifetime but there was no time to congratulate myself. Leaving my bag where it lay I crawled to my ball. The air was full of flapping wings and enraged cries. Without a second thought I stood and stroked the ball with my driver. Thunderbolt got me here, Thunderbolt would save me.

For an instant I thought I had hit it too hard. The ball bounced along the rough surface in a dead line for the stick. Then it hit something, popped into the air, slammed against the pin, and dropped straight down into the hole. There was a rumble and a puff of smoke. The Harpies shrieked in dismay and Lorena dropped from the sky like a stone, landing on the green. She could barely contain her rage.

"You are lucky, mortal," she hissed.

"Maybe, but maybe I'm just good," I said.

"No, mortal," she said, "you are lucky that I am one whose word is her bond. Many of my kind would kill you now for pleasure. Go. Your journey will not end here."

With that she rose up into the air and soared off into the dull gray sky with her band following close behind. The beating of their wings faded into the distance and I stood in silence watching until I was sure they were gone. Some unsuspecting hacker somewhere would be the target of the Harpies rage but it wouldn't be me, not today. I picked up my bag and walked back up to the crest of the hill. I played my hole seven more times, took an average and decided it should be known as a par four, although it never took me less than six to finish. The eleventh would henceforth be known as *Tom's Revenge*.

Before making my final putt, I sat for a moment under the tree and must have dozed, for when I opened my eyes I was back on the part of the Mountain with fairways of rolling grass, blue skies, and yellow sun. The green at my feet was lush and clipped to perfection and my ball was resting close to the pin. Only the tree was the same. I rose and pulled my trusty putter from my own bag and scratched my relatively clean-shaven chin. Everything was back to normal. I putted out for my final six and headed for the twelfth. On the way I wondered if I'd earned the right to call on Heidi for a little help on a dogleg left:

CHAPTER 12

The Tutor

In which Tom learns why it's not a good idea to annoy the teacher's pets

After playing the first few holes of Mount Augustus, I had assumed that Pine Valley and Mount Augustus were somehow related, the "Valley" being like the shadows on the wall of Plato's cave. But the more I traveled, the clearer it became that the Mountain was indeed a very different course.

Having escaped the clutches of the Harpies, I expected no more than a few steps from the eleventh green to the twelfth tee. But instead of finding a well-worn path, I was again engulfed by an overgrown wood. As I pressed forward, brambles caught at my clothing and thin branches whipped me across the face. I pulled my sand wedge and used it like a machete to hack my way through the brush like Buster Crabbe in a jungle movie. Suddenly, the ground became softer and rose abruptly upward two or three feet before leveling off. When my eyes adjusted to the dim light in the forest, I realized that I was standing on some sort of earthwork about ten feet wide and thirty feet long.

I walked slowly up and down the length of the mound looking for some clue as to its purpose, but found nothing until my second circuit. Nestled deep in the ivy off to the side of the mound was a severed head—or to be more precise, a bust. Roughly the size of a cantaloupe, it was the likeness of a faun carved out of flawless black marble.

Was this place an ancient burial ground? The resting place of the gods when they cashed in their last gimmie? But then I realized how truly idiotic that was. What would the immortals at Mount Augustus need with a burial site when they didn't die?

I picked up my sand wedge and began to hack around in the underbrush looking for something, for anything that might solve the mystery. At the far end of the mound I found another object, a shaft sticking up out of the ground crowned with an ornately carved head. If it hadn't been for the head, I would have assumed it to be a young sapling, for green buds were appearing along the sides of the shaft. With one mighty tug, I pulled the object from the ground and recognized it almost immediately for what it was: a driver!

Even with greens buds growing out of its hickory shaft and a beard of fine roots sprouting from its handle, the club was beautifully balanced. Delighted by my find, I moved to the middle of the mound and tried it out, taking a couple of tentative chops and then a full-blooded practice swing that picked the head cleanly off a budding dandelion.

"Oh, please stop! Please stop! It's positively painful to watch!"

I wasn't the least bit surprised to hear a new voice. The woods of Mount Augustus were crowded as Madison Avenue during lunch hour.

"You don't have to look," I replied and took another swing, which was greeted with another exclamation from the forest.

"Ouch! You'll never break par that way, dear boy. You're way off plane and you're uncocking your wrists much too early, spilling all your vital energy on the way down!"

"You have to be a golf instructor."

"I stand convicted, I'm afraid," said the voice. "But I really must protest. Calling me a golf instructor is a bit like calling Michelangelo a good draftsman."

"Well, if you're such an expert, why don't you come out of hiding and show me how it's done?"

"I'd love to, dear boy. But I'm afraid I'm all tied up at the moment."

"Booked solid, huh?"

"No, I'm literally tied up! Perhaps you'd give us a hand?"

"Sure, where are you?" I was intrigued.

"Over here, behind the ferns. Oh, thank you, sir, for your kindness."

I parted the bushes and found a most frightening and pitiful sight. The source of the voice was a painfully thin man completely immobilized and hanging on some sort of medieval torture device—a huge metal circle inside which the victim was suspended by a network of chains, straps, and pulleys. Dressed in green golfer's double knits and a yellow Ban-Lon shirt, he looked like a giant mantis trapped in the center of a spider's web.

"Who did this to you?" I asked.

"It's rather hard to explain," the man replied with an embarrassed smile. "Perhaps you'd undo my right wrist. It's chaffing a bit under the strap."

As I helped him out of the bindings, the man introduced himself as Ichabod, the God of Instruction.

"Can't thank you enough. I had scheduled a lesson with one of the younger gods, and while I was waiting for him, I decided to work on my swing with the Plane Perpetuator here. Well, no sooner had I strapped myself in than Mac-Kenzie decides to work on the thirteenth hole. And we all know what that means."

"I'm afraid I don't," I said, and he looked at me as if I were mad.

"Earth tremors, of course," he replied. "A couple of big

ones, too. Completely knocked me and the Plane Perpetuator off the tee and into the woods."

"Wait a minute," I said. "You mean that's a tee box?"

"Of course, what did you think it was?"

"Wasn't sure really. When I found the carved head, I assumed it was some sort of, eh, sacred site."

"Found one of Ma's tee markers, did you?" Ichabod laughed.

"Who's Ma?" I asked.

"The Goddess Rowena, MacKenzie's first wife. Avid golfer, but headstrong. Couldn't teach her a thing. Terrible reverse pivot problem. Eons ago she had a regular afternoon game with the other goddesses. And every Tuesday evening, she and MacKenzie played a hit-and-giggle round with some of the other divine couples.

"At any rate, she used to complain to MacKenzie that the course needed some sprucing up if it was going to be a proper place for the gods to recreate. Eventually, he gave in and let Rowena have her way."

"What'd she do?"

"First of all she built a huge clubhouse overlooking the eighteenth green. Complete with baths, solarium, and a grand ballroom. Then she placed statuary all over the course including carved tee markers like the one you found. Well, the older gods went crazy. They liked things the way they were before. They liked to drink nectar with their mates and chase giggling wood nymphs through the trees after a round. The last thing they wanted was to eat little sandwiches by the pool with their wives."

"So, what happened?"

"Nothing at first. MacKenzie was more afraid of Rowena than his golfing companions. But one day when Rowena was playing a morning round with her friends she came upon the Great God dallying with a young goddess near the ninth green. Well, she stormed off the course and never returned.

"MacKenzie had to move into the clubhouse for the next two thousand years or so. Eventually Rowena forgave him, but she never did return to the course."

"That explains a lot," I said. "But I still don't understand why this tee box is so overgrown."

"Oh, these are the championship tees, don't you see," explained Ichabod. "Since I've been away, no one's game has been good enough to play from the tips. Bertie used to use them all the time, but he hasn't been off the third tee in hundreds of years, since he became so enamoured of the long ball."

"Just how long have you been here?" I asked.

"Five hundred years exactly," Ichabod replied. "Forgive me for rambling on, it's just that I haven't spoken to anyone in so long."

"Nobody's looked for you?" This was unbelievable.

The man's eyes began to fill and then a tear crested and rolled down his gaunt cheek. "I'm sure they must have. Their games couldn't have survived this long without my attention. Old MacTavish and that terrible slice. And Fergus hits so many balls in the water—although I suspect it's so he can swim after them. Oh, and MacKenzie has this over-the-top move that you simply can't believe. Sometimes it's a dead pull into the woods and at other times a great banana ball off to the right."

"But if you've been tied up for five hundred years, how'd you survive?"

"My friends have fed and cared for me," he replied. "Ah, and here they come now."

An enormous white cockatoo lighted on a nearby branch while a sleek brown mongoose darted out of the bushes and stood erect, looking at me quizzically. Ichabod reached down and gave the mongoose a chuck under the chin.

"Why didn't your friends, as you call them, let anyone know where you were?"

"Oh, they tried of course, but no one paid attention," he replied. "Well, that's not exactly true. Mulligan comes by from time to time, even tried to get me out but he's so clumsy and incompetent. Besides once he leaves he forgets I'm still here."

"None of the other gods would listen to them?"

"Unfortunately no," he answered.

"And why not?" I wasn't sure why I was pursuing this. Even as a kid I never believed Lassie could have convinced anyone to look for Timmy, so it was hard for me to imagine anyone telling a mongoose or a cockatoo to "Find Ichabod."

"Teacher's pets, my boy. Everyone despises them."

"Oh, I see," I responded, but really had no idea what he was talking about.

"Well, enough about me," said Ichabod suddenly. "Let's hear about you. However did you get to Mount Augustus?"

For the next twenty minutes I told Ichabod of my life as a junior associate at Hartless & Craven, my nightmare of a boss, my suspect golf game, and how I met Harry Brady at Pine Valley. Ichabod asked me a great many questions.

The Fable of Ichabod—God of Instructors

In the early years of golf, two or three millennia after the invention of the divine game, the Great God Mac-Kenzie was bored and decided to sojourn upon the earth for a time. Disguised as a common countryman, MacKenzie stepped through the sacred portal into the highlands of Scotland. There he came upon a young Englishman named Ichabod who played the game with a skill not dreamed about on Mount Augustus. Unfortunately, Ichabod had no future. As the youngest son of a nobleman, he stood to inherit nothing upon his father's demise.

Seeing his opening, MacKenzie lured Ichabod to Mount Augustus with tales of gorgeous wood nymphs, endless summer days, and all the mead and nectar he could consume. In exchange, Ichabod would teach MacKenzie's sons the proper way to play golf. The bargain was struck and Ichabod traveled with MacKenzie through the sacred portal to Mount Augustus.

The first few years went swimmingly, but then Ichabod's still mortal mind began to tire of the sameness of it all. The nymphs were too easy, the weather seldom varied, and MacKenzie's sons were idiots incapable of understanding the subtlety of the game. Ichabod longed for the smart-mouthed shop girls of London, malt whiskey, and a fresh supply of students. But when he told MacKenzie that he intended to leave, the Great God informed him that this was possible but only if he met certain conditions. Ichabod must first develop the perfect golf swing, and teach it to everyone on the mountain.

Ichabod agreed, but soon discovered that the gods possessed little discipline or focus and were unable to learn his secrets from example and explanation alone. Eons passed and he was still no closer to his dream of leaving the Mountain. In desperation he began devising training tools to help him explain the mysteries of the swing. His research leaked to the mortal world and he was the inspiration for not only the famous Plane Perpetuator but the Medici Breaker Pro, the Swing Wrap, and the Slicebegon Full Alignment Tool. While sales of these golfing miracles reaped millions Ichabod was never acknowledged for his contributions and received no royalties.

And so, to this day, Ichabod continues to tinker with all manner of bizarre machinery and gadgets, searching for the perfect golf swing and his freedom.

At first I thought he was just being polite, but after a while I realized that Ichabod was genuinely fascinated by my story—or starved for conversation.

"Ah, so you are a mortal, after all," said Ichabod. There was an edge of excitement in his voice.

"Of course. What'd you think?"

"I'm not sure, really," replied Ichabod. "Perhaps a visiting deity from a pantheon that wears really bad clothes . . ."

"You should talk."

"Or possibly the result of one of MacKenzie's affairs with a shepherd girl or milkmaid," he continued. "Happens all the time, you know. The question is, are you *The One?*"

"The one? I'm afraid I don't follow you."

"Oh surely you've heard the stories?" Ichabod said. "The gods have been telling them around the campfires for centuries. Wonderful stuff, wonderful."

"Afraid not," I said.

"Not certain about all the details; I forget so many things. But they go something like this: a mortal enters Mount Augustus through a shimmering portal in the forest. Or on a flaming chariot? Ah, never mind. Anyway, things happen, he has some adventures, and then rescues the game of golf. Or is it a fetching maiden? I forget. At any rate, because he has a pure heart, he rescues something or other and saves the day. And there you have it."

"Sort of like Sir Gallahad and the Holy Grail and *Dante's Inferno* all rolled into one?" I ventured.

"Quite," agreed Ichabod. "The point is, all the gods— and I do mean *all*, believe it, and they are always on the lookout for *Him*. At least they used to be, but I've been tied up for so long and . . . but I would so love to find him first and I believe you might well be him. What do you think?"

"Well, I'm afraid I don't qualify, Ichabod. Whoever The One is, he isn't me," I said with a laugh. "My heart's not all that pure, and the only thing I'm looking for is a way to get out of this place in one piece."

"Hmm, that's too bad," replied Ichabod. "But then you wouldn't necessarily know. I mean, I do hope you are because the old gods don't like to be disappointed. They're rather like children that way. And everyone seems to disappoint them sooner or later. Even our friend Harry." There was a look of genuine concern on his face.

"I'm not so sure he's a friend," I said. "The only reason he brought me here was to supply Weyland with another foundry worker. I figure the only chance I've got is to finish the round."

Ichabod looked at me and smiled engagingly.

"Listen, you'll never make it back to the house with the swing you've got. But I think I can help you. How would you like to have a perfect golf swing—one that would never let you down?"

"Who wouldn't?"

"Then I have a proposal to make," he said. "I will teach you the perfect golf swing this very afternoon, enabling you to hit greens in regulation every time. Absolutely change your life, I guarantee it."

"Sounds great," I said. "What's the catch?"

"In exchange, I will ask a small favor of you."

"Uh-huh."

"Take me back with you to Manhattan when you leave."

"I'm afraid I have a very small apartment," I said, shaking my head.

"Not to worry, dear boy," replied Ichabod soothingly. "You won't even notice me. Besides, I'll get my own place in no time at all. As soon as I sell the Plane Perpetuator, I shall be rich as Croesus."

Chances were I would never get back to New York anyway, so sharing an apartment with Ichabod and his animals wasn't likely to become an issue, and if he could improve my swing . . .

"Okay," I said.

"Well, enough standing about," Ichabod exclaimed. "It's time to get to work. Let's have a look at that swing of yours."

Ichabod pulled a couple of practice balls from his pockets and dropped them in front of me. Auditioning of any sort has always made me freeze up, and this time was no different, so I managed a couple of stiff swipes at the balls, sending them clattering into the woods on the right.

Ichabod chuckled softly and shook his head. "Not the worst I've ever seen, but far from the best. By the way, do you get cable?"

"Yes, it's in my building."

"Wonderful," he said. "Prewar? Rent-controlled?"

"Both," I replied.

"What's the view like?"

"Can't see the river, but there's a good view of midtown by night."

"Excellent."

"How is it you know so much about Manhattan?" I asked.

"Mulligan, of course, he's been there many times, it's his favorite place in the mortal world. He lived there for a while after his mother left MacKenzie, you know. I would just die to see Times Square."

Mulligan loose on the streets of New York and Ichabod in Times Square was surely something to contemplate, but not on my dime.

"So Ichabod, what's your diagnosis?"

"Oh, your golf swing! Yes, mustn't forget that! Not to worry. You can be helped, dear boy. It's just a question of adjusting a few angles here and there."

Ichabod began twisting and bending my joints into positions even the most accomplished yogi couldn't appreciate or approximate. He stepped back to admire his handiwork.

"There, that's a proper setup," said Ichabod. "Now, let's see you hit a couple more balls."

They fared no better than the first, ending up this time in the woods to my left.

"Don't understand it, my boy. You looked marvelous. How did it feel?"

"Painful," I replied.

"Ah, there's the problem," said Ichabod, nodding sagely. "We must get beyond mere mechanics to 'feel.' And there's only one way to do that. The Plane Perpetuator!"

"Wait a minute, you're not getting me in that thing!"

"Oh, there's absolutely nothing to worry about, dear boy. Unless there's an earthquake. And even then I'd be here to get you out of the harness."

So we dragged the Plane Perpetuator back up on the tee and Ichabod strapped me into the elaborate getup of leather straps and steel rings. Once the harness held me fast in the center of the metal ring, Ichabod began to fasten leather bands to my ankles and wrists.

"Are these absolutely necessary?" I asked.

"Essential, dear boy," Ichabod replied. "Without these straps, you'll get no feedback. And without feedback, you won't improve. Let me demonstrate."

Ichabod handed me the five-iron and dropped a couple of balls on the tee.

"Now take it back slowly," Ichabod instructed, guiding the club with his fingers. "If you come back too far inside— setting up an over-the-top downswing path, the strap on your left wrist engages the pulley above your head which, in turn, plucks a tail feather from friend cockatoo on his perch."

As the pressure tightened, the cockatoo turned around warily, but Ichabod backed off before any feathers flew. "And if you take the club back too far outside the target line, then you'll probably hit a severe hook. And when that begins to happen, the strap on your right wrist will yank on the tail of friend mongoose. When he squeals you'll know you've gone too far."

"But doesn't that make them angry?" I asked.

"Of course, dear boy. That's the whole point," Ichabod answered. "Both of these creatures are fearsome biters when annoyed."

Ichabod lifted both pant legs to reveal a pair of white bony calves covered with bite marks and lacerations. "Just look at the scars on my legs, Tommy lad. I don't have to tell you that after a couple of bites like these you'll be taking the club back on the proper plane in no time at all. Now, care to give it a go?"

"Can't wait," I replied. But I had no intention of being fodder for the jaws of Ichabod's wildlife companions. Not only was Ichabod crazy as a loon, he was far more interested in my apartment than my swing. And, once he was my roommate, he'd never leave. I was about to give Ichabod an acting lesson. Drawing the club back I began grimacing madly as if pulling with all my might when, in fact, I was putting on the greatest demonstration of Dynamic Tension since the heyday of Charles Atlas.

"What's the matter?"

"I don't know. It seems to be stuck."

"Try it again, dear boy," he urged.

Again I pretended to pull the club back, straining and holding my breath until my face turned red.

"It's no use," I said finally. "Maybe you'd better show me how it's done."

"Oh, heavens." Ichabod was getting exasperated.

He released me from the harness and I buckled him into the Plane Perpetuator.

"I just don't understand it," he puzzled as I fastened the straps around his wrists. "It worked perfectly the last time I used it."

"Yes, but that was five hundred years ago," I reminded him.

"Well, there you are," he replied. "Perhaps you're right. Now be a good lad and move out of the way."

"Yes, sir," I replied sharply and trotted down the length of the tee box, clubs rattling in my carry bag. I broke for the bright spot in the woods ahead where I knew the members' tee box had to be. Ichabod was shouting "fore" behind me. Half a second later a ball rattled through the trees above my head but I kept running. The cockatoo screeched, Ichabod screamed, and I imagined the foul-tempered bird biting him hard on the calf. Justice was served. The Tutor paid the price for slicing.

As I finally teed up my ball for the assault on twelve, I heard Ichabod's voice echoing through the clearing.

"YOU SEE, IT WORKS!" he screamed.

CHAPTER 13

The Tempest

*In which Tom learns that a golfer swings from sun to sun
but the Great God's work is never done*

When I emerged from the woods near the thirteenth tee, I
was battle scarred and weary. However, despite my encounters with the Harpies and with Ichabod and his nasty
little friends, I felt strangely confident. I had taken everything the gods had thrown at me and survived. And not
only Heidi and Lorena, but Divot, Mulligan, and Fergus,
too! In spite of Ichabod's attempt to "fix" my swing, I had
come back and made a tough bogie on twelve by sinking
a long putt. They had all taken their best shots at me and,
wonder of wonders, I was still standing!

It just didn't figure. I had always thought of myself as a
slightly overweight guy with a pretty good mind, okay
looking, with a slight tendency toward clumsiness—not the
best self-image in the world. But now, I seemed to be suc-
ceeding at something at which I had no previous apti-
tude—something requiring gumption, physical courage,
and athleticism. For the first time in my life, I was caught
between two conflicting self-images. Which was right? Was

I a pudgy MBA with a mind for figures and a spine of Jell-O, or was I Tom Cruickshank, budding superhero? I decided to try the new persona on for size.

According to the mountain of self-help books I had devoured since college, it was all about creating an image of the person I wanted to be, and miraculously, I would become that person. So, as I mounted the tee box, I was no longer the timid overweight junior executive from Hartless & Craven. Okay, physically I was still a forty short with a thirty-eight waistband, but in my mind's eye I pictured a herculean figure with a chiseled chest and rock-hard abdominals.

I tried to picture myself standing firm on the tee and then crushing an epic drive down the middle of the fairway, but had trouble holding the image past the backswing. Each time I ran the movie in my mind, the image began to wobble and fade at the top, and I would see myself once again as a bean counter on holiday. After three failed attempts at holding the picture, I decided speed was the key: I had to eliminate the waggle.

Moving as quickly as possible, I painted a fresh picture in my mind, jammed my ball and tee into the turf, and then without waggle, striped the ball down the middle of the fairway. Before the new image could fade, I pulled my tee out of the ground like a grizzled touring pro, without bothering to see where the ball landed. It was a career drive—a streaking thunderbolt that came low out of the box and then rose inexorably into the fading sky until it reached its apex—a dot of pure white in sharp relief against the blue-black clouds of a rapidly approaching storm. By the time I raised up, dark thunderheads were racing across the sky like advancing armies and a cold wind was whipping dried leaves around my feet.

To my astonishment my ball was still where it was a moment before, some two hundred yards out over the fairway spinning in the air like a yo-yo at the end of its string. Which "god" was responsible this time? I wondered. Fergus? Divot? Or perhaps some other meddling sleight-of-hand artist I hadn't yet met.

Where did they get off calling themselves "gods," anyway? There was nothing particularly transcendent or omnipotent about them. Sure, they could pull off a few parlor tricks, but nothing that couldn't be topped by a good Las Vegas magician twice an evening. As far as I could see, the "gods" of Mount Augustus were little more than a ragtag collection of petty bureaucrats, ex-wives, and civil servants. There were thousands just like them back in Manhattan: arrogant incompetents in charge of postage stamps, driver's licenses, and expense accounts who got their jollies by making everyone else completely miserable. I clinched my jaw and resolved right then and there that no band of second-rate deities would ever kick Tom Cruickshank around again, and that went double for the wage slaves and pension protectors back home.

Tossing my carry bag over my shoulders, I leaned into the wind and marched down the fairway, overconfident and looking for trouble. Twenty yards down the fairway I found it. Reg was coming toward me driving a herd of sheep.

"I should've known it was you," I shouted above the wind.

"Have you gone daft, guv'nor?" Reg replied. "Get off the bleedin' links before all hell breaks loose."

Now, a little bit of confidence can be a dangerous thing—especially to someone like myself not used to the experience. I was convinced that the storm brewing before me was only a figment of my imagination, and I had no intention of giving in to it.

"I wouldn't give you the satisfaction," I said.

Reg laughed bitterly. "Do you honestly think old Reg had anything to do with this?"

By now wave after wave of stinging rain was pelting us. Reg grumbled and pulled up the collar of his tweed jacket to cover his neck.

"Don't act so put out," I added. "We both know it's only a hallucination."

An enormous bolt of lightning struck the ground knocking us off our feet.

Reg raised up on one elbow and shook his head. "Well then it's a bloody good one, mate."

No sooner had we gotten to our feet than we were struck down again, this time by a gale force wind. With considerable effort I managed to right myself, but the winds were too much for the God of Caddies. He formed himself into a ball of tweed by tucking his arms and legs under his coat. With the next gust of wind he was flying down the fairway.

"Don't fight it, guv'nor. Go with the wind!"

In fact, I had little choice. The wind was now at a hurricane pitch, howling eighty or ninety miles per hour and gusting to well over one hundred. Stubbornly, I continued to fight against it, managing to move another couple of yards down the fairway. But then a huge gust straightened me up like a solid right to the jaw, then the wind filled my rain pants and shirt, blowing me up like a cartoon balloon in the Macy's parade.

Suddenly I was airborne, bouncing backward over the fairway like a deranged tumbleweed. After a couple of violent somersaults, I tumbled over a small mogul into a bunker.

A chorus of angry bleeting greeted my arrival. I had landed in the midst of a group of black-faced sheep taking shelter from the storm. The smell of wet wool was overpowering, but I wedged myself in as tightly as I could. All in all, the sheep were a remarkably good barrier against the weather. Despite the howling gale around us, I was reasonably dry and quite warm. Soon I was asleep.

When I awoke several hours later, the storm was more violent than ever. Something had spooked the sheep and they were deserting the bunker as fast as they could. Through the inky blackness I could just make out their heads as they moved away from me toward the woods on the left side of the fairway. It was strange that I could see only their heads. Then I realized that they were swimming. No wonder it was cold; I was in water up to my neck!

In a panic, I broke into my schoolboy crawl, splashing after them through the rising water. Although it was only twenty yards to the woods, it might as well have been the English Channel. The weight of my soggy clothing was dragging me down. Frantically, I called after the sheep, "Don't leave me behind!" A shaggy old ram heard me. He turned and swam back, bleating loudly over the thunder and roaring winds. A large swell broke over my head causing me to choke on a mouthful of water. Just as I started to sink, he gripped my sleeve in his teeth and pulled me to safety.

The ram left me draped over the trunk of a fallen oak on the edge of the woods. "I owe you my life," I sputtered. As a chain of lightning lit up the woods, the ram opened its mouth wide and bleated as if to say, "Think nothing of it." If he had answered me in the King's English I wouldn't have been any more surprised than by what I saw in his mouth. Dental work. The ram not only had fillings, but two gold inlays on his rear molars, and if I wasn't mistaken, his front teeth had been capped.

As the ram swam away into the woods, I yelled after him, "Harry, is that you?" This time the ram didn't answer me, and I had no time to ruminate on the subject of his true identity because the storm was growing in intensity.

Every golfer knows you're not supposed to take shelter in trees during a thunderstorm, but with the water around me continuing to rise, there was little choice but to seek a higher position. Rising above me was a sturdy old oak, veteran of many a violent storm. Using my rain pants as a rope, I lashed myself to a heavy branch about fifteen feet from the top of the tree and prepared to ride it out.

It was the longest night of my life. While the wind continued to roar like a wounded animal, giant thunderbolts exploded across the sky eerily illuminating the landscape of Mount Augustus. The noise was dreadful, but above it all, I swear I heard a man's voice. Sometimes he seemed to be laughing and sometimes he seemed to be shouting angrily. And when he was shouting, the earth trembled violently. Once when lightning struck a nearby tree, a shower of sparks filled the air and I saw something. Perhaps it was my imagination, but silhouetted against the sky was a gigantic man—a bearded figure fifty feet tall. But the next time the lightning flashed, he was gone. At some point in the wee hours of the night exhaustion won out over my terror and I slipped into a dreamless sleep.

When I awoke the storm had gone, leaving in its wake the most glorious morning since creation. The air was cool and fresh, and every tree was filled with singing birds. The fairway below, a tossing sea only hours before had become lush with new grass. In fact, the entire landscape of the thirteenth hole had been completely transformed during the night. Then a man's booming voice called to me from the fairway.

"Wha' are ye doin' up thair?"

Just below me was a barrel-chested old fellow with a white mustache. Decked out in tweed cap and a Norfolk jacket, he reminded me of the paintings of Old Tom Morris.

"Surviving the hurricane," I answered. I untied myself from the tee and began to climb down.

The old gentleman was incredulous. "A hurricane, ye say? Heer at Mount Augustus?"

"A tidal wave crashed right over this fairway," I replied. "Didn't you see it?"

"Canna say tha' Ah did," the man replied. "Bit o' drizzle perhaps, durin' tha reconstruction, nuthin' more."

"Reconstruction?"

The old gentleman gestured down the length of the fairway with a sweep of his arm.

" 'Tis grand, dunna ye think?"

Until that moment I hadn't really looked at how the hole had changed. While it was still a par four, dogleg left, the waste area in front of the tee was now a steep ravine con-

nected to the landing area by a suspension bridge. The
piney woods that framed the hole on the left side of the
fairway had been washed away leaving a grassy hillside
that dropped off precipitously to the ocean. The ocean?

"So, lad, wha' do ye think?" the old man asked again.
He seemed very excited, very pleased with himself. "Do
ye like it?"

"I suppose so," I answered. "But I really don't see what
was wrong with it before."

"Ah donna' take yer meanin'."

"I mean, it was already a challenging hole—at least for
me."

"Ye dinna think 'twas boring? Ah mean, dinna ye think
tha dropoff intae tha woods was a wee bit obvious?"

"Maybe," I answered. "But on the other hand, isn't a
dropoff down a seven-hundred-foot cliff a little out of character for the rest of the course? After all, the ocean's nowhere near here. Or at least it didn't used to be."

"Ah like tha sound o' sea birds," he said wistfully. As
if on cue, a large oceangoing gull lit on his shoulder carrying a sprig of azalea in its beak. "Besides, cliffs make a
dandy hazard," he continued expansively. "Ah'd like tae
see Bertie gie outta this one!"

"Well, it does make for a spectacular view," I admitted.

"Aye, an' ye hae room tae breathe!" he said with pride.
"Ye'll see noone o' those fancy cottages squeezin' tha life
oot o' tha fairways at Mount Augustus, laddie. Playin' on
coorses like tha' is more like billiards than gowf. An' another thing, ye won't find noone o' those wee highways
cuttin' through tha coorse, neither."

"You mean cart paths?" I asked.

"Wha'evir ye call 'em, they're an abomination," he said
passionately. "All they do is encourage gowfers tae race
'round tha coorse like a bunch o' tinkers in their wagons,
scarin' tha birds an' woodland creatures."

"So, who are you anyway?" I asked cautiously. "The
god of architects or something?"

"Me friends call me Mac," replied the old gentleman, extending his hand.

"Tom Cruickshank."

"Aye, tha lad frum New York tha' Harry brought wi' him," said Mac with a twinkle in his eye.

"You know who I am?"

"Aye, Ah've bin watchin' yer progress wi' great interest," Mac replied. Then he turned and from behind him produced a carry bag covered with a thin film of mud. "These wudna' be yer clubs now, wud they?"

"Where did you find them?"

"Oh, heer an' there aboot tha fairway," he answered vaguely. "Where's yer ball, lad?"

"I don't know," I said. "Last time I saw it, it was spinning in the air over the fairway about two hundred fifty yards out."

Mac walked back toward the tee about twenty yards or so, looking skyward every few yards. Suddenly he stopped and snapped his fingers and something landed in his hand.

"Two hundred yards tae be exact," he said, handing me my ball. "Most amateurs wildly overestimate tha lengths o' their drives."

"I usually get a lot of roll," I said, feeling a little defensive.

"Ah'm sure ya do, laddie," said the old gentleman.

"I'm not sure what to do in this situation," I said.

" 'Tis easy enough, laddie. Ye must tae a drop."

"A free drop?"

"Nay, 'twas an unplayable lie, now wasn't it? Either tha' or a lost ball. In either case, laddie, 'tis a one-stroke penalty."

"That's ridiculous," I shot back. "If it hadn't been for that hurricane, or the 'reconstruction' as you call it, that ball would've landed right here in the middle of the fairway."

"True enuff," the old man agreed readily. "But tha's na wha' happened, now is it? Yer ball was held in tha air by tha force o' tha winds. An' how is tha' different frum a ball tha' lodges in a tree on its way tae tha fairway?

Whether 'tis a leafy tree or a pocket o' air, hardly seems tae matter."

"That's completely illogical," I snapped. I could feel the color rising up my neck. "There's no way I'm taking a penalty stroke here."

" 'Tis either tha' or return yer ball tae whar we found it," Mac replied, pointing to a fluffy cloud floating above us. There was now an edge to his voice. "Whar's bloody MacTavish whin ye needs him?"

"MacTavish?" I queried. "He does rules, yes?"

" 'Tis a thankless task, but somebody's ga' ta do it," Mac replied with a grimace.

I remembered Weyland's warning back in the foundry and suddenly thought better of challenging the strange old man on his interpretation of the rules. If there was ever a time when discretion was the better part of valor, this was it.

"No need to get the officials involved," I said, managing a phony smile. "It's probably just a local rule I'm not familiar with."

I extended my arm out from my shoulder and dropped the ball, whereupon it plugged in the soggy fairway.

"Lift clean and place?" I asked with a smile.

"Ye gods, man. 'Tis na tha bloody PGA Tour," Mac replied with exasperation. "All raight, but jist this once," he said. "On account o' tha 'hurricane' an' everything."

Mac walked the rest of the hole with me, and despite his strictness was a fine companion. Perhaps I was a little stiff from spending the night lashed to a tree, or maybe it was the lack of a proper breakfast, but for whatever reason, I was all over the course the rest of the way. I sliced my second shot into the brush on the right side of the fairway about 120 yards up, and like a seasoned caddy, he located the ball nestled under the limb of a hickory sapling.

"Great, now what am I supposed to do?"

"Play it as it lays, laddie," replied Mac with a lift of his bushy brows. "An' be a man about it."

"Play it as it lays," I repeated sullenly. "I've never understood what's so damned magical about that. Most of the time it just means you're the recipient of some hideous accident, or the carelessness of somebody else."

"Yer missin' tha point, laddie," said Mac. "Gowf is na jist a game, 'tis a divination system, if ya will. 'Tis tha I Ching, tha Kabala, an' yer horoscope all rolled into one gigantic fortune cookie. Strikin' tha ball is na different from castin' bones aboot a sacred circle."

"So, if I move the ball, I'll be getting the wrong message?"

"An' more importantly, ye'll be cheatin'."

After considerable slashing around the underbrush, I managed to get the ball back to the fairway. I chunked my next shot and ended up in even worse condition, nestled against the trunk of a tree about fifty yards from the green.

"What's the message this time?" I asked sarcastically. "You're an idiot for thinking you could ever play this game?"

Mac raised his finger to his lips and gave me a stern, reproving look.

"Quiet down, Tom. Yer makin' a powerful lot o' noise whin ye shud be listenin'."

"Listening to what?"

"Tae tha voice inside ya."

"The voice inside me says I'm an idiot for ever taking up golf."

"Tha's noo voice. 'Tis nuthin' but yer overstimulated mind prattlin'. Ah'm speakin' o' tha small quiet voice within, Tommy boy."

"New Yorkers don't have those, Mac."

Totally exasperated, the old man lifted me at least a foot off the ground and shouted in my face, "If ye canna hear tha' voice inside, thin hear me, laddie. And if ye canna hear me, thin read my lips!"

He dropped me like a sack of bones and continued.

"If ye believe tha old Chinaman, Lao Tse, gowf 'tis a lot like war, Tommy. Thair are times whin ye canna overpower tha course, but must run an' hide or tae wha'iver

tha course will give ye. Tha's what bad lies are all aboot, lad. They're tha signposts along tha way."

I looked down at my ball still nestled against the gnarled roots of the oak tree. "So, what's the signpost say about this lie, Mac?"

"Well, each lie has its own special meanin', Tom. If you're lying against a tree trunk or hae a slab o' protruding rock underneath yer ball, 'tis time tae tread carefully in life. 'Tis risky business tae forge ahead like a bull. 'Tis na only true o' gowf, but o' business an' love, too. If ye fail tae take heed, ye could injure yerself or worse! Ah ken a fella down in Florida who tried tae play out o' such a lie. His ball was up against a tree much like yers an' whin he whacked at it wi' his wedge, tha ball ricocheted off the tree an' struck 'em between tha eyes."

"Was he hurt bad?"

Mac took off his cap and shook his head wearily. "A fatal blow, Ah'm afraid."

"You mean the ball killed him?"

"Nay, na tha ball. He was so angry tha' his ticker exploded on tha spot." Mac replaced his cap and clucked. "A classic type A personality, Ah'm afraid."

"Well, I'm not getting killed over a game of golf," I replied.

Leaning over, I plucked the ball from its resting place among the roots of the oak tree.

"Takin' an unplayable lie, are ye?"

"Something like that," I said, and tossed the ball into the middle of the fairway. Since I hadn't taken the official two clubs' distance before dropping the ball, it was abundantly clear to Mac that I had no intention of taking a penalty stroke. In any case, when I turned around the old gentleman had disappeared without so much as a footprint in the soggy fairway.

Suddenly it became unnaturally dark and quiet. A cloud passed in front of the sun and the songbirds that filled the trees along the fairways fell silent. Even the crashing of the waves on the other side of the fairway abruptly stopped. I had the sudden impression I'd made a big mistake.

"Now you've done it." A small man in a jacket and knickers waded out of the tall fescue grass on the side of the fairway.

"Done what?" I asked.

"Don't act innocent with me, mister," he replied. He took out a small spiral-bound notebook and made a notation. "You know damned well what you've done. The Great God MacKenzie reached out to you, and you turned your back on him."

"That old man was MacKenzie?"

"Wearing one of his gentler faces," replied the man with an unpleasant smile. "He has others that you won't find so amusing, I assure you."

"And who are you?" I asked, knowing the answer.

"Why, I'm MacTavish, Lord Protector of the Rules of Golf and Counsel to the Great God MacKenzie himself."

The Fable of the Great God MacKenzie

Although poets have speculated throughout the ages, no one really knows where the Great God MacKenzie came from or when he came into being. Some say that he was a progeny of Zeus, the Ober god of the Greek Pantheon, and like so many younger sons throughout the ages, struck out on his own to conquer new worlds when he realized he would not inherit his father's position.

However, most poets and scribes believe that MacKenzie was there at the beginning when the world was without form and the heavens a dark vault without stars. Though time did not yet exist, MacKenzie slumbered through what would have been millions of earth years, dreaming vaguely of verdant meadows populated by strange bipedal beings.

In his dream these beings entertained themselves by knocking a small white ball through the fields of this imaginary world—a vision that caused the dreaming god to smile though there was no one to see. Now, when a god dreams things they tend to come to life with extraordinary regularity, and that's just what happened in this case. MacKenzie stirred from his slumber to see a shining white ball, like the one in his dreams, spinning before his eyes. And in his hands was a thick branch of wood with a gnarled tip.

Still in his dream MacKenzie swung his legs from the cushion of mist that had held him in sweet repose for so long. He stretched his arms and swept the mist away with his branch of wood, revealing an empty blackness. Only the little sphere, so full of energy and life that it glowed from deep within its center, remained. He placed his boots firmly on the void and floated there for a time before he grasped the shiny spinning ball in his huge hand, and it continued to turn even as it rested. In his dream he smiled, releasing the ball into the void and it spun to his feet where it floated, waiting.

He drew back the stick and hit the ball for all he was worth, exploding it into a billion pieces that began to scatter across the universe forming stars, planets, and comets. Soon thereafter, the delightful little bipedal beings filled the planet called Earth and busied themselves building towns, cities, nations, and ultimately, although it was not yet known to them, golf courses.

While all this was happening, the Great God MacKenzie slumbered until the brightness of the new sun awakened him and he strode onto the Earth to claim Mount Augustus as his own.

This is known as "The Big Drive Theory of the Universe."

Was it possible that this mousy little clerk was the same MacTavish everybody had warned me about?

"I see that you've heard of me, mortal," said MacTavish with an evil grin. "Too bad you didn't heed the warnings, but then I'm not surprised. I've yet to meet a mortal with any real intelligence. Or moral fiber."

I looked out at my ball resting in the middle of the fairway. "So, what am I supposed to do now?"

"Do whatever pleases you, Mr. Cruickshank," the little man replied. He closed his notebook and raised it up for me to see. "It doesn't really matter. I have almost everything I need. Not even Mulligan can save you now."

CHAPTER 14

Tea for Two

In which Tom learns the true nature of cruelty

After my run-in with MacTavish I seriously considered packing it in. The little weasel had made it clear that my goose was already cooked; so what could possibly lie ahead for me but more aggravation and the chance to dig myself a deeper hole—if that was possible? Things looked pretty bleak, no question about it. The Great God MacKenzie—the inventor of golf himself, had taken me under his wing, and not only hadn't I believed it was him but I had had the unmitigated gaul to improve my lie right under his nose. Why he hadn't turned me into a sand devil or consigned me to the lowest job in the foundry on the spot was a mystery. There seemed to be nothing left to do, except continue the round and hope for redemption along the way.

As soon as I left the thirteenth green, I was enveloped in darkness. It seemed fitting. Instinctively I reached out to feel my way forward and found the shaft of an old club stuck in the ground and then another. Somebody had finally marked a trail and I followed it hand over hand through the closely packed trees until I emerged in a clearing that was, in some demented architect's twisted imagination, the thirteenth tee. The pine and oak trees that hugged the edge of the narrow fairway were so huge they turned what had been a bright sunny day into November twilight. The tee box was swallowed in dark shadows and the grass was so damp and cold that I found myself longing for the comfort of Angus's peat fire and even the smell of his haggis. Gnats and mosquitoes began to swarm around my face, and I was afraid to set my bag down for fear of it filling with seepage.

Was it really possible, I wondered, that MacKenzie had actually intended this godforsaken swamp as a golf hole? Or had he created this dank, depressing place moments before to serve as my own private purgatory?

I wasn't alone. Someone was sitting on a wooden bench about ten feet away so covered with moss it was fuzzy as a velour sofa. His back was to me so I couldn't see his face, but it was clear he was a gentleman. The goods he wore were tailored and fit him to a tee. On his head was a straw boater with a black-and-white-striped band. The white collar that emerged from the dove gray woolen suit was high and starched. The handle of an oversized umbrella was hooked to the top rung of the bench.

He had to have known I was there, but he didn't acknowledge me in any way. As I watched, he raised a fine china cup to his lips and sipped from it gracefully before setting it down carefully on a folding picnic bench. The man produced a napkin from his breast pocket with a flourish and gently patted his lips. He refolded it carefully and replaced it, crossed his legs, and waited. I knew he was a god; I just didn't know which one. It wasn't like there was a guidebook.

Damned if I was going to make the first move, I turned my attention to the hole. Branches reached out over the fairway from both sides, touching in the middle to form a dense arch that rose forty or fifty feet in the air and extended out from the tee box more than sixty yards. The center of the fairway beckoned at the end of the leafy tunnel, and the bright sunlight framed by the arch of trees promised warmth and safety. The man recrossed his legs and took another sip from his teacup.

My feet had sunk an inch or so into the soggy turf off the tee box. As I stepped away I lost my footing and staggered to regain my balance. The imprints of my shoes filled immediately, leaving several little swimming pools. The tee box looked like a diagram of the tango at a Fred Astaire dancing school. It was time to break the ice.

"Am I actually supposed to hit from here?" I said.

"You might wait in hopes that perhaps someone will offer to play through," the man answered. "If not, I suppose you would have little choice but to continue." He paused and raised his cup. "Unless you wish to join me in a spot of Earl Grey. A bit too perfumey, but really quite acceptable. Fellow takes his chances when he can't get his own blend." He still hadn't turned to look at me.

"Tea sounds all right."

"Jolly good. Slosh on over, old chap."

I made it to the bench, leaned my bag against the back near his umbrella, and walked around to meet the latest incarnation. Whoever he was, he was not a pleasant man. There was no kindness in his eyes. They were devoid of spirit and feeling. His face was thin and angular, with high cheekbones, a large hook nose, and thin, narrow lips that gave him a disdainful and cruel look. When he smiled perfunctorily in greeting, the effect was chilling. He was classic aristocracy, an arrogant snob with a mean streak.

"Hello, I'm Thomas Cruickshank," I said. He placed his soft pink hand in mine and let it lay there like a catfish sleeping at the bottom of a pond. No question about it, he was upper crust through and through. Suddenly, I felt extremely self-conscious in my ragged rain pants and golf shirt.

"I rather doubt we'll know each other long enough to become familiar so I suggest we leave it at hello." He smiled.

"Okay," I said, "I'm not Thomas Cruickshank after all, and I'm not glad to meet you."

He chuckled politely at my little joke. "Good one," he said. "Now, how about that tea?"

"Please."

The man opened a wicker picnic basket, passed over the china cups and saucers in plain sight, and took out a thick pottery mug with a large handle.

"Hope you'll forgive the servants' tableware, but the good china's been in the family for generations. Mum couldn't tolerate the loss of a single cup."

"No problem," I said, taking the mug. There was a large chip off the handle.

"One lump or two?"

"None, thank you, perhaps a little milk?"

"Ah, just out, I'm afraid."

"Whatever. It's fine as it is."

"I can offer fresh Italian lemon?"

"Sure."

He filled the mug from an ancient thermos, took a tiny slice of lemon from a glass jar, cut it in half with a little silver knife, and handed it to me. A little tea would do wonders to stave off the chill. I took a sip; it was cold as ice. I noticed, however, that steam was rising from the cup sitting on the folding table.

"Satisfactory?" he asked.

"Tastes great," I answered. "A little cold, maybe."

"That infernal thermos is ineffective but I can't offer some from the other or there wouldn't be enough left for myself." He smiled as he added milk to his cup from a tiny container hidden in the bottom of the basket. He shrugged as if he was sure I would understand. I was really beginning to hate this guy.

As we sat sipping our tea on the soggy bench I looked around and decided that the whole effect with the canopy was like sitting in the orchestra of the Metropolitan Opera looking at a painted drop and wing version of the forest primeval. I expected a woman in chain mail and a Viking helmet to enter left and sing forty-five minutes of Wagner. But there was nothing except the silence and the damp and the gentleman who poured cold tea.

"Quite beautiful, isn't it?" he said after a long silence. "Perfect weather, perfect setting."

"All that's missing is heavy rain," I said ironically.

"That would be delightful," he said, "absolutely delightful." He wasn't joking. "A good downpour creates such fantastic havoc, makes the difficult impossible, wouldn't you agree? Perhaps we are kindred spirits after all . . . in spite of your appearance."

"I was kidding," I said.

"Ah, well . . ." He shrugged, pursed his lips, and took another sip. "But that's why this is such a perfect spot, don't you see. Even without rain it's almost impossible to hit away. Creates such exciting opportunities for abject failure. What's better than observing a combination of the elements and the human condition result in total humiliation and embarrassment? More tea?"

"No thank you," I declined politely. "Got to be getting on. I've urgent business to attend to in Calcutta."

"Ah, Kipling, how clever," he said, smiling thinly. "But really, I insist."

"No, really, I've had enough." I turned on the bench to give him my mug just as he balanced his precious cup and saucer on his knee and reached between us to pick up the ancient thermos. We met halfway with a crash and my mug, filled with cold tea, knocked the thermos out of his hand. It fell directly on top of his cup and saucer, smashing them into a million pieces. Shards of delicate bone china littered the bench and the mossy ground at our feet. The mug was fine.

"Oh man, I'm sorry," I blurted.

"Think nothing of it," he answered coldly

"It was an accident. I'm sorry it happened, but it was just an accident."

"It's nothing. I, of course, shall suffer for your clumsiness and you shall suffer nothing, but that's the way of the world. As you say, an accident."

"I guess I'd better go."

He was silent.

Even though I thought the guy was a bore and bad tempered to boot, I actually felt bad about the cup. All my life I'd spilled glasses and broken dishes; it used to drive my mother crazy and I was embarrassed, but there was nothing to be done about it. All I wanted was to tee off and get out of there.

I sloshed back and forth in the muck, looking for a dry spot of ground, trying to pretend he wasn't watching me with unbridled loathing, but I knew he was. I wished he would go away, I didn't want to hit in front of him. But the man was sitting rigidly on the bench, both feet planted firmly on the ground, arms folded across his chest, glaring at me.

Finally, I stopped circling like a bull terrier and staked

my claim on a little piece of marsh. I needed a low power drive to get out of the cave. At least Thunderbolt was the perfect club for the job. With its classic persimmon head, I'd have a much better chance of keeping the ball low. As I lined up the clubhead I realized to my horror that the ball was sinking slowly into the grass. The ground was too wet to hold the weight and, before I could react, the ball itself began to disappear below the surface. Naturally, I was sinking, too, and my shoes were almost covered with water. I scooped the ball out of the muck and re-teed it in another spot, but just as I was at the top of my backswing, the aristocrat started laughing. It was one of the most evil sounds I'd ever heard. Low and deep and so loud the leaves seemed to shake in the trees.

I was so startled I stumbled and fell, landing in an oozing puddle with a resounding splash. As I pulled myself to my feet a peal of high-pitched laughter caused me to fall again. I was completely soaked.

"In my experience a decent golfer has four to six seconds to get the ball off before it sinks too far below ground to hit," he said, smiling broadly. "In your case, however, I'm not certain there is enough time in the world."

"Shut up," I said as I struggled to my feet.

"Frightfully sorry, did I distract you? I certainly hope so."

"Bug off," I snarled as I picked a spot that seemed to hold.

"Oh my, we are cranky today, aren't we?" he replied.

I swung away and came way over the top, resulting in a drive that splashed to earth about fourteen inches from my tee, which had by now all but disappeared into the muck. I was up to my ankles. I leaned over and plucked the ball out of the sucking spongy grass.

"Why you shameless cad," said my tormentor. "I daresay that's another stroke."

"I deserve another shot," I said firmly. "This isn't fair."

"Fair? What, pray tell, is fair? Was it fair that my poor

mum's teacup was shattered because of your clumsiness? Don't talk to me about what's fair, sir."

"Maybe I'll just skip this hole," I said.

"The consequence of that would be severe," he replied. "No one walks the Mountain without playing the game. It can't be done."

"You are one poor excuse for a god," I challenged.

"Perhaps it should rain after all," he answered, popping open his umbrella. Immediately torrents of water cascaded out of the trees. It was raining cats and dogs.

"Hit now, fool," he cried.

"Damn you," I shouted. I was livid. I dropped the ball back on the ground and swung like a demon possessed. In the last second I realized I was forward and way off balance. It was too late.

"NOW, YOU'LL KNOW MY NAME, SIR," he shouted as I was coming through. "THEY CALL MEEEE SHAAAANNNNNK."

I felt the sting as the ball connected with the hosel and I knew that I had indeed shanked a beaut. Again, I landed flat on my butt in the mud and goo. My hands ached from the vibration that had shot up the shaft. I knew the ball had gone hard right, but beyond that I hadn't a clue. Then I heard another loud pop, a crash, and the sound of what could only be my ball ricocheting through the trees.

To my astonishment the ball was flying back and forth, caroming off the limbs near the top of the canopy. The Maxfli deuce had become a crazed white bird flitting maniacally from branch to branch, and it was gaining speed as it flew. Shank folded his umbrella to watch, and the rain ceased. We looked in wonder as the ball moved faster and faster until we realized that not only was it gaining speed but it was losing altitude as well.

"Incoming," I screamed, as the ball zoomed over our heads and banked off a huge oak directly behind where we were standing. The impact echoed through the trees like a rifle shot and we hit the ground just before it streaked back over our heads, disappearing into the blinding sunlight and the fairway beyond.

"Well, it looks as if in spite of my best efforts you've cleared the trees," he sneered. "Just remember you are lying three wherever it is."

"You mean I can go?"

"Unfortunately, yes."

"I am sorry about the cup."

"Don't be absurd, dear boy," replied Shank. "The cup was merely a device to torment you. Frosting on the cake, so to speak." Then he opened his umbrella and as he walked into the woods, the rain started to fall again in buckets.

When I emerged from the trees to find my ball I felt like a soldier who had just walked forty days out of the jungle. The warmth of the sun was a tonic and I raised my face to the bright blue sky, thanking the Lord I had made it out alive. What had started out as a casual practice round with a kindly old mentor had turned into something resembling the Battle of Guadalcanal. I dropped to the dry ground and began to remove my shoes and socks. Of course I had nothing to change into and kicked myself for never remembering to pack spares of anything.

I sat in the fairway scratching my legs like a hobo and feeling more and more uncomfortable. The heat from the sun was turning the mud on my body into dust. I itched all over and was beginning to smell like the Swamp Thing, but there seemed to be little choice except to play on. As I stood to pull an iron from my bag a flock of small birds flew from the trees on the left and attracted my attention.

Almost hidden in the treeline was an arched doorway of carefully manicured boxwood hedges looking like the entrance to a formal garden. The well-trimmed grass of the fairway cut a path through the short rough like a green carpet to the foot of the opening. I walked over to get a closer look.

The Fable of Shank—the God of Cruelty

Of all the gods on Mount Augustus there are no records to prove that Shank was actually born. In fact, it is certain that he sprang like a poison mushroom from one of Fergus's long forgotten compost heaps. As a youth Shank hid deep in the woods, afraid to show himself. Soon, however, he discovered a chilly pleasure in disrupting players' concentration by making unsettling noises as they were about to hit the ball. The resulting loss of focus meant that they would inevitably connect on parts of the club not designed for striking. The resulting shots were so embarrassing and humiliating that even the most stoic of the gods would be reduced to tears of frustration.

Shank grew to godhood and roamed the woods in raging solitude for many years before he was accidentally discovered by Ichabod, who was searching for berries to feed his cockatoo and mongoose. It was the Tutor who took it upon himself to reform the wild lad. But all he succeeded in doing was giving Shank a superficial aura of manners and decorum that allowed him the occasional foray in public. Sadly, Ichabod also gave his charge a basic knowledge of the fundamentals of the game, thereby improving his ability to destroy an unsuspecting golfer's round. Many of the gods are convinced that Shank could as easily have been a serial killer had he not chosen to focus his maniacal energies on the ancient game.

Shank is a solitary god and to this day refuses to involve himself in the business of the mountain, preferring to live on his own without contact of any kind. Even he has no idea why he is so angry and without feeling or why he chooses to wreak havoc on undeserving golfers with a coldness unparalleled in the history of pantheons.

As The MacKenzie put it, "Sum apples are just bad and should be plucked from tha barrel." But he is tolerant to a fault and for reasons of his own chooses to let Shank remain loose in the world.

The entrance was beautifully cared for and I wondered if it was the work of Fergus and his grounds crew. I stepped

underneath the archway and walked a few feet into the
woods before stopping to get my bearings. In the near distance was the sound of running water. My heart leapt. Running water meant there was a stream or something nearby;
I could bathe and rinse off my muddy clothes. I hurried
out into the fairway, retrieved my shoes and socks, and set
off to find the source of the sound. Midway down the path
it stopped.

Ahead of me was another boxwood arch and through it
a clearing. I stepped through the arch and found myself in
an outdoor locker room. Somebody had transplanted the
entire contents of a clubhouse, except for the walls, into
the middle of the woods. Rough benches were arranged in
front of rows of tall, dark green lockers that blended perfectly with the trees around them. No branches blocked the
sunlight here, and the clearing was pleasantly warm and
comfortable. I walked over thick, neatly trimmed grass to
a bank of lockers and listened. There was nothing but silence. The air was still and quiet. It occurred to me that I
hadn't heard a stream at all. Somewhere around here
would be showers, towels, and soap.

There seemed to be acres of lockers altogether. They
formed a giant maze bisected by a wide center aisle. It was
so large the attendants probably had to use an overnight
parcel service to ship towels to the outer regions. Apparently, Mount Augustus had a lot of members. As I worked
my way down the aisle, I heard the murmur of conversation far away but couldn't see a soul.

Taking a deep breath I turned around a corner and crept
down the aisle, passing row after row of identical lockers
and benches. Mirrors were mounted on the ends and I got
a good look at my filthy condition as I tiptoed forward. I
would have crossed to the other side of the street if I saw
myself coming.

Suddenly the silence was shattered by angry shouting
coming from the far end. I darted into a row and plastered myself against the lockers. I was following a basic
rule of survival in Manhattan—avoid loud arguments be-

tween people you don't know in case they're carrying automatic weapons. Then just as suddenly as it had begun, the shouting stopped. Either things had been ironed out or I was sneaking up on the scene of a homicide.

Then someone yelled, "Cruickshank is a bloody fool!" and I realized they were talking about me. The loud crack of a stick hitting a bench echoed through the locker room just as I reached the end of the aisle. Now I wasn't so sure I wanted to be involved.

Planting a foot on one of the benches, I hoisted myself up on the row of lockers and rolled to the far edge. I just missed being discovered as the two men turned the corner and stopped below me. My plan was to jump down into the next row and head for the trees, but then I recognized one of the voices. It was Harry, and he was telling the other man that I was a good guy in spite of my failings. Failings?

I inched my way to the edge and peeked down on Harry's bald head. Soaking wet and wrapped in a large terry cloth towel, he was talking to a man wearing a tweed cap who was furiously searching through an open locker. It was the Great God MacKenzie himself! I pulled my head back and listened as I stared up into the blue and cloudless sky.

"Give him a chance, Mac," pleaded Harry.

"Tha lad improved his lie under me very nose, Harry! 'Tis enuff, na more," MacKenzie shouted. I heard the locker door slam shut. "MacTavish seen him as well. 'Tis outta me hands, 'tis finished."

"C'mon, Mac," said Harry.

"An' ye, Harry, hae let me down, too," MacKenzie continued. "Ye've become part o' tha very thing ye were charged tae prevent. Ah send ye oot intae tha wide world tae keep tha spirit o' gowf alive, an' before Ah know it, ye're rippin' down forests, an' drainin' marshes, drivin' wee creatures frum their natural abodes. . . ."

"That's awfully strong talk, Mac," Harry protested.

"Sure, I've made a few dollars in real estate, but I was buildin' golf courses, spreading the game ..."

"Ach, ye're spreadin' somethin', all right, an' tis na tha game, Harry Brady. Two hundred dollars a round? Canna ye explain tha' tae me, Mr. Protector o' tha Game? An' wha' aboot all these wee pictures o' bears an' crocodiles an' fancy names plastered all o'er tha place?"

"Mac, you're takin' things outta context here ..."

"Am Ah? Wuild tha' Ah were, Harry Brady. Perhaps MacTavish is raight, perhaps all mortals are weak and corrupt. Now because o' yer weakness, auld friend, Ah may hae na choice but tae wi'draw tha game...."

There was a long silence, and I wondered for a moment whether Harry and MacKenzie had left the locker room. Then a soul-wrenching sigh echoed through the locker room.

"Mac, I just want to hang on till the end of the year," said Harry finally. "Then I'll retire. I'm negotiating with a Japanese group to buy my business and then we're going down to Hilton Head for good. Six or eight months and the boy will be ready to take over. I promise I'll come here at least once a month...."

"Harry, six months o' your time 'tis more than twenty years here on tha Mountain," MacKenzie shouted in return. "After forty years o' cuming heer, ye shud know tha'! Ah canna hold oot tha' lang. MacTavish is pushin' me an' he's ga' plenty o' support this time, Harry. Plenty o' support. Cruickshank mus' stay tha coorse, or MacTavish will hae won."

"But the boy needs seasoning, Mac," Harry pleaded. "He never saw the game the way it was supposed to be. He never saw Hogan or Snead in their prime. He thinks Bobby Jones is a line of clothing, for goodness sake."

"Harry, ye know there can be only one. 'Tis always been tha' way. Only one, Harry. 'Tis time, auld friend. Ye know wha' needs to be done."

"The boy will make it, Mac," Harry insisted. "You'll see, he'll make it."

"He'd better, Harry Brady, fer Ah canna interfere more."

"Then wish me luck, Mac."

"Ye'll need more than luck, auld friend. But luck ta ye, Harry Brady, fer all the gud it does," MacKenzie said quietly, and left Harry standing in the aisle.

I wondered if the one MacKenzie was talking about was the same one Ichabod referred to. It was time for a chat. I swung my legs over the edge of the lockers and looked down at Harry.

"Hi, Harry. How's it going?"

"Tom?" Harry was so surprised he almost lost the grip on his towel. "How much did you hear?"

"Enough," I replied as I jumped to the ground.

We stood in the aisle looking at each other.

"So, what was that all about?" I asked as coolly as I could.

"You're going to have to trust me on this, son," he said.

"No problem, Harry, look what you've done for me so far."

Harry snorted and started walking toward the shower stalls at the end of the aisle. I stood there watching him leave, wondering what to do next. I decided to take the bull by the horns.

"Toe Wedge and Hoeffer send their regards," I said.

Harry wheeled around and gave me a long, cold stare. "So, I guess they told you I set them up."

"Not in so many words," I replied. "But they didn't have that long to chat. They're pulling down some long hours in their new careers."

"Let's cut the crap, Tom. They didn't need my help to get where they are; they did it to themselves. And you know it."

"Okay, Harry. Cards on the table. Why did you bring me on this little journey? So you could take me into your business—whatever that is—or because MacKenzie needs bodies to stuff golf balls?"

"Is that what you think, son?"

"I was in the foundry, Harry. Weyland wasn't surprised to see me. I, on the other hand, was a little surprised at what I just heard here in the old locker room. This is supposed to be a game."

"You're not gonna self-destruct on me, are you, Tom?"

"Can it, Harry. Why is all this suddenly up to that runt MacTavish?" I sat down on a bench. "What have you gotten me into?"

Harry seemed genuinely hurt. We stared at each other in the sunlit locker room. As angry and worried as I was, I felt we were very close to crossing a line from which there would be no stepping back. Harry seemed to sag a little. His shoulders drooped and he sighed deeply before he walked to an open locker next to the showers and started to dress. I followed him and leaned against a row, waiting.

"You know why some sayings become old sayings?" he asked as he buttoned his shirt.

"Ah, Harry."

"Because they're so damn true they don't need any explanation. I brought Toe Wedge to the mountain, I brought Hoeffer, too. The fact they didn't leave has everything to do with them and nothing with me. You make your bed, you lie in it. Sound familiar? Well, that's how it is, no matter what I want or you want or anyone else wants. That is how it is. True, you're in a bit of a jam right now, so am I, but you did it to yourself just like Toe Wedge, Hoeffer, and me. One thing I'll tell you is it's worth trying to sort out. What I told you yesterday is still true. You've got a chance to do something special and that hasn't changed. Bottom line, Tom, you've got a choice. You can play on and take your chances, or you can lie down and die like an old dog.

"Personally, I'd like to see you finish the Mountain, play it out. But just like every other damn thing in this life, it's up to you." He paused and pursed his lips thoughtfully as he tied his shoes. "And now, son, I gotta go. I got my own problems."

"Sure, Mr. Brady," I said coldly. "Just do whatever you need to do. Don't worry about me, no sir, I'll be just fine."

"Good," he answered evenly and walked out of the locker room.

Harry didn't look back, he just disappeared into the trees. To hell with him, I thought to myself. I was in this thing up to my neck and I was going to see it through, but first I was going to take a shower.

Quickly I removed my muddy clothes. Might as well face the music clean, I thought, as I helped myself to a rough cotton towel from a neat stack on one of the benches. I took a bar of soap from a khaki bucket that sat near the showers and stepped inside a stall. Above my head a rope dangled from a bulging canvas bucket. I gave it a yank and water warmed from the sun was pouring over me. The soap was rough but fragrant, and as the grime fell away, I began to feel better.

I squeezed the last of the mud from my rain pants, thanking the wizards at Gortex for creating something so synthetic that it dried almost instantly. As I was drying off I walked back to the row where Mac and Harry had their little chat.

MacKenzie's name was engraved on the corner locker. Only a green wooden door separated me from his personal stash. I couldn't leave the clearing without seeing what a god stuffed in his locker. I opened the door carefully. Inside were nothing but a stack of clean boxer shorts and a lonely bottle of Aqua Velva. I was disappointed, expecting to find things like lightning holders or enchanted putters, but clean underwear was awfully appealing. I had nothing on under my rain pants and there was a long way to go.

So, after making sure I was alone, I snatched a pair of shorts and quickly slipped them on. As an afterthought I splashed on a bracing shot of AV. Though I wouldn't have admitted it in a million years the smell was kind of good.

As I closed the door to MacKenzie's locker I felt like a new man. On my way out I grabbed a towel.

My bag was in the fairway where I'd left it. I spent a quiet moment cleaning my clubs, taking special care to shine up my beloved Thunderbolt. I had a feeling I was going to need it.

CHAPTER 15

The Watery Grave

In which Tom takes a walk on the wild side

My round at Mount Augustus began with a feeling of incredible good fortune—like a Hollywood hopeful being discovered at a drugstore counter, but after fourteen holes on the Mountain, I was feeling used. My mind was still spinning from the confrontation with Harry, but amazingly enough, I wasn't really angry or even frightened, just exhausted. Harry Brady had lured me to Mount Augustus just like the fox had lured Pinocchio and the donkey boys to Pleasure Island, and the way things were going, I expected to sprout ears and a tail at any moment.

I had become the pawn in somebody else's game all right. The only trouble was, I still didn't know the rules or even how to keep score. After what I overheard MacKenzie saying, I was beginning to think that Ichabod wasn't a total idiot after all. Incredible as it seemed, the Great God MacKenzie apparently had believed that I was *The One*, the mortal with the pure heart that would save golf, or the maiden or whatever—at least up until the moment I improved my lie right under his nose. But Ichabod's story was vague and confusing at best and I certainly didn't feel chosen. And now, who knew what the golf gods had in store for me? I had the uncomfortable feeling they would all be waiting at the eighteenth green—poised to sacrifice my blood upon an altar, or at least ready to make me cut their lawns for all eternity.

At that moment, however, I didn't care. I was a man desperately in need of a break, and I thought I'd found it when I stood on the fifteenth tee. The hole featured three terraced tees that stepped gently down to an island green ringed by a moat of sparkling blue water. To my weary eyes it was an oasis rather than what it really was—a pitifully small target ringed by diabolical hazards.

Since it was a par three, there was no need to use a peg. Instead, I kicked up a little ridge of turf, balancing my ball on top just as I planned. The pin was on the far back of the green making the hole play out at about 158 yards and it was all downhill. A three-quarter six-iron would allow me to make a nice smooth swing and leave plenty of club to clear the water. Well, I put that nice smooth swing on it just like the plan, but either I caught it a little fat or the wind must've kicked up, because my tee ball splashed down into the water hazard only three short yards from the green.

Normally, this would have provoked a club-throwing frenzy, but I had achieved what my grandfather thought was a major life's goal. I had become a true stoic on Mount Augustus, and losing my ball in a water hazard now seemed little more than an inconvenience. Shrugging it off, I patted down my pockets looking for another ball, but they were stone empty. The cupboard was also bare in the pocket of my carry bag, and the side pocket as well. So much for stoicism. I started to curse.

There should have been at least a dozen old balls in my bag, placed there by my own hand before meeting Harry on the practice tee—balls with corporate logos left over from outings, yellow and orange balls hawked out of the rough, plus a couple of new balatas wearing big smiles that I was too cheap to throw away. There should also have been a sleeve of new balls with Pine Valley logos in my windbreaker. Was it possible all of them were gone in only fifteen holes? Good God, that was better than a ball a hole. Another fruitless search confirmed I was completely out of balls and three holes from the house. A swim in the water hazard would be necessary in order to finish the round.

But I got a break at the bottom of the hill; a small round boat was tucked away in the reeds. Constructed of saplings lashed together with vines and then coated with pitch, the rudderless craft was watertight but difficult to maneuver. My first attempts at paddling forward merely spun the craft around in circles, but I soon got the hang of it and splashed toward the area where my ball had disappeared.

Up close the water was very murky and deeper than it appeared from the tee box. Since the boat was more unstable than a canoe, I slid my right arm slowly into the water until it was over my shoulder, but couldn't touch bottom.

Suddenly there was a splashing sound behind me, as if a fish had just risen for a fly. But instead of the silvery flash of a trout's flank, a man's forearm rose slowly from the middle of the pond.

Muscular and pale as alabaster, it was entwined with water plants, and delicately balanced in the long, slender fingers of its hand was a pristine golf ball. Even at fifteen feet the slightly pink color identified it as the king of balatas—a tour model, undoubtedly 100 compression.

I paddled quickly to the outstretched arm and tried to steady the boat while leaning out as far as possible to snatch the prize away. Naturally the little boat capsized, spilling me headfirst into the hazard with a splash. As soon as I entered the water, my head struck something hard and large hands started pulling me down. Two giant blue eyes closed in on mine and then I felt a violent, hairy kiss upon my lips before losing consciousness.

When I came to, I was coughing up water, confused, and lying on my back inside some sort of stone structure with a vaulted ceiling. Squatting a few feet away from me was an enormous man wearing a green hooded tunic of rough linen, decorated with live water plants. New York survival instincts kicked in immediately and I jumped to the only possible conclusion: a psychotic homeless man had abducted me and dragged me into the bowels of the subway system. A violent spasm of coughing shook my body and I rolled over on my stomach, looking for a door.

"Ah, so he lives!" said the giant.

"I hope you're taking your medications," I said, sitting up.

"Pills and potions, ya mean?" The man's pale blue eyes opened wide in a deranged expression.

"I guess so."

The giant man smiled widely, inflated his cheeks, and spat out a round white object. It was a golf ball emblazoned with a bright blue Hartless & Craven logo.

"There's a pill for ya, laddie."

"What happened? How did I get here?"

"When ye fell in off the wee silly boat, we cracked noggins," replied the man with a grin. He drew back his hood and leaned his head forward. "Ah've ga' an egg on me melon tha size o' a featherie ball. Ye were a gonner fer sure."

"You didn't kiss me, did you?" I asked.

" 'Twas tha breath o' life Ah gave ye," the giant explained indignantly.

"I suppose I should be grateful," I said.

"Yer welcome, Ah'm sure," said the man. He leaned forward and offered his hand. "Ah'm Horace."

As I took the giant's hand, Harry's story flooded into my mind. The same thing had happened to him on his first trip to Mount Augustus. I was following his footsteps.

"Horace, the God of Hazards?" I asked.

"Aye, some calls me tha'," replied Horace. "But nae more prattling now. 'Tis a poor host tha' fails tae feed his guest. Follow on tae me quarters."

Grabbing a stubby torch from the wall, Horace led me down a winding passageway lined with ancient stalagmites and stalactites deeper and deeper into the cave. The sound of dripping water was everywhere. Abruptly the passageway opened into a much larger cavern, a great room with a vaulted ceiling that sparkled like new fallen snow under lamplight. Voices from an angelic choir echoed from every corner of the cave. It was as if the very rocks were singing.

"That's beautiful," I said.

"Jist Eunuch," Horace grumbled. "Up thair on tha wall."

A single angel seemed to flutter near the ceiling, singing in the purest, most heart-wrenching soprano imaginable. Each note multiplied a thousand times over, echoing again and again as it bounced off the walls until Horace's humble cave rivaled the grandest oratories in Europe.

"He's an angel!" I exclaimed.

"Ah hardly think so," laughed Horace. "Eunuch's a gud climber, but he canna fly, so far as Ah know. Around heer, he's known as the God o' Lost Balls."

Eunuch was balanced on two small rocky extrusions high

above us looking like a slightly damaged cherub. His skin was as pale as chalk powder; his lank hair a dirty gold; and even from that distance his eyes glistened like filmy blue stars that were slightly crossed.

"Ah found him wanderin' tha fairways a couple o' thousand years back after tha gods o' Rome had dropped by fer a visit," Horace continued. "Tha lad was always stealin' birds' eggs and round pebbles tae play wi', an' since Ah had a great store o' lost balls frum tha hazards, Ah took tha' poor child under me wing, so tae speak."

"What's he doing up there?"

"He's mortaring gowf balls intae tha walls," Horace replied. "Tha's why they sparkle so. He's na all there, ye ken. So, Ah canna control him. I jist try tae keep him busy."

Over an extraordinary meal of roasted brown trout and fresh berries, Horace and I exchanged our life stories—an increasingly familiar ritual for me at Mount Augustus. While we talked, Eunuch sat happily beside him, tucking into a bowl of oversize blueberries and fish roe.

Horace brushed through the child's golden hair with his fingers, causing him to trill and purr like a house cat. "Tha lad only eats round food," explained Horace in an aside. "But beware, young Tom. Our Eunuch 'tis a terrible nuisance tae mortal gowfers. He luvs round objects so much tha' if he focuses on yer ball, he can will it intae a water hole or a patch o' thick clover wi'out even touchin' it."

After we finished our meal, I recounted the last few days, including my trip to Pine Valley, meeting Harry Brady, and my encounters with the gods. When I told Horace about jousting with Fergus, he spat into the fire with disgust.

"So, you've met the former rodent, hae ye?" said Horace. "Ya should've killed him when ye had tha chance, lad. Can't leave well enough alone, tha' one. Always trying to improve me hazards, as if ye could improve perfection."

"But isn't that his job?"

"Dunna make me laugh," snorted Horace. "His job is tae swim round a pond wi' sticks in his gob, an' he still

----

The Fable of Horace—The God of Hazards

Before settling down with the Goddess Rowena, the Great God MacKenzie ran ripshod through the woodlands, seducing nymphs by the hundreds and siring children by the thousands, much to the disgust of his half-sister, the Goddess Laura. The director of a home for fallen wood nymphs, Laura decided there was but one way to stop MacKenzie's excesses, and that was to gain control over Mount Augustus itself. Disguised as a wood nymph, Laura lured MacKenzie into a dalliance on a summer's afternoon.

The following spring, Horace was born and delivered to Angus, the God of Starters, to raise. Even as a child, Horace, comely and strong, was a daring and bold golfer. Frequently in trouble because of his hell-bent style, Horace could get up and down from anywhere, and, in fact, preferred the challenge of playing from difficult lies to the safety of the fairway.

One day Wendell and Ruppert were skulking about the primary rough. Hearing voices, they hid behind a tree and saw the Goddess Laura telling the young Horace the truth of his birth; how he was born underneath the water on the fifteenth hole, attended by dryads and the nyads and how he would assume power on Augustus. Wendell and Ruppert hightailed it back to MacTavish with the delicious news. MacTavish used this information to his advantage, warning the Goddess Rowena, MacKenzie's new bride, that Horace and his mother intended to usurp MacKenzie's position, and therefore her own. Rowena demanded of MacKenzie that Horace be destroyed and Laura banished.

So MacKenzie banished Laura to the Land of Alleys where the gods played endlessly at bowling and consumed tasteless ale. But he had no heart to destroy his own offspring, who, in fact, had no designs at all on his realm. So Horace was shipped to the nether regions of Mount Augustus—to the out-of-bounds areas, the primary rough, the lateral hazards, the water holes and bunkers. Upon pain of death, he was never to eat the nectar and ambrosia of the gods again or step upon the fairways or greens. Horace accepted the punishment with a gusto that surprised no one, least of all The MacKenzie, who knew how much the young adventurer loved the rough-and-tumble life.

----

wud be if tha so-called Great God MacKenzie had left well enough alone. Did ye evir see tha beaver feed?"

Recalling the tuna fish sandwich I had given Fergus as a peace offering, I nodded yes.

"Disgusting, isn't it? He'll eat anything. An' tha' damn goat o' his. Ah ken they hae more than a professional relationship, if ye tae my meanin'."

"What do you mean?" I asked.

"Well, ye ken tha' naiads and dryads won't hae anything tae do wi' him since he used tae be a beaver. An' tha other beavers won't neither. They treat him somewhere between a god an' a devil. So, who's left ta warm his bones on chilly nights?"

"The nanny goat?"

"Right!" Horace replied. " 'Tis nae natural, Ah tell ye." He paused. But Ah'm bein' rude an' interruptin' yer story. Continue, lad."

He listened intently to my adventures with Divot, Glenda, Ichabod, and finally my storm-tossed encounter with the Great God MacKenzie himself. As I got to the part where MacKenzie instructed me on the meaning of bad lies, Horace exploded.

"What a lot o' rubbish!" Horace shouted. "Tae wha' tha course gives ya? Tha's wha' tha so-called Great God Mac-Kenzie told ye?"

"Yes," I replied. "And he told me if my ball was lying against a tree trunk or in a hazard, it was a message that I should be careful in life. He said it was 'risky business to forge ahead like a bull.' "

Horace leaned back and howled in agony.

"Stop! Stop, man. Me ears canna stand tae hear nae more o' MacKenzie's lies!"

"What do you mean?" I asked.

He leaned forward and whispered conspiratorially in my ear.

"Dunna ye see? MacKenzie's just tryin' tae keep everybody in line wi' tha' stuff. 'Play it as it lays,' he says. 'Keep it on tha short grass,' he says. 'Dunna flirt wi' danger,' he says. 'Dunna ye bite off too much,' he says."

"But isn't that good advice?"

"Fer weaklings an' mewing infants, maybe. But na fer men, laddie. An' certainly na fer gods. Now, answer me this question. Do ye wan' tae play golf like a god or a scared rabbit?"

There was only one answer to Horace's question.

"Like a god?"

Horace laughed appreciatively and threw an arm over my shoulders. It felt like I was balancing a side of beef on my shoulders.

"Aye, there's a good lad," said Horace. "Now cum wi' me above an' Ah'll show ye how gowf was meant tae be played."

We emerged from the cavern near the fifteenth tee. Night had fallen but a full moon illuminated the green below us. I stepped up and took a couple of practice swings in the cool night air, but Horace stood well off to the side in the tall grass.

"Well, aren't you going to show me how it's done?" I asked.

"Aye," said Horace. "But nae from tha short grass, laddie."

He waded back into the weeds until they were nearly up to his waist. Then he took a ball and threw it down to earth as hard as he could.

"Ye mus' make sure tha lie is nice and buried in tha fescue," explained Horace.

"What happens next?" I asked.

"Ya beat tha living daylights outta it!" replied Horace with a hearty laugh. "What else?"

He took a ferocious cut at the ball, ripping through the fescue like a threshing machine. An explosion of grass filled the air and the hapless ball rocketed high into space toward the bunker on the far left of the green.

"Cut," I said to the ball, trying to get it to turn right and onto the green. Meanwhile, deep in the weeds, Horace was yelling, "Draw, ye bastard."

The ball landed on the first cut of the green and then trickled down into the trap. I let out a moan of disappointment, while Horace raised his arms in exultation. "Yes, I still hae tha magic!"

"You're glad you landed in the trap?"

"O' course, manly golf 'tis played from hazard tae hazard!" replied Horace. "Any fool can shoot frum tha short grass. And in future, lad, dunna ye talk tae my ball unless I ask ye."

"Sorry, I meant no offense."

"Nune taken," replied Horace solemnly.

We went the long way around the hole winding through the trees and tall grass, and on the way Horace talked to me about hazards.

"Ye canna fear tha hazard, lad. And ye canna pretend they're nae there. Ye must hae contempt for them. Aye, contempt."

"You're saying I should fire right at them?" I asked.

"Nay, nay, lad. Only if yer playin' a game o' hazards like me. The trick is, ye must be willing fer tha course tae give ye its best shots, an' still cum out victorious. Tha's tha mark o' a true gowfer. Tha's tha mark of a warrior!"

As we passed a line of yellow stakes, he made sure to stay well to the right. "Ya see, lad, hazards are nae something tae avoid, they're what defines tha risk, an' wha' makes possible tha reward."

"So, you mean they're important because they measure your skill?" I asked.

"Aye, tha', but much more, too," Horace answered. "Hazards measure yer heart. Those wi' nae heart wud rather embrace disaster than deal wi' tha demands of success."

"I'm not sure I understand."

"Well, did ye evir see a player hit ball after ball intae a water hazard?"

"Sure," I answered, failing to mention how many times I had done it myself.

"That's a player wi' nae heart," said Horace sadly. " 'Tis like a death wish."

When we reached the back of the hole, Horace waded through the moat until he reached the sand trap where his play lay. I took the small bridge on the back of the green.

"Gravel is luvly stuff, dunna ye think?" said Horace with a grin. He scrunched his feet down into the bunker, delighting in the squeaky sound it made. As he was addressing the ball, Horace stopped and turned to me.

"Ye know, everytime Ah see a man quaking because he mus' traverse a wee bit o' sand, or a puddle before tha green, Ah want tae puke, or cry. Ah dunna know which. Do ye ken my meanin', lad?"

"I think so," I replied.

"Gud, an' now fer me putt!"

Horace's "putt," as he called it, was a classic explosion shot, executed with an ancient niblick—an instrument ill-suited to the task since it didn't carry the heavy flange of a modern sand wedge. Chalk it up to Horace's supernatural strength, his force of will, or extremely deft hands, but for whatever reason, the niblick cut through the sand like a hot knife through butter, lofting the ball gently skyward. It traveled some forty feet in a graceful sweep before coming down in the middle of some lily pads near the other bank. There was a resounding ker-plunk and then several smaller splashes.

Not fully understanding the rules of "hazards" I kept my mouth shut, but it was hard to imagine Horace being happy with the shot. I was wrong.

He threw his arms up in the air and yelled, "Froggy!"

" 'Froggy'?" I asked.

"Aye, 'tis one under par," Horace said with a big grin. "Me putt landin' directly in tha mouth o' a bullfrog. Bullfrogs are what we use fer holes in tha game o' hazards, lad."

"Now what?" I asked.

"We rest a bit till me friends are ready," said Horace.

"Who are your friends?"

"Couple o' dryads named Utha and Gravaine," replied Horace. "Tree people dunna care much fer strangers, lad. No offense. They've been waitin' in tha shadows till yer gone."

He reached under his tunic and pulled out a fistful of brand-new balls that glistened like diamonds in the moonlight. "Heer, these are fer you, lad. So ye can finish tha course. Wait until daybreak an' then start again on tha top tee."

"Shouldn't I take a drop? I mean, I did land in the water after all."

"Nay, nay. 'Tis nae necessary. Ye hit a perfectly gud shot, but yer ball had a death wish or 'twas infected wi' a ball worm and went insane. Jist this once, Ah'll give ye a special dispensation." He placed the balls in my hands.

"I wish I could give you something in return."

"Did ye bring any cheese wi' ya, lad?" Horace said hopefully. "Ah've been living off o' trout, wild berries, an' the occasional frog for two thousand years. Evir since MacKenzie's curse, Ah'm nae allowed tae hae mead, nectar, nor ambrosia nae more. But every so often Harry brings me a cheese when he visits."

"No, I'm sorry," I said. "If I had known . . ."

"Ah love a really ripe brie," Horace continued wistfully. "And tha kind with wee caraway seeds in it, too."

"I wish I could help," I said.

"Nae matter, lad, 'tis a small thing," said Horace, smiling. " 'Tis time tae continue tha round."

"But where's the next tee?" I asked.

He tossed a ball into the deepest part of the water hazard. "A' tha very bottom, lad. Gettin' off this tee requires a manly blow indeed."

And with that, Horace dove into the hazard with all the subtlety of a giant hippo. As the ripples subsided, two of the oak trees on the far bank began to shimmer and then move forward out of the shadows. As they reached the water's edge, the trees had changed into muscular young men with wild, tangled hair. With barely a look in my direction, they followed Horace into the deepest part of the water hazard. I had just seen Utha and Gravaine, my first dryads.

When the last ripples had settled and the bullfrogs had resumed their throaty roars, a golf ball suddenly exploded out of the depths of the hazard like a missile. Streaking across the sky in a splendid arc, the ball cut across the full moon before disappearing in the direction of the sixteenth hole. Although I wouldn't swear to it in a court of law, based on the trajectory of Horace's tee ball, I'm pretty sure it landed in A-number-one position—the giant fairway bunker on the left side.

CHAPTER 16

The Ancient Curses, Runes, and Laws Considered

*Tom discovers that ignorance may be bliss
and that imperfection has a price*

Finding the sixteenth tee was a test worthy of an Eagle Scout. After winding through a tangle of goat paths wrapped around one another like a nest of garter snakes, I lost my way in a grove of torturously gnarled hardwood trees. Suddenly, after passing the same giant maple four times from four different directions, there it was, like a perfectly arranged still life in the middle of the forest: an elevated tee box, a wooden bench, and a ball washer with the number 16 painted neatly on its side in white letters.

Dropping my bag to the ground, I sank wearily onto the bench. Being up all night with Horace and his buddies had only succeeded in further exhausting me. Heaven, I decided, was nothing more than a really great place to sit. For the moment, at least, there were no pressing engagements and no new gods knocking on my door, so I slumped further down in my seat, wiggled my toes, cracked my knuckles, and started to doze. My dreams were of saving the Mountain from a diabolical Harry with cloven hooves, horns peeking out from under his battered Pine Valley cap, and a tinker's cup in his left hand.

Upon awakening, I was startled to see Harry in the flesh, sitting on his carry bag and writing in his crumbling old diary. When he realized I was awake, he capped his fountain pen and smiled.

"You should be getting to bed earlier," Harry said.

"Appreciate your concern," I said, hoping the sarcasm showed. At that moment, I was considering ripping out his throat.

"How's it been going, son?" he asked casually.

"Oh, fine," I answered in my best midwestern evasion mode.

"Good," he replied in his. "Glad to hear it."

"Yep," I continued. "Couldn't be better."

"You must be angry with me," Harry said carefully.

"Me, angry? What for? Because you tricked me into becoming part of somebody's science experiment? Harry, you got me running around like a rat in a maze here. Turn the wrong corner and whammo, I get zapped with a jolt of electricity. If I get lucky and do the right thing, somebody tosses me a couple of pellets of food. Angry? No, I love being set up, old buddy."

"You'll find this hard to believe, son," Harry replied, "but I'm on your side. Really was trying to help you. Still am."

"Don't give me that," I spat back. "I heard what Mac-Kenzie said to you back in the locker room. You're in up to your neck, and you're selling me down the river to save your own skin."

"Don't jump to conclusions, son. It's a lot more complicated than that. Give me a chance to explain."

"I'm listening, Harry," I replied skeptically. I looked at my wrist but then remembered I had surrendered my watch to Weyland. "I've got all the time in the world. They're probably still asleep back at Pine Valley."

"Yeah, probably," Harry agreed, but his voice told me

time was no longer on my side, that maybe I had bigger worries than missing my tee-time with Craven.

"So what's the story, Harry?"

"First off, son, you're right, I am in trouble with the big guy. But not the way you think." He carefully closed the diary and wrapped it with the large rubber bands that held it together.

"See, when I first came here forty years ago, MacKenzie was looking for somebody to act as a liaison—sort of a delegate to the gods from the world of mortals, you might say. Mac wanted me to keep the pantheon abreast of what was going on in our world, and to defend the actions of mortal golfers the best way I knew how."

"Why was it necessary? After all, if these guys are gods, why do they need your help to see what's going on?"

"True, they can see what's going on," Harry replied patiently, "but it's awfully hard for them to understand why mortal men do what they do. Hell, even I don't understand it half the time. Anyway, that's why they thought they needed me."

Well, a few years after I took the job, all hell broke loose. Golf started to explode back in the States. When President Eisenhower wasn't running the country—which was pretty much of the time, he was on the golf course. Ben Hogan was a national hero; and young Arnold Palmer was just starting to make his mark. Because of television, even Joe Six Pack was starting to play the game." Harry shook his head and laughed. "It was a complete disaster."

"I don't understand. I mean the game didn't start in palaces. It started in pastures. It was supposed to be for the common folk. You'd think the gods would be pleased."

"At first they were," he replied. "But then things started happening so fast, even I couldn't keep up with it. Nicklaus hit the scene and they started making golf clubs by the carload and building courses by the thousands. Green fees shot up faster than the national debt and golf carts multiplied like rabbits.

"Anyway, instead of keeping the gods advised, I guess

I got caught up in the fever. I started investing with my father-in-law in desert resorts and tacky golf retirement communities down in Florida. During the '80s, I was so busy making money out of golf, I didn't play more than two rounds at Mount Augustus. As Mac said, I became part of the problem. And then something else happened that I hadn't counted on."

"What was that?" I asked, expecting a tale of some terrible accident or financial misfortune.

"I got old, Tom," said Harry, shaking his head. "Simple as that. Everyone thinks it's not going to happen to them, but it always does. One day I was fresh out of Yale with the world at my feet and then I was cashing my first Social Security check."

"So what happened, Harry?"

"Old MacKenzie got tired of waiting and had me shanghaied one day while I was playing golf with some clients out in Arizona. I went into a sand trap and didn't come back again for two weeks. Glenda threw this huge three-day retirement party at the turn. Afterward, Mac read me the riot act, saying I'd neglected my duties and the game was suffering because of it, that the gods had lost confidence in me, and it was time to replace me with a younger man."

"And that's where I came in, I guess."

"Right, I brought you here because I needed an apprentice—somebody to fill my spikes here on Mount Augustus."

"Why didn't you just run an ad in the golf magazines?" I joked.

Harry didn't crack a smile. "It's not the kind of job you can apply for, son. You have to be approached."

"So that makes you some kind of headhunter for the pantheon?"

"You might say," Harry replied.

"Well, you did a helluva job with Dick Jackson."

"That's below the belt," said Harry, suddenly very angry.

But I had him and he knew it. Harry stared down at his shoes.

"No, you're right actually. Never should have brought him here. Deep down inside, I knew Toe Wedge could never cut the mustard, and that's why I picked him. Same with Ken Hoeffer. I just wasn't ready to retire yet but I never dreamed they'd end up in the foundry. Honest, Tom, you've got to believe me there."

I let it slide. "So, out of all the hackers in the world, why'd you pick me, Harry? What makes me so special?"

"I dunno, son. Just something I could feel in you. You'd been damn near ruined by trying to shinny up that greasy flag pole at Hartless and Craven, but there was still a smoldering ember in your heart, amidst all the ashes. You were pretty far gone, son. But I wasn't wrong. Mac thought so, too."

"You mean I am *The One?*"

"The one?"

"*The One.* Like Ichabod and MacKenzie said."

"What the hell are you talking about?" Harry was looking at me like I was crazy.

"Ichabod said there was this myth or story or whatever about a mortal who comes to the Mountain and saves or rescues something and, I don't know, I guess he thought maybe it was me. Everything kind of fit."

"First of all, what Mac actually said was there can only *be* one. As in one mortal advocate like me at a time. No time shares, I had to find a replacement and hang it up. He was hoping you'd be *that* one. Not *the* one, get it? The second thing is, I can't believe I've got to explain this to you. Geez, Tom, do you actually think you're some kind of messiah just because some flake who's been tied up in the woods for five hundred years tells you so? You've got enough problems without succumbing to delusions of grandeur."

Which is exactly what I had done; Ichabod had unwittingly planted the seed, but I had watered the damn thing and allowed it to grow. The whole thing was a little embarrassing and Harry seemed genuinely angry. Unable to meet his gaze, I looked over his shoulder. Thunderheads were building up on the horizon. They appeared to be rolling up out of the collar of his golf shirt. I wondered if the Great God MacKenzie was about to rearrange another hole.

"Okay, let's forget the one business, the question's still the same. If I was supposed to be your replacement, why'd you leave me alone so much? Why'd you let me get into so much trouble?"

"There wasn't any choice. I knew in my heart you had it in you, but the pantheon would never have just taken my word for it. They had to know for sure. Besides, the tests are a tradition, son. Each time a new mortal comes to the Mountain, MacKenzie allows the other gods to test him."

"Well, I'm not sure things are going too well, Harry," I said.

"Yeah, Mac told me about thirteen," said Harry, shaking his head. "Didn't you know who he was?"

"I probably should have guessed."

"Well, he's not your big worry right now. I'm more concerned about MacTavish. Has he shown his ugly little face yet?"

"Yep, right after my little incident with MacKenzie. Basically, he said to kiss my ass good-bye."

"Well, I wouldn't worry as long as you've been doing your accounting," said Harry.

"My accounting?"

"Yeah, counting the stones. Keeping your score. You have been keeping score, haven't you?"

"I may have missed a hole or two, but I've got a pretty good idea," I answered.

"Okay, what's your score through fifteen?" Harry asked.

"Hey, I nearly had another par on fifteen, Harry," I said excitedly. "Hit the green in regulation, but took too much club, so I had to lag it about forty feet. But my par putt lipped out. . . ."

Harry just looked at me. I was beginning to feel like a

kid who hadn't finished his homework. So, after poking through the stones in my scoring sack, I looked up at Harry and shook my head.

"I don't have the slightest idea. To tell you the truth, I'm surprised I made it this far."

"Not good enough, I'm afraid. MacTavish will have you for lunch if you're not right on the money. When was the last time you moved the stones?"

"The ninth hole, I guess. I've been busy."

Harry nodded and sat down on the bench next to me, rubbing his eyes. Then he leaned back, tipped his hat down over his forehead, and was silent. I wasn't sure what was supposed to happen next. He seemed to have settled in for the long haul.

"Aren't we going to play?"

"No point, might as well wait."

"For what?"

Thunder rumbled again in the distance and the wind began to pick up. I wanted to move on.

"For MacTavish. He's right around the corner."

Another peal of thunder echoed over the mountain and under it I heard the sound of wheels grinding through the underbrush. I looked toward the sound. Harry didn't move. The little man in the jacket and knickers I had met on thirteen fought his way through the brush toward us. He was strapped into a leather harness and pulled a two-wheeled wooden cart reminding me of the prairie schooners I had seen on *Wagon Train*. It was obviously heavily weighted and he was straining as he made his way out of the bushes and onto the fairway.

When he saw me jump to my feet and grab my bag he stopped and raised his fist, screaming at the top of his lungs.

"Yes, yes, yes, scoundrel," he shouted, "don't even think of playing on. Produce your papers, cheater, and produce them now. You are a 1674B. Oh yes, a 1674B and you are mine."

His fury gave him new energy and he practically ran

The Fable of MacTavish—God of Rules

In the earliest days Angus brought a small, unkempt man named MacTavish to meet the Great God MacKenzie. He had devised a means of recording thoughts that he called writing. MacKenzie decided that the man would help him record the creation of Mount Augustus.

Some months later MacKenzie and MacTavish were walking the high ranges of the Mountain when MacKenzie began to kick a stone toward an outcropping of rock. It disappeared into a rodent hole and a memory of a dream before time sprang forth from the recesses of the Great God's mind. Feverishly, he began to explain it to MacTavish, who wrote it down. After eight days on the high range golf was remembered. And they returned to the lowlands with a game fit for the gods.

MacKenzie gathered his sons together and explained the game to them, enlisting them to play in order to test its worthiness. MacTavish explained the First Six Rules. MacKenzie then equipped his sons with sticks and stones and they played the First Round. He beat them soundly because he had been practicing and was pleased, saying, "I'll whip ye the same on the morrow."

Unfortunately for all golfers, MacKenzie was soundly beaten during the Second Round by his eldest, Bertie. The Great God met with the weasel, MacTavish, in secret and bade him create more rules to give him advantage over his sons. MacTavish agreed only if MacKenzie would make him a god. MacKenzie granted his wish and then regretted it for centuries. MacTavish took to the task with a passion and in less than twenty-four hours created The First 100, which he recorded in a cheap ledger. It is said that he devised the idea of penalty strokes during the Third Round when poor Bertie's ball moved after he had addressed it because a volcano was erupting nearby.

Over the centuries MacTavish continued to invent perverse and intricate confusions that were only clear to him. When he had filled 1,000 ledgers MacKenzie shouted, "Stop, weasel, ye ha' dun enough." He despised his rulemaster for making the game so complicated he held no more advantage. But MacTavish was now a god and MacKenzie could never admit to making a mistake, so the God of Rules terrorizes and baffles all golfers to this very day.

---

toward us, parking the wagon so it blocked a straight shot down the fairway. There was no escape. He eased himself out of the straps and shot his cuffs, drawing himself up to his full 4' 2". He preened and fussed with his clothing like a demented guinea hen. Although dressed in typical 20s golfer fashion—a Norfolk jacket, woolen knickers, V-necked sweater and school tie—he seemed totally out of place on the fairway. His skin had the chalky pallor of one who spent too much time in dark rooms and he squinted at us as if the muted sunlight hurt his eyes. His back was slightly crooked, suggesting someone who spent many happy hours hunched over a counting desk zealously tallying duffers' sins by candlelight. If Ebenezer Scrooge had had a brother he could easily have been the God of Rules.

MacTavish reached into the wagon, grabbed a battered leather satchel, and stepped resolutely up to the tee. He smiled at me like a feral dog about to chow down on a rotting carcass.

"Well, we meet again, Mr. Cruickshank." He smirked. "And unless I'm mistaken we have much to discuss. Produce, my fellow, produce."

"Don't overstep, MacTavish," Harry called out from under the brim of his cap. "The round isn't over yet."

"Ah, if it isn't Harry Brady," MacTavish said. "My but you're looking frail, sir. But that's the problem with you mortals. You get old and need to be replaced like a worn-out coat or a pen that's outlived its usefulness."

He snapped his crow quill in half for emphasis.

"The boy's got a good heart, MacTavish," said Harry. "Leave him be."

"A good heart, indeed, Harry. And what do you know of good hearts, Mr. Developer? Stay out of my business, Harry. Your time is through here. Now, Mr. Cruickshank, produce before I weary of asking you."

He folded his arms and waited.

"I assume he means the pouch," I said to Harry as MacTavish smiled.

"It is something we've discussed," said Harry. There was a tone of resignation in his voice.

"The thing is, Mr. MacTavish, I can't exactly put my hands on it right now. I mean I've got it but ..." The excuse sounded lame even to me.

"Enough," MacTavish screamed. "It will be our counting then."

With a flourish he flipped up the canvas top and revealed the interior of the wagon that was stacked high with ledger books of various sizes and loose piles of yellowing paper tied with red string. A musty, ancient smell poured out and settled in the clearing.

"Behold the Ancient Rules and Laws of the MacKenzie's game. By these ye shall be judged and by these ye shall be punished. I am The MacTavish who keeps the Ancient

Rules and Laws, revealing them as required for the Gods." He stood proudly by his wagon, rubbing a finger lovingly along the crumbling spine of one of the books.

MacTavish opened the tailgate of the wagon and removed a stool, which he placed on the ground. He pulled himself up into the back of the wagon and began going through the books, selecting several and placing them on the tailgate along with a wooden writing box. He jumped to the ground. The clumsy leap proved beyond a doubt that he possessed the necessary lack of coordination to be an accountant. He hauled himself up on the stool and opened the writing box, removing paper and quill pens that he arranged around his work space with obsessive care.

"Name?" MacTavish asked, pen poised over paper.

"Answer him," Harry whispered.

"Uh, Tom, Tom Cruikshank," I said.

"Mortal?"

"Oh yeah."

"Answer yes or no."

"Yes."

"Have you provided the necessary documents?"

"I'm not sure."

"May I see your tally pouch at this time, please?" he said with slight exasperation.

"I already told you I didn't . . ."

"This is for the record, answer the question."

"No."

"As I feared. Were you not given the scoring pouch by Angus McLeod and instructed by him to keep your tally current and available for inspection?"

"Well, sort of but he never told me . . ."

"Just answer yes or no."

"I don't remember if he told me or not."

"I'll take that as a yes."

"Listen, Mr. MacTavish, it got a little hard back there to keep track, I mean a lot was going on . . ."

"Then you admit to being lax as regarding the tally?"

"Yes, but I can get pretty close. I was in pretty good shape until around nine. Then on ten my tee shot went . . ."

"Don't worry, Mr. Cruickshank," he smiled thinly, "we can get close as well." There was a knot forming in the pit of my stomach. "Now, did you at any time improve your lie? Think carefully before you answer."

Not only couldn't I answer I couldn't even speak. Of course I'd improved my lie. Sometimes there'd been help but sometimes I'd done it on my own. Harry was sitting on the bench shaking his head. I was overcome with a very empty feeling.

"This is without precedent. Your silence speaks for itself. I invoke the right to expand the scope of this proceeding. As of this moment we are involved in a 1145 Article 9 Subsection 876.451. Prepare as best you can."

MacTavish turned and shouted toward the forest.

"BRING YE FORTH THE STONES."

Wendell and Ruppert emerged from the woods. Ruppert was carrying two leather duffel bags—one was huge, the other about the size of a golfer's weekend carry bag. Ruppert greeted me with a cheery, "Meet again, mate." Wendell was dragging a litter that held a large and ornate brass scale. He was sweating and his face was so red I was afraid he would keel over. The crack accounting team set up in front of the wagon.

"Tom Cruikshank, we will now proceed with a full accounting of your score to this point and at this time we will also assess the necessary adjustments and penalties, adding them to your total and making a judgment as to whether the indiscretions are flagrant enough to warrant extreme punishment. You may not speak and your right to appeal is limited by my analysis and recommendation. Is that understood?"

I nodded. As MacTavish continued to speak, Wendell and Ruppert each took a bag of stones and stood at opposite sides of the scale.

"The bag in Ruppert's hands represents the number of strokes that are considered to be par. The bag in Wendell's hands represents the number of strokes you have been observed to have taken."

MacTavish gestured to Ruppert. "Place par for the course less the count for seventeen and eighteen."

Ruppert lifted his bag and dumped the stones on the scale, then took seven of them away.

MacTavish gestured to Wendell. "Place the counting stones."

"With pleasure," he said as he carefully opened the bag and poured a mountain of rocks into the other tray. The scale tipped quickly back to his side and it was clear as a fat slice over the fence and out of bounds, my side was Everest, the other side was an ant hill.

Using a large brass dish with handles they began to pull stones out of my tray and place them in the dish. The scale began to swing to the center and by the time they were finished it was perfectly in balance. The pile of stones in the counting dish was clearly my extras; I couldn't believe it. Wendell and Ruppert counted them out and whispered the results to MacTavish, who whistled softly to himself and went to work. Silence descended on the clearing as he wrote. Wendell and Ruppert stood quietly and Harry slept on the bench. MacTavish would have been a more than worthy addition to any IRS field office. Finally, he placed the quill back into its inkwell and looked at me.

"It's not good news," he said somberly.

"Give it to me straight," I said.

"You have an aggregate and adjusted total score, including increments and assessments as well as penalties, of 436 strokes through the fifteenth hole. If you will sign this document to verify my findings we will proceed to the punishment phase."

"You said 436 strokes through fifteen holes? That's impossible! Maybe I don't remember them all, but I sure would remember hitting the ball 436 times."

"Are you asking for an itemized account?"

"Yes, I believe I am," I said.

MacTavish nodded and took me through the round

stroke by stroke, patiently explaining the penalties, penalties upon penalties, penalty strokes with increments and rollovers, and assessments that compounded incrementally. As I listened I leafed through the regulations he had excerpted and applied to my case.

By the time he reached the sixth hole, I had had enough. "Okay," I interrupted, "enough. No more. What's next?"

"Are you ready to sign?" MacTavish asked evenly.

"What if I don't?"

"If you don't, I will institute proceedings against you now, outlining the many and devious ways you have cheated and lied and give you the maximum punishment as specified in Book 1000."

"And if I sign?" I had no interest in an express route to the foundry.

"You will be agreeing to my tally, and will be allowed to finish the round where the final judgment awaits you in the scorer's tent. There, perhaps, you may argue your case."

"I'll sign," I said, hoping that something good would happen before the end of the round. Harry nodded his head in agreement.

Thunder rolled in the heavens; the black clouds were moving closer. I saw a flash of lightning in the distance. MacTavish smiled and held out the quill. Harry walked back to the bench. MacTavish stood graciously and offered me the stool. He spread the documents awaiting my signature in front of me. I took the pen and dribbled ink all over the parchment as I scratched my name across the bottom.

"I've never used a real quill pen before," I said apologetically, and my fate was sealed.

MacTavish gathered up the papers and tied them with a piece of red string, sealing the knot with a metal clip. Wendell and Ruppert were already repacking the wagon. They harnessed up and rolled off into the woods, laughing wildly.

Harry broke the silence.

Excerpts from the Books of Law and Regulation
Applicable in the Action Against Thomas Cruikshank, Esq.

 Book 9; Sec. 13; Article 2: Interest on uncounted strokes can result in negative handicap that requires golfer to play specified holes with the opposite hand.

Book 112; Sec. 843; Article 19: Failure to report strokes over the amateur "10" level is punishable by seizure of all equipment purchased since 1946.

Book 56; Sec. 1; Article 856: Gimmies are not allowed and failure to putt out on each hole results in an 18-stroke addition regardless of the actual number of gimmies.

Book 219; Sec. 4B; Article 11-3: The use of a ball washer constitutes an undesignated penalty stroke because the ball is set in motion by means other than contact with flesh. See: Hand in pocket. **(Article 269; Section 46; Subsection 27:98754-R)**

Book 14; Sec. 6; Article 55: The imagined replacement of a lost ball regardless of whether or not the action is taken results in a penalty stroke and an adjustment leverage equal to but not less than ⅔ of the total count of Mulligans taken on the practice range between April 23 and June 16 of the preceding fiscal year.

Book 78; Sec. 12; Article 1346: All assessments and incremental modifications will be determined by the tallykeeper and he alone is responsible for all action taken by the members of his foursome. It is the tallykeeper's responsibility to manage and monitor the activities of all members of the foursome as well as caddies, greenskeepers, stray dogs, and bartenders.

Book 8; Sec. 10; Article 12: A five-stroke penalty will automatically be assessed for each failure to complete the journey from green to tee in less than 1.36 minutes (based on actuarial tables provided by the starter). See: Round Limits and Footspeed based on age and temperament.

Book 563; Sec. 119; Article 32: Travel and entertainment between holes 9 and 10 will be limited to a trip to the designated relief facility and the refreshment fountain provided under **Article 12: Section 17, Part 94b.** A penalty equal to the number of tees or remnants of tees in the left zipper pocket will apply, although a waiver in the form of an **Application 1238645 BC19-0** will be considered if the Tee Count Verifier is under the age of 4 and has not had access to *Sesame Street* repeats and is therefore unable to count to the maximum penalty (24) accurately without using fingers and toes more than once.

Book 1000; Sec. 1; Article 1A (supplemental): If an audit reveals the willful or unwillful concealment of strokes on the part of a player, caddie, or invested relative, no matter whether or not the player, caddie, or invested relative is aware of the infraction, the willful or unwillful concealment will result in no less than 18 years of training and rehabilitation in the Foundry of Weyland and will be enforced without appeal. The term of rehabilitation will begin upon conviction or semblance of proof of wrongdoing as determined by the God of Rules and no authority or deity may overturn the verdict without going to a lot of trouble.

"Tom, he's going to send you to the foundry no matter what."

"Can he do that?"

"You're under his jurisdiction, son. Book 1000; Sec. 1; Article 1A is the rule, if I'm not mistaken."

"Oh, this is just great . . ."

"Unfortunately there's more, Tom," said Harry. "If Mac-Tavish succeeds in sentencing you to the foundry, he'll have won his struggle with MacKenzie. You see, MacTavish has always been against guys like us playing golf. Says it's a game for immortals only, and he's been trying for thousands of years to get MacKenzie to withdraw the game."

"Could MacKenzie do that?" I asked incredulously.

Harry's face was ashen. "Oh, in a heartbeat," said Harry. "But not like you think. He wouldn't withdraw the knowledge of the game, just our passion for it. Suddenly, people would just fall out of love with golf, and one by one the courses would begin to close. Within twenty or thirty years, golf clubs would be nothing but curiosities like kerosene lamps or Civil War relics."

"So, is this it? Is it over, Harry?" I asked. A cold shudder rippled through my stomach. "The game is history and I'm going to spend eternity pumping a bellows in Weyland's foundry? Come on, Harry, you got me into this. There's got to be a way out."

"There is," said Harry. While lightning flashed around his head, Harry unzipped the side pocket of his old canvas carry bag and pulled out his diary once again. "I remember seeing something once, long ago . . ." he said, and began ripping off the rubber bands and leafing rapidly through the pages of the book. As he ran his fingers over the pages, the wind began to whip up and swirl around him, tearing scraps of paper from in between the pages of the diary. Harry started running after the scraps frantically, snatching at them as the wind scattered them about the ground.

"Harry, we don't have time for this right now," I shouted above the wind.

"You're wrong, Tom," Harry shouted back. "The book is the answer."

"What are you talking about?"

"Open your hands, son," said Harry. "Open your hands and brace yourself. It's your turn. Now it belongs to you."

Solemnly, Harry took the crumbling old diary and placed it in my hands without letting go. To my surprise, the book was pulsating with life and its weight almost brought me to my knees. It was like being thrown a medicine ball full of plutonium. The air crackled around my head and suddenly a bolt of energy surged from the book and coursed through Harry's body and then into my own. I thought I had been struck by lightning, but the power was coming from the book.

Harry was grasping me so tightly I couldn't get away. He began to laugh and as he did the wind began to wail even louder. I looked at my hands, and they were glowing as streaks of blue light danced back and forth. Harry's face was like seeing into the very center of an expanding galaxy—his teeth were yellow and jagged, and his eyes, two glowing embers straining in their sockets.

"It's all yours now," Harry shouted and then he collapsed on the tee box in a heap. A fireball spun out of the woods, enveloping me in cool bright light. A sense of peace overcame me, and I crumpled to the ground as well.

When I awoke seconds later I felt more alive than I had ever felt in my life. Every sense tingled and the world seemed in sharper focus than ever before. Harry was stirring as well, mumbling quietly to himself. The storm was gone and I knew that the center of it had been in Harry's mind. He stirred again and sat up. I couldn't believe my eyes. The Harry Brady sitting cross-legged on the ground looked fifteen years younger than the man who brought me to Mount Augustus. He was grinning like an idiot.

"Tom," he said as he struggled to his feet, "you okay?"

"I'm great," I answered, and I was, but the last few moments were a jumble in my mind. "What happened?"

"It worked," he said, laughing. "Let's play on."

It seemed like the right thing to do.

"You're up, as usual," I said as I pulled out my driver.

"You take it, Tom. You're the man, now. I'm just along for the ride."

"Can't kid a kidder, Harry." I laughed.

I stepped up to the tee, set my ball, and took a practice swing. I felt strong and confident and utterly at peace. As I addressed the ball I knew what was going to happen and it did. My drive was solid as a rock, straight down the middle. I didn't even look to see it land. There was no reason to. In the background I heard Harry cackle with glee and begin to laugh.

"Great shot, my boy. I couldn't have done better myself."

Harry mounted the tee like an excited child. He set the ball and took a careful practice swing, then promptly shanked a nasty little dribbler about twenty yards off the tee into the deep rough. I couldn't believe it. Harry tossed his driver into the air and shouted with joy.

"That's more like it," he screamed. "Let's play golf."

And with that he was off after his ball at a trot. Harry seemed to have lost his mind. I grabbed my bag and saw his diary lying on the tee. I gathered it up and put it in my bag. As I approached the ball for a second shot I was already a step ahead, confidently picturing a short putt for a birdie three. Was this what it was like to be in the zone? Or was it some divine state of grace? Then, something told me not to think about it anymore, just to play. So I played on, and got my bird when I sank the four-footer. Harry didn't volunteer his score and I didn't ask. As we walked briskly to seventeen, ever mindful of the 1.36-minute rule contained in **Book 8; Sec. 10; Article 12,** Harry could be heard singing "Honky Tonk Angel" with great gusto, and way, way off-key.

CHAPTER 17

Playing Harry's Game

In which the tables are turned

Something had happened between Harry and me after the accounting with MacTavish, something important. At the time I just couldn't remember exactly what it was. But, there wasn't a doubt in my mind it was a defining moment, as momentous as losing one's virginity, joining the army, being bar mitzvahed, or committing a felony—something that changes your life completely. And whatever it was that happened to me, had somehow also happened to Harry.

The man on the seventeenth tee resembled the Harry

274

Brady I met three days earlier in appearance only. His worldly wise crochetiness was gone, replaced by an almost giddy "lightness" as if he had just shed an incredible burden. But the most striking difference about Harry was his golf game. It stank. He'd hit a few indifferent shots earlier in the round, but I had chalked them up to exhaustion, and even when he'd made a blunder he always got himself out of trouble. But now Harry's errant shots had taken on a new quality. It was as if the reservoir of ineptitude that had built up in him for years had finally been tapped and was rushing out in a torrent. Maybe the law of averages had just caught up to him but, somehow, I didn't think so.

Right off, Harry cold-topped another drive, dribbling it down into the bush only twenty yards in front of the box. After he finished hacking it out of the rough, he was lying four and still only just on the front apron of the landing area. By contrast, I hit an absolutely pure drive that split the fairway about two-seventy from the tee. It was so effortless a swing it felt like I had hit a dandelion puff instead of a golf ball. Holding my finish in perfect balance, I heard the unmistakable sound of clapping. That's when I realized we had suddenly acquired a following.

It was only a small group of fauns and minor gods. Oh yes, Wendell and Ruppert were also walking with us, quite openly this time, carrying their ridiculous sack of rocks.

"Harry, we've got a gallery," I said.

"Yeah, we started picking them up right after we left sixteen, you just didn't see 'em 'cause they're shy," Harry replied. He stood over his ball tentatively and took a couple of practice swings.

"You think I'm laid off at the top, son?"

"Looks fine to me, Harry."

Like a real Saturday morning hacker, Harry took a vicious swipe at the ball and caught it fat sending it a mere 70 yards down the fairway. Harry laughed ruefully and pounded down the edges of his divot. Meanwhile, the gallery was swelling. Some of Weyland's dwarfs had joined the throng as well as some wood nymphs from the ninth hole, and none of them were paying the least bit of attention to Harry Brady. Gods, nymphs, and fauns alike were hurrying past him as if they had never met him, as if he were invisible.

"What in the hell is going on?" I asked Harry as we watched the swelling crowd jockey for position near where my drive had landed.

"They've all heard what happened at MacTavish's wagon," said Harry. "And they want to be there at the exciting conclusion."

"I don't understand."

Harry put his hand on my shoulder. "Let me put it this way, son. Right now that's less of a gallery than a mob."

"A lynch mob?"

"They don't really want your head, son. But if someone were to take it off, they wouldn't mind having front-row seats. Sort of like rubberneckers slowing down on the freeway so's they can get a really good look at an accident."

"Oh, great," I muttered.

"Don't take it personally, son," said Harry softly. "Besides, it's gonna be all right. Take my word on it."

I striped my next shot right past the pin and then watched as it bit hard and spun back within two feet of the cup. The swelling throng around me erupted in enthusiastic applause. Apparently they weren't all rooting for my demise. I caught sight of Glenda standing in the back row of the gallery. As our eyes met, she gave me a warm smile that moved me down the fairway with new energy.

"Great shot, Cruikshank!" came a raspy growl from the crowd.

It was a voice created by many years of late-nights, unfiltered cigarettes, and strong drink: the unmistakable signature of Toe Wedge Jackson. I searched the faces in the gallery as I walked toward the green, first the left side and then the right. Then I saw him crossing the fairway in front of me, using two of Reg's sheep as a shield. He raised his head briefly and gave me a thumbs-up and whispered,

"Go get 'um, boy! I'm bustin' out." Although I couldn't see him, Noopes the dwarf couldn't be far behind. Toe Wedge didn't have a chance.

Once again Harry was in trouble, lying 6 on a patch of hardpan well to the left of the green. He had come over his approach shot and dead-pulled it to the left, but Harry was amazingly nonchalant about it. In fact, as we walked toward the green, he twirled his wedge with his left hand and began to whistle "I'll Be Seeing You."

Whatever whistling the old standard did for Harry, it didn't help his game. The wheels had completely come off his wagon. After skulling it over the green from his hardpan lie, it took two more shots for him to reach the green and then he three-putted for an eleven. Oh yes, and I sank that three-footer for a bird.

"Great day to be alive, isn't it, son?" said Harry exuberantly as we walked to the eighteenth tee.

"What the hell's going on, Harry?"

"Whatever do you mean, son?" he asked innocently.

"You just took an eleven on a hole you could've parred with your eyes closed yesterday!"

"While you birdied the hole like a scratch golfer, is that about the size of it?" he asked. "Well let's just say, 'it's your turn.' " He looked out over the eighteenth fairway from the eighteenth tee and then pointed to a spot. "You'll want to hit your drive about there. That's the best spot for the approach."

And it was my turn in more ways than one. I was playing Harry's game but I was playing it better than he ever did. Harry hadn't had a single bird in the entire round and I made two in a row with another one coming up.

Thunderbolt was singing. I hammered the drive, but released through it a little too much, giving the ball hookspin. I thought for sure that it would run through the fairway into the rough on the left side, but as soon as it hit it kicked right and rolled down the center of the fairway, stopping just where Harry had pointed. The gallery exploded in applause and loud huzzahs.

"Huh," I muttered. Good bounces had never been a large part of my game.

"Member's privilege," said Harry as he teed up his ball. "Get used to it."

Harry's drive was a great big banana ball that landed in the tall grass on the right side of the fairway.

"Guess I'd better book a lesson when I get back home," said Harry gleefully. "Unless you've got any tips?"

Harry took two shots to hack it back to the fairway, but still ended up with an unpromising lie about ten yards farther up than my tee ball. I figured I had no more than a five-iron to the green, but it was elevated and well protected so it looked like an easy cut with a four-iron to come down softly and clear the traps. As I addressed the ball, Harry raised his hand.

"Hold up a minute, son," said Harry. "There's someone on the green."

"Are you sure that's not the gallery?" I asked, squinting into the sun. It didn't seem possible that someone else was on the eighteenth green. No one had been ahead of us for the last three days.

"No, two of them have putters," said Harry. "Looks like MacKenzie and Twitch. Let's wait a minute and let them finish."

"MacKenzie's on the green?"

"Looks that way."

"And Twitch? Who's he?" I asked.

"God of Putters," Harry replied. "And a crafty one. You gotta hold onto your wallet around that old devil."

Harry walked back to me and placed his hand on my shoulder. "They're probably just practicing, son. Mount Augustus doesn't have a putting green. I wouldn't worry about it."

"No problem," I replied, but I was worried and Harry knew it. It wasn't about dealing with yet another god either. It was about dealing with the great god himself. Whatever else MacKenzie was doing at the eighteenth hole the odds were pretty good he was also waiting for me. All that, however, was for later. Right now I was playing the best golf of my life and I'd come too far not to take it all the way home. While we were waiting Harry started fishing around in his pockets until he pulled out a small metal container about the size of an egg timer on a gold chain. He wrapped the chain around the thing and handed it to me.

"This is the last bit of magic I have to give you, Tom," said Harry solemnly.

The charm was surprisingly heavy. There was a tiny glass window on one side of the container, but it was scratched and cloudy with age and I couldn't really see what was inside.

"What the hell is this thing, Harry?"

"Just a reliquary—something to help you putt."

I shook the object and heard a grainy rattle. "What's inside?" I asked.

"Sacred objects," he answered. "A splinter from Calamity Jane's hickory shaft. A piece of leather from the tip of George Low's brogans. Cuticles from Dave Stockton's fingers—got those from a manicurist in Palm Springs. And last, but not least, nickel flakes from Ben Crenshaw's putter."

"Nickel flakes from Little Ben? How'd you get those?"

"Son, do you have any idea how many times Little Ben has been stolen?" asked Harry.

"I don't know, maybe once or twice."

"Five, son, and those are just the times it was reported," Harry said smugly. "And just why do you think it was taken so many times?"

"I don't know. For ransom?"

"Close, but no cigar. The putter was always returned gratis but each time it was missing just a little more nickel plating."

"You mean . . . ?" I shook the charm again and looked at him.

"Yep."

"Harry, thanks. Thanks a lot."

"They're waving us up, son. You can hit," was his answer.

Now I've always hated being waved up. It doesn't save any time at all, and it usually, at least in my case, ensured a hurried shot. The result is always less than optimum and occasionally downright disastrous. But this time, I didn't think twice. Luck or something even more mystical was riding with me and even if it wasn't, another couple of strokes on the old scorecard were just a drop in MacTavish's bucket.

I opened my stance a little and took the club back smoothly. After a slight hesitation at the top I came down slowly, letting my legs lead, and then held on after impact to ensure a fade. It was a textbook shot starting out left of the target and then fading back to the center of the green where it landed softly. Once again, the gallery responded with thundering applause, and over the din I could swear that I heard a raspy voice shout, "You da man!"

Harry's didn't fare so well with his approach. He caught it a little heavy so it spiraled and dove like a wounded duck directly into the stream running in front of the green. Once again, the gallery treated Harry like he was invisible. Even after he dropped and managed a nice pitch shot to the middle of the green there was absolutely no reaction. But when we crossed the footbridge, the gallery clapped in unison like rock fans seeking an encore. As I pushed through the adoring crowd, Harry barred my way to the green with his arm and held a finger to his lips. "They're back on again," whispered Harry. "Twitch is putting." I made my way to the front of the gallery to get a better look.

Twitch was unlike any other god I had seen on the Mountain. First of all, he had a distinctly "modern" look, as if he had been abducted from the men's grill at Bel Air around 1957. He was wearing a canary yellow alpaca sweater with a white polo shirt underneath. The slacks were a powder blue plaid, pleated and cuffed with a razor-sharp crease, and on his feet were a pair of black-and-white wing tips. Completing the ensemble was a large Cuban cigar stuffed in the side of his mouth and an oversized Panama hat on his head.

The God of Putting faced a fifteen-foot double breaker that ran downhill. Pacing back and forth along his line, he puffed his cigar, incessantly pouring a volume of white smoke into the air and reminding me of a railroad switching engine at work in the yards. Finally he stopped and stood over his ball, and then I understood why he was called "Twitch."

As he gripped the putter, his hands began to tremble and vibrate rapidly. Ten times a second, twenty, and thirty times a second until his hands and the putter were a blur of motion making a whirring sound audible clear across the green. Beads of perspiration formed on his forehead and he stepped back from the ball to steady himself. But when he addressed the ball again the same thing began to happen. He stepped back until the horrible twitching stopped, but as soon he stood over the ball violent vibrations overtook him and the sweat began pouring from his face.

"That's the worst case of yips I've ever seen," I whispered to Harry. "Why doesn't he use a long putter and take his hands out of the swing?"

"Be too easy," Harry replied. "Nobody would ever bet with him."

Finally, he moved back to the ball, his hands whirring away at warp speed, but this time Twitch positioned the putter three or four inches behind the ball. Satisfied that his hands could vibrate no faster, Twitch began edging closer and closer to the ball. When he was within an inch he moved his shoulders slightly, bringing the whirring putter blade into the back of the ball. It made a distinct buzzing sound like an orbital sander taking the finish off an old dresser.

The ball started off slowly down the incline, took the first break, and picked up speed. Just when I thought it was going to run three feet past the cup on the high side, it abruptly broke right and rattled into the bottom of the cup.

The gallery applauded and Twitch bowed theatrically. MacKenzie threw a leather purse into the center of the green and stomped off disgustedly. I took his leaving as a good sign.

"Hey, let's hear it for the Great God MacKenzie!" said Twitch to the gallery. "A great sport and a great competitor." As the gallery erupted in another round of applause, he picked up the purse and stuffed it into a back pocket.

"Now, who's got my drink?" he asked jovially. A redheaded wood nymph wearing high heels stepped forward carrying a Del Monico glass filled with ice and an amber liquid.

"Scotch?" I asked.

"Single malt," replied Harry. "I brought him a case the last time I was here."

"High heels, too?"

"Yep. Straight from Vegas," Harry replied.

"Now, who's next?" bellowed Twitch. "Surely there's someone here that's a match for this old codger and his shaky hands?"

"That's our cue," said Harry.

As we pushed our way onto the green Twitch pretended to be afraid and backed away from us, much to the delight of the crowd.

"Oh, a mortal," his voice trembled theatrically. "I'm shaking!"

As I marked my ball, Twitch threw his arm around my shoulders and offered me his other hand.

"Hey, ol' buddy, my name's Phil," he said jovially. "But all my friends here at Mount Augustus call me Twitch."

"Tom Cruikshank," I said.

"Well, I knew that, Tom. Hell, you're on your way to becoming a legend here on the Mountain. What say you and I play a little game to see who's the best putter, Tom ol' buddy?" said Twitch. "I'm sure the crowd would love to see that." Twitch turned and faced the gallery. "Hey everybody, wouldn't you love to see Tommy and me go head to head?"

The Fable of Twitch, the God of Putting

Of all the gods, Twitch was undoubtedly the laziest and the most gifted—an all too common combination. Although not a big hitter, Twitch could work the ball like nobody else, hitting low fades, high hooks, or gentle draws whenever they were called for, and there was no putt he couldn't sink blindfolded. But unlike the other gods, Twitch seldom liked to go out on the course, preferring to lie around the clubhouse drinking nectar, playing games of chance, and chasing wood nymphs and goddesses around the pool.

When the Great God MacKenzie took the fair Rowena for a wife, Twitch's life changed forever. The first time Rowena showed up at the club, the gods were charmed, the goddesses were jealous, and Twitch fell deeply in love. But Rowena wouldn't give Twitch a tumble so he devised a scheme to gain her favors. Knowing that MacKenzie, like most golfers, was nowhere near as good a player as he imagined himself to be, Twitch enticed him into a match, spotting MacKenzie three holes. If MacKenzie won, Twitch would have to vacate the clubhouse and organize a junior golf program for Mount Augustus. But if Twitch won, MacKenzie would be forced to grant anything that Twitch desired.

Well, after pretending to struggle for the first few holes of the match, Twitch pulled away from MacKenzie easily, winning 6 and 5. When Twitch demanded a night with the fair Rowena as his prize, MacKenzie went ballistic causing earthquakes and thunderstorms throughout the Mountain. Ultimately he had no choice but to grant Twitch's wish.

Rowena, on the other hand, was not about to be had so easily. She placed a curse on the randy god of putting so that he would no longer be able to reach consummation, either in the bedroom or the golf course. On the appointed night Rowena showed up at Twitch's apartment perfumed and alluringly dressed. Through the whole night long Twitch's attempts to make love to the goddess were met with one embarrassment after another. When Rowena stomped off in the morning feigning insult, Twitch called after her coining the lament that inept lovers and golfers have been using ever since. "I don't understand. This has never happened to me before."

All the assembled gods, dwarfs, and wood nymphs applauded loudly and stomped their feet in response, and Twitch egged them on.

"Now you wouldn't want to disappoint all these nice folks, would you, Tom?"

"I'm not much of a betting man," I replied cautiously. "Besides, I really don't have anything to wager."

"Why, everybody has something to bet," Twitch replied. He looked me up and down carefully, letting his eyes rest upon each item of my apparel while he considered its value. Finally, his eyes came to rest on my shoes and he smiled broadly.

"I tell you what, Tom. Just to make it interesting, I'll wager this purse of gold I just won from the Great God MacKenzie himself against your wing tips."

I turned and looked at Harry, who was smiling at Twitch as if they were long-lost brothers. He whispered just loud enough for me to hear.

"Go for it, son. He can be had."

I pretended to think it over for another moment or two and then replied, "Okay, but I get to call your putt."

"Why, I think we can handle that, ol' buddy," said Twitch expansively. "So, what do you want me to do? A downhill forty-footer across three breaks with my eyes closed? How about a horseshoe putt?"

"What's a horseshoe putt?" I asked.

"Why, it's one of those putts that start uphill before swinging wide and falling back the other way to the hole," he explained.

"Golly, that sounds good," I replied with mock innocence.

"Or how about an obstacle course?" he asked. "Where I putt over a series of pitch marks, ball markers, and spike marks to reach the hole, which by the way, has a raised lip all around it. Everyone of them is a guaranteed crowd pleaser. So, what'll it be?"

Harry dropped to one knee and pretended to tie his shoe. "Make him putt short, Tommy. A real knee knocker," Harry whispered, a little louder this time.

"Why don't we start off with something simple," I said. "How about a straight putt."

"Fine and dandy," replied Twitch. "How long? Forty feet? Fifty? Just name your poison."

"How about a little two-footer?" I replied, deadpan.

Sweat began to break out on Twitch's forehead. "But that's child's play," he protested. "At least make it interesting for the crowd."

"Okay, one foot six inches," I said with a smile.

When he looked at me, there was murder in his eyes but he just nodded in agreement and a nymph with a yardstick ran onto the green to place his ball.

As soon as he stood over the putt it became clear that Harry knew exactly where the God of Putting lived. Not only was he sweating profusely and his hands trembling, but as he stepped up to the putt his entire body began vibrating and humming worse than when he had beaten MacKenzie. Twitch labored fiercely to control his shaking frame as he inched closer to the ball but it was no use. As soon as he was within a millimeter a tremendous spasm shook his body sending the Cuban cigar flying out of his mouth and causing the vibrating putter blade to rip into the side of the ball. It made a *ziiiipppp-chunnnkk* kind of sound as if some yah-hoo handyman had just gouged a chunk out of Grandma's prized walnut dining-room table with a router. The last I saw of that ball, it was skittering sideways across the green with its rubber windings hanging out of one side.

"Well, today must be your lucky day, mortal," said Twitch, barely suppressing his rage. He pulled a mono-grammed handkerchief from his vest pocket and mopped his brow. "But don't celebrate too soon," he continued with real menace in his voice. "You still have to make yours. And don't forget, if you miss, we go to a second round and then I'm the one who gets to call."

"Just ignore him, son," said Harry. "He's dead meat and he knows it."

Although my four-iron had caught the middle of the

green, the pin was tucked behind two traps near the front—a real sucker's placement if ever there was one. Going for the middle of the green had been the right play, but unfortunately that left me with a slippery downhill putt of some thirty feet and who knows how many breaks. As I squatted behind the ball, Harry stood behind me trying to read them.

"What do you think, Harry? Double breaker or worse?" I muttered. "I don't think I can do this."

"Course you can, it's in the bank. Don't worry about the breaks, son," said Harry soothingly. "Just roll it real smooth and trust the ball."

As I stood up I looked for a coin to re-mark the ball. I wanted to make sure that I had the logo lined up with my target. That's when my fingers found the reliquary Harry had given me. It was giving off a pleasant warmth. A wave of confidence surged through me and I stepped up to the ball without bothering to re-mark it. Thanks to Harry I had my edge.

I stroked the putt, and just as he had said, the ball seemed to take on a life of its own. It skittered for a moment over the slick, wet surface of the dew-laden green and then began to roll. It took the first break at too quick a pace, and then gathered speed as it broke down and to the right through the big swale. At the speed it was traveling, the only way it would not run clear through the green into the large trap on the other side was if it hit the hole, and even then there was no guarantee. But then inexplicably, the ball slowed as it reached the deepest point in the swale. It turned softly to the left, then took another quick break to the right, heading for the cup like a racing pigeon coming home after a cross-country trek. The ball approached the cup almost cautiously from the left side, ran along the rim, and then at the back of the cup it suddenly fell back toward me. I heard the still unfamiliar clatter of a birdie three dropping into the hole.

As the gallery cheered wildly I gave Harry Brady a bear hug. My round at Mount Augustus was finally over. I had birdied the last three holes and I had beaten Twitch. I had played the best golf of my life and I had won. But my celebration was to be a short one. There were too many questions.

"Was it me, Harry, or was it the charm?"

Harry patted me on the back strangely, almost in consolation. "I think you know the answer to that, Tom. You've got the secret, now you just have to decide what to do with it."

I saw Wendell drop a pebble into the open sack that Ruppert held, and then they advanced across the green toward me with MacTavish, the God of Rules following close behind.

"Uh oh," Harry shrugged, "showtime."

MacTavish stopped in front of me and unrolled a sheet of parchment. Then in a voice loud enough for the entire gallery to hear he asked, "Are you Tom Cruikshank?"

"You know who I am," I replied.

"The same Tom Cruikshank that's employed by Hartless & Craven on the island of Manhattan and who traveled here three days ago in the company of one Harry Brady."

"Yep."

"Then, I have here a warrant for your arrest," MacTavish said loudly, "signed this day by the Great God MacKenzie, himself!"

"What's the charge, MacTavish?" Harry interjected.

"Stay out of this, Harry Brady," said MacTavish as he consulted the parchment and intoned solemnly, "This time you have gone too far."

"What is the charge, MacTavish?" Harry shouted.

"Five hundred separate infractions of the rules of golf!"

"That's ridiculous," I yelled. "Let me see that."

"Place Cruickshank in shackles and bring him to the clubhouse." MacTavish smiled.

Wendell and Ruppert grabbed my arms but I wrestled free long enough to grab the "warrant" from MacTavish's hands. There was nothing on it but a crayon drawing of a tabby cat holding a mouse in its mouth. Scrawled underneath the image in big block letters was a single word, PUSSYCAT.

MacTavish snatched the parchment back before anyone else could see it and stuffed it inside his jacket pocket. As I was led away in chains, MacTavish whipped the crowd into a frenzy, leading them in a blood-chilling chant, "TO THE FOUNDRY, TO THE FOUNDRY!"

I was being framed.

CHAPTER 18

At the Court of the Great MacKenzie

In which Tom Cruickshank accounts for his sins

The clubhouse at Mount Augustus loomed ahead like the Addams family mansion come to life. A dark, monstrous edifice with a mansard roof, it was pure Victorianna, except for a few additions that must have been added at a later date, such as some side buildings that could have come from a 1950s Iowa farm, Italian Renaissance walkways, and a rustic English garden bordered by overgrown hedges. The effect was so surreal even the soft glow of late-afternoon sunlight couldn't conceal the menace.

Inside, the place felt as old as the Mountain itself, and the atmosphere was incredibly oppressive—probably enhanced by the fact that two extremely sour dwarfs named Diego and Meldrick were dragging me around in chains. We made our way through long, winding hallways whose walls were a massive collage of paintings, photographs, yellowing scorecards, newspaper clippings, and letters—all related to golf. Tucked away in every nook and cranny was an incredible collection of clubs, balls, hats, and golf clothing from many eras. One door was open as we passed, and I saw an antique billiards table with balls and cues carelessly scattered on the felt as if a game had been suddenly interrupted.

Too soon for my taste, we stood in a large vestibule with huge doors on three sides. Hung by a chain to the middle doors was a gleaming brass plaque that said, "Members Executive Boardroom, No Admittance, Tribunal In Progress."

Diego, the taller of the dwarfs, took a piece of black cloth from his pouch and jumped on Meldrick's shoulders. They walked around my back and I felt the blindfold slip over my head. I took a deep breath as they knocked in unison on the massive doors that opened immediately with a mighty wrenching sound.

"Move it, cheater pig," said Meldrick, poking me between the shoulder blades.

The clank of my chains on ancient floorboards marked out a rhythm reminiscent of a funeral march as we walked deeper into the room and loud voices signaled that the gallery was pouring into the chamber behind us. My trial was to be a very public event.

Suddenly we stopped and strong arms guided me down into a hard, straight-backed chair. The noise level was rising steadily.

"SILENCE!" a voice blared like trumpet over the assembly. I knew it was MacTavish. "REMOVE THE MORTAL'S BLINDFOLD."

My head was pulled roughly back and the blindfold was yanked away. I was staring up into a towering semicircular alcove with tall windows that soared to a vaulted half ceiling. Frosted on the edges, each contained a stained-glass inset—tableaus that depicted the legends of the Gods of Golf. The shouting began again in earnest.

As my eye traveled down the windows to ground level my heart began to thud in my chest. Seven circular wooden pews rose out of a low stage forming a tiered amphitheater that faced the huge room. The top row must have been fifteen feet in the air. The pews were packed with the Gods of Mount Augustus.

The Great God MacKenzie was sitting dead center on an ornately carved wooden throne built into the first pew. Angus, the God of Starters, was on his left wearing a dour expression, and on his right was Fergus, the God of Greenskeepers. Then came Bertie, the God of the Long Ball—apparently paroled just for the trial; Divot, the God of Bad Lies; the ravishing Glenda, Goddess of Golf; Reg, the God of Caddies; Dirk, the God of Tactics wearing a bear's head as a helmet; Weyland, the God of Equipment; the vile Harpies, Heidi and Lorena; Ichabod, the God of Instruction; and Twitch, the God of Putting, who was dozing quietly in his pew with a tumbler full of whiskey held precariously in his fingers.

Even Horace the God of Hazards was there, separated by a boundary line of red paint. Cruel Shank, also off by himself, rested his patrician jaw on the handle of his black umbrella while he glared at the other gods in disgust.

With the exception of Mulligan, who had yet to make an appearance, the tribunal consisted of almost everyone I had met on my round plus a few minor deities on the back benches whom I didn't recognize. Although there wasn't a smiling face in the crowd, they were all decked out for a festive occasion, wearing matching Highland kilts and natty green blazers with the emblem of Mount Augustus sewn on their breast pockets.

MacTavish stood opposite me at the prosecutor's desk, looking like a cat who had swallowed not only the canary, but a whole family of finches. Over his kilt and blazer he wore a black barrister's robe, and sported a powdered periwig on his balding head. Satisfied that the room was full, he approached the throne and bowed grandly, causing his wig to fall on the wooden floor. Ruppert was at his side in a flash and replaced the hairpiece as MacTavish rose to face MacKenzie. In his haste, however, Ruppert got the thing on backward so that its pigtail hung down between the barrister's eyes, making him look very foolish indeed. Several of the gods snickered.

"Get on wi' it. Me robe is gettin' hot an' scratchy," commanded MacKenzie, who had traded his comfortable tweeds for an ermine-lined tartan robe, and a golden wreath of heather for his snap brim cap.

At MacTavish's signal, Eunuch stood up from his bench on the left side of the room and banged a vintage bottlenose driver on the floor three times, singing in his high soprano, "OYEZ, OYEZ, THE TRIBUNAL OF THE GREAT GOD MACKENZIE IS NOW IN SESSION. HEAR ALL ON THE MOUNTAIN THE TRIAL OF THOMAS CRUICKSHANK, ESQUIRE. AND MAY JUSTICE BE SERVED."

Eunuch smiled shyly and sat down. Horace reached down and patted him on the shoulder. The gallery responded with a smattering of applause and a few rude guffaws.

MacTavish pompously adjusted his powdered wig and began.

"M'Lords, this is a very grave day in the history of our benighted realm. The mortal Tom Cruickshank stands before us today, accused of crimes so heinous, that if you find him guilty, he should never again see the light of day. And as you shall see shortly, the evidence against him is overwhelming. But, m'lords, the real question before this august body is whether the noble experiment we began some four hundred years ago—as mortal man counts time, should be allowed to continue."

Just then, a figure in a baggy seersucker suit and Panama hat pushed through the crowd carrying a bulging leather briefcase. Despite the fact the room was chilly, he was mopping his brow with a large linen handkerchief.

"Yore honor, Ah really mus' protest," the man bellowed in an orator's voice dripping with the languid accent of the Mississippi Gulf Coast. "They-ah has bin a gra-a-a-ve miscarriage uv justis, hea-ah. Aah move for an immediate dis-missal, yore honor, on tha grounds that the prosecution has no evidence at all to support these spurious charges."

Placing his briefcase on the table in front of me, he removed his jacket, revealing a spectacular set of crimson and cream braces. Then he turned around and winked at me. It was Mulligan, the God of Excuses.

"Who are you supposed to be?" I asked. "Atticus Finch?"

"Keep yore shorts on, boy," he answered, hooking his thumbs under his suspenders. "I'm yore dee-fense attorney appointed by tha court to keep yore sorry ass out of tha foundry. I believe you already have mah card."

"Perfect," I replied, positive that now I had no chance at all.

MacTavish smiled wryly at Mulligan's bumbling entrance and cleared his throat loudly to settle the room.

"Yes, m'lords, it has been four hundred years of earth time," he continued. "Long enough, in my humble estimation, to have established the game in all of its divine symmetry and exquisite subtlety among men.

"Yet, in all that time, we have never found a single mortal worthy of the game. They lie, they cheat, they throw their clubs and whine like babies, and now it must come to an end. So today, if you find the defendant guilty as charged—as I'm sure you will, the time will have come to withdraw the pleasures of the ancient game from mortal man."

Expecting my defense attorney to leap up and shout his

objections to the rooftops, I leaned over and saw that Mulligan was busy writing on a legal tablet. My esteemed counsel was playing a game of Hanged Man. I slumped back in my chair in resignation. I was toast.

"The evidence, if you please," MacTavish continued.

Wendell approached the bench, dragging the bag of rocks MacTavish had confronted me with on the sixteenth hole.

"This is the mortal's tally, m'lords," said MacTavish solemnly. As he tipped the bag and dumped the stones on the floor, it sounded like someone pulled off a sustained burst on a machine gun. "It contains 442 pebbles, one for each stroke played and/or penalty stroke assessed—proof positive that Thomas Cruickshank is guilty as charged."

As if on cue, half the gallery stood up and began chanting, "TO THE FOUNDRY! TO THE FOUNDRY!"

"Hoss-feathers," cried Mulligan, pounding the table for emphasis. "Surely y'all can't count tha rocks those idiots Wendell and Ruppert picked up. Why those ol' boys couldn't count their fingers and toes with a calculator."

"M'lords, I really must object," said MacTavish.

"I'd object, too, if I had two lamebrains like that workin' fer me," Mulligan interjected. "They're so stupid they think asphalt is a hip disease. Furthermore, yore honor, their brains're slicker than peeled onions. Their bells don't ring on Sunday morning. . . ."

"SILENCE!" roared MacKenzie. As his voice echoed through the chamber, the earth trembled beneath us and rain began to beat against the windows.

"Yer tryin' mah patience. If yer nae careful, Ah'll turn ye both intae wee beavers." Fergus rose angrily from his seat, but MacKenzie silenced him. "Tae na offense, Fergus. Ah've na time fer prideful feelin's ta'day." He turned to MacTavish. "Now, git on wi' yer evidence, roolemaker."

At MacTavish's signal, Wendell rolled in a rude wooden barrow overflowing with objects identified with paper tags. MacTavish covered his eyes and withdrew what appeared to be the wheels of a hand-pulled golf cart.

"M'lords, these were found in the reeds off the fifth tee," he said solemnly. "Proving beyond a shadow of a doubt that the wheels came off of Tom Cruickshank's game early in his fateful round!"

"But I wasn't using a cart," I objected. "I was carrying my bag. This is a frame-up!"

"TO THE FOUNDRY!" cried the gallery, a little louder this time.

"And here is a bag of some fifteen golf balls recovered from the rough and water holes of the course," MacTavish continued, "many bearing the logo of the accused's employer, I might add. Proof that the accused is not only a terrible hacker, but that he should have been assessed at least fifteen penalty strokes and possibly many more."

"TAKE HIM TO THE FOUNDRY! TO THE FOUNDRY!" shouted the gallery in unison. Not only were they louder now, but there more of them, and their mood was turning uglier by the minute.

Warming to his task, MacTavish jumped on top of the prosecutor's table, raising a sheaf of papers aloft for all to see.

"Here are affidavits from ten different trees that have been struck and permanently damaged by the accused."

MacTavish's latest bit of "evidence" was met with absolute chaos and vociferous booing from a group of dryads from the back of the room. "BUTCHER! DEFILER! LET'S TAKE HIM NOW!" I turned to see hand-painted signs with slogans such as DEATH TO THE ABUSER OF INNOCENT TREES waving in the air. Several of the dryads had their arms in slings.

"Are ye nae finished?" asked MacKenzie.

"Why, I'm only beginning, m'lord," replied MacTavish. "There are scorecards from Pine Valley, Pebble Beach, Firestone, and Eisenhower Park covered with eraser marks, balata scrapings from the toes of his golf shoes, and more than one hundred plaster impressions from his divots. And last, but not least, a pair of muddy socks recovered from the bench on the sixteenth tee!"

"MUDDY SOCKS!" MacKenzie bellowed from his throne. "Ye mean tae tell me tha' he's been playin' tha last three holes wi' nae socks?"

"Yes, m'lord," said MacTavish grandly. "A felony infraction of the dress code if I'm not mistaken."

"And you never are," Ruppert piped in.

"TO THE FOUNDRY! TO THE FOUNDRY!" the mob chanted.

"SILENCE," yelled MacKenzie. "Hae ye more, MacTavish?"

Wendell rushed to MacTavish with a sheaf of papers and whispered urgently in his ear. MacTavish nodded, read them quickly and turned to MacKenzie, looking shaken.

"M'lord, we have just come into possession of shocking new evidence that will reveal the perverse nature and true character of the defendant. In all my centuries on this mountain, I have never seen the like. I am deeply saddened by what I must bring before the tribunal this day," Mac-Tavish said so quietly the gallery had to strain to hear him.

"Well, what hae ye got?" asked MacKenzie impatiently.

"Transcripts, m'lord! Recordings of every instance in the last ten years when Tom Cruickshank called upon the Gods of Golf."

"Proceed," said the Great God MacKenzie.

MacTavish opened the first transcript.

"July 23, 1989. Fifth hole at Eisenhower State Park. Long Island, New York. The defendant was heard to say, 'Oh please, Gods of Golf, please let me make this putt and I'll never take a mulligan again.'

"How about this," said MacTavish flipping several pages. "September 14, 1990. Corporate Outing. Twelfth tee at Sleepy Hollow Country Club, Scarborough, New York. The defendant was heard to say, 'Oh, don't let me slice, Gods of Golf, please don't let me slice another ball in front of my boss. Please, please, please.' "

"Disgusting," snorted Angus from his pew.

"Gutless coward," muttered Dirk.

I wondered what the food was like in the foundry cafeteria. I wondered if there was food.

"What a wimp!" sniffed Twitch. I hadn't realized he was awake.

MacTavish closed the transcript and let it drop to the ground dramatically.

"M'lords, we have 792 pages of such incidents, and on some occasions, the members of this club saw fit to grant the defendant's request. And when we didn't, he complained bitterly, saying, 'What are you doing to me?' some 536 times, 'What have I done to deserve this?' 825 times. And 'Why is it always me?' 1196 times."

The gallery gasped, and then the chamber was as still as a tomb.

MacKenzie leaned down and glowered at me. "So, ya dunna like how tha Gods are treatin' ya?"

"Well, I . . ."

"Think tha Gods are only sendin' bad breaks yer way, do ya?" Fergus cut in.

"I must admit that it seems that way sometimes," I replied.

"Well then, what have you ever done for us?" roared Divot.

"I don't understand . . ." I stuttered.

"When was the last time ya dumped a sleeve of new balatas into a water hole?" asked Horace evenly. Up to that point, I had thought he was my friend.

"And when was the last time ya fixed a ball mark that was na yers?" asked Fergus.

"When was the last time ya tipped yer starter more than a fiver?" snarled Angus.

"Sir, if I might . . . ?" It was Reg. He rose from his pew. Raymond stood as well, balancing himself with his hooves on the pew in front of him.

"Aye, caddie, speak," waved MacKenzie impatiently.

"Perhaps I could put this in perspective for our errant mortal." As he addressed me he gently stroked the sheep's woolly head. "All right, guv'nor, have you ever—at any time, sacrificed a goat, pig, or other small animal to his nibs, The MacKenzie?"

"Sacrifice a pig? A goat? You mean like . . ." I was speechless. I had never even cleaned a fish for dinner.

"Ach, ya dunna hae tae slit its throat on a stone altar or nuthing," MacKenzie jumped in. "A simple barbecue in mah honor wud hae been enough. Ah'm na a bleedin' savage . . ."

"It is your basic *quid pro quo,* after all," MacTavish noted sanctimoniously.

"I . . . I didn't know . . ." was all I could say.

"Ignorance 'tis na excuse," said MacKenzie sternly.

The tribunal broke into a rumble of jeers and loud conversations. Waiting for the noise to subside, MacTavish paced around the room looking up into the faces of the gods, obviously pleased with the impact of his latest barrage of evidence. It was my darkest moment, or so I thought.

"Now, are ye finished, man?" MacKenzie asked MacTavish.

"There's one more exhibit, m'lord," he replied. "A piece of evidence that proves beyond a shadow of a doubt that Tom Cruickshank is not only a liar and a cheat, but . . . A THIEF!"

At MacTavish's signal, Wendell and Ruppert pulled my rain pants down to my ankles, revealing a pair of bony knees and the clean new pair of boxer shorts I had taken from MacKenzie's locker.

"Mah boxers!" exclaimed MacKenzie. He sat bolt upright in his throne with a look of horror on his face and the rumble in the chamber rose to a deafening crescendo.

"I put it to you, m'lord," MacTavish shouted over the noise, "that a man that would steal another's underwear is capable of absolutely anything!"

MacKenzie looked over at me with a mixture of sadness and revulsion. He was close to tears.

"So, how do you vote, m'lords," MacTavish harangued the gallery, "shall we take him to the foundry?"

Mulligan jumped on top of the table and waved his seersucker jacket around his head like a banner. To my utter astonishment, he threw back his head and yelled, "TO THE FOUNDRY!"

The chamber promptly went berserk. By acclamation, the entire assembly voted to condemn me. A mob of dryads, nymphs, fauns, and gods of all description began to close in and I felt myself being raised up in the air. MacTavish was standing on his table shaking hands with Wendell and Ruppert.

Suddenly, a shrill whistle cut through the air. Mind you, this was no ordinary whistle, it had pitch, resonance, and volume—in short, the kind of authority needed to find a cab on a rainy day in Manhattan. The mob parted like the Red Sea as a man wearing a green member's jacket made his way to the front.

Harry Brady had finally arrived.

Freshly shaved and showered, Harry jumped on top of the defense table. He looked hale and hearty, seeming to have dropped another ten years since I left him on the eighteenth green. In fact, I could have sworn that a little color was creeping back into his hair.

"Take your hands off him!" shouted Harry and whistled again to make sure everyone was paying attention.

"You can't save him, Harry Brady," barked MacTavish. "The evidence is overwhelming, and the mortal must pay the penalty."

Several of the dwarfs started to chant again, "To the foundry! To the . . ."

Harry put a stop to the chanting by leaping across the room onto MacTavish's table, chasing away the prosecutor and his two assistants.

"Here's what I think of your evidence, MacTavish," he said, kicking transcripts and ledgers to the floor.

"You've gone too far this time, Harry," MacTavish spat. "There's room enough at Weyland's forge for one more, I'll warrant."

"ENUFF!" the Great God MacKenzie shouted, raising his golden mashie overhead. "Ah'll decide who goes tae tha foundry on me own mountain! Now, Harry Brady, ye'd better hae a guid reason fer disruptin' these proceedin's."

"Well, Mac, I just can't stand idly by and watch a miscarriage of justice."

"But, Harry, tha roolemaker has made his case," MacKenzie replied gravely, "an' tha evidence is overwhelmin'."

Harry walked to the end of the table, kicking off more ledgers on the way, and sat on the edge facing MacKenzie. "Oh, I guess Tom did all those things all right. Probably enough to send him to the foundry—even if you subtract some of MacTavish's ridiculous penalty strokes."

"To the foundry!" the dwarfs began chanting again.

"Now just hold on everyone and let me finish," said Harry, raising his hands to quiet them.

"I didn't bring this boy here because I thought he was perfect. It's obvious he's not. I selected Tom Cruickshank to replace me on the Mountain because of his heart—that's the important thing. This boy really loves the game. And that's all that matters."

"What a touching story, Harry. I'm sure there's not a dry eye in the house," said MacTavish. He dabbed at the corners of his eyes theatrically. "However, you are hardly a shining example of mortal perfection, and I won't bother to document your failures, they are well known to us all. But the law is clear and it applies to everyone who comes to Mount Augustus."

"Everyone?" asked Harry with a devilish grin.

"Well, everyone except . . ."

A troubled look crossed MacTavish's face as he realized what Harry had done.

"Everyone except the Keeper of the Book," said Harry, finishing MacTavish's thought. "As the delegate from the mortal world, he's got diplomatic immunity, isn't that right?"

"You didn't . . ." MacTavish muttered.

"Oh, but I did," Harry replied. "Tom Cruickshank has been the Keeper of the Book ever since I passed it to him on the sixteenth hole."

"You have the sacred book of golf?" asked Mulligan in astonishment.

"Sacred book of golf? I don't know," I stammered. "You don't mean Harry's old diary, do you?"

"It's right there in his bag," said Harry simply.

"Oh, my god," screamed MacTavish. "Harry's passed him the power! He's got the secret!"

MacKenzie raised his hands to quiet the room, and then in a somber voice, he asked Harry, "Do ye ken wha' this means, man?"

"All too well, Mac," said Harry. "I can never return to Mount Augustus, because there can only be one Keeper of the Book at a time."

Harry paused and slowly removed his green blazer before continuing.

"I'll miss you, Mac. I'll miss a lot of you in this room, but I finally figured out what most of you have known for a long time—it's time for me to retire. And now according to the bylaws of the Divine and Ancient Golf Club of Mount Augustus, my membership, with all its rights and privileges, belongs to Tom Cruickshank. Remove the shackles, Meldrick, so the boy can put on his jacket."

While the dwarfs fumbled with my chains, Harry readied the green member's jacket for me to slip into.

"Boy, am I glad to see you, Harry," I said. "What took you so long?"

"Why, I always shower after a round, son," said Harry, smiling broadly. "Don't you?"

"Yeah, when I'm not all tied up," I replied as Meldrick finally freed my hands.

I slipped on the jacket and Harry smoothed away the wrinkles, eyeing the effect like a veteran tailor.

"A little snug in the chest, but all in all not a bad fit, son," said Harry finally. Then he buttoned the blazer and wheeled me around for the gallery to admire. I was greeted by waves of applause. At MacKenzie's signal, Angus stood up in his pew.

"Welcome tae tha club, Tommy lad," said Angus. "Has

mah ol' friend Harry tole ye tha' ye mus' now ask a boon o' Tha MacKenzie?''

"A boon? I'm afraid I don't understand," I replied.

Angus explained that as long as there had been delegates from the mortal world, the Great God of Golf had traditionally granted them one special wish to seal the bargain. It seemed that when Harry's time came, he had told MacKenzie that he had always wanted to be a scratch player. And so, that's what he became, a scratch golfer—nothing more and nothing less.

From the look on Harry's face, the "boon" was a sore subject, but it went a long way toward explaining his uncanny ability to make par from just about anywhere on the course.

"Weel then, wha's yer decision, lad?" asked Horace.

"Will ye be a scratch player like Harry?" asked Angus. "Or will ye be a tournament player an' always be under?"

The gallery became so quiet and still they didn't seem real as they waited for me to speak. It was like being alone in the sculpture collection of the Metropolitan Museum early on a Saturday morning.

"Neither," I said finally. "I don't want either one."

"The mortal insults the Great God again!" shrieked MacTavish. "Take him to the foundry!"

Chaos descended on the room. MacKenzie clapped a hand over his forehead and slumped down in his seat while the rest of the gods jumped up from their pews, and everyone started talking at once.

"And if it means I've got to carry the secret with me from now on, I'm afraid I'll have to return the book, too," I shouted over the din, unbuttoning the blazer and slipping it off.

"Thanks, but I really can't accept this," I said, handing it back to a dumbfounded Harry Brady.

"But why?" asked Harry.

"Aye, laddie," Angus joined in. "Ye owe us an explanation. Quiet doon everyone an' let tha lad speak."

"Well, it's kind of hard to explain," I began. "I've been

playing golf since I was a kid, but I'm beginning to see that it's been for all the wrong reasons, like trying to please my dad or to help me up the ladder. And because of that, I've done some pretty dumb things—things I'm ashamed of now."

"Are ye saying yer givin' up tha game, laddie?" asked Horace quietly.

"Oh no, not at all," I replied. "Before I came to Mount Augustus, I never knew how much I loved it. And now that I know, I just can't imagine giving any part of it away. Especially its mystery."

Angus thumped his shillelagh hard on the floor several times. "Heer, heer!" he said, and nodded his approval.

"Well spoken, dear boy," called Ichabod from an upper pew.

MacKenzie was sitting forward on his throne listening intently.

"You see, when it comes to golf, I want to be just like everybody else. I want to be devastated by my failures and thrilled by my successes. And, I want to have memories, so that on long winter evenings when the course is resting under a blanket of snow, I can think back on one of those perfect shots that came to rest within the leather, or remember making a double-breaker of forty feet to win a tough Nassau from the guys at the club.

"And on my bad days, I want to be free to moan and groan over my rotten luck. And yes, like every other golfer, I want to be free to call upon the Gods of Golf to keep my drive from slicing or to help my ball find its way to the green through a grove of trees. And maybe, just maybe, when I call, one of you in this room will see your way to helping me out. That would be all right, too. Anyway, that's why I've got to turn down the membership, and the secret, too."

When I finished, MacKenzie's face was twitching and his robe was writhing like a sackful of eels. Every head in the chamber was craned in his direction, watching in suspense as his agitation mounted, just waiting for the volcano to blow.

"NAY! NAY! NAY!" MacKenzie shouted, shaking the timbers of the clubhouse till the air was filled with plaster dust.

"M'lord, are you all right?" asked MacTavish, rushing to his side.

"NAY, AH'M NAE ALL RIGHT, YE BLEEDIN' FOOL!" MacKenzie continued at the top of his lungs. "AH'M BLOODY PISSED! IF HE'S NAE CUMIN' TAE MOUNT AUGUSTUS, AN' HARRY'S NA CUMIN' AGIN, WHO'S GOIN' TAE BRING ME MAH BOXER SHORTS FRUM BROOKS BROTHERS?"

MacKenzie's realization began to filter down to the rest of the pantheon and pure pandemonium broke out in the boardroom. Gods were leaping up from their pews and shouting simultaneously at the top of their lungs. And of course, no one was listening to anyone else.

"Who's goin' tae bring me mah cheese? Mah wheels o' brie?" shrieked Horace, looking even more unhinged than usual.

"Where am I going to get my scotch and Havanas?" wailed Twitch.

"An' what about tha latest clubs?" whined Angus.

" 'Tis time ye stopped usin' crutches anyway," Weyland shouted from the other side of the room, "and get back tae nature!"

"Git back in yer hole, vermin!" Angus yelled back. "An' ye can tae yer blocks o' persimmon wi' ye!"

Every god seemed to have their secret itch that only Harry Brady could scratch. The Goddess Rowena liked a special shade of blush that he picked up at the Ritz, while Glenda fancied cream-filled chocolates from Belgium. Fergus liked tins of sardines—the cheaper the better, while Weyland coveted flawless hickory shafts from Tennessee, and on and on. And now the entire pantheon at Mount Augustus faced the very real prospect of going cold turkey.

As the hysteria grew, objects began to fly around the

room. Featheries, balatas, gutta perchas, and balls of all descriptions filled the air, as well as tees, ball markers, and dried divots.

With his gnarled starter's stick, Angus took a round-house swing at Dirk who was brandishing his dagger menacingly, but instead of clipping the God of Tactics, Angus caught MacTavish square in the back of the head, felling him like a miniature redwood. The God of Rules tumbled over the prosecutor's table and then lay quite still among his books and papers on the floor. That's when Harry pulled me under the defense trestle for safety.

"I'm afraid this is all my fault," Harry shouted into my ear. "It's the salesman in me. I've been treating them like clients for forty years, and now they're hooked. They'll never let us leave, you know. We need a plan."

"Any ideas?" I asked.

"Fresh out, you're supposed to be the brains here." Harry had passed the buck. The battle raged above us, projectiles of all description flying like Bat Day at Shea Stadium.

Then it struck me.

"Okay," I said. "Got one."

"What is it?"

"Trust me. How do we get their attention without being killed?"

Harry smiled and whispered in my ear. On the count of three, we cupped our hands over our mouths and with all the power we could muster, yelled the international golfer's distress signal:

"FORE!"

Every single god, nymph, faun, dwarf, and dryad hit the deck with a resounding thud. The room was silent as the mob covered their heads and searched the sky. As order was being restored I told Harry my idea and he took the floor, laughing. Harry proposed to the gods that I should be offered an out-of-town membership—a compromise that would allow me to visit Mount Augustus now and again, but that would not require me to compromise my stature as a hopeless duffer.

When Harry finished, MacKenzie's brow was knitted in deep thought and the room was silent as a tomb for at least a minute. Then the great god leaned forward from his throne and spoke to me directly.

"Clever," he said slowly. "A very clever compromise, indeed. But in order tae seal tha bargain, ye mus' still ask a boon o' the Great God MacKenzie, otherwise Ah could niver accept yer services."

"Can I ask anything at all?"

"Anything wi'in me power," MacKenzie replied, raising his eyebrow.

"Then, I ask that you correct an injustice," I said. "I want you to release Toe Wedge Jackson and Ken Hoeffer from the foundry and send them home."

MacKenzie's divine face shone like a thousand suns. He raised his arms and Eunuch thumped the floor three times with his stick to signal the Great God's pronouncement.

"Hear now and spread tha news to every part o' Mount Augustus," MacKenzie began, his booming voice filling every corner of the hall. "I, Tha MacKenzie, find 'tis much sense in this plan. An' so it shall be frum this time forward. Step forward, Tom Cruickshank. Ye hae been found worthy o' tha Mountain an' are bestowed tha gift o' out-a-town membership wi' all tha rights an' privileges tha' pertain tae it. Ye may cum an' go as ye please an' tend tae tha responsibilities tha cum wi' this honor wi' great care an' devotion."

"Well, I guess that about does it," Harry chuckled.

But then from behind us came a screeching noise—the sound of furniture being dragged across a hardwood floor. Like a sea monster rising from the depths, MacTavish, the God of Rules, was emerging from his scattered papers and ledgers, pulling himself up hand over hand on the leg of the prosecutor's table.

"Hold everything!" he roared. "Our business is not over here, m'lords. Not by a long shot. Yes, the mortal has squirmed like through a loophole in the law and has avoided the jaws of the foundry. But there's still a question that remains to be resolved. The primary question if you will . . ."

"Aw, come on, MacTavish," Harry said. "You're not still talking about withdrawing the game?"

"A bargain is a bargain, Brady," MacTavish shouted, pulling a yellowing parchment from inside his robe.

"Forty earth years ago, the Great God MacKenzie himself affixed his seal to this document declaring that if we could not find a mortal golfer worthy of the divine game by the end of Harry's tenure as mortal advocate and Keeper of the Book, that the game would be finally and irrevocably withdrawn from mankind. And I submit to you that even though the prevaricating mortal has escaped justice because of Harry Brady's cunning, he has in no wise demonstrated his worthiness, or the worthiness of mankind to play the game of golf."

MacKenzie was clearly annoyed, but knew that despite the fear of losing Harry's booty, MacTavish still had plenty of followers in the room. So he proceeded cautiously when he addressed the tribunal.

"Are thair na gods tha' wish tae speak on this matter?"

After a moment of silence, MacKenzie turned to me.

"Weel, Tom," he said, "tha' leaves you. Yer tha mortal advocate now. Wha' hae ye tae say in defense o' mortal man?"

"You want me to answer him?" I stammered.

"Go ahead, Tom," said Glenda.

"You've got the power, son," said Harry. "That's what it's for." He gave me a little nudge, and I stepped forward to address the great god one on one.

"Look, I'll admit I've got my failings; I never pretended otherwise, but that's no reason to withdraw the game from mankind. I don't know where you've been looking, but there are a lot of folks out there who play the game just because they love it. Players who wouldn't dream of taking liberties with their scores . . ."

"Oh, and in what fantasy land is this?" MacTavish sneered.

"You probably won't find them in your fancy country clubs where they double-cut the greens every morning," I continued. "The people I'm talking about are just average folks. Grade school kids down in Alabama playing with their fathers' cut-down clubs. Farmers in Nebraska relaxing after the plowing's done on a little nine-hole course with sand greens. A Tex-Mex kid down in San Antonio playin' the grown-ups for quarters, and dreaming of being the next Lee Trevino. . . ."

"You're making me ill," whined MacTavish, holding a rag to the lump on the back of his head. "Next thing you'll have them harvesting crops between holes . . ."

"Thair really are such people out there?" asked MacKenzie, leaning forward.

"Thousands," I replied with growing confidence. "Maybe more."

"As lang as Ah thought sich gowfers as these still walked tha earth," MacKenzie replied, "Ah could niver wi'draw tha game."

"Oh, wonderful," MacTavish steamed. "You're going to take the word of a man who underestimated his score by a modest three hundred strokes?"

"No, MacTavish," said the Great God angrily, "but Ah'm gonna give him a chance to prove his case. Jist as ye hae bin given tha opportunity tae prove yers. If it makes ye feel any better, consider it a stay o' execution. Fer one year's mortal time. Then, he mus' return tae tha Mountain wi' proof tha' sich gowfers exist. Do ye agree tae tha', Tom?"

"Yes," I said, "I'll do that."

"An' wha' about ye, roolemaker? Can ye stifle tha bile in yer throat lang enuff tae strike a compromise?"

"It's a waste of time," MacTavish snapped bitterly. "The result will be the same . . ."

MacKenzie shot the God of Rules a look that caused thunder to rumble outside and the windows to rattle.

"But then, what's a mortal year?" said MacTavish with a brittle smile.

"THA MACKENZIE HAE SPOKEN," the great god shouted to the gallery, and then in front of the roaring crowd he shook my hand.

We had a deal.

After the dust had settled Harry and I were standing on the member's terrace with flagons of mead recently freshened by one of Glenda's nymphs. We were looking out over the Mountain. The sun was beginning to set and once again the richness and bounty of the world of Mount Augustus outlined in light and shadow was breathtaking. There was a chill in the air but my new member's jacket was more than enough to ward it off.

"Aren't you going to miss it?" I asked.

"A little," he smiled ruefully. "A lot, actually, but not enough to have it the way it was."

"And you can't come back, ever?"

"Not without a member, Tom. When I walk through the trees I won't remember the way back."

"That's kind of sad."

"No it isn't. The world is full of golf courses and I intend to hack around as many as I can while I can still swing a club. I'll be all right, Tom. Like I said before, it's your turn now and you made a far better deal than I did. Enjoy it. That's the real secret."

"Thanks, Harry." We shook hands and I think there was a trace of a tear in both our eyes. But Harry Brady was far too Protestant to end on a note as sentimental as that. As a matter of fact, so was I.

"I knew I made the right choice back in the grill room," Harry said seriously.

"How?" I asked.

"You hated the snapper soup." He laughed as we shook hands. "Well, I guess I'd better clean out my locker."

Then he set down his drink, winked at me, and walked outside. It was to be the last time I saw Harry Brady.

As I left Mount Augustus, I was escorted down the Mountain by a large throng of well-wishers, all of whom wanted to tell me about some little thing or other they desired. By the time I reached the base of the Mountain, a blanket of mist was covering the first fairway and I had filled four pages back and front in a little spiral notebook Harry had given me. As I started a fifth page, I noticed for the first time that my escort had dwindled down to Angus, the God of Starters.

"Where'd everybody go?" I asked.

"There's a scramble startin' jus' after dinner," Angus replied. "They'll see ye tha next time ye cum."

"When will that be?" I asked. "I mean, how will I know when to bring this stuff, and how will I pay for all of it, and . . ."

"Keep yer britches on, laddie. MacKenzie will tae care o' that. And speaking of britches, I think I'd better return yer 'ga-tae-hell pants.' Yer a bit broader in the beam than myself, laddie, and besides, tha color hurts me eyes."

So Angus returned my kelly green pants with the little whales on them, but he also was careful to give me his exact size—just in case I found myself in Brooks Brothers anytime in the near future.

"And now Ah mus' be leavin,' too, Tommy lad. Ye cannae hae a shotgun start wi'out a starter, now can ye."

Angus stepped into the mist and began to disappear. I suddenly realized that there were still questions to be answered.

"Angus, come on, how do I get back?" I called.

He continued to recede into the swirling vapor.

"Ye'll know," he answered.

"How do I pay for all this stuff?" I called again.

"Tha MacKenzie will reveal all when 'tis time."

And Angus was gone. I turned and walked into the trees.

EPILOGUE

Pine Valley

In which Tom learns with some regret that you can come home again

Retracing the path Harry and I took through the woods three days earlier, I could feel Mount Augustus slowly release its hold on me. The air was becoming warmer and the colors a little less vivid. At last I reached the place where I had tumbled down the embankment and knew I was on the way home.

Emerging from the trees, I found Pine Valley's practice range spread before me just as Harry and I had left it. From the look of the sky and length of the shadows it had to be pretty early in the morning, but there was no way to be sure how long I'd really been gone. High overhead a jet plane cut double lines of white through the pale blue sky; I was back in the world. I turned to the treeline to fix Harry's shortcut in my mind, but the portal had closed.

I took a deep breath of Pine Valley's fragrant air and brushed some dirt from the knees of my "ga-tae-hell" pants. I could recall Angus handing them back to me with the comment that they were "a wee bit broad in the beam"

311

for him—a little dig that still annoyed me, but I couldn't remember slipping them back on. Hefting my bag, I walked up the gravel path through the trees to the guest house, my mind and spirit still full of the Mountain.

Only minutes after leaving Mount Augustus, I was desperate to return. Pausing on the path, I looked back once again at the treeline, hoping to see the parting of branches that could lead me back. But there was no shimmering portal, no magic gate, just a wall of very ordinary trees. Then I remembered the mission that MacKenzie had charged me with, and of course, the shopping list tucked away in my shirt pocket. Maybe I'd walk through another shimmering portal on some other course, or like Harry, be shanghaied from a sand trap in the middle of a summer day, but however it came about, the Gods would show the way.

As I climbed the stairs to my room, the rattle of pots and pans from the kitchen told me the Saturday Breakfast Buffet was being prepared by the staff. The question was, which Saturday? Depending on which day it was, my journey could have taken less than an hour or as long as a week.

The window behind the little writing table was open and the curtains were billowing softly in the breeze. Someone had already been in to tidy my room. Setting my bag down by the bed, I suddenly remembered Harry's book tucked safely in the side pocket. What had MacTavish called it, "The Book of Golf"? Yes, that was it, and as "Keeper of the Book" it was my responsibility to look after it, add to it as I choose, and to be the advocate for mortal golfers everywhere. Perhaps the book held the answers.

Removing the ancient volume from my bag, I marveled anew at its incredible weight and the powerful vibrations it threw off. Since I didn't want to be knocked flat on my behind again with such a full morning ahead of me, I considered leaving the book until later.

Out of habit, I looked at my wrist to check the time and then remembered that old Weyland was now the proud owner of my training Rolex. But the clock radio by the bed and the *New York Times* on the writing table told me everything I needed to know. Only forty-eight minutes had passed since I went to meet Harry at the range, and the scheduled tee-time with old man Craven was still two hours away. In less time than it took me to walk to work, my entire life had been changed. I shook my head in amazement and sat down at the writing table to read Harry's diary.

The wine-red journal was worn and battered; the obvious result of spending forty years in the pocket of a golf bag. At one time, however, it had been a thing of rare beauty. The leather was still soft as butter, and you could just make out the remnants of idyllic landscapes embossed into the covers. I removed the rubber bands that Harry had used to hold it together and placed them carefully to the side. Before opening the journal, I glanced out the window and studied the fairways and greens that lay before me, hoping to catch a glimpse of Mount Augustus in the morning light. But it was only Pine Valley so I opened the tattered covers.

The book was not what I expected, but then how could it possibly be? It was something far more mysterious and wonderful than anything I could have dreamed up. According to the introduction, as the newly anointed Keeper of the Book, I was the most recent link in a chain of mortal visitors to Mount Augustus, going back thousands of years. And over all the centuries, each was charged with the solemn responsibility of writing in his own hand the ongoing history of the game of golf and the immortals who play it on Mount Augustus. I also learned that in the passing of the book from one mortal golfer to another, Harry, like all the others and eventually myself, would forget about its existence. As MacKenzie reminded Harry that day in the locker room, "There can be only one."

The entries in the diary were written in many different hands, narrative styles, and languages. The first entries were not a language at all—at least as I understand them, but a series of pictograms like you'd see on the walls of an ancient temple. Then came entries in Greek and Latin, and many other ancient languages, but surprisingly, I could understand them all. The last entries were written with a leaky old fountain pen in Harry Brady's cryptic style. Unlike his predecessors, Harry hadn't just captured the myths and legends that abounded on the Mountain, but had undertaken a golfer's guide to each of the gods in the pantheon at Mount Augustus. That was what he had been so feverishly working on during every spare moment of our round. I guess in his heart of hearts, even Harry knew that when we began three days ago it would be his last trip to Mount Augustus.

Stuffed randomly between the stories were loose pages of lists as well, notes that Harry had taken over the years to remind himself of Twitch's single malt whiskey and Horace's brie, The MacKenzie's Aqua Velva and Fergus's seed catalogues, Reg's textbooks on animal husbandry, and Ichabod's patent applications. I laughed aloud and knew that they would be useful references for when I returned to the Mountain myself, although the list in my pocket was plenty specific.

Harry had left no note of explanation or greeting and, for a moment, I was disappointed. We had been through a lot together. Then I realized that, in choosing me to be Keeper of the Book, Harry had said all there was to say. With great care and patience he had helped create and preserve a guide to the world of Mount Augustus and the Gods of Golf and it was up to me to decide what my contribution would be.

Fresh breezes ruffled the curtains and once again I glanced out the window over the flowering dogwood trees to the course beyond. This time I didn't really expect to see Mount Augustus. It was just a stolen moment to enjoy the promise of a beautiful spring morning, but if MacTavish had pressed me for the truth, I would have had to admit I was really looking for Harry.

The smell of breakfast wafted up from the kitchen through the open window and I realized I was hungry. I went to my suitcase and unpacked a simple pair of blue slacks and a matching polo shirt. While it was open I took out an extra pair of socks and a shirt for my golf bag just in case. While changing from my "ga-tae-hells" with the little whales, I realized I was still wearing the Great God MacKenzie's boxers. They fit pretty well.

On my way down to breakfast I had the feeling it was going to be a good day to play a little golf.

THE GOLFER'S GUIDE
to the
Gods of
Mount Augustus

The Golfer's Guide to
Angus, the God of Starters

Angus, the God of Starters, lives in a tiny hut at the gates of Mount Augustus. He guards the gates to this heavenly kingdom with the ferocity of a brigade of Gurkhas. It is said by many that it would be easier to shinny over the Pearly Gates themselves than to sneak past Angus.

Description:
Usually seen wearing a tartan kilt and a tweed jacket festooned with tournament badges and other golfing mementos. Tools of office: a starter's ledger, a pocket watch that is always ten minutes fast or slow, a fierce-looking shillelagh that occasionally doubles as a driver, and of course, his ever open palm.

Dominion:
Angus is the patron god of all golf course starters, doormen at upscale nightspots, bouncers, toll booth collectors, maître d's, and civil servants—especially DMV employees. Also patron of trolls, valet parking attendants, rent-a-cops, and subway panhandlers.

Hazards:
When annoyed, Angus can create miserable conditions for gods and mortals alike. Among his favorite tricks:

- *The Oldest Living Member Outing*—Scheduling the morning rounds with foursomes of octogenarians

319

and heavy betting Asian physicians, thus ensuring lengthy and tedious rounds for all who follow.

∘ *Bogus Frost Delays*—Typically declared on balmy spring mornings.

∘ *The Dreaded Shotgun Start*—Usually used in tandem with bogus frost delays, to virtually guarantee a five-hour round.

∘ *The Disappearing Tee-Time*—Your name magically disappears from the starter's sheet only to reappear with a timely application of the secret handshake. (See *Preventive Maintenance* below)

∘ *The Mismatched Foursome*—Three 30-plus handicappers are matched to your hard-won 8ster. Alternatively, you are stuck with a new member giving his grade school children their first golf lesson.

Sacrifices, Charms, and Amulets:

For Better Tee-Times and More Congenial Foursomes
Remove the labels from three pricey pro-shop shirts or sweaters. To them, add a scorecard from Merion, Pine Valley, or Pebble Beach, two white tees, and a crisp new five-dollar bill. Grind the ingredients into a powder and place the contents into a drawstring pouch. Must be worn next to the wallet throughout an entire round. For more immediate and dramatic results, sprinkle the contents on the four corners of the first tee after midnight.

Preventive Maintenance
Of all the golf gods, Angus is the simplest to propitiate. Although susceptible to charms and other golf hoo-doo, it's easier and more efficient to make a contribution to Angus's foundation.
Take a crisp, new five- or ten-dollar bill and fold it in half. Make sure the four corners meet exactly, and then crease the

bill sharply at the fold. Take the folded edge and fold the bill in half again. Make another crisp fold. Place the small green rectangle in the palm of your right hand and let it rest lightly on your life line. Close your hand. Now you are prepared to greet the starter. Remember to smile broadly when you shake his hand.

A Veteran Linkster's Tip
At regular intervals—say once a fortnight, you must give Angus similar handshakes so he won't completely forget your name or more importantly your starting time. Although no substitute for cash, you may also render other kinds of tribute from time to time such as golf merchandise from the pro shop. And if you're smart, you will leave all the tags on.

The Golfer's Guide to
Fergus, the God of Greenskeepers

As the God of Greenskeepers, Fergus has been given charge over both the upper and lower eighteens at Mount Augustus, and like all greenskeepers would prefer that no one ever be allowed to play in his carefully manicured garden—especially while he works. But when they are, his mission is to ensure that the golfer's round is neither easy nor pleasurable.

Description:
Easily recognizable by his diminutive stature and fur poncho, Fergus is usually found in the company of grazing animals and is often seen riding a goat. His instruments of office include a large pair of clipping shears and a shepherd's crook, emblematic of the first flag used in the game of golf.

Dominion:
Fergus is the patron god of all golf course superintendents, architects, and greenskeepers. Also of employees of lawn services, stadium groundskeepers, horticultural societies, and English gameskeepers.

Hazards:
When you get on Fergus's bad side, one or more of the following hazards is bound to befall you:

- *The Greenskeeper's Dance*—Known to all greenskeepers throughout the world, this dance is marked by

322

an apparently aimless pacing around the green while golfers are trying to hit their approach shots. When accompanied by a contemptuous stare, the dance is particularly effective at unsettling golfers.

- *Weekend War*—This is the most mean-spirited of all of Fergus's tricks. It involves delaying all course upkeep to the weekend because of wet weather, dry weather, or any excuse at all, and then taking it out on the members on Saturday and Sunday. One of the tactics in this strategy is . . .

- *Mower Blitzkrieg*—Just what it sounds like, mowers racing over the fairways and greens like a Panzer division while you're trying to play. In ancient times, Fergus would cause a herd of grazing animals, usually sheep, to suddenly cross the fairway while players were addressing the ball.

- *Geese*—Despite what most people think, geese do not arbitrarily adopt golf courses. Evil greenskeepers feed them. Greenskeepers control a virtual Noah's Ark of wildlife to annoy you, from geese to crows—which steal your sandwiches—to rabbits, squirrels, and of course sheep and goats.

Sacrifices, Charms, and Amulets:

Ball Mark Bingo
This strategy is employed to alleviate minor problems with the greens. Simply put, it is good citizenship in the extreme. It involves repairing five ball marks on each green for a full eighteen holes. If your membership is anything like the average, there should be ample opportunity to do this.

Franklin's Fork
Take twenty-five collectible ball markers from high-profile courses and/or major tournaments. Spot weld them into a shape resembling a pitchfork or candelabra with the ball-

The Gods of Golf

mark tools pointing upward. Mount on the end of a telescopic ball retriever or a one-iron. On the first stormy night of summer, take the implement to the highest point on your home course and hold the instrument as high into the heavens as your arms and height allow until you attract a spark from the heavens. If you live, you should have no further problems with Fergus the God of Greenskeepers.

Feed the Greenskeeper

Many experts feel that greenskeepers let the rough grow too long, or let clover invade the fairways because, harkening back to their animal origins, they are simply hungry. True or not, many golfers have had great success with feeding the greenskeeper, both literally and figuratively. So, try inviting the greenskeeper out for a burger next time you're around the club, or take the direct approach and slip the greenskeeper a tenner when you see him. Tell him what a great job he's doing despite the "dry summer" or the "awful winter" we just had.

The Golfer's Guide to
Bertie, the God of the Long Ball

A perpetual adolescent, Bertie is always in pursuit of the "cheap thrill" both in golf and in life. When Bertie is on, he's awesome, and when he's not, everything he does is awesomely inappropriate.

Description:
In contrast to his blond youthfulness, Bertie wears a traditional sweater with a shawl collar and a woolen tie, and favors knickers and plus fours. Although not overly tall, Bertie is built like a baby bull with a barrel chest and massive forearms. Tools of office: an extraordinary gilded driver with a living eye inset in the face of the club.

Dominion:
Bertie is the god of long-drive champions, drag racers, shot-putters, arbitrageurs and takeover artists, home-run sluggers, caber throwers, high-stakes gamblers and commodity traders, mad-bombing quarterbacks, bungee jumpers, power lifters, and all those whose motto is "too much ain't enough." Suspected to be the god of the idiots who shout, "You da man."

Hazards:
If you get on Bertie's bad side, he can cause you all manner of embarrassment of the tee.

- *The Red Ball Special*—Also known as the Ten-Yard Dribble, the Red Ball Special involves a pathetic topping of the ball off the tee so that it only travels as far as the ladies' tees.

- *Sherwood Express*—As Harvey Penick used to say, "The woods are full of long hitters," and you'll get to meet them all while looking for your tee ball if Bertie afflicts you with this particular malady.

- *Bertie's Blindness*—This curse involves the inability to see any club but the driver in your bag—even when you're playing abrupt doglegs and well protected short par fours. Also referred to as "attack of the stupids."

Sacrifices, Charms, and Amulets:

Harry's Goo: A General Tonic for Driving Woes
To the contents of one cherry bomb, add tablespoon of wheat germ. Grind fiber insert from old driver and then mix well. Add the liquid center from a three-piece ball and ½ oz. powder from superalkaline battery and the needle from a Boy Scout compass. Mix with 2 oz. of engine additive till it has the consistency of shoe polish. Optional: add ¼ teaspoon of chopped rubber windings. Apply to face of driver before each round.
Makes enough for two small containers.

Date With Your Driver
Along with the putter, the driver is among the most sensitive clubs in your bag. If you ever give it cause to doubt your affection and confidence in it, say by trying out new drivers once a month when manufacturer's reps come by your club, or worse yet, by platooning it with another driver, then there is only one way to regain its cooperation. Every driver likes to be pampered. So, to begin with, treat your driver to an expensive new grip—genuine leather if you can find it, and perhaps a refinishing job if it's a classic persimmon. And how about a new head cover to

show you really care? Next, refuse to hit range balls with it and let it know that from now on you'll only use soft-cover balls off the tee. Take it with you everywhere you go, but *not* in the trunk. Let it sit up front with you. And if all else fails, take it to bed with you. Don't worry, this measure will either end your marriage, or it will greatly improve your sex life.

The Golfer's Guide to
Reg, the God of Caddies

Reg, God of Caddies, and personal looper for the Great God Mac-Kenzie, comes from a long line of herdsmen and is in fact the storied shepherd who stole the Divine and Ancient game from the golf gods and introduced it to mortals.

Description:
A soft man with rounded features and eyes blue as the Scottish heather in spring, Reg is short and stout and wears a tattered corduroy jacket with leather elbow patches over a gray sweatshirt that proclaims, Property of the London School of Economics in faded burgundy letters, and a pair of khaki flood pants hiked high above the ankles revealing black Converse hightops. Tools of office: a blue New York Knicks cap festooned with a pin cushion with colored tees, ragged towels, stubby yellow pencils, golf balls (at a nominal charge), spare spikes, and his "New Testament," a dog-eared yardage book of Mount Augustus covered with thousands of years' worth of hand-scribbled notes.

Dominion:
Reg is the god of all who serve and are underappreciated: mailmen, hod carriers, bicycle messengers, diplomatic couriers, airport bag handlers, locker room attendants, rock 'n' roll roadies, landscape gardeners, and pool boys are some of the many who fall under his protection.

Hazards:

Annoy or insult your caddie, and you will discover some of the tricks Reg has perfected throughout eons on the Mountain.

- *The Clang Rattle*—This involves picking up a bag from the wrong end, raising it high in the air, and spilling all the clubs on the ground, creating a loud and distracting noise just as you are about to putt.

- *The Sly Smirk*—A devastating confidence crusher that almost always occurs upon returning a club after sclaffing an approach shot.

- *The Tourist Game*—In this game, your caddie wins points by giving you a series of intentionally misleading observations and advice. Examples: "Naw, the water's not a problem on that side of the green," or "Don't worry, nine-iron is plenty of club to clear that trap." The Tourist Game is usually begun without warning after an argument over remuneration. Variations are played by farmers and lost motorists throughout the world.

- *The Muddy Rag*—If you happen to score points in the Tourist Game by overruling your looper, most likely he will retaliate by using the infamous Muddy Rag to clean your clubs after the round. Next time you will discover that the grooves of your irons are caked with mud and if they're forged, the faces are speckled with rust.

- *The Heel Mashie*—A Divot-like retaliation for real or imagined offenses in which the caddie searches endlessly for your lost ball and then discovers it smashed into the turf beneath his shoe.

Sacrifices, Charms, and Amulets:

The Caddie Yard Confessional

At the beginning of each season go to the caddie yard and distribute alms of golf shirts, cartons of unfiltered cigarettes, and cases of beer to all who loll there. Then seek out the caddie master, kneel before him, and apologize in advance for what is certain to be a terrible season and plead in a loud voice for aid and assistance. Offer a sacrifice of freshly minted twenties rolled into tubes and placed in a deck of Lucky Strikes saying, "I don't smoke anymore, but maybe you'd like these."

Shameless Sucking Up

While there are many variations on this theme, history has shown the following gambits to be effective. Arrange for a catered lunch from a four-star restaurant at the turn. If your club uses carts and fore caddies, let the caddie ride while you walk. On hot days, offer to pay for an assistant caddie to carry your putter and sand wedge. Memorize the names of the last ten caddies who carried bags for winners of Majors and sprinkle them in conversation throughout the round. Examples: "Squeaky's (or Greg Rita's) got nothing on you." Or "You're good, ever think about working the tour?" Offer to sponsor a caddie/guest tournament.

The Golfer's Guide to
Mulligan, the God of Excuses

Mulligan is the weekend golfer's advocate. Sees in each shot an opportunity to right the imbalances and injustices of the universe. Creator of the insanity defense in golf and the current USGA handicapping system.

Description:
Studious looking with thick, wire-rimmed glasses, three-piece suit with plus fours, and a tightly buttoned vest. Often carries several heavy-looking law books and meteorological devices for measuring random physical events and a large pocket handkerchief—Mulligan is a heavy weeper at the first sign of injustice.

Dominion:
Patron of defense attorneys, constitutional lawyers, psychologists, liberal Democrats, social engineers, historical revisionists, and, of course, all public links golfers. Mulligan is widely reputed to be the patron god of the Senior Tour.

Gambits:
Mulligan is the master of deflection. If you are a devotee of Mulligan, no errant shot need ever be considered your fault. Here are some of Mulligan's favorite conditions leading to an automatic do-over:

- *Random Acts of Nature*—Sudden gusts of wind, falling leaves during one's backswing.

- *Concentration Breakers*—An opponent jingling his pocket change, the sudden chirping of a bird, golf cart noise, clubs rattling. . . .

- *Meteorological Anomalies*—Unusually high humidity affecting trajectory or distance; unseasonable heat or cold.

- *Equipment Problems*—New clubs, borrowed clubs, new grips, slick grips, thick grips, cracked heads, loose whipping, loft and lie need adjusting. . . .

- *Biological Problems*—Head cold, allergies, arthritis, backache, biorhythms, just ate lunch, need to eat, low blood sugar, hangover, etc.

- *Course Problems*—Everything under repair, hit sprinkler head or cart path, immovable obstructions (including trees and rocks). Fairway too heavy, narrow, or thin. Greens just sanded, aerated, or cut.

- *Local Rules*—While most local rules were inspired by Mulligan, the lift, clean, and place rule in use on the PGA Tour during inclement conditions is Mulligan's masterpiece—a variance of the rules of golf for those who need it least.

Sacrifices, Charms, and Amulets:

Golfer's Panacea

Take a copy of the official USGA rules of golf. Burn it. Scatter the ashes to the four winds from the top of the tallest building in your state.

The Written Excuse

Get notarized notes from your doctor, your priest or rabbi, your bartender, and your psychiatrist testifying to your need for: a cart, low-stress experience, and a break in life. Also for various medical conditions such as tics and partial blindness. Bind them in plastic sleeves and carry with you at all times.

Caution: While Mulligan can be useful in small doses, if used indiscriminately, he will completely destroy your self-esteem and any pleasure you might get from the game.

The Golfer's Guide to
Dirk, the God of Tactics

Dirk, the God of Tactics, is a wild Highlander who lives for the pleasures of battle, whether against other gods or against the ultimate opponent, a wily golf course.

Description:
Easily recognizable because of his long red hair and full beard, Dirk wears the traditional dress of a Highland warrior, including a tartan kilt and sash. Always armed against the possibility of aggression, Dirk carries both a dagger and a short sword under his belt. Tools of office: an ancient niblick used both as a cudgel and a golf club; and a rude set of bagpipes with which Dirk plays the elements, causing trees to creak and moan, rivers to roar, and the wind to whistle.

Dominion:
Dirk is the god of all military strategists, surveyors, political campaign managers, and marketing directors. Also the patron of tempters such as telephone solicitors, especially stock and bond salesmen; commercial voice-over announcers; human potential quacks; and compulsive gamblers.

Hazards:
If you get on the wrong side of Dirk, he will cloud your judgment, making both your golf and your personal life miserable.

○ *The Gazillion to One Society*—You'll never get a membership card or attend a meeting, but you'll pay very heavy dues when Dirk inducts you into this particular fraternity. All members of the Gazillion to One Society play long odds in every facet of their game with typically disastrous results. They go for par fives in two even if it means carrying large bodies of water; they always try for impossible recoveries from the trees instead of pitching back to the fairways; and they carry long irons instead of fairway woods.

○ *Foursome Blindness*—Fueled by Dirk's cheerleading, you'll become so aggressive on the course that you'll be blinded to the existence of all other foursomes. Typically, this means that you'll drive into other groups at least three times before having your lights punched out by the foursome in front of you. Hence: Foursome Blindness.

○ *Full-Tilt Harrying*—When really pissed at you, Dirk's magnetic voice will follow you off the course and compel you to do all manner of ill-advised things in your personal life such as an attempt to fill inside straights at poker and making a pass at the boss's "niece" at out-of-town conventions.

Sacrifices, Charms, and Amulets:
Dirk is among the hardest of all the gods to propitiate, because he only goes after those who lack aggression. So, to inoculate yourself against his compelling vision, you must catch a little bit of his disease.

Iron Bruce
To keep Dirk at bay, you must find the wild man in your soul. First, fashion a kilt from an old army blanket and let your hair and beard grow long. Then repair to the woods where you spend a long summer night with your mates, tell-

ing tall golf tales and playing bagpipes you've made out of a cow's stomach and a couple of wooden recorders.

Charge of the Dewsweepers
Organize the second and third flights from your club into battalions. Dress them in camouflage fatigues and muffle the wheels of your golf carts. Then at first light, you move out in a shotgun start and hide in the woods near each green. Precisely at the moment the sun breaks over the horizon, squads of dewsweepers will simultaneously attack the eighteen greens, bringing the course to its knees.

The Golfer's Guide to
Divot, the God of Bad Lies

A foul-tempered but impish creature who lives in the forest around Mount Augustus, Divot has full charge over the course. Assisted by an army of bugs, lizards, and other crawling things, Divot has a million methods of making sure your ball is virtually unplayable.

Description:
Divot is a young faun—that is, he has the lower body of a goat and upper body of a human boy of about fourteen. Known for his skills with magic and sleight of hand, Divot can also transform himself into a real boy or, more often, as something noxious like a scorpion.

Dominion:
Divot is the god of croupiers and roulette dealers, Three Card Monte con artists, aluminum siding salesmen, and short sellers in the stock market. Also god of mine sweepers, lottery winners, and bad hops in baseball.

Hazards:
When Divot is around, the worst thing that you can do is to appear "lucky." Divot abhors lucky breaks of any description and will go to any length to balance out your good fortune with something awful. Some examples:

- *The Plain Vanilla Bad Lie*—Your perfectly good drive ends up in an old divot mark, a bare patch, on gravel, or in a small fairway depression filled with uncut grass. And of course, there's the sudden appearance of U.S. Open rough minutes after the course has been cut.

○ *Pick-Up-Sticks*—These are lies that defy description. Your ball balanced on a single strand of straw or sitting precariously on a delicate lattice of twigs, pine needles, and pinecones.

○ *General Bad Luck*—If you get gum on your boat shoes in the club parking lot, or pick up a nail in your tire on the way home, Divot is usually to blame. Also responsible when you lose a critical spike or break a shoelace during a round.

○ *Rocks and Ricochets*—Your ball ends up on a slab of granite, wedged between petrified tree roots, or sitting in a bunker atop a large rock covered with a thin layer of sand—lies sure to ding your expensive irons or injure your person.

○ *Trade 'Em*—Like a pack rat, Divot is fond of replacing your ball with something wildly inferior. For example, a powder blue ladies ball is substituted for your brand-new three-dollar balata.

○ *Manly Lies*—Your ball lands on the edge of a precipice at Pebble Beach, plugs into a wasps' nest, or lands between the coils of a sleeping rattler. Not for the faint of heart.

Sacrifices, Charms, and Amulets:

For perfect lies all the time
Sell all you have and give the proceeds to the poor, or the Republican National Committee. Give up golf and live a life of humility, poverty, and good works. (See: Shank, the God of Cruelty) If this is too extreme, try the following:

Luck Loading
For the next fortnight, run over every pothole you see, step on every irregular piece of sidewalk, deliberately scratch during pool games, and go out of your way to pick up tacks and gum with your shoes. Since nature seeks balance, it will seek to redress your run of bad luck with a run of good luck on the golf course. Not even Divot can overcome this.

Bent Grass Window Box
Plant a window box with bent grass and carefully cultivate it through the spring. Manicure it on Friday afternoons and then leave two brand-new tour balatas on its freshly cut surface overnight. This is sympathetic magic at its best.

The Golfer's Guide to Wendell, the God of Winter Rules, and Ruppert, the God of Preferred Lies

Wendell and Ruppert are the Trickster gods of Mount Augustus, bent on visiting divine and mortal golfers alike with periodic storms of chaos, while at other times they are the authors of sublime moments when good luck shines upon the golfer. Nevertheless, Wendell and Ruppert are not to be trusted under any circumstances.

Description:
Although they are able to change size at will, Wendell and Ruppert prefer to be no taller than a brand-new pencil, and when they are that size, Wendell is about as thin as a pencil, too, while Ruppert carries the girth of a can of motor oil. Lovers of costumes, Wendell and Ruppert often sport morning suits, but just as often they will appear in boaters and red-striped blazers like underclassmen at Oxford, punting on the river. Tools of office: an old wooden WWI shell box filled with all the necessaries to convince a wavering duffer to stretch the rules.

Dominion:
Wendell and Ruppert are the gods of hucksters, used car dealers, mob accountants, crybabies, whiners, and anyone who is willing to take advantage and believes that the rules

are made for others. Consequently, they are also the patron deities of undercover vice cops, industrial spies, federal sting operations, and the Committee to Re-elect the President— either party.

Hazards:

Wendell and Ruppert are not as dangerous as they are incredibly annoying. Even so, if they are angered, prepare for a long afternoon.

- *Stool Pigeon Pie*—Your minor peccadilloes on the golf course—such as improving your lie in a patch of shaggy fairway, will be reported in stunning detail to the membership committee who will then ban you from all future member guest tournaments.

- *Jokers Wild*—Your life becomes a series of pratfalls and social gaffes worthy of a Max Sennett comedy. You fall off the first tee after your spikes get tangled in the grass; a tow truck will have to be called to extract your cart from the soft fairway near the water hazard on the course's signature hole. Also, in a single round you will be given exploding golf balls, exploding cigars, and a dribble glass to drink from at the 19th hole.

Sacrifices, Charms, and Amulets:

The Trojan Clubhouse
Sometimes known as "the roach motel" this involves planting an elaborate doll's house with a steel reinforced roof and a one-way door near the eighteenth green of your course. Place a bowl of beer nuts in the living room. If you succeed in trapping Wendell and Ruppert, the world of golf will be your oyster. On the other hand, should they escape, you'll have to find a new sport—say, lawn bowling.

Join the Lollipop Guild
In brief, become an advocate for the vertically challenged. Buy a Yorkshire terrier or a toy poodle and become a breeder. Memorize the words to the Lollipop Guild song from *The Wizard of Oz*—but for God's sake, keep them to yourself.

The Golfer's Guide to
Glenda, the Goddess of Golf

Glenda is the female principle that balances the Great God MacKenzie and animates Mount Augustus. Responsible for the joys of nature in golf, Glenda is the bitter enemy of all that threaten her domain such as encroaching condos, railroad ties, and herbicides.

Description:
Like MacKenzie, Glenda can appear in many guises—most often as the ideal of any mortal she graces with her presence. Whether blond or brunette, pale or dusky, blue-eyed or brown, Glenda is always the most beautiful woman the golfer has ever seen. Since Glenda is responsible for the grass, trees, and wildlife of Mount Augustus, she is often seen in the company of woodland creatures.

Dominion:
Glenda is the patron deity of horticulturists, allergists, ecologists, highway beautification programs, equal access to membership activists, mistresses, cart girls, fertility clinics, and the LPGA. Also considered to be the goddess of the benevolent first grade teacher and good witches.

Hazards:
At first placid and beautiful, Glenda can turn on you suddenly—just like a great golf course. Then she becomes a fortress, forbidding and impenetrable. Mess with her, and you

will become like Adam driven from the garden with a flaming sword.

- ○ *Creepy Crawlies*—At every turn you will be assailed by tiny creatures. Ticks bearing Lyme disease and God knows what else will swarm up your pant legs, malarial mosquitoes will take chunks out of your neck, and fire ants will colonize your fairways.

- ○ *Barks and Bites*—Your fairways will be honeycombed by gophers, leaving holes for your ball to tumble into and vast areas without an even lie. Coyotes and stray dogs will roam the course at will.

- ○ *Birds Unlimited*—Crows will abound, annoying golfers with their strident calls and stealing snacks from the unwary at the turn. Canadian geese will decide to winter and summer at your course leaving mounds of droppings in their wake.

- ○ *Mal-Aire*—The fresh air you normally exult in on the golf course will become fouled with noxious cart fumes, rank odors from suddenly stagnant water holes, and world-record amounts of pollen causing everyone to gag and hack.

Sacrifices, Charms, and Amulets:

Glenda is a jealous goddess and wants more than anything else that you have no other loves but her. So the most effective charms for Glenda are the most traditional.

The Token

In an act of chivalry, request an item from the cart girl or female assistant pro you've fallen head over heels for, and prominently display the item on your person during the next member guest tournament. Tip: Gloves and scarves are excellent choices, but steer clear of intimate apparel.

The Festival
Organize an annual festival in Glenda's honor at your club.
Since there is no one traditional day of observation, Nancy
Lopez's birthday would do nicely.

The Shrine
Leave gifts for Glenda near the halfway house at the ninth
hole. Bouquets of flowers, potpourri, perfume, and chocolate
truffles are always appreciated. If you're really in trouble with
her, bury small items of jewelry among the flowers once a
fortnight for three months. Caution: Glenda may redouble
your curse if you try to slip a zircon past her.

Oath of Fealty
Compose a sonnet to Glenda and recite it at the turn within
in the hearing of your foursome. Then leave a copy of the
sonnet along with other supporting evidence of your undying
love, such as facsimiles of your divorce papers, in a hollow
tree.

The Golfer's Guide to Weyland, the God of Equipment

Weyland, the God of Equipment, is the only god of golf who lives and works underground. Opinion is divided as to whether Weyland is the golfer's friend or the mortal enemy of all hackers. Illustrating his basic ambivalence is Weyland's favorite saying: "It's a poor workman who blames his tools, but it's a stupid bastard who buys cheap ones to begin with. . . ."

Description:
A largish woodland faun with the upper body of a man and the lower body of a goat, Weyland sports a white goatee and wears rimless spectacles. He is usually seen wearing a leather apron cinched at the waist by a tool belt containing a blacksmith's hammer and a pair of wrought-iron tongs.

Dominion:
Weyland is the god of all club and ball makers as well as club repairmen. He is also the patron deity of manufacturers of garden tools as well as the craftsmen of other arcane arts such as fly fisherman and egg tempera artists.

Hazards:
Although a relatively mild-mannered god, Weyland will not abide club abusers. If observed tossing your clubs into water hazards, slamming them into trees, or dragging your misbehaving putter behind your car, one of the following things may happen to you:

346

○ *The Missing Club*—No matter how many times you count your clubs and lay them along the flag during putting, when you return home, your bag will be short a seven-iron. Don't even bother looking, this club will be never be turned in.

○ *Possession*—If your crime is severe, one or more of your clubs will be possessed by malevolent spirits such as hoselwiggs or shaftweevils. Once possessed these clubs will visit upon you with frightening regularity all manner of errant shots including the shank, the pull, the fat shot, the thin shot, and the dreaded whiff.

Sacrifices, Charms, and Amulets:
Fortunately, Weyland does not often interfere with mortal golfers. However, it is well documented that Weyland will come to the aid of the suffering if they employ some of the following techniques:

Observance of the Festival of Irons
At the beginning of each new season, devotees of Weyland make sacrifices to him by purchasing brand-new irons. Typically this act of devotion costs his followers anywhere from $400 to $1,200. Strict observers of this ritual claim that for maximum benefit irons must be purchased from your pro shop at full retail.

Feeding the Putter Barrel
Each time a putter loses its magic, it must be retired with respect to a putter barrel in your garage or basement. Warning: *Putters must never be sold or traded. They are personal effects like dentures or eye wear.*

Annual Absolving of the Clubs
Another springtime rite, the annual absolving of the clubs is usually performed by the elected chaplain of your club. If there is no club chaplain, your local Episcopal minister will make a dandy substitute. Traditionally during this ceremony,

all curses placed on clubs or bad karma incurred during the previous year are dissolved by pouring a measure of vodka and tonic over one's irons. In recent times, it has been considered acceptable for the participants to drink the mixture themselves.

The Balata/Nickel/Persimmon Poultice
Grind up two genuine balata ball covers, one square inch of persimmon wood, and combine with the nickel plating from a vintage forged iron or putter. The combined mixture may be sprinkled in the bottom of your bag where it will come in daily contact with your clubs, or worn in a gris-gris bag around your neck as a charm. Good for a variety of club ills, it does not work in cases of possession.

The Golfer's Guide to
Lorena, Goddess of Slicers, and
Heidi, Goddess of Hookers

*Recruited from the Greek Pantheon by MacTavish, the God of
Rules, to assist in his campaign against mortal golfers, Lorena and
Heidi possess an uncanny ability to deflect projectiles away from
their intended targets, sending them careening wildly off the right
or to the left—but almost always out of play.*

Description:
Also known as Charon's Angels, the anti-angels, and the
Butcher's Daughters, Lorena and Heidi are frightening creatures with the heads of beautiful women and the bodies of
large predatory birds. They are often found in the company
of carrion birds such as crows, ravens, kites, and vultures; but
Heidi has also shown an inexplicable affection for mallards.

Dominion:
Lorena and Heidi are the goddesses of all who give directions
for a living, most notably traffic cops, mothers-in-law, information booth attendants, and gas station pump jockeys. They
are also patrons of manufacturers of road signs, traffic lights,
gyroscopes, and compasses.

Hazards:
The Harpies are a foul-tempered pair at best and they specialize
in hazards that will take the starch out of a golfer's sails for the
entire round.

○ *The Ultimate Birdie*—Also known as "taking one for the sisters," or "Kamikaze Kites," this is the ultimate sacrifice a bird can make for the Harpies. Basically, it involves swooping down on your drive and catching it in the chest. Anyone who has ever seen the explosion of feathers and the lifeless form on the fairway after a Kamikaze mission knows why this is so debilitating to the mortal golfer.

○ *The Slice of Life*—A humiliation usually visited upon high-profile hackers such as retired presidents and Hollywood stars. The slice of life involves hitting a big banana off the first tee into the crowd as it leans into the fairway to get a good look at the celebrities. If properly executed, no fewer than three members of the gallery will require medical assistance and at least one will call Jacoby & Meyers.

Sacrifices, Charms, and Amulets:

There's only one tried and true way to mollify the Harpies: Live a pure life, give generously to the poor, never cheat at golf, cards, or at marriage, control your temper, and be generally self-deprecating. Face it: if you could do those things, you wouldn't be playing golf, so try something from the list below. It couldn't hurt.

Army Penance
If you're alternating hooking and slicing, you must walk three times around the circumference of the golf course wearing your spikes on the wrong feet. So, instead of going left, right, left right, you are in reality going right, left, right left ... In extreme cases, try walking backward.

The Cloak of Virtue (to be worn under your regular golf attire) Obtain hair or nail clippings from your priest or rabbi or other small articles belonging to them, and sew these items into a vest. This should sufficiently confuse the Harpies to let you get through the round unmolested.

The Mercy Date
Dinner and a movie is probably out with the Harpies, but it's still possible to get on their good side with a little old-fashioned courting. For example, before teeing off you could shout in the direction of the rough, "Hey, great-looking talons!" or "Beautiful feathers, doll. Who preens them?" Okay, a little lame, but it will probably get their attention enough so that you can proceed.

Gifts for the Girls
Once a fortnight, walk the perimeter of the course leaving a little care package for the sisters in the left and right roughs. Cuttlebone, bird seed, emery boards, and beef jerky have proven to be a winning combination. For those extra special rounds, like the club championship, you might want to throw in a little roadkill.

The Scarecrow
This is to be used in extreme situations. Make a scarecrow out of straw and your best golf attire and hire one of the kids from the cart garage to drive it around the course while you play. Tell the starter he's your brother-in-law, but keep the starter away from him, or the starter will try to talk his ear off. *Tip: Use a sweater on the upper body or the arms will give you away.*

The Golfer's Guide to
Ichabod, the God of Instructors

Ichabod, the God of Instructors, is Mount Augustus's teaching pro. Like a highwayman lying in wait, Ichabod is likely to set upon unwary golfers at any time or place in their rounds, prescribing bizarre drills, confusing swing thoughts and the use of torturous swing training devices.

Description:
All legs, pointy elbows, nose and Adam's apple, Ichabod has the build of an egret, but none of the grace. Ichabod wears all manner of golfing gear, although he tends to favor an outfit Harry Brady brought him in the 1970s: a pair of beltless double-knit slacks, a clinging nylon polo shirt, and a pork-pie style golfer's hat.

Dominion:
Ichabod is the god of all who sell hope to the desperate and quick fixes to difficult problems. Apart from golf pros and ballroom dance instructors, this includes: television evangelists, trickle-down economists, and infomercial pitchmen who sell unnecessary kitchen appliances, fold-up fishing gear, Elvis mementos, home exercise machines, and miracle beauty aids.

Hazards:
Caution! Although Ichabod seems like one of the more harmless gods, he can make your life a living hell if you cross him. Here's how.

- *Plague of Swing Thoughts*—Standing over your approach shot to the first green your mind will suddenly darken with a million contradictory swing thoughts. which will quickly devour your self-confidence like a plague of locusts.

- *The Nether Zone*—The Golf Swing is a dialectic, finding the right balance between flat and upright, strong and weak, laid off and crossing the line, swinging and hitting. If angered, Ichabod can send you to the "nether zone" where nothing is comfortable and no matter what you do, you're always doing a little too much of one thing and not enough of another. This curse can last for years.

- *The Tin Man*—Another diabolical sentence, "The Tin Man" consists of an obsession with mechanics and an absolute absence of "feel." After failing to arrive at the home hole, chronic sufferers of this syndrome have been discovered by search parties standing in the middle of the fairway rigid as statues—presumably frozen in mid-swing thought.

Sacrifices, Charms, and Amulets:

Group Flagellation

Since lessons are often given in groups, group propitiation is often effective in lifting Ichabod's curses. Form a conga line of not more than eighteen golfers, each carrying a training belt designed to keep the arms close to the sides during the golf swing. At the lead man's count, the members of the line beat themselves across the back with their straps (four lashes a hole, minimum) while chanting "head down, hit the ball before the ground." The conga line then travels the golf course, staying on the cart paths and strictly obeying the 90-degree rule when calls of nature make it necessary to cross the fairway.

The Rack

For golfers who find themselves in extremis, it is sometimes necessary to construct "the rack." The rack consists of an altar constructed in the woods to the "slice" side of any fairway. Upon the altar, the propitiate must place all the gold instructional books, videos, and swing trainers he has ever owned. Then he must place his handicap card upon the altar and set it ablaze. Some advocate keeping a vigil at the altar until the new handicap cards are issued, but this has seldom proved necessary in our experience.

Hogan's Amulet

Place five range tokens, an ounce of plastic grass from a new range mat, the surlyn covers from the three-striped range balls, and five shredded pages from "Five Lessons" into a leather valuables bag. Wear the bag under your hat the next time you take a lesson. *Tip: Make sure it is a large hat.*

Note: *While Ichabod can be a particularly vindictive god, one must bear in mind that like all pedagogues, he just wants to be loved. So, if none of the prescriptions listed above are effective, try inviting your teaching pro home for dinner.*

The Golfer's Guide to
the Great God MacKenzie

*The Great God MacKenzie is the father god of Mount Augustus
and the creator of the divine game of golf. A righteous and jealous
god, the MacKenzie is without pity when it comes to those who
transgress against the immutable laws of golf.*

Description:
Since no man alive could look upon the true face of MacKenzie
without coming down with a terminal case of the yips, he wears
many disguises, including the rough tweeds and rubber boots
of a simple Scots countryman. And other times he appears like a
terrifying colossus striding across the earth, his footfalls causing
earthquakes and his breathing, gale force winds. Tools of office:
on formal occasions the MacKenzie carries a gigantic golden
scepter shaped very much like a 1950s MacGregor driver.

Dominion:
MacKenzie is the patron of all those in charge of great enter-
prises: kings, queens, and other heads of state, CEOs, chairmen of the board, and all other all-powerful dictators and
despots such as owners of professional sports franchises,
presidents of PTAs, and chairmen of membership committees
at golf clubs throughout the world.

Hazards:
A jealous and often capricious ober god, the MacKenzie is
not to be toyed with. Those who have run afoul of him have
suffered the following consequences:

- *Snead's Scourge*—Even though the cause may be the transgression of a single person or foursome, if MacKenzie is sufficiently angry, he will take it out on an entire club through the following instruments: burning the clubhouse down; destroying the course through brush fire, flood and/or windstorms; EPA shut down due to chemical run-off or for endangering the habitat of something as endearing as the burrowing nematode.

- *The Anti-Manager*—Your club—if it still exists after all this—will suddenly hire the blackest heart in the Western world as its new general manager. The new manager who will thereupon book the week solid with corporate outings; announce backbreaking assessments on the membership; and make cart use mandatory.

- *Attack of the "Youdamans"*—As surely as Jehovah visited the Babylonians on the Israelites for their sins, MacKenzie will visit the Youdamans, also known as Yahoos and barbarians, on your quiet little club if you have crossed him. Known by their obnoxious behavior, loud clothes, and propensity to shout "YOU DA MAN" whenever anyone they remotely like hits a reasonable drive, the Youdamans will suddenly come into money and join your club when the economy is weak and your assessments are high.

Sacrifices, Charms, and Amulets:

The Graven Image

Collect from your membership all plastic bag tags from fancy resorts and out-of-town clubs. This should yield roughly two bushels of plastic. Place bag tags into a large cauldron and over a slow persimmon fire, slowly reduce to a liquid. Let contents cool until it reaches the consistency of spackling paste, then mold into an effigy of the Great God MacKenzie

356

(Old Tom Morris will do as a model). When cool, place garlands of azaleas around the bust and worship it.

MacKenzie's Jihad, a.k.a. "Kiltie Raids"
There's nothing a god likes more than a good holy war. Like beautiful women, gods love to be fought over or have their honor defended from infidels, and MacKenzie is no different.
Organize the members of your club into squadrons and then perform daylight raids on other country clubs or municipal golf courses in your area.* The preferred modus operandi involves camouflaging yourselves with old divots and painting your faces with Foot-Joy polish. Your group hides in the woods until a rival foursome comes along, and then swoops down upon them in golf carts bearing the logo of your country club. When they surrender, cut the kilties off their shoes as trophies. Attach them like scalps to an extra-long putter or Senior Tour driver and display outside the pro-shop at your course.

---

*Raiding other clubs' locker rooms at night is not considered manly and may cause MacKenzie to reject your sacrifice.

The Golfer's Guide to
Shank, God of Cruelty

*Shank, the God of Cruelty, is the dark prince of golf. A being totally
without light in his soul, he feeds off the pain and humiliation
suffered by mortal golfers.*

Description:
Tall, rail thin, and aristocratic in bearing, Shank is a classic
bully. He takes great pride in his appearance, affecting the
dress of an Edwardian gentleman, including high-starched
collar and bespoke suits from Savile Row. Tools of office:
a large black umbrella with meteorological powers, and a
straw boater.

Dominion:
Shank is the god of all those who take pleasure in humiliating
their fellow man in public situations: bill collectors, personnel
directors, Marine drill instructors, Senate committee chairmen,
maître d's in four-star restaurants, Parisian taxi drivers, gym
teachers, and tech-support operators for software companies.

Hazards:
If you have the bad manners to display a modicum of grit and
confidence, Shank will come after you like a scorned lover.

- *Shank's Revenge*—Midway between the clubhouse
  and the turn, you suddenly come down with a violent and humiliating case of the trots.

- *Shank's Splits*—For minor infractions, Shank will merely humiliate you by having your trousers split completely open when you bend over to pick up your ball. Normally used in mixed foursomes.

- *Fool's Foursome*—When one of your regulars drops out, the starter teams your group up with a loud-mouthed Lothario covered in gold chains. The newcomer spends the next three hours describing his most recent sexual conquest who, as anyone from the foursome can tell from the description, can be none other than your wife.

- *May the Farce Be with You*—When you're entertaining your boss and some important clients, Shank arranges an impenetrable force field around your tee ball on the first hole. After no fewer than five whiffs, you watch your ball dribble down to the ladies' tee, taking your career with it.

- *The Shanks*—The single most soul-destroying shot in golf is Shank's most cherished accomplishment. Not only is this lateral shot into the woods incredibly embarrassing, it strikes without warning at virtually any time within the round.

Sacrifices, Charms, and Amulets:

Casting the Balata Bones

Place nine balata balls that have deep cuts or "smiles" in their covers into a mahogany humidor. Place the humidor in the middle of a felt-covered poker table in your clubhouse and spin counterclockwise. After three full revolutions open the lid; if more of the balls are frowning at you than smiling, under no circumstances should you play that day. Repeat for each member of your foursome.

The Country Club Coven

Imitation being the sincerest form of flattery, sometimes the best thing you can do to propitiate old Shank is to humiliate others in his name. Select twelve of the most venal, low-down, prevaricating, foul-mouth members of your club—the first twelve you meet should do nicely, and form a coven. Every Sunday morning, all twelve of you should gather around the first tee to criticize and otherwise unnerve other golfers as they go off.

Warning: Many clubs already have such covens and they do not take kindly to competition.

The Golfer's Guide to
Horace, the God of Hazards

Horace, the God of Hazards, is pretender to the throne and leader of the shadow government of Mount Augustus. Banished to the hazards and out-of-bounds territories by the Great God MacKenzie, Horace waits for the day that he can unseat MacKenzie and make Mount Augustus a real macho test of golf.

Description:

A figure of frightening proportions, Horace is well over seven feet tall, bearded, and has skin as pale as ivory. Although Horace wears a hooded tunic of rough green linen the most striking feature of his ensemble is a net of living water plants that clings to his body. Horace's favorite saying: "Tha' which doesn't kill me, really really pisses me off."

Dominion:

Horace is the god of highway robbers, first wives, deposed dictators, squeegee-men, rag pickers, ball-hawks, junkyard men, janitors, and garbage men. He is generally the patron of the dispossessed, including kids at summer camp and military school, and all who have been banished to unsavory areas of the earth including penal colonies such as Devil's Island, Australia, and parts of New Jersey.

Hazards:

- *Perfecta*—Also known as "a day at the beach," this curse involves the golfer hitting into every greenside bunker on the course and then tripping into the last water hazard.

○ *Quinella*—Also known as "Army Golf," those who are cursed with the quinella never see the fairway, but hit from right rough to left rough all the day long.

○ *Daily Double*—Sometimes referred to as "buried treasure," this curse involves the golfer finding large rocks buried directly under his ball. If this happens to you, the best you can hope for is that your club will be damaged, at worst a ricochet will hit you somewhere in the head.

○ *Ball Swallowing Clover*—You're two feet off the fairway and you might as well have dropped your ball down a dry well. And if Horace has his way, and he will, you'll never find it unless you discover the nether region of the universe where all your missing socks have gone.

○ *March of the OB Markers*—Some believe this curse is an optical illusion, but those who have suffered it swear otherwise. As soon as you hit your tee ball, out-of-bounds markers encroach like an advancing army, narrowing the fairway even while your ball is in the air.

Sacrifices, Charms, and Amulets:

USGA Gambit
This is the ultimate in preventive medicine. Allow the rough to grow in dramatically, severely narrowing the width of the fairways and then allow it to grow to a minimum of six inches. Allow the greens to dry rock hard and slick so that errant shots naturally flow off the green into bunkers and thatches of greenside rough. Some classical scholars believe that USGA tournament setups are throwbacks to ancient

times and practices when Horace was routinely celebrated and propitiated in a weeklong festival during the middle of June.

The Alternate Game

Also known as "Hazards," this is Horace's favorite game. To play, participants must tee off on the night of the full moon and then endeavor to keep their balls either in the rough or in hazards throughout the round. Today's most skilled practitioners tend to be professional ball collectors, though wearing wet suits while playing Hazards is frowned upon by purists.

Preventive Maintenance

(a) Bring a sleeve of new balls with the receipt to the largest water hole on your course. Dump two of the balls in the water beyond the reach of ball retrievers. Wrap the receipt around the third ball and secure with a rubber band and toss it in, too.

(b) Select a very ripe wheel of brie or camembert from a gourmet shop. Slice it into eighteen pieces and bury the pieces in the greenside traps or other hazards of each hole. *Tip: Bury them DEEP.*

The Golfer's Guide to MacTavish, the God of Rules

The most despised and small-minded of all the gods, MacTavish's great pleasure is catching unwary men and gods in snares constructed entirely from words.

Description:
MacTavish looks like a haggard version of Moses, that is, if Moses were a British barrister. Usually dressed in three-piece woolen suits with celluloid collars, MacTavish wears black robes and periwig for formal occasions such as trials. Tools of office: A magnifying glass with which to read the fine print and half a ton of rule books. Favorite expression: "Ignorance of the rules is no excuse. In fact it's a crime itself."

Dominion:
MacTavish is the deity of IRS agents, accountants, Calvinist theologians, Kabbalists, corporate lawyers, and insurance claims adjusters. Also of writers of consumer electronics warranties, and union negotiators.

Hazards:
The most mean-spirited of the Golf Gods, MacTavish robs the golfer not with a bad bounce, a gust of wind, nor a sudden case of the hooks, but with the proverbial fountain pen. Among his favorite tricks:

- *The Surprise Golf Audit*—At any point in your round, or indeed at any point in your life, MacTavish or his agents may call upon you to justify your recorded score for any round you've ever played. If you fail to satisfy MacTavish, you may be sentenced to a minimum of two years of playing executive golf courses exclusively and a forfeiture—with interest—of any monies won in Nassaus during the rounds in question.

- *Membership Recall*—The results of your golf audit will be forwarded to your club with the recommendation that your membership be recalled, pursuant to a full vote of your club to take place at the next meeting of the membership committee.

- *Invoking the Code of MacPhearson*—An alternate set of rules charted by one Andrew MacPhearson, said to be the most foul-tempered, mean-spirited, perennially out-of-sorts man that ever dragged his wife by the hair across the heath. Each infraction of MacPhearson's narrow code—whether imagined or real, called for the golfer's partner to hammer the perpetrator across the head with a cudgel. For practical reasons, the Code of MacPhearson has never been employed when more than three holes remain in the match.

Sacrifices, Charms, and Amulets:
While there is little that the golfer can do to shield himself against MacTavish's cruel excesses short of avoiding the game altogether, there are a few measures that provide some protection.

The Golfer's Protection Program
You will be given a new identity and smuggled out of your club via the Underground Cart Path. After you have been debriefed, you will be resettled in a locale where golf is still considered an oddity. Popular choices include Switzerland and the Sudan.

The Gods of Golf

Membership Amulet

To one letter of invitation from a swank club like Wingfoot, add one single digit handicap card, three tungsten-tipped spikes, and an expired American Express gold card. Grind into a paste with macadamia nut oil. Place a dab behind each ear before meeting with the membership committee.

Change of Venue

When MacTavish and his minions knock on the door to the men's locker room and demand an audit or when the membership committee demands a recall, you request a change of venue to some really swell club you've played in the last year—where you can be judged by a membership committee that doesn't know you. At best this is a delaying tactic, but it could buy you some time and a free trip to Scottsdale or Bermuda.

The Golfer's Guide to
Twitch, the God of Putting

Also known as Shakey, Yips, and Nerves, Twitch the God of Putting hangs around the putting green enticing the unwary into games of chance. The "good buddy" of every man with the wherewithal to run a bar tab, Twitch is not to be trusted with one's wife, wallet, or livestock.

Description:
Usually seen wearing a yellow cardigan and powder blue glen plaid trousers, Twitch is a model of sartorial splendor. Twitch has thick wavy hair that he keeps well combed and favors gambler's jewelry such as golf ID bracelets and pinkie rings.

Dominion:
Twitch is the god of all manner of hustlers and gigolos including tennis pros, pool boys, pool sharks, bridge bums, male escorts, hangers-on, and the common freeloader. Also known as the patron of premature ejaculators and sexual therapists.

Hazards:
As demonstrated by the following hazards, Twitch can be among the cruelest of gods when he is angry.

- *The Shield of Chastity*—A curse often used to confound foursomes as well as individual golfers, the

Shield of Chastity consists of a cup that seemingly cannot be entered no matter how short or straight the putt. Typically, the situation is resolved with "gimmies" all around.

○ *The Yips* (Garden Variety)—Those afflicted experience an involuntary tremor of the hands just when they are about to putt, typically sending their ball far off line.

○ *The Yips* (Grand Mal)—A grievous affliction indeed that typically strikes the golfer even as he contemplates the putt. Tremors begin in the hands and then travel throughout the body, loosening dental work and dislodging contact lenses and hairpieces.

○ *Garden of Stone*—Not regarded as a separate affliction by all, Garden of Stone is often considered the end-stages of severe Grand Mal Yips. Those afflicted find themselves totally immobilized when standing over their putts, unable to draw back the putter or step away. For this reason, sufferers of Grand Mal Yips are strongly cautioned not to play solitary practice rounds late in the day.

Sacrifices, Charms, and Amulets:

Harry's Putting Reliquary
Contents: a splinter from Calamity Jane's hickory shaft, three flakes of nickel from Ben Crenshaw's Wilson 8802 putter, a piece of leather from the tip of George Low's brogans, and cuticles from Dave Stockton's fingers.* Place the contents in a small metal container such as a locket or reliquary and keep in your pocket or wear around your neck.

---

*Note: We cannot guarantee the effectiveness of the reliquary if substitutions for these ingredients are made.

Round the Horn
If you have really annoyed Twitch, Round the Horn is the strongest medicine available. Have a friend place a new golf ball in each of the nine holes of your club's practice green. Then walk on your knees to each hole and suck the ball out. Do this four times for a total of thirty-six holes. After soaking the balls in disinfectant overnight, donate them to Junior Golf.

Preventive Maintenance
See: Ball Mark Bingo (Golfer's Guide to Fergus)